RETURN TO JALNA

BY
MAZO DE LA ROCHE

Whiteoak Edition

BOSTON
LITTLE, BROWN, AND COMPANY
1946

FIRST EDITION

Published October 1946

ATLANTIC—LITTLE, BROWN BOOKS
ARE PUBLISHED BY
LITTLE, BROWN AND COMPANY
IN ASSOCIATION WITH
THE ATLANTIC MONTHLY PRESS

W
·D3753r

167097

Fiction

CONTENTS

I	YOUNG MAURICE'S RETURN	3
II	FINCH'S RETURN	30
III	THE SISTERS	44
IV	BREAKING THE NEWS	51
V	TUG OF WAR	71
VI	A CHASTISEMENT AND A TEA PARTY	80
VII	THE WANING OF THE YEAR	92
VIII	PIERS'S RETURN	115
IX	DAYS OF SPRING	124
X	GEMMEL AND MR. CLAPPERTON	140
XI	ADELINE AND THE ORGAN	150
XII	ROMA IN THE MOONLIGHT	167
XIII	RENNY'S RETURN	177
XIV	THE WHEELBARROW, THE ORGAN, AND THE MODEL VILLAGE	196
XV	ALMOST A PROPOSAL	213
XVI	GRANDMOTHER'S ROOM	222
XVII	THE THEFT	232
XVIII	CONCLAVE	252
XIX	A CHANGED LIFE	263
XX	OTHELLO	269
XXI	PIERS AND HIS SON	298
XXII	RENNY AND HIS DAUGHTER	308
XXIII	THE PROPOSAL	312
XXIV	AFTER DARK	319
XXV	THE FINDING	330
XXVI	ALAYNE HEARS THE GOOD NEWS	350

viii   CONTENTS

XXVII   THE CHILDREN 365
XXVIII   THE CLEAR AIR 375
  XXIX   FROM CHURCHYARD TO VAUGHANLANDS 390
   XXX   A MORNING CALL 400
  XXXI   FINCH AND HIS SON 409
 XXXII   A DEBT REPAID 424
XXXIII   INTO THE YEAR 1945 440
XXXIV   SETTLING DOWN 454

RETURN TO JALNA

The Whiteoak Family

CAPTAIN PHILIP WHITEOAK (of the British Army)
b. 1815 (deceased)
m. 1848
ADELINE COURT (of Ireland)
b. 1825, d. 1927

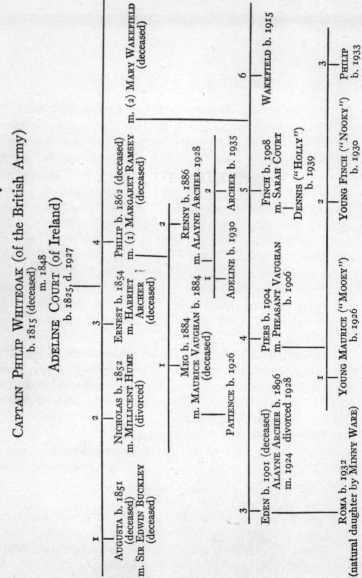

YOUNG MAURICE'S RETURN

It was more than four years since Maurice Whiteoak had left his native land and now he was once again within its borders. Then he had sailed by passenger ship from Halifax to Cóbh. He had returned in plane and warship by way of Portugal and New York. He smiled as he considered the change wrought in him by those four years in Ireland. He was a different being, he thought, from the child of thirteen who had gone to live with Cousin Dermot. How timid he had been then! The very marrow of him had shuddered as he had stood waiting with the maid in the hall while old Dermot Court had interviewed Wright, in whose charge Maurice had been. When Wright had come out of the room he had winked at Maurice as they passed and whispered — " I hope you 'll like the old boy better than I do."

Maurice had slowly but steadily entered the room where Dermot was waiting. Dermot had looked very old, sitting there in the high-backed chair, but his voice had been strong and his handclasp warm. Maurice clearly remembered the first words they had exchanged.

" How do you do? " Dermot had said.

" Quite well, thank you, sir," he had answered. And the conversation had continued — " I hear you were seasick coming across."

" A little. After that it was fine."

Then Dermot had given him a penetrating look and asked: " Do you think you can bear to visit me for a while? "

" Yes. I 'm sure I can." His own voice had sounded very small and wavering even to himself.

" Remember — " Dermot had continued — " if you don't like me you may go home whenever you choose."

" Mummie told me that."

" But I 'll say this for myself — I 'm not hard to get on with.   Some of the Courts were, you know."

" So I 've been told."

Dermot Court had laughed.   " Your great-grandmother was among 'em," he had said.   " But of course you don't remember her."

Maurice had been terribly homesick on that first night in Ireland, but the next day had been warm and sunny; Dermot had shown him the lawns, smooth as bowling greens, the yews clipped into fanciful shapes, the lodge embowered in ivy, the pasture where the mares and their colts grazed. Later, by himself, Maurice had crossed the bluish-green fields and climbed the hill, from where he had a glimpse of the sea.   It was all so different from his own home.

Jalna had seemed very old to him.   The house had been built almost ninety years ago, but ninety years was as nothing in this place.   Surely those gnarled oak trees were as old as the Druids!   At home he had been the eldest of three small brothers.   His father had been sharp with him.   At Cousin Dermot's he became the young, tender, cherished heart of the house, the apple, as everyone said, of the old man's eye.

At the end of his first summer in Ireland the war had come.   It had now been going on for four years.   In spite of all the letters from home Maurice had felt remote from the war, as Cousin Dermot felt remote from it.   Even when his father and his uncles had gone overseas to fight, even when he had heard that his father was a prisoner in Germany, he had felt remote from the war, leading his peaceful life with his tutor and the old man.

Now Dermot Court was dead and young Maurice White-oak was on his way home.

Again he thought of the change in himself.   He had gone

over in charge of Wright, doing just what Wright had told him to do; he had come back by himself, doing just as he pleased. He had left home wearing the clothes of a small boy. He was returning in the garb of a man. He tried to feel the unconcern of the seasoned traveler, a man who had been abroad and knew all about life. But, as the train neared the city, a tremor ran through him and his mouth became suddenly dry. Who would be there at the station to meet him? Not his father, for his father was still a prisoner in Germany. Perhaps his mother would come! At the thought of her his heart gave a quick thud. It moved in his breast as though it were a thing apart from him, imprisoned there. Her figure rose before him, as he had seen her at the moment of their parting more than four years ago. Her arms had been held close against her body, as though she forcibly restrained them from clinging to him, but her eyes had clung to him in anguish. She had feared she might never see him again. Now he had a sharp stab of jealousy as he thought how his brothers had been close beside her all these years, and he far away. He was almost a stranger.

He looked out at the fields baked brown in the late summer drought, at the wire fences and the ugly little houses of the suburbs. The train was nearing the city. People were beginning to gather their things together. Two officers in the seat in front of him rose to their feet, looking very rigid and erect. Maurice thought of his uncles and supposed they would look like that. And his father in the prison camp! He pictured him in an old uniform, almost ragged and his hair unkempt, but his face still fresh-colored and authoritative. He had a guilty feeling of relief that his father would not be at home when he arrived there. He remembered his father's eyes and how they could give you a look that made you tremble. It would be easier to return home with only his mother and his brothers there.

While he was thinking he had got to his feet, scarcely knowing he did so, and was moving slowly toward the door of the railway carriage with the other passengers. Agitating memories crowded in on him. He almost shrank from alighting from the train. But now he was on the platform surrounded by people struggling to find porters. There were very few of them and they were almost overwhelmed by luggage. At last he managed to capture one. He was among the last to pass through the station. He kept on the watch for his mother and had a sudden fear that he might not recognize her.

There was no need. He was in her arms before ever he saw her. She had darted from among those who waited and flown straight to him.

"Mooey," she was saying, "why Mooey darling, how you've grown!" She was holding back the tears from her eyes but they were in her voice.

He put his arm tightly about her and they walked together so linked. "Mooey!" He had not heard himself called by that old pet name for four years. Instead of bringing her closer it had set her apart in a half-forgotten life. He dared not look into her face.

"I have the car here," she was saying rather breathlessly. "Is that your luggage? Why, Mooey, you're almost a man! Traveling alone — with all those things! Oh, to think you are back again! I can scarcely believe it."

She was smaller than he had expected her to be. He remembered having looked up into her face. Now she was looking up into his. The pain of their parting distorted the joy of their reunion. Even as they held close to each other they felt that they were about to be torn apart. They made slow progress through the station crowded with men in uniform.

"How much shall I give the porter?" he asked, displaying some silver coins on his palm.

She took one and gave it to the man. The luggage was in the car. The early morning sunlight was dazzling on the expanse of clean pavement. Pheasant said: —

"Hop in, darling. Let's get out of this — to where we can talk." He got in and she started the car. There was something new about her, Maurice thought, as though she were used to looking after herself, doing things in her own way. She wore a funny little black beret and she had on quite a lot of lipstick. Somehow he did n't like that. He wanted everything to be just as it had been before he went to Ireland.

They spoke little until they reached the less busy road that ran alongside the lake. The lake was animated by small bright waves and the air was fresh. She asked questions about his journey, trying to keep her voice steady, trying to drive carefully. Really she scarcely felt capable of driving this morning. She had slept little the night before and her nerves were strung up. She did not dare look at Maurice.

"How are Nook and Philip?" he asked. "I expected they would come too."

"They wanted to but I would n't let them. I felt that I must have you to myself at the very first. It was selfish of me. Are you disappointed?"

"Oh, no. I expect they've grown a lot."

"Terrifically. But Philip the most. He's almost as tall as Nook and weighs more. It's very annoying to Nook." She went on talking rather hurriedly of Philip's escapades. She did not speak of Maurice's father.

However he said — "Home must seem strange without Daddy. I can hardly imagine it."

She nodded, her lips compressed into a thin line. Then she said — "You know, we — myself and the boys — lived at Jalna for a time but it did n't work. The children were so noisy — Philip especially — I was thankful when I could get rid of my tenants and go home again. Mooey, it will be heavenly having you with us!"

Maurice smiled but he wondered if ever he would feel at home in Canada again. That four and a half years in Ireland, in Cousin Dermot's house, rose as a barrier of more than a thousand days of misty sunshine, quiet rain, more than a thousand nights — surely there had been nearly two thousand days and nights — nights in that great quiet house where he and the old man had been so happy together. The tranquil life had suited Maurice. Even the longing for his mother had at last subsided. Now that he was with her again he had a strange, an almost bereft feeling, as though of awareness that his old childish self was lost and would never again be found. With memory's eye he surveyed the two pasts of his life, so completely separated by ocean and by war that they made him into two people. His mother had seen nothing of his life in Ireland. He had no one with whom he could talk about it. In this moment of his return he felt deeply lonely.

They were in the country now, with farmlands all about. There was a dry, pungent smell to the air, as though of dry vegetation, crisped by the sun, and of distant wood smoke. He remembered the moss-grown oaks of Cousin Dermot's park, the rich vaporous meadows, the flowery hedgerows, the pollarded willows — but Cousin Dermot was dead and the place belonged to him. He wondered if his mother realized that that estate in County Meath now belonged to him.

Pheasant went on talking, trying to pass lightly over these moments of reunion with her boy. It made her feel suddenly quite middle-aged to see him so grown. Well, she was thirty-seven but she still felt like a girl. They were silent when at last the car sped along the quiet side road and turned in at the gate. On either side of it the two small boys were waiting. They stood very still but ready on the instant to spring into action.

"Here we are!" called out Pheasant. "Here's your big brother!" The car stopped and she and Maurice alighted. What a difference there was between him and them! They were just children. Maurice had an air of calm, a manner of the Old World, acquired from Cousin Dermot in those years of close companionship. Oh, to think that she had had to part with him — to lose all those years out of their lives! Nothing she could do would bring him wholly back to her. He was part stranger and always would be. The loss was not made up by his inheriting Cousin Dermot's fortune. That somehow made the loss greater. Maurice was independent of her and Piers. He did not need them. He had learned to do without them. But she said gayly: —

"Here he is! Now give him a big hug."

She added this last because the brothers had stood staring shyly at each other, speechless. But now Maurice gravely shook hands with each of them and they in turn gravely shook hands with him. "Just like old gentlemen being introduced!" she thought. She exclaimed: —

"What a marvelous complexion you have, Mooey! You used to have no color. You're just peaches and cream. You make us look like Indians, does n't he, boys?"

She and her younger sons were, in truth, deeply tanned after a summer's exposure to the Canadian sun. The boys' arms and legs were as brown as their faces. Maurice, with his creamy skin, the rosy flush in his cheeks contrasting to the brown of his hair which he had got from Pheasant, looked like a garden flower beside two tough-fibred little weeds. Their fair hair was bleached to tow, it was dry from the hot sun, it stood out in wisps. Maurice's hair was glossy, softly waving. He looked cared for. They had the look of running wild.

"I expect it's the climate," answered Maurice. "We have a lot of damp, you know."

We! He identified himself with Ireland. But why not?

It was natural. He had spent his most impressionable years there. But it hurt her. It hurt her. She said: —

"Now we'll go in and have something to eat. You must be starving. Does the house look natural?"

It looked natural, as the remembrance of a dream might seem natural, but so small, half-hidden behind its lilacs and syringas. He recalled the imposing façade of Glengorman. Surely you might put this small house, built almost eighty years ago by a retired naval officer and named by him The Moorings, into one corner of Glengorman and scarcely notice it! He answered politely: —

"It looks very natural."

"And do I?" Pheasant asked tremulously.

"Oh, yes."

"Now, Nook and Philip, help Mooey to carry his things upstairs. Your room is waiting for you — just as when you left it. I'll make coffee."

She hurried indoors. The two small boys flung themselves on Maurice's hand luggage. They clattered up the narrow stairway and deposited it, with thumps and bangs, on the floor of the bedroom. Maurice looked about. It had not changed at all, except to look smaller. There was the little bed where he had slept as long as he could remember! He thought of that night when he had first been told of the proposed visit to Ireland. He had been in his pyjamas and had just knelt down to say his prayers. His father's voice had come up from the hall below. "Mooey, come down here!"

He had been frightened, wondering what he had done. He had scrambled quickly to his feet, then more slowly, hesitatingly, moved to the top of the stairs. He had seen his father standing below, waiting for him, his strong figure erect, his face upturned. But he had not looked angry. When Maurice had reached the bottom step his father had put his arm about him and led him into the sitting room. His Uncle Renny had been there. All three grown-ups had worn curious strained smiles. Then Uncle Renny, newly returned from Ireland, had told him how old Cousin Dermot lived all alone and how he liked boys and wanted Mooey to pay him a visit. The very thought of going away from home had been terrifying. He had never in all his life been separated from his mother.

" Wake up," his father had said, " and tell us how you like the idea. Mind, you don't have to go unless you really want to."

" How long should I stay? " he had asked.

Uncle Renny had answered — " As long or as short a time as you want."

His mother had exclaimed, as she watched him standing silent and bewildered — " You don't want to go, do you, Mooey? " Her eyes had yearned towards him.

The thought of leaving her had been terrible, but how glorious it would be to leave the school he hated, to be free from the strain of riding horses he feared, helping to school polo ponies under his father's critical eye, pretending he liked to ride when even the horses were aware of his fear and made the most of that awareness. And it would get worse as time went on, not better. It had been a shadow constantly darkening his days.

Uncle Renny had taken him into the dining room and had said, when they were alone — " Now, what is it you would like to ask me? "

He had twisted his fingers together and whispered — " Uncle Renny, will you please not tell Daddy what I 'm going to ask? "

" May I drop dead if I do," had been the answer.

" Well — " he had got out haltingly — " I want to know if I 'll have to ride to hounds or school polo ponies."

Uncle Renny had reassured him. He was to do just as he pleased, never mount a horse during the whole visit un-

less he wanted to.   And he had said — " I 'll do it.   I 'll go.
Tell Daddy."   Then he had run swiftly up the stairs to this
very room.   How far away it now seemed, like a dream.
But what he had heard pass between his parents, after Uncle
Renny had gone, stood out with terrible clarity.   They had
just closed the front door after him.   He had heard his
father say, with an exasperated note in his voice: —

" I don't want you to think for a moment that I 'm urging
this.   I don't want to part with Mooey — except for a visit.
But you look as though you were giving him up forever."

Then her voice had come, a voice choked by tears.   " I
am! I know I am.   And another thing — you don't love
Mooey! You never have!"   Yes, she had said that, her
voice coming up clearly and loudly to where he was standing
shivering in his pyjamas.

There had been silence for a space, then his father had
almost shouted — " That 's a lie! I 'll not let him go! I 'll
go right upstairs and tell him not to go!"   He had begun
to run up the stairs but she had run after him and stopped
him.   She had burst into tears and sobbed: —

" I did n't mean it, Piers! I don't know what made me
say such a thing.   I want him to go to Cousin Dermot.   I
know he 'll have a lovely time — poor little boy!"   They
had gone downstairs again and he had got into his bed.

Now he was back in that room again.   Nook and Philip
were staring at him.   Nook asked politely — " Shall we
bring up your trunk?"

" Yes," agreed Maurice, " we had better bring it up."

They ran down the stairs together and dragged the
steamer trunk from the back of the car.   With puffings and
gruntings on the part of the small boys they carried it to
Maurice's room.   Maurice wandered about looking at the
things that were so strangely familiar.   Pheasant's voice
came from below.   " Wash your hands, boys, and come
straight down."   They could smell bacon frying.

Nook and Philip stood respectfully watching him from the doorway of the bathroom while he washed. Maurice did not know what to say to them. He was not used to small boys. They went soberly down the stair.

"Now," said Pheasant, when they stood about the table, "I'm going to put you in Daddy's place, Mooey. You are the man of the family — till he comes home."

How pretty the dining room was, Maurice thought, with its gay curtains, the sun pouring in, the pretty breakfast cloth and vase of marigolds! There were bacon and an egg for Pheasant and each of the small boys, but for Maurice two eggs. Nook and Philip looked on him with respect. He was a man.

"Nook," adjured Pheasant, "sit up straight and stop holding your fork like a shovel. I don't know where you get such manners. Just look at Mooey! He doesn't sit or eat that way."

Nook sat upright at once but it was not till Pheasant fixed Philip with a stern eye that he obeyed.

"After breakfast," she went on, "I'm going to take you to see Auntie Meg and then we'll go to Jalna. Oh, Mooey, it's so wonderful having you home! And just think what it will be when Daddy's home! I can scarcely imagine the joy."

Philip put in — "Daddy's got only one —"

"Not now, Philip. Eat your toast. Pass him the marmalade, Nook."

She was not hungry. She talked eagerly, her eyes drinking in the sight of Maurice sitting there. She could not relax.

"What a time we've had," she said, "running Jalna without any help to speak of! In the house, just Mrs. Wragge and she quite unequal to those basement stairs; she's fatter than ever! And the two old uncles need a good deal of waiting on. Then there are the three children

to get off to school. You should see Adeline, Mooey.
She's lovely. . . . Poor Alayne! The house would be
enough to cope with, but there are the stables — twelve
horses still — the stock, cows, pigs, sheep, and poultry! If
it were n't for Wright we 'd have gone quite crazy. That 's
to say nothing of the farmlands and the fruit. I 've worked
like a farm hand and I guess I show it." She looked wist-
fully at him across the table.

"You still look lovely," Maurice replied, with a little
bow and in Dermot Court's own manner.

"Oh, how darling of you to say that, Mooey!" She
jumped up and ran round to him and hugged him. Oh, the
feel of that brown head of her first-born on her breast once
more!

He put both arms about her.

When they had cleared away the breakfast things —
Maurice, carrying a toppling load of dishes, remembered
the formality of meals at Glengorman, the white-haired
butler and his air of making even breakfast a ceremony —
Pheasant led him into the living room and closed the door.

"There is something I think I ought to tell you," she
said, in a low voice. "About Daddy."

"Yes?" He stared at her startled.

She took his hand and held it. "Oh, Mooey, he has lost
a leg! I never told you in my letters. I could n't bear to.
I could n't bear to tell you, when you were so far from
home." Her eyes filled with tears.

Maurice did not know what he was expected to do. Cry?
Turn pale? His father had lost a leg. It was a calamity.
But so far away. He remembered Piers on two strong legs.
He had stood strongly on them, as though it would take a
great deal to knock him over. And now only one! Mau-
rice said, in a low voice: —

"I suppose it happened years ago — when he was taken
prisoner."

" Yes . . .   Oh, I 've been terribly broken-up about it . . .
Of course now I 'm getting used to the thought of it. . . .
But it 's new to you, darling." She put both arms about
him. He breathed, against her shoulder : —

" I 'm sorry."

She drew a deep breath. " Well, we will do all we can
to make him forget it, when he comes home."

" Yes. Is he pretty well ? "

" I think so."

They separated and Maurice's eyes moved toward the
open window.

" We 're going now," said Pheasant, then hesitated and
added — " It will seem strange to you not to see Uncle
Maurice at Vaughanlands. Poor Auntie Meg and Patience
are alone there now. You must be sympathetic but cheerful when you meet Auntie Meg."

" Yes," said Maurice dutifully. He had not been much
moved when he had been told, more than a year ago, of the
death of Maurice Vaughan, his mother's father. Pheasant's
children had always called him " Uncle Maurice " because
he had been married to Auntie Meg. He had never seemed
in the least like a grandfather.

" It was very sad," went on Pheasant. " He was ill such
a short time. His heart, you remember."

" Yes. I remember." But he had forgotten.

" Auntie Meg has been very brave."

" Yes. She would be brave."

" Now we shall go ! " Pheasant spoke cheerfully.

Maurice thought — " I 'm glad that 's over." He asked
— " Could n't we go to Jalna first ? I 'd like to see Adeline."

" No. Auntie Meg would feel hurt. Nook and Philip
will want to come. Oh, Mooey, I do hope you will have
some influence over Philip ! He 's completely out of hand.
There is no one here who can do anything with him."

The two small boys now came running in. Philip at ten

did indeed look a handful to manage. He looked courageous and self-willed; while Nook, with his gentle amber eyes and sensitive mouth, had an air of reserve and shyness. Pheasant looked the three over.

"You're not a bit alike," she declared. "Mooey, you are like me, I think. Philip is the image of Daddy. And Nooky," putting an arm about him, "you are just yourself."

Now they were in the car passing between fields of sunburnt stubble and orchards bright with apples. "This is home," thought Maurice. "How strange it seems! This is my mother and these are my two brothers. My father has lost a leg and Uncle Maurice is dead. It's as though we were a colored glass window that had been broken and then put together in a new pattern."

Philip would put his hand on the steering wheel. "Philip, *will* you stop! You'll have us in the ditch," Pheasant said but she could not stop him. It ended by his keeping his hand there. "You see I can steer as well as anyone," he said.

What a dusty car! thought Maurice. The windows grimy, mud dried on the wheels. Cousin Dermot would have refused to set his foot inside such a car. But it could go! In a few minutes they were at Vaughanlands, the low, verandahed house standing in its hollow almost hidden in greenery, in which the yellow note of fall was already struck. A bed of scarlet salvia and many-colored dahlias made the background for a matronly figure in a mauve cotton dress.

She looked more familiar to Maurice than even his mother and his brothers had done. Among the curving masses of foliage, Meg Vaughan looked nobly in her place. Her hair had become almost white and this set off her fine complexion and the clear blue of her eyes. She clasped Maurice to her breast and exclaimed:—

"Home at last! How you have grown, Mooey! Oh,

what sad changes since you left! Your father a prisoner with a leg lost, your uncles gone from Jalna and our sad loss here." Yet in spite of this sad recital there was a comfortable look about Meg. She did not make Maurice feel unhappy, as his mother had done.

Now his cousin Patience appeared on the scene, a slim edition of her mother but with gray eyes. Maurice held out his hand but Meg exclaimed — "What formality! You must kiss each other. To think, Pheasant, that they both are seventeen — and practically fatherless!"

"Mooey is n't practically fatherless," said Pheasant, almost fiercely. "Piers is likely to return quite soon. There is talk of an exchange of prisoners."

Maurice saw the flash of antagonism between the two. Then, turning to Patience, he said — "How you have changed, Patience. You 're a woman grown."

"You speak differently," said Patience. "I suppose you got it from Cousin Dermot. Is it Irish?"

"Heavens, no!" cried Meg. "An Irish gentleman does n't speak with a brogue."

"I suppose you 'll despise our ways now," Patience said, with a teasing look.

Maurice was embarrassed. He could only say — "Oh, no, I 'll not."

"And you 're rich too," she persisted, "and we are all so terribly poor."

Maurice was scarlet. "Indeed, and I 'm not."

"Listen to the Irish of him!" laughed Patience. "Indeed and I 'm not!"

Meg considered Maurice contemplatively. "What a pity," she said, "that you don't come into the money till you are twenty-one! You could do so much with it right now."

"Yes, I suppose I could," he agreed, still more confused.

"Is n't it a strange thing" — Meg turned to Pheasant — "that Granny's fortune was inherited by Finch, a boy of nineteen, and Cousin Dermot's by Mooey, a boy of seventeen! It does n't seem fair."

"I hope Mooey's money lasts longer than Finch's did," said Pheasant. "It was shameful the way Finch's money disappeared."

"Shameful!" Meg's eyes became prominent. "What do you mean *shameful?* I certainly never had — " Suddenly she remembered that Finch had paid off the mortgage on Vaughanlands. It had been only a loan but the interest had been paid more and more irregularly, till at last it was quite forgotten. Meg concluded: "Anything Finch did for us he did because he *wanted* to."

"Of course," said Pheasant. "I always thought Finch acted as though he wanted to get rid of everything Gran left him."

"And now," put in Patience, "he has got rid of his wife."

"With all her wealth!" mourned Meg.

"I 'm afraid," said Pheasant, "that Mooey will think we are very cynical."

"You may be cynical," retorted Meg, "but I have only the welfare of the family at heart and always have had and always shall."

As she stood planted firmly in front of the rich foliage of late summer, she looked the very spirit of benevolence and there was no one there to contradict her. Patience regarded her with amused devotion; Pheasant, in controlled irritation; Maurice, in admiration; Nooky, in wonder; Philip, speculating as to whether she would give him anything. She gave him a kiss and exclaimed: —

"He grows more like Piers every day! He 's the one perfect Whiteoak among all the children. Poor Alayne, I feel sorry for her, with that boy of hers!"

Pheasant gave a sigh. "Well," she said, "we must be off. The old uncles will be anxious to see Mooey."

"Give them my love — the old dears! You 'll see a

great change in them, Mooey. I doubt if they 'll survive till all my brothers are home again."

"I don't think they 've changed much," said Pheasant stoutly. "I think it is remarkable how little they 've changed."

"Remarkable — for ninety — yes. Quite remarkable for ninety."

"Gran lived to be a hundred."

"Men don't endure like women. Heavens, if a man had gone through what I have! Well, he just could n't do it."

Again no one contradicted her.

On the way to Jalna, Pheasant exclaimed — " She may have gone through a lot but — what care she takes of herself! And Patience is just the same. They do nothing to help, though we 're at our wit's end at Jalna."

"Patience is a lazy lump," said Philip.

The car was entering the driveway of Jalna. The spruces and hemlocks stood close and dark. To Maurice it seemed not so much an entrance as a defense. The trees reared themselves to conceal the house, to protect the family. Not only the evergreen trees, but the great weeping birch on the lawn, and the oaks and the maples. The Virginia creeper, nearing its ninetieth year, now had difficulty in finding fresh space for its growth. Long tendrils were festooned from the eaves and dangled from the porch, swayed by every breeze, seeming in their avidity to reach for support down to the very humans who passed under. But at one corner of the house the vine had been cut away in order to make some repairs, and in that place the rosy red of the old bricks was prominent and bathed, as it were consciously, in the sunshine. Two old gentlemen were seated on chairs near to the birch tree. These were the two great-uncles, Nicholas and Ernest Whiteoak. Nicholas had a plaid traveling rug over his knees. He was somewhat sunk in his chair, his massive head, well thatched by iron-gray hair, looking a little large for the body which in the last four years, that is the years of the war, had considerably shrunk. But his shoulders still were broad though bent, his face because of its strong and handsome bony structure was still impressive, and his hands, which were his one remaining vanity and which he had inherited from his mother, looked the hands of a much younger man. His voice too had power, as he now called out : —

" Hullo, hullo, hullo, Mooey! Come and kiss your old uncle! Come and kiss him quick! "

Now this was the expression which his mother, Adeline Whiteoak, had often used in her very old age and it annoyed his brother to hear it on Nicholas's lips. Did Nick imagine that, by repeating expressions so peculiarly hers, he could live to be a hundred, as she had? Ernest could not help feeling annoyed but he smiled eagerly, as he held out both hands to Maurice, and murmured : —

" Dear boy, how you 've grown! And how like your mother you are, though you have blue eyes."

Nicholas was rumbling on, still uttering expressions used by old Adeline — " Bring all the boys here, Pheasant. I like the young folk about me."

His great-uncles had many questions to ask about Dermot Court and more especially about his last illness. Maurice could not recall those days without a feeling of great sadness. He wished he need not talk about them. The three boys had dropped to the grass but Pheasant still stood. Now she looked at her wrist watch exclaiming : —

" How the day is going! And I have about fifty baskets of early apples to grade and pack. You two small boys must come and help. Mooey, when the uncles have finished their talk with you, you must go into the house and see Auntie Alayne and Adeline."

" This lawn," observed Ernest, " badly needs mowing. I have never before seen it in such a state. The south lawn

is no better than hay.   It will take a scythe to prepare for
the mower.   I wonder if you would undertake to mow this
front lawn, Mooey."

"Oh, yes," agreed Maurice, doubtfully.

Pheasant supplied the heartiness.   "Of course he will —
he'll love to.   Come along, boys!"

Nooky and Philip dragged themselves to their feet and
limply followed her.   A quarter hour had scarcely passed
when Philip rejoined the group on the lawn.

"I thought you were helping your mother," said Nicholas
sternly.

"I couldn't do it properly," he returned, and lay down.

The front door of the house now opened and Adeline
Whiteoak came out to the porch.   She wore riding breeches
and a white shirt.   For a moment she hesitated, looking at
Maurice, then ran down the steps and came to him.

"Hullo!" she said.   "So you're back."

Maurice took the hand she held out.

"Dear boy, kiss your cousin!" urged Ernest.

The two young faces bumped softly together.   "How
firm her cheek is!" thought Maurice.   "And as smooth as
satin."

Nicholas and Ernest looked at each other as though to
say — "What a pretty pair!"

"Mummie had to take Archie to the doctor," Adeline
said.   "It's his tonsils.   Roma went too because she needs
new shoes.   But they'll not be long.   Are you glad to be
home again?"

"Yes, indeed," he answered politely.

Ernest said to Nicholas — "He has true Irish politeness.
He speaks like Dermot."

"How long are you staying?" asked Adeline.   "Always?"

"Till I'm twenty-one."

"Are you glad?"

" Yes, indeed."

He was a puzzling boy, she thought. You could not tell whether or not he meant what he said.

" Rags has homemade grape wine for us," she went on. " Will you come in and have some? "

" Thank you. I 'd like to," he answered, with a little bow.

" Uncles, will you have some? " She leant over them, solicitously.

They gratefully declined but Philip sprang up. " I 'll have some," he said.

" Wait till you 're asked," returned Adeline severely.

She led the way into the house. On the table in the dining room stood a squat bottle of grape juice and a plate of small biscuits. Presiding over these was Wragge, the houseman. He was a cockney who had been batman to Renny Whiteoak in the first Great War, had returned with him to Jalna, had become the devoted though critical servant of the family, further entrenching himself by marrying the cook. Again he had followed the master of Jalna to war, helped to save his life at Dunkirk, had later that year been himself severely wounded and in 1941 been discharged from the army and returned to civilian life. His wife, the cook, had always been fat while he was thin. Now she was enormously fat while he was thin to emaciation. She suffered considerably from arthritis, and he more than a little from his old wound. Her temper had always been quick, his of the sort that smouldered and sputtered. Now both were highly explosive. Still she was thankful to have him back in the basement kitchen and he was thankful each morning to discover her mountainous body beside him when he woke. He would put his arm about it, clinging to it as a shipwrecked man to a raft.

Together they did the greater part of the work in the house that was far from convenient to work in, where there were two old gentlemen who had, from infancy, been waited on and who expected summoning bells to be answered with celerity. To Alayne, Renny's wife, fell the task of bed-making and dusting, of getting three children off to school in term time, of mending, of darning, of making the little girls do some share of the work, of supervising their studies.

Early in the war Pheasant and her two boys had come to live at Jalna, their house being let. At the time it had been considered a good arrangement but it had not worked out well — two women with different ideas of how a house should be run — too many children — too much noise for the uncles. At the end of six months Pheasant's tenants departed and she thankfully returned with her boys to her own home, a general thanksgiving arising at the same time from Jalna.

Now Wragge came forward beaming to greet young Maurice.

" Welcome 'ome, sir. This is a 'appy day for the family, sir. Not only to see you return but to see you return with a fortune."

Maurice shook hands with him. " Thank you, Rags," he said, rather embarrassed.

" I remember," said Wragge, " when you were born, as if it was yesterday. I remember when you was a little codger and your father used to carry you about on his shoulder. A great pity about your father, is n't it, sir? "

" Yes, it 's a great pity."

" He was a well-set-up gentleman and one with a good walk — a soldierly figure. Ah, well, we 'll be glad to see 'im 'ome, no matter 'ow he comes. War is hell and no mistike. I ain't the man I was, Mr. Maurice. You may 'ave noticed."

" You do look a bit thin, Rags."

" Thin is no nime for it! But — 'ave you seen my missus? She weighs fourteen stone, she does."

He filled two glasses with grape juice, remarking —

"We've reached a low ebb here, where liquid refreshment is concerned, sir. It's not like the old days. To be sure, the old gentlemen keep a small supply for their own use but they guards it fierce. This 'ere grape wine my wife made last year and it's pretty good, if I do say it. Miss Adeline enjoys it. Don't you, miss? Wot do you think of our young lidy, sir?"

"I think she's grown."

Rags looked dotingly at Adeline. "Grown! Why, she might pass for fifteen and she's only thirteen! Give her another year and she'll be 'aving admirers — if she 'as n't already. I suspect that she 'as, if the truth was known."

Adeline smiled imperturbably. But Maurice did not like the man's familiarity. It was of a different quality from the familiarity of Irish servants. Seeing Adeline standing there under the portrait of her great-grandmother, the wine-glass in her hand, Maurice had the desire to protect her. There was a new something about her that appealed to his developing manhood. After all, he thought, I am almost a man, I am the only young man at Jalna. Adeline needs looking after.

"'Ave a biscuit, sir?" asked Rags, proffering the plate. "I'll bet you don't get biscuits like these in Ireland."

"No, thank you. I've had a very late breakfast."

Rags exclaimed — "Well, I must be off. I've promised to pluck two chickens for Mrs. Wragge." He hastened down the basement stairs, warning as he left — "Don't you go drinking too much of that there grape juice, miss. It 'as a real kick in it."

Left alone, the two cousins were silent for a space. Adeline was systematically eating the cookies. Presently Maurice asked, in a new intimate tone: —

"Do you like that fellow?"

"Yes," she answered laconically. "Don't you?"

"No. I don't. I think he's cheeky."

"Oh, Rags is all right. As a matter of fact, he and I almost run this house."

Maurice stared. "You do?"

"Well, when we want a thing done, we generally get it done."

"Oh, I see."

"This place," she went on, as she finished the last biscuit, "is going to rack and ruin."

"Is it really? Why is that?"

"Well, in the house everything is out of repair. The roof. The plumbing. Everything. There's no money for repairs. But the farm is far worse. We've one farm hand. We used to have four. Wright is the only man in the stables. Wright and I run the stables. If it wasn't for us they'd be sunk."

"You must be pretty busy."

She nodded her head vigorously. "You bet I am. Like to feel my muscle?" She drew up the sleeve of her shirt and flexed the muscle in her round brown arm.

Maurice laid his hand on it and pressed.

"By George!" he exclaimed.

"Let's feel yours."

He drew back. "No."

"You're ashamed of it!"

"No, I'm not."

"I'll bet it's as flabby as a poached egg."

"Feel it then." He extended his arm.

She felt his muscle and looked aghast. "Gosh!" she exclaimed. "Don't you take any exercise?"

"Well, I play some tennis and I walk a good deal."

A smile lit her face, imparting an almost sardonic quality to its childish beauty. She said: —

"You'll soon get a muscle here."

"How?" Maurice spoke defensively, deciding that she was not as pretty as he had at first thought.

" Oh, hammering in the heads of apple barrels — digging potatoes — there are lots of ways. You don't like horses, do you? "

" I don't like riding," he answered resolutely.

" I 've always heard that about you. Wright says it 's because you had too many falls schooling polo ponies. But falls have n't turned me against riding. Like to come and see the horses? "

" I think I ought to go and find my mother."

" Come upstairs first and see my room."

" Very well."

She led the way to the room that had been her father's. Inside she tried to soften the look of pride that had come over her face. " I used to sleep on the top floor with the other children," she said, casually, " but last spring I moved down here. It 's more convenient in case the uncles or Mummie need me and I like it because it is Daddy's."

He would get even with her, Maurice thought, for what she had said about his muscle.

" I guess you like it because it makes you feel important." He smiled.

She answered quickly — " I 'd feel important if I slept in the basement."

" I 'll bet you would. In any case, it 's not a bit like a girl's room."

" I don't want it to be."

" You wish you were a boy then? "

" No!   I just want it to be like Daddy's room."

Maurice did not think it was an attractive room but he felt that he was expected to praise it. " It 's very nice," he said.

" Those pictures are famous horses.   Here are his pipes." She ran her finger across the rack on which they hung. " There are nineteen of them. He just took one with him. His clothes are still in the cupboard. I use only half of it."

She displayed the interior of the cupboard where her childish garments hung among tweed and serge and corduroy. "All his ties and shirts and things are in the drawers waiting for him."

" You think a lot of him, don't you? "

" Oh, yes. I suppose you do of your father too."

" Yes, indeed."

" Is n't it awful their being gone so long? "

" Yes, it is pretty awful," he agreed. " Especially, of course, for our mothers."

Adeline looked at him almost sombrely. Then she said — " Well, we 'd better go and find the others."

Walking with her to the orchard, Maurice thought he had never before known what September heat could be; or perhaps he had forgotten. The sun seemed to have drawn the last drop of moisture from the land. The path beneath Maurice's feet felt like cement. There was no breeze to stir so much as a grass blade. He wondered how the laborer he could see ploughing in a distant field could endure the heat. He glanced at Adeline. She looked warm — no more.

" This heat is awful," he muttered.

" You 're dressed all wrong. But, if you call this hot, you should have been here last week. It took a terrific storm to clear the air. It 's nice now. There 's Auntie Pheasant with the boys."

Philip had returned to the orchard. Boards laid on trestles made a table for the array of baskets which Pheasant and Nook were packing with the reddest apples, Maurice thought, he had ever seen. Philip was bringing them the apples from a great mound on the ground. Pheasant cried: —

" It 's a perfect shame to be working on your first day home, Mooey, but these apples must be put on the train at two o'clock. We 're slaves here, are n't we, Adeline? Don't be so rough with the apples, Philip! And look here,

Nook, don't you go putting the best ones on the top or we shall get a bad name."

"I don't do it to be dishonest," said Nook. "But just because they look prettier that way."

"Everyone expects the best apples to be on the top," said Adeline, tersely. "I looked into some baskets at the market and they all had. And I asked the man and he said they were all that way."

"I'd put the best on top," Philip declared, "and I'd put rotten ones underneath."

"You little scoundrel!" Pheasant gave him a look half-stern, half-laughing.

"Not rotten," said Adeline. "Just not quite so round and rosy. They'd taste just as good."

"What would those underneath be like in Ireland, Mooey?" asked Pheasant, her eyes caressing him.

"Oh, they'd be rotten enough."

He took off his jacket and set to work. But he was slow, unaccustomed. The heat was almost intolerable to him. Every time he was near to Pheasant she touched him. She could scarcely believe that she had him back. She said: —

"No one of us is going to do a hand's turn of work this afternoon. We shall just give ourselves up to the joy of having you back. We're going to have a picnic tea on the lawn and Mrs. Wragge is making ice cream!"

"Hurrah!" shouted Philip.

"Hurrah!" shouted Nook, putting a misshapen apple in the bottom of the basket he was packing.

Maurice felt like one in a dream. The half-forgotten life of his childhood had opened to receive him, had taken him back. Its walls had closed behind him. He thought of September in County Meath. He drew back to him the picture of Glengorman in September, the hushed cool meadows, the river that seemed scarcely to move, and how it gave back, almost unbroken, the reflection of the slow-flying heron.

And the life with Dermot Court! He had been the cherished child of the old man. From the moment he had entered the house he had done just as he had pleased, he could do no wrong. He had been the white-haired boy.

And now he was home again — where it had once seemed to him that he could do nothing to please his father. Now he was one of many. He did not know what to say to his young brothers. All about him was an activity in which he would be expected to take a part. There was something new, purposeful and practical, in his mother. She was asking: —

"Can you drive a car, Mooey?"

"Yes, indeed I can," he answered.

"Oh, that's splendid! You will be able to drive the truck to the station. It takes such a lot of Wright's time and puts him completely out of temper."

A strange feeling of loneliness came over Maurice.

II

FINCH'S RETURN

A MONTH later Finch Whiteoak was walking along the country road, on his way from the railway station to Jalna. He had taken the local line from the city, not sending word home to say when he would arrive. He wanted the exercise of the walk after the long rail journey across the continent and he wanted to be alone. Yet he was scarcely alone, for with him walked, ran, trudged, or loitered, the many selves of his childhood and boyhood who had traversed this road.

It was October and the countryside had already felt the sharpness of frost. Summer was reluctantly giving way to the coming of winter. Like the banners of a defeated army the trees hung out their scarlet, their gold, and their green. Finch took off his hat that he might feel the crispness of the air on his head. Three days, four nights on the train — he could still feel the vibration.

He had a vision of himself as a small boy seated beside his grandmother in her phaeton, moving sedately along the road on a summer's day, behind the glistening flanks of the bays. He could see her handsome old face, framed in her widow's veil which fell voluminously over her shoulders and down her back. Her expression was purposeful, as it always was when she set out on any expedition however small. Sitting beside her in the phaeton with Hodge's, the coachman's, broad back looming in front of him, with the hoofs of the bays thudding rhythmically on the smooth road, he had felt more secure, more sheltered from the world than at any other time. Well, she had been dead sixteen years, a long while. A good deal had happened to him since then. He threw back his shoulders, as though he were freeing them from a burden, and took a long breath. He would let the freshness of the morning penetrate through all his being.

He had not seen Jalna for a year. During the winter and spring he had given a series of concerts in the large cities. Now he was returning from a trip to the Pacific Coast where he had played to Canadian and American servicemen. He was going home for rest he badly needed. He felt humiliated that he was so often tired, that periodic long rests were so often necessary to him. What was wrong with him, he wondered. There was his youngest brother, Wakefield, who had been a delicate boy with a weak heart and a poor appetite, while he himself had been strong and able to digest anything — always hungry. Yet Wakefield had outgrown his weakness. He was a flier who had seen long hard service, had been decorated for great courage, and now was an instructor in a flying school out West. He had had hard experiences in his private life too.

Finch Whiteoak was a distinguished-looking man. He strode along the country road, long-legged, with a kind of angular grace. His features were strongly marked, his lips sensitive, the hollows in his cheeks emphasizing these qualities. He walked so fast that a fresh color had appeared in his face when he turned into the drive. He ran up the steps of the porch and entered the house. At that instant his brother Renny's wife came out of the library and almost collided with him. She was carrying a vase in which there were little bronze and yellow chrysanthemums. She had worn a look of anxious concentration which had turned, first to dismay, as she had almost dropped the vase, then to pleasure at the sight of Finch.

"Why, Finch," she exclaimed. "You here! How nice! Why didn't you send us word to meet you?"

"I wanted the walk." He kissed her cheek and took the vase from her. "Where shall I put it?" he asked.

" Just there on the table. Do come and sit down. I want to talk to you before you go to see the uncles."

They went into the library, where at this hour the sun blazed.

" Where are the dogs? " he asked, feeling a lack in the room.

" Outdoors." She spoke firmly, as though it had not been without struggle that she had kept them there.

" Oh . . . How are the uncles? "

" Just fairly well. They 're still up in their rooms. Are you hungry, Finch? Will you have something to eat now or wait till lunch? "

" I 'll wait, thanks."

" Have some coffee."

" I 'd love that. But first tell me how you are getting on."

Alayne made a gesture of despair. " You can imagine. It 's impossible to get help. There 's an enormous crop of apples. How they 're to be picked, graded, and shipped, heaven only knows. Rags and his wife are out in the orchard now. We had the threshers yesterday. We 're half-dead."

He made noises of sympathy. " No wonder," he exclaimed. Then he added admiringly — " But you always look so nice, Alayne."

She gave a faint smile. " Thanks. See how white my hair has got."

" It 's lovely. Becoming too."

" It 's not much wonder I 'm white."

" No. Have you heard from Renny lately? "

" I had a letter last week. He 's still in Italy. He 's well. I believe he could have got leave if he 'd tried hard enough. But he seems to think he 's indispensable. Other officers are n't."

" Of course he 's a colonel now."

" Yes. Just think — he went over in the fall of 1939.

When he and Piers come home — if they ever do — they 'll be different men."

" They 'll not change, Alayne."

She gave a little shrug. " Perhaps not. But they 'll find the rest of us greatly changed. They 'll not recognize their own children. Why, Finch, you should see Maurice. He 's a young man. He 's charming. But Piers won't understand him or get on with him — even as well as he used. As for Philip, his mother can do nothing with him. Maurice has had several actual fights with him, trying to make him behave."

" Hmph." Finch's expression became grim. " I pity him when Piers comes home. How are your own children, Alayne ? "

Her face lighted in pride. " Oh, they are developing wonderfully. Adeline amazes me. When I think of what I was at her age ! Really I was a baby. She will take on any sort of responsibility. I honestly believe she thinks of herself as the Master of Jalna while Renny is away. She 's as strong as a pony."

" And Archer ? "

" He has a remarkable mind and a will like iron. He thinks everything out for himself."

Again Finch muttered " Hmph." A nice lot were growing up at Jalna. He did not ask for Roma, his dead brother Eden's daughter. He knew that the child's presence in the house was a sore point with Alayne.

They went to the basement kitchen and Alayne made coffee. The kitchen, with its brick floor, its deep fireplace, was quiet and warm. They sat down by the table to drink the coffee and Finch lighted a cigarette. It was not till then that Alayne said : —

" Would you like to tell me something about your — separation from Sarah ? "

" It 's not a separation. It 's a divorce. Or soon will be.

As you know, she went to Reno and got what they call a divorce there. Now I've filed a petition in Ottawa. God knows I have grounds for it!"

" She has married again, hasn't she? "

" Yes. To a Russian."

" And you will be free to marry! "

" I don't think I shall risk it again."

" I think you 're very sensible."

He gave a little laugh. " But you did, Alayne. You married again."

" Yes," she returned calmly, " but I was in love with Renny before my divorce from Eden. I don't think you 're in love with anyone, are you? "

" Not a bit. And don't intend to be."

After a silence she said — " I think you should go to see the uncles. They 'll be so delighted. Life is pretty dull for them these days. We all are so busy." She felt that Finch did not want to talk about himself. She saw that he was nervously tired.

He looked about the kitchen. " How peaceful it is here! " he said. " God, what a world! I 'd like to stay down here till the war is over."

" You 'd not find the Wragges very peaceful company. They 're really terrible but I don't know how we should have got on without them."

A bell jangled violently. Alayne looked up at the row of bells on the wall. " That is Uncle Nick's," she said. " I wonder what he wants."

She sighed, like a poor overworked housewife. Was this the Alayne, Finch wondered, who, in the old days, had never raised her hand unless she chose? Now she said: —

" They 're not so feeble as they think they are. It is simply that they 've been waited on hand and foot all their lives. They 're spoilt."

"Don't you come," said Finch. "I'll get whatever it is Uncle Nick wants."

"Thanks. But don't go in too suddenly."

"I'll whistle as I go."

The bell rang again.

"That's the way they go on," exclaimed Alayne. "I wonder the Wragges stand it."

Finch ran up the stairs. Nicholas was standing in the passage outside his bedroom. He extended both arms to Finch. He gathered him in and embraced him. He said: —

"I heard your voice below. I couldn't wait. I wanted to see you. Gad, what a long time it seems! Ernest! Here's Finch!"

Ernest came out of his room. "Come right into my room," he said. "We'll have a good talk. You look well, dear boy, but a little tired. How nice it is to have you home again! Mooey is back. Did you know that Mooey is back? A different boy. So improved. Such good manners. Not that he wasn't a gentle boy. But now he has a manner. He's grown up. Ireland's been good for him."

The two old men placed Finch in an armchair and beamed down at him.

"Did you get the newspaper cuttings I sent?" asked Finch.

"Yes, yes," answered Ernest. "They were very good. Very appreciative. We're very proud of you. Proud of all our nephews. But we do miss you. Things are very different here. Alayne does the best she can, poor girl, but she has no real executive ability."

"Alayne does very well," put in Nicholas.

Ernest continued — "But she has no real authority over the Wragges. They do as they like. She cannot control the children and, if we try to do it for her, she doesn't like it. She gets quite upset."

"I pulled Archer's ear for him yesterday," muttered Nicholas.

"She did n't like that — not at all," said Ernest.

"Neither did he! Neither did he! But have you seen Adeline? She 's a beautiful girl, Finch."

"No, I have n't seen her. I 've just come."

Nicholas regarded him quizzically. "Been getting divorced, eh?"

"Yes, Uncle Nick."

"Just like me, eh?"

"Yes."

"That 's right. If wives misbehave, get rid of them. Who 's this fellow she has married?"

"A Russian. I can't pronounce his name. Ends in *sky*."

Nicholas blew out his breath. "Well, well — *sky*, eh? I 'll bet he gets away with every dollar of her money."

"What a pity!" said Ernest. "So much could have been done with a nice fortune like that."

"I don't want any of it," exclaimed Finch, hotly.

"Not for your family's sake?" Ernest asked reprovingly.

"Well, perhaps for them."

"What does this Russian do?" inquired Nicholas.

"Nothing that I know of."

"What about your little boy?"

"I am to have him with me a part of the time."

"How old is he?"

"He will be four on Christmas Eve."

"Yes, I remember."

Ernest remarked — "It seems strange to think that a man with a name ending in *sky* should bring up a Whiteoak."

Finch laughed. "He will have nothing to say about the bringing up. Sarah allows no interference."

"You seem oddly detached about your son," said Ernest. "That is unusual in our family."

A flush came into Finch's cheeks. He said — "Everything has been unusual in my connection with Sarah. Even my relations with her child."

"*Her* child!"

"Our child, then."

"Sarah was a damned queer woman from the first," rumbled Nicholas. "When she went off with that Russian you should have got an order from the courts to give you complete possession of the boy."

"Sarah is an adoring mother. I'm not an adoring father. Dennis scarcely seems like my child."

"Yet you have always been so fond of the children of the family!" exclaimed Ernest.

"I know."

"Are you in doubt as to whether the child is yours?" asked Nicholas, his large, deep-set eyes searching Finch's face.

"I'm positive he is." After a moment he added — "If I were n't so positive I might have been a happier man — if you know what I mean."

"That woman," said Nicholas, "concentrated every atom of her queer being on you. I've never seen the equal of it. It does n't do." He took his pipe from his pocket and began to fill it.

"How do you think Alayne looks?" asked Ernest.

"Rather tired."

"She fusses too much," declared Ernest. "From morning to night she thinks of things that ought to be done or should n't have been done. Now I look at it this way: here we are — helpless, you might say. There is a war. We've got to accept things as they come. Our little doings are so paltry compared to the stupendous happenings in Europe, they 're not worth worrying about."

"Then why do you worry," asked his brother, "when your meals are late?"

" Because late meals give me indigestion. I am fearful of becoming ill and adding to the burdens of the household."

Nicholas winked at Finch.

" Grand old boy, your Uncle Ernest," he said. " Never fusses. Never gives any trouble."

Ernest smiled good-humoredly. The two settled down for a long conversation with Finch. The familiar quality of this atmosphere which was of the very essence of Jalna closed in about Finch. His concerts, his long train journeys, seemed far away and unreal. Here was his reality. No matter if it were extraordinary to other people, it was his reality. Looking back on his life with Sarah he saw how she had laid waste its freshness and its vigor. Almost from the first he had felt something insensate in her. She was a figure in porcelain who somehow had managed to inspire passion in him, to devastate his life. But now he was free of her. Never again! The grip of those arms . . . those lips . . . but now he was free and in his own place! He was not the man he might have been if he had never known her. On the other hand he could look back on the poignant spasm of his desire for her as a thing conquered, outlived. Perhaps the great love of his life lay ahead. With the surface of his mind he basked in the company of the two old men. In its depths he explored his past.

Late in the day he wandered alone through the fields and woods. The land lay in the dreaming beauty of Indian summer. It was many months since he had been weary from outdoor exercise. He turned toward the stables, thinking he might find Adeline there. It was likely she would pay the horses a visit soon after her return from school. He remembered his own school days and how hard it had been to spend the lovely fall months in those journeyings on train and long sessions in classrooms.

The doors of the stables were wide-open to let in the mild sweet air. The horses had been bedded and fed. The smell of clean straw came to him and, when he stepped inside, the sounds of placid enjoyment of the evening meal. The occupants of stalls and loose boxes looked out at him, as he passed, with a kind of noble unconcern, as though recognize him they could, if they but thought it worth the while. He was a part of Jalna, they knew, but a being of no importance.

How different he was from the young girl who stood beside the aged mare, Cora, in the loose box at the farther end of the passage! The very sight of her, the sound of her voice, created a stir of pleasure that was transmitted in some mysterious way from stall to stall. Finch now saw her leaning against the mare's shoulder, her auburn hair touched by sunlight slanting through a small window so that there was a look of the young crusader about her, or the young saint.

Finch smiled at this fancy. Adeline, he guessed, was a very human child and probably badly spoilt. She was looking up into the face of Wright, who lounged beside her, and they talked with the air of intimates. Wright had put her on her first pony when she was five. Since then horses had been the absorbing subject of all their conversations. Finch heard her say: —

"If we can't show our horses properly, what's the use of keeping them?"

Wright returned glumly — "That's just what the mistress thinks. She don't see no sense in it. She'd like to see the lot of them sold."

"And have my father come home and find empty stables!"

"Sure. Except for Cora here and the roan and the work horses. She'd like to see 'em all sold."

"Never!" exclaimed Adeline hotly. "We'll never do it, Wright! You'll stand by me, won't you?"

Wright threw the most profound feeling into his voice. "I'd rather," he said, "part with my wife and child than with these here horses. But the mistress — she don't understand how you and me and the boss feel."

"Let her keep out of this! Let her attend to her own affairs!"

Finch now thought it better to appear. He did so with an air of innocence, as having overheard nothing. He kissed Adeline. It was like kissing a flower, her cheek was so cool, so fresh. The freshness, the newness of her was so potent. Her nose no longer looked too large for her child's face. It was superb. And what nostrils — designed to express pride, fierceness, if need be! The mouth no longer a rosebud but with the smiling lips of a happy girl.

"I was pretty sure," said Finch, "where I should find you."

"Wright and I," returned Adeline proudly, "run the stables."

"It keeps us busy, I can tell you, sir," put in Wright, grinning. Then he added soberly, "I don't know what I'd do without Miss Adeline. There's nothing she won't turn her hand to. She rides at all the best shows. Of course, there aren't any real big ones since the war but there's a good many. Gosh, you ought to see her ride, sir! I often say to my wife that one of the reasons I hope the boss will come out of this war alive is so he can see her ride."

"I hope he will," said Finch.

Wright went on — "I can't say we get all the co-operation from the big house that we should, sir. It makes it hard to carry on. There's things that need doing about the stables and we can't get permission to have them done. It will be different when the boss comes home."

"I write to him every week," said Adeline.

"To tell him how well you are getting on at school, I suppose," said Finch.

"I hate school!"

"So did I."

"It spoils everything. You can't get on with what you really want to do."

"I never bothered much about school," said Wright. "They learned me how to read and write. That was enough for me. Now take Mr. Maurice, he likes book learning. But he has n't got no use for horses."

"He has n't got any use for anything that looks like work," declared Adeline. "We thought when he came home he'd be an extra man. But he's a lazy dog. Gosh, is n't he lazy, Wright?"

Wright, with a straw between his teeth, laughed derisively. "Say, I'd back one of his two little brothers against him for work, any day. Just to see him take a hold of anything manual shows he has n't any interest in it. But he's got the dough, so he'll be able to do what he likes."

Finch said, "Come along, Adeline, I want to talk to you."

"Don't you want to see the horses first?"

"I'll see them to-morrow. It's Saturday. You'll be at home."

Outside he said to her — "Look here, I don't think you ought to discuss family affairs with Wright. He's too familiar."

Her fine brows went up. "Who shall I discuss them with?"

"I don't think you should have said what you did about your mother — just as I was going in I heard you."

"Pooh — that was nothing!"

"It was n't respectful to her."

"I'm always respectful to her."

"But you should be, behind her back, as well as to her face."

"I know. But you can't think how hard it is for Wright and me, with her always interfering. Do you know she wants to send me to boarding school? She knows we can't afford it but she wants to send me away from Jalna. Yet we sold the horse I rode at the Yelland show, for eighteen hundred dollars! What do you think of that?" Her eyes flashed pride at Finch. Her slender body was taut with pride.

"Splendid!" he exclaimed.

"The American who bought him said he would n't have made an offer if he had n't seen me ride him."

"Fine!"

"Well, that was a lot of money, was n't it, Uncle Finch?"

"It was. Does your father know?"

"I wrote right away. I guess he 'll have my letter by now. You can see how it 's necessary for me to be here. Yet Mummie 's always talking of sending me to boarding school."

The calm golden beauty of the October evening was descending on the orchard as they passed by. It was dusk already beneath the trees but great mounds of apples could be seen, and some of the branches hung low with their weight.

"It looks a profitable crop," remarked Finch.

Adeline drew her brows together in a line of troubled responsibility. "If we can harvest them! We simply can't get men."

"I will turn in to-morrow morning," he declared.

"Tell Mummie that. She will be glad."

Adeline's tone was so heartfelt that Finch turned to look down at her, striding beside him. There was something pathetic, he thought, in the little figure, for all its courage. Above it arched the immensity of the sky; behind rose the bulk of the stables, their occupants to be cared for, exercised, exhibited at shows; there stretched the army of apple trees, their fruit to be garnered and sold; ahead the dark shape of vine-embowered house with all its problems. The child, he felt sure, was eager to thrust her slender shoulders under the weight of responsibility, never considering herself a responsibility or problem.

Oh, it was good to be home! He put out his hand and took one of Adeline's in it. They swung along together.

"To-morrow morning," he said, "you'll have a new hired man. The thought of physical work is bliss."

"Good," she returned stoutly. "To-morrow is Saturday. I'll be working with you."

As they neared the house he looked across the ravine where dark night was settling. "How are those girls who live at the fox farm?" he asked.

"They're a funny lot. They keep to themselves. They lead a very confiscated life."

"Do you mean *isolated?*"

"I expect I do. Their sister's an actress and she supports them. They're queer but I like them. Do you know them?"

"A little. I think I'll go to see them on my afternoon off — if you can spare me."

III

THE SISTERS

ON the following day the three sisters who lived in the house called the fox farm were gathered about a round table eating their evening meal. The house had once been occupied by people who bred silver foxes, and though that had been years ago the name still clung. The three Griffiths had lived here since the first year of the war. Their stepsister had brought them out from Wales that she might better provide for them. Though they were grown-up they were helpless as children when it came to looking after themselves. Before coming to Canada they had lived on a remote farm in the heart of the Welsh hills. They had seen almost no one outside their own family. Then their father had died, and their brother had been killed in an airplane accident. They had been helpless, like frightened children, and had obediently and eagerly journeyed to this new world to which their stepsister, herself only a young girl, had urged them to come. She was an actress whose occasional appearances on the screen made it possible for her to provide for them. Yet her heart was with the legitimate stage and it was there she hoped to make her name.

The three about the table showed little physical resemblance to each other, but there was a resemblance that was visible to the most casual observer. It was the likeness of people who have lived identical lives since birth. The thought of being separated, one from the other, would have been terrible to them even while they were filled with curiosity for the outer world. The journey from Wales to the fox farm had been their one adventure.

Though the table was round, the dignity of a place at its

head was given by the presence of the teapot in front of Althea, the eldest, a silvery-fair girl in her middle twenties. At first sight she looked very thin till it was seen that her bones were unusually small. She wore an attractive dress of a light green color which was in contrast to the careless, almost shabby attire of her sisters, both of whom were eating much more heartily than she.

Gemmel, the one next to her in age, had a pale, pointed face, wide at the temples, with large greenish-blue eyes and lively dark hair. The dominant expression of her face was an almost ruthless interest in those about her. The circle of her activity was small, for she had been unable to walk since early childhood because of a fall. Her hands were supple and very strong. By means of them, half-sitting, half-kneeling, she propelled herself about the house.

Garda, the youngest, was a sturdy girl of twenty, with rosy cheeks and childlike eyes, but she had a temper. She was by far the strongest of the three and took it as a matter of course that she should do the rough work. Between times of working she was indolent, loved her bed, and had to be routed out in the morning. In the early hours Althea wandered through woods and fields, secure in the thought that she ran little risk at that time of meeting her neighbors, for she was restrained by an unconquerable shyness.

Now Garda exclaimed — " It does seem unfair, Althea, that you should be the only one of us who can wear Molly's clothes. Look at that lovely dress you have on and no one to see you ! "

" If you were n't so greedy," returned Althea, " you might n't be so fat."

" I 'm not fat! It 's you and Molly who are so tall and thin." She buttered another piece of bread.

" I 'd gladly give you the dress if you could get into it."

" I know you would but it 's hopeless. Nothing that

Molly casts off will fit me. I might as well eat and be merry."

Gemmel broke in impatiently — " Do let 's stop talking about clothes and talk about the Whiteoaks. To think that you 've had three encounters with them to-day, Garda! Now begin at the beginning and tell all over again."

" Goodness, I shall be tired of the very name of Whiteoak!"

" Rubbish! Now which was it you met first? "

Garda, with an air of resignation that did not conceal her gusto for the recital, began — " It was Mrs. Piers Whiteoak. I was coming from the village with my arms full of packages when she overtook me in her car. She was on her way from the railway station. She 'd been seeing about a large shipment of apples. She had her eldest son with her. He 's home from Ireland, you know."

" We ought to," laughed Althea. " We 've heard of him a dozen times in the past month."

" Oh, I wish I might see him! " Gemmel drew a long sigh. " He must be sweet. How old do you say he is? "

" Seventeen. But he seems older. He has what I call polished manners."

" And they gave you a lift? "

" Yes. Oh, she 's so happy to have him home again! And she 's heard that next spring there will be an interchange of prisoners and her husband may be returned. Her eyes shone when she told me that. I asked Maurice where he was going to school and he said they were looking about for a tutor to prepare him for the university. He is to be in Canada till he is twenty-one and then he is going back to Ireland."

" He has lots of money," said Gemmel. " Owns a mansion and large estate."

" Don't interrupt. When he goes back his mother is to

go with him for a long visit. She 's dying to see his place. You can see that she adores him."

" What a pity he 's so young!" exclaimed Gemmel. " You might marry him, Garda."

" I 'm not so old as all that."

" Seventeen and twenty! Let 's see! When he goes back to Ireland he 'll be twenty-one and you twenty-four. No, it would n't be impossible. Especially as he is old for his years and you young for yours."

" So you want to be rid of me!"

" No, but it would be fun."

" Well," Garda went on, " she let me out of the car at our gate and I was just turning in through it when who should appear but Finch, with two dogs at his heels. He arrived only yesterday."

" To think," cried Gemmel, " that I was n't looking out of the window!"

" Never mind. He 's coming to see us."

Althea flushed. " I 'll not see him."

" You 're the one he wants to see. He asked after you at once."

" Not after me?" Gemmel's eyes were tragic.

" Yes. After you too. But he likes Althea best. It 's easy to see that. Well, we talked for a bit and he told me quite simply that he 's divorced."

" Good heavens!" exclaimed Gemmel. " Would you marry a divorced man, Althea?"

" I would marry no one."

" But you do admire him?"

" Yes."

" He has such an interesting face," said Garda. " He looks as though he 'd experienced every emotion."

" I should like to give him a new one," said Gemmel boldly.

" It 's shocking to hear you, Gemmel," Althea protested. " You sound positively brazen."

Garda spoke soothingly. " She does n't mean it."

Gemmel hunched her flexible shoulders and gave her reckless laugh. " Offer me the chance," she said. She took a cigarette from her pocket, where she carried them loose, and lighted it. There was something impudent about her that caused her sisters to look at her half-disapprovingly, half-admiringly.

" I pity him," said Althea, " for I think I 've never seen a more selfish face than his wife's."

" She 's not his wife now."

" People don't forget cruel experiences, Garda."

" But it makes them appreciate kindness all the more."

" What else did he say? " asked Gemmel.

" He said he was very tired and so glad to be at Jalna again. He 's going to help with the work. They are filling the silos to-morrow. They have tables set out in the old carriage house. Quite a feast, he said. I can't see him working. He 's every inch an artist."

" Now then, tell us of the third encounter," demanded Gemmel.

" Oh, how persistent you are! " exclaimed Althea.

" You enjoy gossip just as much as I do."

" I know I do but I 'm ashamed of myself for it."

Garda continued — " The third encounter was with Mrs. Vaughan. I do like her. She 's so unaffected and so friendly. Finch had just left me when she came down the road. She was on her way to see her uncles and she was taking a jar of apple jelly to them. She seemed to think it would ease the blow she had in store for them. I 've already told you what it is."

" Yes, yes, but tell us again."

" It is simply that she has sold Vaughanlands. The entire property. And to a Mr. Clapperton — a widower."

" How marvelous! " cried Gemmel.

Althea gave a small derisive smile. " That she has sold Vaughanlands or that she's sold it to a widower? "

" Both. A new neighbor to watch. "

" She has known for some time that she must sell it, " went on Garda. " She simply cannot run that big place alone. It's going to ruin. But at the last she settled everything quickly. The papers are signed, the first payment made. She moves out at the end of the month. "

" Where to, I wonder. "

" She would have liked to go to Jalna till the end of the war but she practically said that her sister-in-law, Mrs. Renny, is very difficult to get on with. Mrs. Piers tried to live there with her two little boys in the early part of the war but she had to give up and go back to her own house. So Mrs. Vaughan is buying a house on the road where the church is. It will be a sad change for her, she says. "

" Tell us about the widower, " said Gemmel.

" He's a retired business man who has always wanted to live in the country — work in a garden, read books — that sort of man. Very nice, she says. Would it be proper for us to call on him, Althea? "

" Heavens, no. " She rose and began to collect the plates.

Gemmel watched her admiringly. " You are exactly like the drawings in fashion advertisements, " she said. " Impossibly slim and tall, with an impossibly lovely face. It's a pity you're so — whatever you are that makes you hate people. "

" I don't hate people. I only ask to be let alone. " She carried the dishes to the kitchen. As though in defiance she began to sing.

" How that song takes me back to Wales! " exclaimed Gemmel. " Oh, we were happy there, were n't we — when Father and Christopher were alive? "

" Be careful, " said Garda, " or you 'll make me cry. "

"You're pretty too. You can do anything you want to do. I am the only one who has need to cry."

Garda patted her on the back. "You are the happiest person I know, Gemmel. I often wonder why. And when it comes to faces, you have the most interesting one of the three of us. You could do anything — if you were n't handicapped."

Gemmel looked straight ahead of her, inhaling the smoke from her cigarette.

"I do very well," she said.

IV

BREAKING THE NEWS

MEG had presented the pot of jelly to her uncles, been complimented on its color and clearness. Now she sat down by the open fire and prepared to tell her news. But first she remarked: —

"It seems so strange not to see three or four dogs stretched on the hearth, as there used to be."

"Yes," Ernest agreed, "it does. But since old Merlin died, Alayne has been able to keep them more or less under control. The bulldog has taken up with Wright and spends most of his time in the stables. The sheep dog has a fancy for the kitchen. It's a good thing too because the amount of mud he carries in on his long coat is extraordinary. He was actually ruining the rugs. I think Alayne is quite right to encourage them to keep out."

"I miss them," growled Nicholas.

"So do I, Uncle Nick. And so I'm sure will Renny when he comes home, if he ever does come home, poor darling. I sometimes doubt it."

Nicholas shifted in his chair. "He'll come home, all right," he muttered.

Meg drew a deep breath and plunged into her disclosures.

"He will find other changes too. For one thing, he will not find me at Vaughanlands."

Her uncles stared at her speechless.

"I have sold it," she said, dramatically. "Lock, stock, and barrel. To a Mr. Clapperton."

The two men repeated as one voice — "Sold it!"

"Yes. Sold it. Now don't say I have done this without

consulting you, because I have been talking of selling ever since poor Maurice died. You all have known that it 's impossible for me to run the place alone. Every month it 's got harder. Every month I 've had a greater loss. Three days ago an agent brought this Mr. Clapperton to see me. He is a widower, a retired business man. His wife hated the country but he loves it. He longs to settle down and live a quiet country life, breed prize stock. That sort of man, you know. He just wants something he 's never had. He has plenty of money. He 'll pay cash. Now should n't I be foolish to stay on in that big house? Some day Patience will marry. I shall be left alone." A pathetic quaver came into her voice.

"But where will you go?" asked Ernest.

"It seems providential." She smiled, though tears were in her eyes. "The old Pink house is for sale. The house where that awful Mrs. Stroud lived, after the last war. They 're asking a ridiculous price for it but nothing is cheap nowadays. It 's a good time to sell."

"What are you getting for Vaughanlands?" asked Nicholas.

She hesitated. She hated to tell. Not that her family would resent her getting a good price. They would rejoice. But — she hated to tell. However, she said quietly: —

"Fifty-five thousand dollars."

"Whew!" exclaimed Nicholas. "Quite an advance since pioneer days when the first Vaughan bought it."

"Think of all that has been spent on the estate! Think of the amount of land!"

"I know. I know. Well, I shall try to be glad for your sake, Meggie. But it will seem queer to have a stranger at Vaughanlands."

"But he is so nice, Uncle Nick. All he wants is peace and quiet and books and a garden and prize stock. It 's quite touching to hear him talk."

" How old is he? " asked Ernest.

" Between fifty and sixty. Very well dressed. Very carefully dressed. Quite immaculately turned out."

" Humph," growled Nicholas.

" Meggie," said Ernest, " I am hurt that you should have done this without consulting us."

" Uncle Ernest, I dared not wait to consult you. Mr. Clapperton had another place in mind. He was wavering between the two. I might have lost him."

" Well, I hope he 'll be a nice neighbor."

" He will. Never doubt that. I should say that he 's the very personification of a nice neighbor."

At this moment Alayne came into the room. She had been aware that Meg was with her uncles and had given them time for conversation before entering. Now she was told of the sale of Vaughanlands and the proposed purchase of the small house. She congratulated Meg. She thought Meg had done well for herself and for Patience. They talked more congenially than was their custom.

" It will be a great relief to you," Alayne said. " I know what a burden these large places can be." She gave a sigh and clasped her hands tensely in her lap.

The three Whiteoaks bent looks on her that made her feel an outsider in spite of her twenty years' residence among them.

" Do you consider Jalna a burden? " Ernest asked, in a hurt tone.

" We have been at our wit's end to keep things going since the war, have n't we? "

" We have. But when the war is over there will be plenty of help. Renny and Piers will be home."

" If ever they come home, poor darlings," said Meg.

" How can you say such a thing! " exclaimed Alayne. " It is only the thought of their coming that makes it possible for me to keep things running."

"They 'll come. They 'll come," said Nicholas. "And it can't be too soon for me."

"Or for me," declared Meg. "I don't want them for what they can do, but just for themselves. Now that I have lost Maurice I yearn more and more for them."

Ernest laid his hand on hers. "Poor girl, you have had a hard time. Now do tell us more about this Mr. Clapperton. I do so hope he will be a congenial neighbor."

The talk circled round and round Mr. Clapperton and Meg's plans for the future. She had barely gone when Rags entered, with an air of importance.

"Excuse me, ma'am," he said, "but I 'ave to tell you that the oil 'eater 'as gone off. I can't do nothing with it. Shall I telephone for the repair man to come out?"

"Oh, Rags." Alayne spoke despairingly. "Can't Wright do anything to make it go?"

"Naow, ma'am. Wright 's 'elpless as I am. I expect there 's a fuse blown out."

"That oil heater," said Nicholas, "is a pest. I sometimes wish you never had had it installed, Alayne."

"You must acknowledge," she returned, "that the house has had a more even temperature than ever before. You have said repeatedly how comfortable it has made every room."

"I know. I know." Nicholas spoke testily. He did not like to be reminded, as Alayne so often reminded him, of what he had said on another occasion. "But it 's always getting out of order. Do you remember the three days of last winter when it was zero weather and we had no heating?"

"That I do, sir," said Rags. "And a quite bad cold Mr. Ernest caught."

"What I most object to," observed Ernest, "is that it keeps the drawing-room and library so warm that we no longer feel the need for the grate fires. They were undoubtedly cheerful."

" We still often have one in the evening."

" Yes, but it 's not the same as when one comes downstairs in the morning and sees a blaze crackling on the hearth."

Rags spoke with that unctuous quality in his voice which Alayne detested. " It was indeed cheerful, sir. And I never grumbled at carrying the coals or wood, did I ? "

" Indeed you did n't."

Alayne rose abruptly. " I must go to the children," she said. " They will come to the table without washing unless I oversee them."

" Speaking of the children, ma'am," said Rags, " I have a note 'ere from Master Archer's teacher. I met her on the road and she 'anded it to me."

" Why did n't you give it to me before? " asked Alayne.

" W'y, ma'am, I should think you 'd know. Everything was knocked right out of me 'ead by the behavior of that there oil 'eater."

What an impudent way of speaking the man had, thought Alayne. She gave him an icy look as she took the note. She read: —

Dear Mrs. Whiteoak,

I do so dislike to complain of dear little Archer, but he has been very late for school every morning this week and yesterday he did not appear till afternoon. This is very bad for his work which, as you know, is uneven. He is *so* clever in some ways. But . . .

" Is anything wrong? " interrupted Nicholas.

" No — not exactly."

" You look very disturbed," observed Ernest, peering at her. " It 's bad to get upset over minor irritations."

Rags was listening. To him Alayne said — " You may telephone for the repair man." When he had left the room she exclaimed, almost tragically: —

"It's about Archer. He has been playing truant again. Really, I don't know what to do about him."

"Boarding school is the place for boys," growled Nicholas. "The Spartan life there makes men of them."

Ernest said — "You are not severe enough with Archer. You should give him a punishment he'd remember."

Alayne loved her son with an almost painful devotion, painful because he fell so short of being what she would have him, fell so short of the large nobility of her father whom he physically resembled. She said: —

"Miss Pink is not the type of teacher to hold Archer's interest. She is far too old-fashioned."

The door opened and a boy of eight years came into the room. He looked at his elders with an air of profound pessimism. As this was his habitual expression it roused no concern. He had a high white forehead, clearly cut features, a rather thin face but a sturdy body and legs. His eyes were intensely blue, his hair very fair, straight and dry. He stood planted in the middle of the room, as though inviting attack.

"Now then, sir," said Ernest, "what about these complaints of you?"

"We know what you've been up to," added Nicholas. "So there is no use in hedging."

"I don't like going to school," said Archer. "It makes me tired."

His mother looked at him anxiously. "Archer, when you say school makes you tired, do you mean it makes you tired in a slangy sense or do you mean that it tires you?"

Archer looked as though he had the weight of the universe on his shoulders as he considered this. Then he replied: —

"Miss Pink makes me tired and lessons tire me."

Nicholas slapped his thigh. "Good man! You've explained it perfectly."

"Don't praise him," said Ernest. "It's bad for him when he's been obstreperous."

"A little praise hurts no one," returned Nicholas.

"But he should not be praised for a cheeky answer."

"I don't think Archer intended to be that," said Alayne.

Ernest fixed a penetrating look on Archer. "Which did you intend," he demanded, "to be cheeky or clever?"

"Both," Archer answered promptly.

"We are getting nowhere," said Alayne. "Archer had better come up to my room with me." She rose and took the little boy's hand.

"A switching is what he needs." Ernest clenched his delicate white hand, as though it held the implement of chastisement. "Perhaps Finch would do it for you."

"Why doesn't Roma see that he gets to school?" asked Nicholas. "Where is Roma?"

Roma was standing just outside the door with her ear to the keyhole. She drew back as Alayne and Archer came out. Alayne asked suspiciously: —

"What are you doing here, Roma?"

"Waiting for Archer."

Roma spoke in a quiet little voice, and she had a quiet little face, an air as though she consciously made herself someone to pass unnoticed. When she was just old enough to run about she had been brought to Jalna, the fruit of dead Eden's connection with Minny Ware, an English girl. The child had been conceived in Rome whence came her name. She had known, almost from the first, that Alayne did not like her. She did not like Alayne. Roma was not shrinking or timid. If she had a self-effacing air, it was because she chose to be so. At eleven she looked more than two years younger than Adeline. To judge by her limbs she might later be tall but now she was small for her age. She had an odd charm, with her glistening fair hair, her narrow strange-colored eyes, her high cheekbones and the sensitive full-lipped mouth which she had got from her father.

"Are you sure you were not listening at the door, Roma?" asked Alayne.

"Quite sure." Roma smiled a little.

"That question was not intended to be amusing," Alayne said sternly.

Roma took the smile from her face.

"I want you both to come in here with me." Alayne led the children into the sitting room.

They stood facing her, where she seated herself, looking imperviously small and innocent. Roma thought — "She has heaps of lines in her forehead when she's worried. Why should she care if Archer goes to school? He won't do what Miss Pink says. He won't do what *she* says. He won't mind anyone but Adeline. I wonder if I dare smile again." The smile flickered across her lips.

"Roma," said Alayne, "you knew very well that you were doing wrong in letting Archer play truant. You are older. You should guide him to do right."

"He won't let me."

"You should have told me he was not at school."

"That would be telling tales."

"Archer must be told of, when he does anything so wrong as this."

"I'm hungry," said Archer. "Could I have my tea?"

"Yes. But no cake. No jam. Just salad and bread."

"Salad gives me indigestion."

"Then you may have an egg."

"Thank you, Mother." He spoke in a sweet, soothing voice. He got on to her lap and laid his cheek against hers. She said: —

"Go upstairs and wash and brush your hair, Roma. I wish to talk privately to Archer. I am deeply hurt, and very displeased with both of you."

Adeline was going up the stairs as Roma closed the door of the sitting room behind her.

" Hullo," said Adeline. " Who 's in there? "

" Aunt Alayne and Archer. He 's been late for school all week. About ten or eleven o'clock. And yesterday he did n't come till afternoon."

Adeline whistled, then said — " Come on up to my room." She darted up the stairs. Roma followed.

Inside her room, Adeline shut the door and locked it.

" Goodness! " said Roma. " Your back 's all over mud. So is your leg."

" Jester threw me. He was in a bad mood. Gosh, it hurt! I want you to rub liniment on me. I don't want Mummie to know. She would n't let me ride him at the show."

" She won't anyway. I heard her say so."

Adeline was drawing off her muddy pull-over. She dropped it to the floor. " We 'll see about that," she said.

" Could n't Wright ride him? "

" Jester is in the ladies' saddle-horse class, you duffer."

" Could n't Auntie Pheasant ride him? "

" She could n't possibly handle him. She has n't been riding. She has n't the time."

Having stripped her upper part, she got a bottle of liniment from the cupboard and handed it to Roma. She turned her beautiful sun-tanned back to her.

" Rub here," she commanded, and indicated the area below the small of the back. She groaned as Roma rubbed but repeated — " Harder."

The handle of the door was rattled. " Let me in," came Archer's voice.

" Go away! "

" No! I want to come in."

" We 're busy."

A kick resounded on the door.

Adeline went to it, opened it, grasped a handful of his dry tow hair, and half lifted him into the room by it. Again she locked the door. Archer made no outcry but, when she freed him, examined her back with scientific interest.

" It does n't look sore," he said.

" I wish you had it."

" I 'd rather have it than my tonsils. They have got to come out, the doctor says."

" I saw a horse at the Queenstown fair that had had his tonsils out."

" Did it bleed much? "

" I don't know. I was n't there. But it saved his life."

" I expect having mine out will save mine."

" A lot of expense and trouble for a small thing," observed Roma.

Archer made a pass at the bottle of liniment. Adeline took it from Roma. " That 's enough," she said. " Now I must attend to my leg." She pulled up the leg of her breeches and disclosed a knee with a deep rasp on it.

Roma drew back but Archer leant close, his high white forehead giving him a profound look. Adeline produced a bottle of iodine. He begged: —

" *Please,* Adeline, let me put it on! I won't hurt you half as much as you 'd hurt yourself. Please do! " He tried to take possession of the swab she had made.

She hesitated, then said firmly — " No. I 'll do it myself." She immersed the swab in the iodine, looked at the bloody knee, looked at Roma and Archer pathetically. " Oo, how I hate to! " she said. " It will hurt like the dickens."

" Let Archer do it," said Roma.

" No."

" I 'll put my arm round you," said Archer.

This he did, leaning rather heavily on her. She set her teeth. She pressed the swab to her knee. Color flooded her face. Again and again she sterilized the rasped place.

She handed the swab to Roma, then sat down and rocked herself.

A knock came on the door. The handle turned. Alayne's voice said — " Why have you locked the door, Adeline? "

" So Archer would n't bother me."

" Well, let me in, dear, I want to speak to you."

Adeline pointed under the bed. Silently Archer scrambled beneath it. Adeline kicked her muddy pull-over after him. She drew down the leg of her breeches and opened the door. Alayne came in, noting with distaste that peculiar air of squalor which children are able to impart to the rooms they occupy. She said : —

" So you are changing, Adeline. That 's right. What a smell of iodine ! "

" I scratched my finger," said Roma. She went to the medicine cupboard and, before returning the bottle to it, stuck her finger in the iodine. She held up the finger in front of Alayne, who remarked : —

" That is right. It 's well to be careful." Then she turned to Adeline. " Did you know," she asked, " that Archer has been playing truant from school? "

" I knew he 'd been a little late."

" How did you know? "

" He remarked that he 'd been a little late."

" A little late ! " cried Alayne. " Yesterday he did not arrive till afternoon."

" I expect it 's his tonsils. They 're poisoning his system and making him tired."

" I suppose they are, poor little fellow. But how I dread his having them out ! "

" He 'll be all right, Mummie. If you 'll let me, I will go with him to the hospital."

Alayne gave a little laugh. " You know you are suggesting the impossible, Adeline."

The child flushed. Alayne noticed her beautiful back, her

shoulders where the dark auburn waves of her hair floated. Alayne gave her a pat, then sniffed her hand. "Liniment! What is the matter?"

"I'm a bit stiff. Roma was rubbing my back. Jester is quite a one to pull, you know, Mummie."

"Adeline, if you knew how I dislike your riding that horse! If your father were here I don't think he'd want you to. I don't think Jester is suitable for a girl to ride."

"Oh, Mummie, you don't know what you're talking about!"

Alayne's voice came sharply. "Adeline, I will not have you speak to me like that."

"Sorry. But, really, if you'd ever ridden him you'd think he was perfect. He canters like an angel."

"Well, someone else can ride him at the Ormington Show. I'll not endure the thought of your riding that temperamental creature, in such a big show. He's terrifying."

"If I don't, who will?"

"Wright can ride him."

"He can't! Jester loves me! I'll get a big price for him, you'll see."

"Adeline, don't be foolish. You must listen to me. We can hire someone to ride Jester. Anyhow we are not dependent on the sale of one horse."

"It will make three I've sold."

Alayne tried to speak patiently. "I know. You have done very well. But the time has come for you to — to — " She hesitated.

Adeline's luminous eyes, with the changeful lights in their brown depths, were fixed on hers.

"To what?" she asked.

"Well, you're thirteen. You're not just a little girl. The people you meet at these fall fairs and horse shows aren't always the sort you should associate with. It isn't as though I were there with you."

"Come with me then."

"And stand for hours among horses and grooms and queer people? You know how I'd hate it."

"Lots of the people aren't queer."

"I know. But the atmosphere would be very uncongenial to me. It would be impossible. You are quite aware of that."

"Auntie Pheasant and Maurice would go with me, in the car."

Alayne was losing patience. She said — "Now, let us have an end to this. I forbid you to go."

Adeline's breast heaved. She gave a hard sob, then controlled herself. "Just this once," she pleaded.

"At the next show it would be just the same."

"It's almost the end of the season."

"You are getting behind with your school work."

"Who cares!" Adeline cried, defiantly.

"Now you are being just stupid," Alayne said coldly. "I care. Your father cares very much. You think because he likes to see you ride, that your riding is most important to him, but he is anxious to see you well educated. I think I have made a mistake in letting you have his room. Because it is covered with pictures of horses and trophies, you have got the idea that he cares for little else! You are quite mistaken. He admires culture in a woman and, I may tell you, he admired it in me."

Roma kept blowing on the finger she had dipped in the iodine. Alayne asked irritably: —

"Why do you do that?"

"It stings."

Roma held up the finger.

"I can see no cut."

"It's under the nail."

"I think you are making an unnecessary fuss over it."

Roma's eyes grew large, as they did when she was reproved.

Alayne had had to turn from Adeline. There had been

something in her face that had the power of rousing a desire to hurt her, not physically but by a calculated thrust against her personal egotism. Now Alayne, her hand on the doorknob, turned away.

"Tidy this room. I must go to Archer," she said and left.

Archer threw Adeline's pull-over from under the bed, then crept out, got stiffly to his feet like an old man, and walked over the pull-over. He went to the window and observed : —

"I see three men in a car going to the stable." Adeline leaped to his side.

"It's Mr. Crowdy and Mr. Chase!" she cried excitedly. "They've brought a man to see Rosina. They said they would. Wright and I've been expecting him all the week!"

She snatched her pull-over from the floor and dragged it over her head. She pulled up her breeches and tightened her belt.

"I'm coming too," said Roma.

"No. You stay and tidy the room. Tell Mummie I'm studying. I'll buy you a big chocolate bar to-morrow. I've got to see these men."

"I'm coming," declared Archer.

She turned to him fiercely. "No!" She ran lightly down the stairs and out of the house. The three dogs were waiting outside. When she opened the door the little cairn terrier darted into the house and up to Nicholas's room but the other two ran with Adeline to the stables, the bobtailed sheep dog in loose shaggy movements, the bulldog solidly, with sturdy purpose.

The stable was brightly lighted by the electric lights, though outside the western sky was still aflame. The four men were in Rosina's loose box. She was a delicately made mare who could be intractable when things did not go to please her. She moved toward Adeline as she entered, as though to tell her that at this moment she was not too well pleased.

" Here 's my young lady," said Wright, and the other three took off their hats.

One of them was a stranger to Adeline but the others she had known as long as she could remember. Chase was a lawyer who had been too indifferent to his profession to succeed in it. He had drifted quite naturally into the profession of horse dealing. He did not make a very good living at it but he was a single man who wanted little. If it had not been for his friend Crowdy, he might often have been in financial straits, but Crowdy had the flair for picking a likely horse at a low cost, while Chase supplied the gentlemanly element that carried many a deal through. Now, with ceremony, he introduced the somewhat nervous buyer to Adeline.

" This young lady," he said, " knows as much about horse-flesh as any man. She 's carrying on the business with Wright here, while her father, Colonel Whiteoak, is overseas."

" She," declared Crowdy, " is A 1 in all respects."

Adeline gravely shook hands with the stranger.

" Welcome to our stables," she said, as she had heard her father say.

" This here gentleman," said Wright, " has come to look at Rosina. He likes her looks but he thinks she 's high-strung. He 's buying for a lady friend who 's not much of a rider."

" She 's as nervous," said the stranger, " as seven thousand cats."

Adeline gravely considered this. Then — " This is her horse," she said; " your lady friend could n't fall off her if she tried. Any more than she could fall off a rocking chair."

" And she 's pretty as a picture," put in Chase.

" And dirt cheap at the price," added Crowdy. " Did you

say to me the other day that someone has an option on her?"

"Well, no," answered Adeline, "not exactly an option. But he's coming back to-morrow."

"Well, well, to-morrow you say? Would you mind telling me his name?"

Adeline turned to Wright. "What is his name, Wright?"

"Miller," answered Wright. "In the brewery business."

"Would that be R. G. Miller?" asked the stranger.

"No, sir. This is J. J. Miller."

"John James," amended Adeline.

"A large portly man," said Chase, "with a cast in his left eye."

Crowdy tapped the thick palm of his left hand with the forefinger of his right. "My God, sir, I caution you, don't let that man buy her. Your lady friend will never forgive you. You'll miss the chance of a lifetime. I have no personal interest in this sale, mind you. I only do what I can to help Colonel Whiteoak who is off fighting his country's battles while we're safe at home."

"That's the truth," said Wright, "and it comes from one who has ridden her in half a dozen shows."

"Perhaps your lady friend doesn't want a real show horse." As Adeline spoke, a remote look came over her face.

"But that's just what she does want. She may not ride at shows herself but she wants to show the animal and win prizes."

Adeline turned to Wright. "Do you think it is light enough for me to put Rosina over a few jumps, just to show what she's like?"

"It's still bright in the west, miss."

Still wearing the remote air, Adeline went with the men to the paddock where half a dozen white-painted hurdles lent an air of purpose. She mounted the mare and, in a pre-

liminary canter, showed her style. The mare's beauty and
the child's grace were well matched. The swallow on his
flight was scarcely better poised. Then, thudding over the
turf they came and cleared the hurdles, one after the other,
without a tick.

Crowdy turned to the prospective buyer. " Ever see the
like of that? Ain't she a winner? " But whether it was
mare or child he designated he did not say.

" That 's a sight," said Chase, " in these contemptible
days, when the motorcar has pushed the horse into limbo and
all a young fellow thinks of is getting a swell car or, if he
has n't means for that, a motorcycle. God! " The Deity's
name was uttered on a note of indescribable despair.

When Adeline had dismounted, Wright, with the bridle
over his arm, said — " Well, sir, have you made up your
mind? "

" I 'll buy her," returned the man, " if you 'll take fifty dollars off the price."

Without hesitation Wright answered — " I could n't think
of it, sir. I 'm here to get a just price for Colonel Whiteoak's
horses. I could n't face him if I 'd been giving them away."

" Especially," said Crowdy, " when he 's fighting for his
country and we 're safe at home. It would n't seem right to
beat down the price."

" If he were here," added Chase, " he 'd say take it or
leave it and be damned."

As Adeline limped back toward the house she sang a joyful, though rather tuneless, song of triumph. The bargain
had been clinched. The mare sold. She had done her part
and done it well. But how her knee hurt! She would
bathe it in hot water before she went to bed.

Inside the house she could hear that the family were at
table. She limped softly upstairs. She washed face and
hands and then brushed her hair, not attempting to get out
the tangles. She took off pull-over and breeches and put

on a little cotton dress she had outgrown but which still served for evenings at home. She must not wear socks. She must not show that awful-looking knee. She drew on a pair of the long black stockings she wore at school and hastened down to the dining room. She was about to seat herself when Alayne stopped her.

"Wait a moment," she said, peremptorily, but with a quiver in her voice, "and tell me why you went back to the stables after I had told you to dress."

"Yes," added Nicholas, "we want to know what you were up to." There was a mischievous gleam in his deep-set eyes.

Oh, that ever-recurring "we," thought Alayne. It dragged her down to the level, in authority, of old great-uncles!

Adeline answered — "I had left my books in the stable. I had to go back for them."

"And it took you three quarters of an hour to find them! You can scarcely expect me to believe that."

"When I got to the stable there was something interesting going on, so I stayed."

"That's right," put in Ernest, "tell the truth. You'll get a lighter punishment if you are truthful." His forget-me-not blue gaze beamed encouragement at the child.

"If I'd dared to be truthful about my doings at her age," said Finch, "I'd have got a clip on the ear that would have knocked me flat."

"Oh, would you really, Uncle Finch?" cried Archer.

"You can bet I would. And a yank on the other ear to pick me up."

Archer gave a shout of laughter. He fell back in his chair and laughed helplessly.

Alayne sprang up, went to him, lifted him upright and whispered in his ear — "Archer, do you want to go straight up to your room?"

"Oo," he giggled, "your hair's tickling my ear! Ooo!"

Roma, sitting next him, pinched him on the thigh. He uttered a squeal, then collapsed giggling. He shut his eyes tight and showed the interior of his mouth in an insane grin.

" Archer ! " ordered both great-uncles at once. " Behave yourself ! "

He straightened himself, hiccuping.

" Come and sit down, Adeline," said Alayne, in a tense voice. She felt nervously exhausted. For the remainder of the meal she discussed sedulously with Finch a critical article in a musical magazine. The children were silent except for an occasional hiccup or smothered giggle from Archer. Rags brought a dish of hot soup for Adeline, setting it in front of her with a solicitous air.

When she had returned to her room she took the pile of textbooks that lay on her bed and slammed them on to the table. The door opened and Archer came in.

" I 'm on my way to bed," he remarked.

" That 's good news."

He advanced to where he could look into her face. " You lied to Mummie, did n't you ? " he said.

" Yes," she answered tersely. Then she added, while she sorted the books — " I had to. It was for her own good. It was for her good to sell Rosina. I had to help. It was n't a bit like *you* pretending you went to school when you did n't. That was just for your *own* fun."

Archer's brow became noble. " Mr. Fennel says we should pray for forgiveness when we 've told a lie. Have you ever ? "

" No."

" I 'll bet you 're afraid to."

" Why ? "

" Well, God might say out loud that He forgave you. You 'd not like that, would you ? "

" Of course I should."

" To be spoken to out loud from the ceiling ! "

" Mummie does n't believe in that kind of God."

" Does Daddy ? "

" I think he believes what Mr. Fennel believes."

" I guess you ought to ask God to forgive you."

" All right, I will.   Now, get out."

" I wish you 'd ask Him while I 'm here."

" People don't pray in front of other people."

" If you 'll pray, just this once, in front of me, I 'll promise not to stay away from school again."

" All right.   But, if you break your promise you 'll be sorry."

With a decidedly grumpy expression she threw down the book she held and, limping to the bed, knelt beside it.   She could not kneel on the injured knee, so that leg, in its long black stocking, stuck stiffly out to one side.   She folded her hands, closed her eyes, and said : —

" Please God, forgive me for lying to my mother.   Please make her understand it was for her own good.   And please fix things so I shan't have to do it again.   Amen."

Archer stood with one hand holding his chin, his intense blue gaze bent on her.   About once in three days Archer smiled, and now he did.

Alayne's voice came from without.   " Archer !   Archer ! Where are you ? "

Adeline took him by the shoulders, opened the door, and thrust him into the passage.

" My throat 's sore ! " she heard him whine, as he went to meet his mother.

Adeline arranged her books on the table.   Then she went to the rack where Renny's pipes were hung.   She selected one she knew to be a favorite of his.   She took it from the rack and returned to the table.   Seating herself, she put the amber mouthpiece between her lips and drew a few reflective puffs.   Then she laid the pipe on the table and applied herself to her studies.

V
TUG OF WAR

ADELINE attended a large girls' school in the city and an arrangement had been made by which she was taken there each morning and brought back in late afternoon by the Rector's son, George Fennel, who went by car to his business. As his business was connected with the army he had an extra allowance of gasoline. Pheasant's two boys also were taken to town by George. In fine weather Adeline walked through the fields to the church road and was there picked up by him. In bad weather or in winter he came to the house for her.

On this morning there was no reason for him to call for her. The weather was perfect. Yet Adeline did not see how she could endure the walk. Fresh and clean in her school tunic and long black stockings, she limped to the stables to find Wright. He was lounging in the open doorway smoking a cigarette. It was a quarter to eight and he had been up and at his work for two hours. He gave her a quizzical grimace as she advanced toward him.

" Good morning," he said. " It 's nice to be you — all dressed up and off to a swell school to get yourself made into a lady."

Adeline looked about her for something she could throw at him. Nothing of the sort was in sight, so she slung the textbooks, which she carried in a strap, against his shins. " Stow that! " she said, using an expression she had picked up from him.

Wright saw that she was not herself.

" What 's up? " he asked.

" I have a sore knee.   Will you drive me to meet George's car? "

" Is that the knee you hurt yesterday? "

" Yes.   It 's not very bad.   Just stiff.   Will you take me to meet George? "

" Sure I will."   He brought out the car.   She threw her books into it and climbed stiffly on to the seat.

Wright regarded her with concern.   " You don't look much like riding Jester at the show," he said.

" Don't you worry.   I 'll ride him."

" What about your mother? "

" She 'll never know."

" She 'll know, if you win a prize."

" I 'll bear the consequences."

As they sat in the car waiting for George Fennel they made their plans.

The following day Adeline went to school as usual, but after the school lunch she went to the mistress of her form and, pleading that she was not well, asked to be allowed to go home.   Indeed the mistress thought the child did not look well. She looked flushed and tired.

But Adeline's spirits were high as she got into Mr. Crowdy's car, in which he sat waiting for her outside the school.   She gave a little grunt of satisfaction when they left the city streets and sped along a country road.

" How 's the knee? " he asked solicitously.

" Pretty fair," she answered noncommittally.   " Might be better and might be worse."

" When you 're at the show you 'll forget all about it. That 's the way when I 've anything wrong with me.   Now I 'll tell you a little story to cheer you up.   There was once a man who had n't much money but he had a hunter he loved better than anything on earth.   One day he went into the stable and found that the horse had got a terrible bad chill.   It was shaking from head to foot.   He put its blanket on it but it did n't stop shivering.   Then he went to the house and found his wife in bed with a cold. He went straight to the bed and pulled the blankets off her and carried them out and heaped them on the horse."

" Good for him! " said Adeline. " Did the horse get better? "

" Sure."

" And did the wife? "

" Sure. When he went back to the house she was up and laying the supper table."

As there were no longer any large shows, the small ones drew large crowds. When Adeline and Mr. Crowdy arrived there was already a dense throng about the ring. Wright met them with Adeline's riding clothes in a suitcase. She changed into them in the clubhouse. There were a number of people about who knew her so she did not lack companionship, but she was not in a sociable mood. To await the events in which she was taking part, in stoical endurance of the throbbing pain in her knee, then to take her part with credit to herself and to her mount, was her one concern. No one would have guessed, to see the gallant little figure taking the jumps, that each jolt of landing caused her acute pain. A small set smile was on her lips and remained there when the judges awarded her a first and a second, and when photographers took her picture, mounted on Jester. In the applause of the crowd she forgot the pain for a space. She had upheld the honor of the Jalna stables. Wright too had done well. He beamed at her as he helped her to alight.

" I guess you 're feeling pretty good now, eh? " he said.

" No, Wright, I 'm not," she answered, in a trembling voice. " I want to go home." Tears rained down her cheeks.

Back at Jalna, when the horses had been taken out of the van and after he and the farm hand had made them comfortable, Wright turned anxiously to the child. She had been sitting on a low wooden stool watching them.

" Come into the office," he said, " and let 's see that knee."

He led her into the little room that Renny used as an office and lifted her to the desk. She sat there relaxed, her legs dangling. "It does n't pain quite so badly now," she said, in a small voice. But she gave a sharp cry when Wright pulled off her boot. When the knee was bared he drew back horrified.

"Cripes!" he exclaimed. "This is an awful leg. Why, miss, you ought n't have ridden at that show to-day. You ought to have told me how bad it was."

"It does look pretty bad, does n't it?" she agreed, with a certain pride.

"Bad!" he repeated desperately. "It 's a hell of a knee."

At that moment he saw Rags passing the window carrying a basket of broccoli. Wright tapped sharply on the pane and beckoned to Rags, who, scenting trouble of some sort, hurried in. When the knee was exhibited to him, he scratched his grizzled head and threw Wright an eloquent look.

"Could your wife make some sort of a poultice for it?" asked Wright.

"Nao. The only thing to do for that there knee is to send for the doctor."

Wright and Adeline looked at each other aghast.

"We can't," she declared. "Mummie must n't know."

"Now, look 'ere," said Rags, "would you rather lose your leg or 'ave your mother knaow?"

Adeline grinned. "Lose my leg," she said.

Rags said to Wright — "If I was you I 'd 'ate to take the responsibility of keeping this from the missus."

"I guess you 're right."

"I 'll take the blame," said Adeline, "if we 've got to tell. Come on, let 's have it over with."

Wright gave her a reproachful look. "You should n't have let me in for this, miss," he said. "If ever you 'd showed me that knee! By gum, I 'll catch it for this!

Come, get on my back and I'll carry you to the house." He bent himself in front of her. She bestrode his back, clasping his neck. So they went to the house, Rags, with a desperate air, carrying her boot.

Alayne was leading Archer upstairs to oversee his preparations for the evening meal. To-morrow she had to take him to the hospital to have his tonsils out. She was filled with shrinking from the operation. As she looked down at the little boy she had a painful yearning to protect him. She was halfway up the stairs when Rags appeared in the hall below. He said, mysteriously: —

"Please, madam, would you mind stepping down 'ere? Wright 'as something he feels 'e ought to show you."

"Whatever is wrong now?" demanded Alayne, irritably.

"I think you ought to come down and see, madam. It's Miss Adeline — she's 'urt 'erself."

Alayne flew down the stairs, Archer close behind.

"She's 'ere at the back of the 'all." Rags led the way to where Adeline was standing. Wright skulked in a dim corner behind her.

"Adeline!" cried Alayne. "Where are you hurt?"

The child, standing on one leg, held up her knee.

Alayne, bending over it, gave a cry of distress.

"It's dreadful!" she exclaimed. "It's not a fresh injury. When did you do it? Was it the other evening when I smelled iodine in your room? Why — you have on your riding things! Adeline, were you riding at the show?"

Adeline hung her head. "Yes, Mummie."

Alayne now saw Wright. "This is your doing!" she exclaimed, in a voice tense with anger.

"No, Mummie, it isn't! Truly, it isn't!"

Wright said — "I never saw the knee till a quarter of an hour ago."

"That has nothing to do with it. I told you expressly

that Miss Adeline was not to ride at any more shows this
fall."

"I thought you'd changed your mind."

"When I change my mind you can be certain I'll let
you know. Adeline, go to your room and get into bed. I
must telephone for the doctor. You will please wait here,
Wright."

"Shall I carry the young lady upstairs, ma'am?" he
asked.

"I don't need any help," said Adeline. She began to
mount the stairs, helping herself up by the banister. Archer
followed close behind her.

Alayne, rigid with anger, went into the library and telephoned to the doctor. Rags ostentatiously took the sheep
dog by the scruff and pushed him down into the basement.

Alayne, returning from the telephone, laid her hand on the
carved newel post. From there she spoke to Wright.

"I have had quite enough," she said, "of your interference and your opposition to everything I wish to do. I
will not endure it any longer. You can take a month's
notice from to-night."

The man went white. He had expected a severe repri-
mand — not this. He knew that it would be easy for him
to get another situation, one with higher wages, but he had
been at Jalna for more than twenty years, he had reached a
time of life when he did not like change. He had trained
many horses for Renny Whiteoak. He had ridden at innumerable shows on Renny's horses, at Renny's side. He
had looked forward to keeping the stables in good order
against his return. He had a real sense of loyalty toward
Renny's daughter. He said: —

"That's pretty hard, ma'am, considering the way I've
worked here. You won't get another man to do it."

"I don't wish to discuss the matter with you," Alayne
said coldly. "You will consider yourself discharged. If

my daughter has a serious illness, you will be entirely to blame." She turned and left him. Her legs felt heavy, her whole body dragged down, as she climbed the stairs.

Wright, seething with anger, descended the stairs into the basement. Rags was mounding a tray with dishes to carry up to the dining room. His wife, crimson-faced, was drawing a pan of baked fish from the oven. Both turned expectant faces on Wright.

" Well," he said, " I 'm fired."

" Nao! " exclaimed Rags, unbelievingly.

" What 'll she be up to next! " cried Mrs. Wragge.

" Firing us, I 'll bet," said Rags. " Thinks she can run the 'ole blooming plice alone."

" She 's got a superiority complex, if ever anyone had," added his wife. " Now she come down here yesterday and tried to tell me — "

Wright interrupted — " If she thinks she can fire me she 's mistaken. I won't go."

" Waon't gao! " echoed Rags. " 'Ow can you 'elp yourself? "

" The boss engaged me and he can fire me — if he wants to — when he comes home. She ain't got the authority." Color was returning to his ruddy face. " Why, this here place would be sunk, if I was to leave."

He remained in the kitchen expatiating on this subject till the ringing of the front doorbell announced the arrival of the doctor.

Stout, white-haired Dr. Drummond took a serious view of Adeline's knee. If the hospital were not so overcrowded, he said, he would recommend that she should be taken there. Alayne declared herself capable of doing everything necessary. She would telephone Pheasant to come to her aid. Hot compresses were to be applied all night to the knee.

When she and Adeline were alone together the child said ruefully — " Oh, Mummie, it 's a shame that you should have to stay up all the night with me, when you have to take Archer to the hospital to-morrow."

"Don't worry about me." With an effort Alayne kept her voice calm. "But let this be a lesson to you. In future try to remember that sometimes I know what is best for you."

"I will." Adeline gave a little moan and turned her face to the wall.

It would have been logical for Alayne to ask Meg to come to her aid but they never had got on well together. She disliked the thought of asking a favor of Meg so she telephoned to Pheasant, who gladly undertook to share the nursing. Adeline became more and more restless. By midnight she was delirious. Alayne again sent for the doctor. The little girl was in acute pain and only a strong sedative relieved her.

It was a haggard Alayne who set off the next morning with Archer, dressed in his Sunday suit, a look of mingled self-importance and apprehension in his eyes. Wright was there with the car to drive them to the hospital. He avoided Alayne's eyes as he held open the door of the car. It was a wet morning with the first chill of autumn in the air. If only, thought Alayne, Renny were there to take some of the load of responsibility from her shoulders. It was too much for her. She felt weighed down by it.

At the entrance to the hospital Wright asked, half-sullenly: "How is the young lady this morning, ma'am?"

"Very ill indeed," returned Alayne icily. "I had to send for the doctor again, in the night. He is very anxious about her."

Wright made no reply. "The brute!" thought Alayne. "To think that he had nothing to say. I'm glad I discharged him. I'm glad."

She had been able to get a private room for Archer. He was pleased by this and stood docile while the nurse prepared him for bed. Alayne could see that the nurse admired him.

"He's an old-fashioned little boy," said the nurse.

"He is being very good," said Alayne.

"I promised I would, did n't I? I always keep my promises. I 'm not like some people."

"Listen to him!" exclaimed the nurse.

How tiny he looked, standing there in his pyjamas! How helpless when the orderlies came with a cot on wheels and the nurse, with a jolly air, lifted him on to it. Alayne went to the door with him, holding his hand. When he was gone she came back to a chintz-covered chair and flung herself into it, almost too tired to think.

She felt numb. A long while passed. Then she sprang up as the door opened and the sickening smell of the anesthetic reached her. The cot appeared and Archer was put into the bed. "It is over," thought Alayne. "Thank God, it is over."

"Is he all right?" she breathed.

"He 's fine."

But a miserable time followed when he came out of the anesthetic and painfully vomited up large gobbets of blood. His first remark was to make sure that the tonsils had been saved for him in a bottle.

Alayne had intended to return to Jalna in the afternoon but Archer so clung to her that it was evening before she could bring herself to leave him. She alighted from the car and went into the house without a glance at Wright.

Finch met her in the hall.

"How is Adeline?" she asked.

"Quieter. I 've helped Pheasant with her. At this minute they both are asleep. Meg 's been here and wonders why she was n't sent for. She 's coming back to spend the night. So you can have a good rest. Rags has coffee waiting for you." He tucked his arm under hers and led her comfortingly into the hall. All three dogs were there, the sheep dog's coat wet, every disreputable hair of him beaded with mud. At sight of Alayne he rose and descended majestically into the basement.

VI

A CHASTISEMENT AND A TEA PARTY

MAURICE had settled down quite comfortably into the life of home, with his mother and his two small brothers. Now he seldom had the lost feeling that had made heavy the first days of his return. But, when it did come upon him, he was submerged by it, drawn down by a painful longing for the ordered life of Glengorman, the love of old Dermot Court, the intellectual companionship of his middle-aged tutor, the congenial friendship of Patrick Crawshay. He liked his great-uncles but either they talked of their past in the social life of London, discussed the complications at Jalna, or worried about their nephews who were taking part in the war. After the first few visits to them, Maurice found them rather boring. His cousin Patience was a nice girl but she was interested only in outdoor things and in preparations for the removal from Vaughanlands to the small house. She and her mother were always busy. Intellectually Patience was years younger than he, yet she was rather superior in her attitude toward him and had a way of making fun of him that was very amusing to her and her mother but was disconcerting to Maurice.

The problem of his education loomed large in his thoughts. A perusal of the University curriculum and the examinations necessary made it clear that in the classics, in the study of English and French and in ancient history, he was far in advance of what was required, but in mathematics and science, far behind. It would be necessary for him to be crammed but the thought of entering a cramming school was repugnant to him. He would have to find a capable tutor but where to find him he did not know. They seemed either to be at the war or already engaged in teaching. However, Maurice was willing to drift for a time. The fact that he would have independent means contributed to his natural indolence. He had a generous allowance and so was able to do pleasant things for his mother, for which Pheasant was touchingly grateful. He would bribe his brothers to be obedient and otherwise behave themselves.

On this Saturday morning when she was at Jalna helping to nurse Adeline, Maurice was examining a large packet of books for which he had sent to the town. He had promised each of the small boys twenty-five cents for washing the dishes and making the beds. But they seemed to be possessed by the idea of doing everything with as much confusion and noise as possible. Maurice shut himself in the living room with his books but nothing could shut out their noise, their giggling and scuffling. He went out to them.

"Do you boys," he demanded, "want me to give you those quarters or don't you?"

"We do," they yelled in unison.

"Then stop this row and get on with your work." He returned to the living room.

There was a short interval of quiet, then noise and laughter broke out again. Maurice laid down his book and marched back to the kitchen. Nooky was washing the cutlery, Philip drying it, and as he dried each knife, fork, or spoon, he flung it across the room on to a table. Nooky was in a state of helpless laughter, spilling more water on the floor than he expended on the cutlery.

"Stop it!" shouted Maurice. He caught Philip by the collar and gave him a shake. Philip flung the silver tablespoon he was drying at Nooky and hit him on the head, sending him into hysterical squeals of mirth.

"Here comes the Irishman!" shouted Philip. "He's a holy terror, bedad and he is!"

Nooky leant against the edge of the dishpan, overturning

the water on his own legs and the floor. Philip tore himself from Maurice's grip and ran through the open door into the yard. Here were scattered half the contents of a tool chest which Pheasant had forbidden him to touch. He ran over these and into the tool house and tried to slam the door behind him. But Maurice had caught him. As he held his young brother in his grasp, Maurice felt only cold anger, but when he got a sharp kick on the shin it changed to primitive rage.

" Bend over ! " he ordered.

" I won't ! " yelled Philip, kicking him again. " I won't — I won't! *Mother !* "

But Mother was far away. Maurice heaved him across a work table and, picking up a short piece of lath, belabored him where the trousers were drawn tight across his seat. Philip's howls were such that a young man who at that moment was turning in at the gate hastened to the tool house in alarm. He stopped when he saw what was going on.

" I 'm sorry," he apologized, backing away. " I thought something was wrong."

Maurice laid down the stick. Philip stopped screaming and rolled over. Maurice, his cheeks flushed, came forward.

" Just a little necessary discipline," he explained, and he looked inquiringly at the visitor.

He was a young man of about twenty-eight, fair-complexioned, prepossessing and self-assured. He said — " I wonder if you are Maurice Whiteoak."

Maurice nodded gravely. " I am," he agreed.

" My name is Sidney Swift. I 'm Mr. Clapperton's secretary. I was talking to your aunt, Mrs. Vaughan, yesterday and she told me you are wanting a tutor. Now I believe I could fill the bill. I 'm a Rhodes scholar. I was at Oxford when the war broke out. I joined the R.A.F. but I had a crash while training. I was discharged and came back to

Canada. I've been secretary to Mr. Clapperton for two years. I have a good deal of spare time and he is quite willing to let me take on some part-time job, so I can add to my income. I'm afraid I've appeared at rather an inauspicious time."

"Come into the house," said Maurice, "and we'll talk about it." He led the way into the living room and offered his visitor a cigarette from his case that once had been Dermot Court's.

When they were seated Maurice remarked — "I've never spanked anyone before and I must say it's a delicious sensation."

"The next time you do it I hope you'll invite me to be present. I've never witnessed a more spirited domestic scene. What had he been up to?"

"Making an infernal row doing the dishes. There's another one of them in the kitchen. Will you excuse me while I speak to him?"

Maurice found Nook meekly collecting the cutlery. He said, with severity — "That's right. And clean up the floor when you've finished the dishes. Then make your bed and mine. When you've done I'll give you your quarter. If I have any nonsense from you, you'll get just what I gave Philip."

Nook hung his head and applied himself to his task.

Seated again beside Sidney Swift, Maurice told him of his difficulties in preparing himself for the University.

"I'm sure I can help you," said Swift, and he briefly outlined the work they would take up.

"I suppose you're very glad to be back in Canada," he went on. "Life in Ireland must have been pretty tame for you."

"It suited me very well. Still, of course, I am glad to be with my mother again."

"Well, for my part," said Swift, "I've no use for the

Old World, except as a curiosity. This is the country for opportunity for the young man. Mr. Clapperton was deploring the destruction of all those ancient buildings and works of art but I said — 'Let them be destroyed. We don't need them in this modern world. They're out of date and they may as well go.' Don't you agree?"

Maurice laughed. "I expect," he said, "that each one of us will drift to the place that suits him best."

The telephone rang. It was Pheasant speaking.

"Are you boys getting on all right?" she asked.

"We're getting on splendidly."

"No trouble with Philip?"

"None to speak of. How is Adeline?"

"Poor child, she had a very bad night but she's quieter this morning. However, I must stay on. Alayne is completely exhausted."

"How is Archer?"

"He's getting on well. But Alayne has worried herself ill over the pair of them."

"What a pity! Look here, Mummie. Mr. Swift is here and he and I have talked things over. He's Mr. Clapperton's secretary and he'd be willing to coach me. He's a Rhodes scholar and very nice. Are you agreeable to it?"

"Why — yes. But first find out what he asks. Don't consent to just anything — as though we were millionaires."

"Oh, no . . . Anything I can do to help?"

"No, thank you, dear, except to carry on at home. Tell the children to be good."

"Yes, I will."

Maurice returned to his guest. Soon they had made their arrangements. Maurice agreed to the remuneration asked by Swift. It was not in him to haggle. When Pheasant returned home and learned what the fee was she thought it excessive. Still, it would be paid by Maurice's solicitors, so she need not worry.

It was fortunate that the fall work was over before the illness of the children. Archer was brought home in a few days but remained in bed for another week and after that he was ailing and irritable for a fortnight. Three weeks of suffering passed before Adeline was able to be up. Then she had become thin and her pallor was such that her hair and eyes were shown in striking contrast. But, where Archer had been difficult to nurse, she was amenable and deeply conscious that she had, by her own fault, brought all this weariness upon her mother. She would ask for her needs in a small sweet voice; she would catch Alayne's hand in hers and press it to her lips. She would catch Alayne's skirt and say, " Little Mother," in a cajoling voice. It was almost as though Renny were holding her by the skirt and saying, " Little wife." They're a pair, thought Alayne. There is nothing of me in the child.

Roma was constantly helpful in those days. Perched on the side of Archer's bed she played halma or parcheesi with him and, when he was able to be up, set out his lead soldiers and engineered campaigns. Whatever went wrong he blamed her for it. She ran endless messages to the basement, carried up glasses of milk and fruit juice. She hastened home from school to be on hand to help. Alayne was grateful for this, but it drew them no nearer together. Alayne's eyes often rested on Roma's face, sometimes seeing on the childish lips the resemblance to dead Eden's smile, sometimes in her slanting eyes the very look of Minny Ware. It was curious that Alayne seldom spoke to Roma as to a child. She might reprove her but it was as a grownup, in a superior position, might reprove another grownup. Roma in return spoke to Alayne in a cool, self-possessed tone.

Meg and Patience had removed from Vaughanlands to the small house. Fortunately Mr. Clapperton had been glad to purchase some of the large furniture that for three generations had stood in the Vaughans' home. Meg was able to make the small house look very attractive indeed. Patience was clever with window curtains and cushions. They were very happy and quite reconciled to the change in their situation. In truth Meg found herself with less responsibility and more means for the pleasures of life than she had enjoyed for many a year. She liked Mr. Clapperton and looked forward to the day when his affluence might be added to the support of the church built by her grandfather. Mr. Clapperton was at present a Christian Scientist but Meg looked on this as only a phase in his life. He had been born a Presbyterian but had joined the Christian Science denomination soon after his marriage. If he had changed once he might change again. Already Meg had introduced him to Mr. Fennel, the rector, and the two men had got on well together.

One day Mr. Clapperton accompanied her to tea at Jalna. It was a dark wet day toward the end of November. As they alighted from the car he paused to look up at the old house, and the old house seemed to gather itself together to look at him. There was open admiration in his eyes as he raised them to the walls which were of a peculiarly rosy-red brick closely interlaced by the tendrils of the stout Virginia creeper, now bereft of its leaves save for a few bright scarlet ones in the shelter of the eaves. Spirals of smoke rose from several of the five chimneys and mingled with the gently falling rain. Firelight could be seen reflected on the ceiling of the drawing-room. Inside the deep stone porch, the heavy door was scarred by the pawings of many generations of dogs. On Mr. Clapperton the house seemed to reserve judgment. It appeared to draw itself together as though saying — " You 're a bird of a new feather. I 'll not say what I think of you — not yet."

The door was ceremoniously opened by Rags, who that morning had had a very close haircut and in consequence looked a hardened little criminal.

"Good afternoon, Rags," said Meg.   "I think my uncles are expecting us.   I hope they are well."

"They are indeed expecting you, ma'am, and as well as can be looked for in this weather.   Mr. Nicholas's knee is pretty bad."

He escorted them to the drawing-room, which seemed to Mr. Clapperton quite full of people.   All fixed their eyes on him.   "Can this old gentleman be ninety!" thought Mr. Clapperton.   "He certainly doesn't look it."   He said — "Your niece, Mrs. Vaughan, has talked a lot about you to me, sir."

They shook hands.   Ernest was favorably impressed. He saw a man a little past middle age and middle height, fresh-colored, with light inquiring eyes and thin gray hair carefully brushed.   He wore spats, a pale gray suit, and an air of businesslike friendliness.

"Excuse me.   Can't very well get up," mumbled Nicholas. "Gout.   Had it for years."

"Too bad, too bad," sympathized Mr. Clapperton.   "I gathered from your niece that your health is not very good."

"Perfectly good otherwise," growled Nicholas.

Ernest put in "Have you met my niece, Mrs. Piers Whiteoak?   Pheasant —"

She interrupted — "Oh, yes, we've met.   Long ago."

Meg brought forward Finch and Wakefield, who had lately arrived.   They were almost of a height but Wakefield appeared the taller, with the straightness of his training on him and the proud carriage of his head.   There was a look about his mouth that showed he had known great fatigue, and a look in his eyes of one used to risking his life. The Air Force blue of his uniform made his skin a little sallow.   Meg was proud of them both and, with that air, introduced them to the visitor, explaining the fact that Finch was not in uniform by saying : —

"Finch is a concert pianist.   He has made a tour right across the continent."

"Is n't that fine?" said Mr. Clapperton.

"Troops too much entertained. Too little trained," growled Nicholas.

"This is my youngest brother, Wakefield," said Meg. "He is home on a short leave, on his way to England."

"You 've been an actor in London, I hear," said Mr. Clapperton as he shook hands with him.

"Bad actor, from the first," added Nicholas.

"We are very proud of him," said Ernest. "He has been given the Distinguished Flying Cross by the King, for gallantry."

"Too many decorations in this war," said Nicholas, winking at Wakefield.

"And here," cried Meg, "is your own young man, Mr. Swift, and our nephew, Mooey, whom he 's tutoring."

Mr. Clapperton was not entirely pleased to find his secretary already at Jalna. He was a good-natured man but he had a firm idea of his own importance. He gave Sidney Swift a frosty smile. Then his face lighted as he looked about the room. He exclaimed:—

"May I remark the beauty of your furniture? I thought I had some nice pieces! But *these!*" After an admiring contemplation of the well-polished Chippendale, he added, on a deeper note — "And to think that just such pieces as these are being bombed!"

"Yes, is n't it terrible?" said Meg.

"Too much old stuff in the world," growled Nicholas. "World cluttered up with antiques — material and human. Is n't that so, Mr. Swift?"

"I quite agree," cried the young man. "I often say — " But, after a glance from Mr. Clapperton, he did not say what he often said.

At this moment Alayne entered the room with the air of elegance that always distinguished her. The party was now complete and, after welcoming Mr. Clapperton, she sat down behind the tea tray which Rags had just carried in.   The new neighbor sat near her while the four young men busied themselves in carrying about teacups and plates of thin bread and butter and cakes.   Mr. Clapperton remarked sympathetically to Alayne : —

"I hear you have had two very ill children."

"Yes.   My little son had his tonsils taken out.   It was an unusually bad case but he is better now, I 'm thankful to say."

"Tonsils," said Nicholas, "just disappear naturally if you leave 'em alone.   Mine did."

Ernest said — "I sometimes think my health would be better if I 'd had mine out."

"It 's not too late.   Have 'em out next week."

"And your little girl," said Mr. Clapperton to Alayne, "is she better?"

"Thank you, she has quite recovered.   She is a very strong child."

Nicholas heaved himself in his chair, so that he faced Mr. Clapperton.   "Now I want to know," he said, "why you should choose to live in the country.   You strike me as a man absolutely of the town."

"Not at all, sir."   Mr. Clapperton spoke a little huffily. "I 've always had the ambition to end my days on a country estate where I could play at being farmer."

"Life in the country is n't what it used to be, you know. Help question 's terrible."

Mr. Clapperton smiled.   "I plan to use modern business methods.   Everything up to date.   Wages to tempt the most experienced men.   Oh, I have many plans!"   He gave a silent chuckle.   "I 'll surprise you by what I 'll do."

"My father," said Ernest, "used to employ twenty men at Jalna.   Farm hands, gardeners; we had our own carpenter's shop — our own smithy."

"And cheap labor, I 'll bet," returned Mr. Clapperton. "Those were the days!"

"Certainly," said Meg, "we now have to scrabble along as best we can. I'm thankful to see Vaughanlands in the hands of someone who has the money to run it properly. I've had enough of making shift."

There was a silence in which Nicholas noisily supped his tea. Mr. Clapperton gave him a quick look, then turned to Maurice. "So you are the young gentleman my secretary is teaching."

"Well, he's trying to, sir. I'm afraid he finds it pretty heavy going at times."

Pupil and tutor exchanged smiles. "This lad," said Swift, "has been mentally submerged by the classics. I'm doing what I can to bring him to the surface."

"And a mighty unpleasant surface it is," said Finch gloomily.

"Just wait till we get the rubbish cleared away."

"Meaning our kind," said Nicholas, putting a small muffin whole into his mouth.

"Oh, no, Mr. Whiteoak. I mean the accumulation of outworn tradition."

"Description answers perfectly," growled Nicholas, through the muffin.

"People like you," put in Mr. Clapperton, "have been the backbone of this country."

"Very handsome of you to say so."

"Development and change are necessary," said Ernest, "and I always like to feel myself in the forefront of such."

"Good man!" said his brother.

Meg now brought the conversation to personal affairs, from where it led quite naturally to the financial difficulties of the church. Mr. Clapperton was sympathetic but showed no disposition to offer financial aid. Before he left he expressed a wish to see the other rooms on the ground floor. A group progressed into the library and dining room. Mr. Clapperton might have been a connoisseur of old furniture, to judge by the profound expression with which he stood before each piece. But the truth was he knew little and gave his rapt attention to things of no value, such as the ugly and ornate whatnot which stood in a corner of the library, its shelves covered by photographs, papier-mâché boxes, and Victorian china ornaments. But when, in the dining room, he stood before the portraits of Captain Philip Whiteoak and his wife, Adeline, his enthusiasm increased, if that were possible.

" There," he exclaimed, " is what I call a perfect example of a gallant English officer ! "

Captain Whiteoak, blond and bold in his Hussar's uniform, looked unconcernedly over their heads.

Meg said — " My brother Piers, the one who is a prisoner in Germany, is the image of Grandpapa."

" And you should see my little boy, Philip ! " cried Pheasant. " The likeness is remarkable."

" As an officer," said Nicholas, " my father was overbearing to his inferiors, insubordinate toward his superiors, and was never so happy as when he got out of the army."

" And what a striking woman your mother was ! " exclaimed Mr. Clapperton, rapt before the other portrait.

" Right you are," agreed Nicholas. " She 'd hit any one of us over the head as lief as look at us."

When the guests had gone, Meg asked — " Now what do you think of my Mr. Clapperton ? "

" I think," said Nicholas, " that he 's a horrid old fellow."

" Do you indeed? Then what is your feeling about that good-looking secretary of his ? "

" I think," returned Nicholas, filling his pipe, " that he 's a horrid *young* fellow."

VII
THE WANING OF THE YEAR

ALAYNE had met with much criticism from Meg and the uncles because of her dismissal of Wright. He had been at Jalna for more than twenty years. He had been Renny's right-hand man in the care of the horses. He had ridden beside him in many a show. He could be depended on. To be sure he was no farmer, nor did he pretend to be. To grow sufficient hay and oats for the horses satisfied him. Where the stables were concerned he was extravagant and nothing could change him. Alayne had had little to do with him before the war. Since Renny's departure there had been a constant tug of war between them. He, in her opinion, demanding, headstrong, and inflexible; she, in his, close-fisted and interfering. Now they stood facing each other. She had in her hand a check for the amount of his wages.

"You know what I think, ma'am," he said. "I was hired by Colonel Whiteoak and I don't feel like taking notice from anyone but him. In fact I ain't going to."

Alayne felt her anger rising. "This is ridiculous, Wright," she said, "and you know it is. I am in complete authority here. I have given you notice. Now I intend to pay you your wages. So let us have no more arguing about it."

He thrust his hands behind his back. "Listen here, ma'am. The farm hand has given me notice. What are you going to do when he's left?"

"Given *you* notice!" she exclaimed. "If he wishes to give notice let him give it to me."

"He'll do that fast enough. He wants to leave at the end of a fortnight."

"Well, let him leave. There are others. In fact, we can get along quite well with one good man at this time of year."

Wright smiled grimly. "Perhaps you can find one," he said.

Alayne proffered him the check, but he kept his hands behind his back.

"Please take this," she said sharply, her color rising.

"No, Mrs. Whiteoak, I ain't going."

"Do you like the idea of staying on without wages?" she asked.

"No. I don't, but I'll do it sooner than let the boss down."

"Your flat over the garage will be needed for the new man."

"You can't put me out of there for three months, ma'am."

"Then he can live in the cottage. You are doing yourself no good, Wright, by behaving like this."

"I ain't out to do myself good, ma'am."

Alayne turned sharply away and left him.

Finch was her comfort in these days. Now he went to the town and at the office of the Selective Service interviewed several men. He engaged one who had been discharged from the army, and he was installed in the one cottage which remained of those built for farm hands in the early days at Jalna. He was a clean, bright-looking young man and Alayne felt that Finch had done well in acquiring him. Wright would not let him do anything more for the show horses than to clean their stalls, but put the farm horses in his care, with many injunctions as to feeding.

A few days after his coming the weather turned bitterly cold. The new man gave ice-cold water to the horses to drink and one of them, a handsome Clydesdale mare, took a chill. All that Wright and the veterinary could do to save her failed and the next day she lay, a mountain of solid flesh, dead in her stall. Wright did not bring the bad news to Alayne but entrusted it to Wragge, who told it with the air of one bringing tidings of a national disaster. She was greatly distressed and felt in this misfortune some sinister negligence on the part of Wright — a cruel desire to get even with her.

Now Wragge stood before her, his hands clasped on his stomach, an almost clerical look on his face. He was saying: —

"I think we shall just 'ave to put our pride in our pocket, madam, and let Wright stay on. 'E understands the 'orses and the 'orses understand 'im. These 'ere fellers you engage 'ap'azard, they 're no good."

She stood silent, twisting her fingers together.

Wragge went on — "Dear knows what disaster will come next, if this feller stays on."

Adeline entered the hall from the side door. Her eyes were swollen from crying. She said, in a choking voice: —

"How can I tell Daddy! Whatever will he say!"

"You had better go up to your room, dear," said Alayne.

"Ow," put in Wragge, "she 's 'eartbroken — just like I am!"

Alayne said — "You may tell Wright to come and I will see him here."

She did see him and, in a controlled voice, revoked her decision to discharge him. The new man was sent away. But all this did not bring back the grand Clydesdale, and Alayne's heart was heavy.

But the house was far from gloomy. Finch and Wakefield were happy in being once again at Jalna, even though Wakefield's time there would be short. Since Sarah's marriage, Finch felt a new freedom. He was done with that phase of his life — done with it! Never again would those slender arms wind themselves about his neck as though to suffocate him; never again those narrow eyes, set like jewels in the head, discharge their cold passion into his soul. He had seen the last of Sarah, the very last. If ever again he loved a woman, and he doubted that, it would be a woman normal — yes, absolutely normal — equable, one who knew neither ecstasies nor despairs but mild temperatures, like settled May weather.

He and Wakefield had had their disappointments, he in his marriage, Wakefield in his broken engagement. He had been engaged to Molly Griffith, whose stepsisters now lived at the fox farm, but it had been necessary, because of a tragic circumstance, to forgo the marriage. That had been four years ago. In the bitter months at the first, Wakefield had hardened into manhood. He had an imperious way with him which took the place of his former air of a spoilt boy. He was animated; he was gay but he had within him the memory of the bliss that had borne no fruit. In their attitude toward money, the brothers were a complete contrast. When Finch had been possessed of a fortune, he had lent or given it away with scarcely a thought. He had seen Sarah's wealth depart with her, with only relief. Now that he had little money it did not at all trouble him. He liked old clothes, he liked old possessions. He had given much of what he had made in his concert tours to war charities.

Wakefield, on the other hand, had inherited the extravagant tastes of both Courts and Whiteoaks. He liked spending money for the sheer exhilaration of spending it. He enjoyed acquiring anything new, from a thoroughbred to a pair of shoes. Old possessions depressed him, with the strong exception of Jalna and its furnishings. To him these retained their lustre unimpaired. During his short leave he constantly caused concern to Finch, vexed Alayne, delighted the children, half-worried, half-gratified the uncles, by the manner in which he threw money about — when he could lay hands on it. He reminded Nicholas and Ernest pleasurably of their own spendthrift youth, though his expenditures were insignificant compared to theirs. Now he seldom was with them for long without getting money out of them on one pretext or another. He was able even to get something from Meg. Poor boy, she would think, he may never come back to us again! The things he thought he needed were amazing, and he would store these away in his room against the time of his return. In a curious way it made him more sure that he would return, to have all these possessions awaiting him.

Finch several times had urged Wakefield to go with him to see the Griffith girls at the fox farm. Wakefield had refused because of his last painful meeting there with Molly, but now, on this dark afternoon in early winter, he consented.

There was light snow on the ground as the brothers crossed the ravine. Through it showed the brown leaves and the rough brown grass. The brown stream hurried past tiny snow-mounded islands and, stalking by himself, in lonely masculine grandeur, was a cock pheasant, his wide blue collar bright as though burnished.

The three sisters were sitting by the fire in the living room when the knock sounded on the door. Althea swiftly gathered up the sketch she was making; Gemmel closed the book she was reading aloud; Garda suspended her knitting needles. So apart was their life that a knock at the door was enough to send them into confusion.

" For heaven's sake, see who it is! " whispered Althea to Garda, who flew to peep between curtains.

" It's Finch and Wakefield Whiteoak! " she exclaimed, getting scarlet.

" Sh! " hissed Gemmel. " Fetch my lipstick — quick! " She had lately taken to using lipstick, which neither of the others did. She took a small comb from her pocket and began to comb her dense dark hair. In spite of the affliction that cut her off from the pursuits of other young people, she thought more of her personal appearance than either of her sisters.

Garda flew noiselessly upstairs and brought back the lipstick which Gemmel lavishly applied. The knock sounded again. Althea was gliding from the room. Gemmel caught her by the skirt.

"Let me go!" Althea whispered fiercely.

"No! You must n't. They 'll think it strange if you don't show up."

"Tell them I 'm ill." Her beautiful wan face was flushed by color. "Let me go, Gemmel!" But Garda had already opened the door. She greeted Wakefield as an old friend, for he had visited them in Wales. But Althea's lips barely moved in a soundless greeting.

Garda ran to put the kettle on. Finch seated himself where he could look at Althea.

"Been sketching?" he asked.

She inclined her head.

"She 's been doing the loveliest trees," said Gemmel, "but you may be sure she won't show you. If I had a talent I 'd love to show off."

"You have a talent," said Wakefield. "I remember how splendidly you recited in Wales. I thought then you 'd make an actress if —"

"If!" she cried, with an expressive gesture of her flexible hands. "It 's always *if* with me. And always will be. Oh, if I could lead the life Molly does!"

"How is Molly?" asked Wakefield.

"Flying between New York and Hollywood. She has n't had a big success yet. For one thing she 's too thin to photograph well." She poured out the tale of the plays Molly had been in and what parts she had had. Althea marveled at her, for she could say nothing. Wakefield hungrily drank in all this news of the stage, wondering if ever he would act again.

Garda brought in the tea tray. She was bent double under its weight, for she had loaded it with all the cakes and scones she could find, to say nothing of buttered toast and fruit loaf. Wakefield sprang to help her. They gathered about the table, all but Althea talking. She kept thinking of things to say and how she would say them, coolly or laughingly, as her sisters might speak, but before she could bring herself to utter them, the conversation had turned to another subject, the chance was gone. Finch's hands fascinated her and the way he used them, but she never let her eyes meet his.

Tea was not half over when another knock sounded on the door, and Sidney Swift and Maurice came in. It was not the first time they had visited the Griffiths. Indeed Swift settled himself beside Garda with an air of familiarity. Gemmel was so exhilarated by the presence of the four young men that she talked almost wildly and her greenish-blue eyes glittered with excitement. Swift was a fluent talker. He spoke with authority of painting, Althea never daring to contradict him; of music, Finch laughingly disagreeing with most of his dictums and being glibly talked down; but it was Wakefield who, when Swift laid down the law about the theatre, turned his own remarks on him and brought a laugh against him. When it came to literature, young Maurice was the only one whose reading in any way compared with Swift's. As Swift's pupil he was respectful but already he had discovered his tutor's limitations. On Swift's part he found Maurice indolent and fully convinced that no teaching he could have in Canada would equal that of his old tutor in Ireland.

On the way home Wakefield remarked to Finch — " If Swift is all he makes himself out to be, why is n't he doing something more important than being secretary to that old gaffer, Clapperton, and tutoring Mooey?"

"Meg says she believes he is clinging to Mr. Clapperton in the hope of inheriting his money. He's some sort of relation."

"I believe he's gone on Garda."

"No. He just has that snuggly manner with girls."

"What do you think of the other two? Aren't they an amazing contrast?"

"It would be a strange experience," said Finch musingly, "to love a girl like Althea. You'd always be pursuing — and she eluding."

"Damned strange," answered Wakefield and thought to himself — "Especially after a hussy like Sarah."

"But Gemmel is the one who interests me most."

Wake opened his eyes in surprise. "Really! Well, of course, her being a cripple is a tragedy. You can see that she's mad for experience — and she's chained. I guess she lives in the experiences of her sisters."

"She wouldn't find much there. She's so different."

"They're all three different. All four — counting Molly."

"We are not very lucky, you and I . . . In love, I mean. Are we, Wake?"

Wakefield's face grew sombre. "No more of that for me," he said. "We'll settle down at Jalna, when we're old men — like Uncle Nick and Uncle Ernest."

Finch gave a grim assent. Then suddenly one of his boyish fits of hilarity came upon him. He began to chase and wrestle with Wakefield as they descended into the ravine. The moon cast their active shadows on the snow. The stream uttered its last gurglings before it turned to ice. A frightened mouse ran across the bridge. Finch found himself no match for Wakefield, whose body was hardened by military training. By the time they had mounted the other side of the ravine, his heart was thumping. He would not cry out for mercy but surrendered himself dumbly to Wakefield's iron grasp, as in the old days he had surrendered to Piers.

The lights of the house streamed out across the snow. The three dogs waiting in the porch rushed out, in a fury of barking, at the two dark figures rising from the ravine; then, as they recognized members of the family, circled in joy about them. Finch exclaimed: —

" I wish to God that I could live a country life — never step inside a town from one year's end to another — never play in front of an audience — never be sick of the sight of people — belong utterly to myself! "

" You 'd tire of it. You 'd soon be panting for the excitement and the applause."

" Never! Excitement is mostly apprehension for me. Applause just means — thank God I have n't failed! It would suit me to work in one of the arts where you need n't see your public — to be a writer, a painter, a sculptor."

" Tame! Tame! " exclaimed Wakefield. " Give me my visible public — even if it throws rotten eggs at me! "

They were at the door. " You always were a showy-off little beast," Finch retorted, and was inside the house before Wake could lay hands on him.

Their companionship was precious to them in these days. They were inseparable. Neither said what was in his mind. But Finch looked with ever-increasing foreboding toward the day of Wakefield's departure. His eyes followed Wakefield's tall lithe figure, rested on the dark beauty of his face and wondered if this would be their last time together. They spent many hours at Meg's, helping her and Patience to settle in the small house. Meg clung to Wakefield as the little brother to whom she had been a mother, and when the hour of parting came she was swept by a storm of weeping. She made no pretense of being brave. But when he was gone the ranks of the family, depleted though they were, closed behind him and life went on as before.

Now the December days marched coldly on toward Christmas. There were five children to consider. There had always been a Christmas Tree and a Santa Claus. Piers had marvelously well played the part and, since his departure, Nicholas. What he lacked in rosiness of countenance, Pheasant applied from a rouge pot. The sonorous jollity of his Santa Claus voice was contagious. But this year he declared that he no longer could do it. Something had gone out of him, he said. He was too old. He could not read the labels on the packages. Ernest or Finch must be Father Christmas.

But no one could, by any stretch of imagination, picture Ernest or Finch as Santa Claus. Nicholas must hold the Christmas fort till Piers came home. " Hmph, well," growled Nicholas, " he 'd better hurry. I 'm ninety-one."

" Why Uncle Nick," chided Meg, " think of Granny! She lived to be a hundred and two."

" She was a woman," said Nicholas, " and she had n't gout. She was sound, you might say, to the last."

" And so are you! " cried Meg, kissing him. " You 're just as sound as a dear old nut."

He was won over. He would do it, he declared, just this one time more.

The cloak of family custom hung heavy too on Finch's shoulders. From the time when the church was built, a Whiteoak had always read the Lessons at Morning Service. After Renny had gone to the war, Ernest had capably and with much more elegance filled this office, but for the past year it had obviously been too much for him to undertake. There were Sundays when the weather was not fit for him to venture out. So Mr. Fennel had himself read the Lessons. Now he and Meg and the two uncles had put their heads together and decided that Finch was next in order.

He was to be home for some months and it would be good for him to fill the niche in the ordered sequence of things. Family custom must not be allowed to flag but must be kept firm and upright by Whiteoak mettle.

To Finch the idea of standing up behind the lectern and reading from the Bible was more intimidating than playing the piano in a concert hall. Yet he was pleased and even flattered by being chosen. He was thankful that neither Renny nor Piers would be there to see him. He could not have faced their amused gaze from the family pew.

The morning dawned cold and cloudy, with much snow in the sky but little on the ground. As he descended the stairs to breakfast, the resinous scent of the Tree filled the hall. Alayne and Pheasant had decorated it the day before and it was safely locked inside the library. On how many Christmas mornings had he come down those stairs, made dizzy by the wonder, the mysterious strangeness of that scent? He stood a moment alone in the hall. He was indeed alone, for Sarah had gone out of his life. He felt oddly young and untouched at this moment.

Alayne and the children were at the breakfast table. She was having a time of it to persuade Archer to eat anything. He desired only something that was not on the table. Finch looked at him severely.

" I can tell you this, young man," he said, " if I had demanded things like you do, I'd have been taken by the scruff and put out of the room."

" What 's the scruff? " asked Archer.

" This." Finch laid a heavy hand on his neck. Archer wriggled away. " Who would have done it to you? " he asked.

" Your father."

" Mother would n't let him do it to me. She 'd —"

" Archer," interrupted Alayne, " I want to hear nothing more from you."

Wragge entered the room with a portentous air. " Mrs. Whiteoak, please, my wife would like to see you in the kitchen as soon as convenient."

Alayne rose. " I have finished," she said, and went with him to the basement.

" I 'm *not* going to church," said Archer, " and I *am* going to see the Tree. I 'm going right now to get my presents off it."

Finch sprang up and lifted the small boy from his chair. He strode with him into the hall. Archer lay, stiff as a poker, in his arms.

" What are you going to do with him? " asked Roma.

" Open the door," ordered Finch.

Adeline opened the front door and Finch stepped into the porch. All three dogs came into the house. Finch carried Archer to the steps and held him head downward over a snowdrift.

" Want to be dropped into that and left there? " he asked.

" I don't mind," answered Archer impassively.

" All right. Here goes! " He lowered Archer till his tow hair touched the snow. He lowered him till his head was buried. The little girls shrieked. Alayne could be heard talking, on her way up the basement stairs. The bell of Ernest's room was loudly ringing below. The two old men were having breakfast in bed, in preparation for a tiring day. Now Ernest wanted his. Two short rings meant that he wanted porridge, toast, and tea. One prolonged ring indicated that he wanted an egg. This was a prolonged ring. It went on and on.

Finch reversed Archer and stood him on his feet. His lofty white brow was surmounted by snowy locks.

" Now are you going to behave yourself? " asked Finch, grinning.

" I still don't want my breakfast," answered Archer. " And I still want to see the Tree."

"Wherever is that terrible draft coming from?" cried Alayne. "And who let the dogs in?"

Finch leaped up the stairs.

Oh, if Renny and Piers and Wake were home, how happy he could be! He pictured them, one after the other, at their various pursuits. What a Christmas it would be when they all were at Jalna once again! He knocked at Ernest's door and went in.

"Merry Christmas, Uncle Ernest!" He went to the bed and kissed him.

"Merry Christmas, my boy! Will you just prop those pillows behind me a little more firmly. How cold it is! Please don't touch me again with your hands. They 're icy."

Finch tucked the eiderdown about him. "Is that better?"

The old gentleman looked nice indeed, with his lean pink face, his forget-me-not blue eyes and his silvery hair brushed smooth. Nicholas, when Finch visited him, was a contrast. His hair, his eyebrows, his moustache, still iron-gray, were ruffled. His bed was untidy and on the table at his side lay his pipe and tobacco pouch, with burnt matches strewn about.

After the season's greetings, Finch asked — "Have you rung for your breakfast yet, Uncle Nick?"

"No, no. I never ring till I 've heard Rags bring your Uncle Ernest's. No matter how early I wake he always gets ahead of me. So now I just smoke a pipe and resign myself to waiting. How many times did he ring?"

"One long one."

"Means he wants an egg. Does n't need an egg when he 's going to eat a heavy dinner. To-morrow he 'll be taking indigestion tablets, you 'll see."

Nicholas stretched out an unsteady handsome old hand, found his pipe and a pigeon's feather with which he proceeded to clean it. What did it feel like to be ninety-one,

Finch wondered. Very comfortable, to judge by the way Uncle Nick pulled contentedly at his pipe.

"So you 're going to read the Lessons, eh?" the old man asked.

"Yes, and I 'm scared stiff."

Nicholas stared. "You nervous — after all you 've done!"

"This is different."

"I should think it is. A little country church, as familiar to you as your own home. Your own family there to support you."

"That 's just it. When I see you all facing me while I read out of the Bible, it will seem preposterous. And I have n't had any practice. I don't know how to read out of the Bible."

"Good heavens, you 've been often enough to church!"

"It 's not the same."

Nicholas thought a minute, then he said, "I 'll tell you what. You get my prayer book out of the wardrobe, then you can let me hear you read. I 'll tell you how it sounds."

Finch went with alacrity to the towering walnut wardrobe that always had worn an air of mystery to him.

"Door to the left," directed his uncle. "Hatbox where I keep my good hat."

Finch opened the door. A smell which was a mixture of tobacco, old tweed, and broadcloth, came out. He took the lid from the large leather hatbox. There inside was his uncle's top hat and in its crown lay his prayer book, the gilt cross on its cover worn dim by the years.

"I remember," said Finch, "when you wore that silk hat every Sunday."

"Ah, there was dignity in those days! On this continent we shall sink before long to shirt sleeves and not getting to our feet when a woman comes into the room — to judge by what I see in the papers. Well, you boys were n't brought up that way. Now, let 's hear you read."

Nicholas had in his younger days played the piano quite well. He was convinced that Finch had inherited his talent from him. Though his fingers had long been too stiff for playing, he still kept his old square piano in his room and sometimes when he was alone fumbled over the few stray bars he remembered. Now Finch sat down before the keyboard and placed the open book on the rack. He read the Epistle through. He looked inquiringly at his uncle.

"Too loud," said Nicholas.

"Not for the church, Uncle."

"You must learn to control your voice. It 's a good one but it 's erratic."

"I expect I 'll make a mess of the whole thing."

"Nonsense. You read far better than old Fennel."

The jingling of dishes on Ernest's tray could be heard.

"There he is!" exclaimed Nicholas. He searched the top of his bedside table and found two envelopes. Wragge appeared at the door.

"Merry Christmas, sir!" His small gray face, with its jutting nose and chin, took on an expectant beam.

Nicholas handed him the envelopes.

"One for you — one for your wife. Merry Christmas to you both. Bring me porridge — thick toast, gooseberry jam."

"Yes, sir. Thank you, sir. It 's very nice to be remembered. Mr. Ernest did the sime for us. Mrs. Wragge will thank you later, sir."

When he had gone, Finch groaned. "Gosh, I completely forgot to give them anything! No wonder he gave me a chilly look. How much was in the envelopes, Uncle Nick?"

"Five in each. Ernest gives them the same. Well, it keeps 'em good-humored. They have a lot of trays to cope with."

Finch walked alone across the fields to church. A slight
fall of snow had made them freshly white. There showed
no human footprint, but the winding path was clearly defined
among the tall dead grasses, the stalks of Michaelmas daisy
and goldenrod. In and about ran the footprints of pheasants. Rabbits had been there too, leaving their Y-shaped
prints, and field mice their tiny scratchings. From a twisted
old thorn tree, a chickadee piped his last recollection of
summer.

Now Finch could see the church tower rising from its
knoll and in the graveyard two figures. They were Meg and
Patience. As he drew near he saw that they were standing
by the plot where the Vaughans were laid. It was the
second Christmas that Meg's husband, Maurice Vaughan,
had been gone from her. Yet Finch felt that it would
scarcely be seemly to call out " Merry Christmas " to Meg and
Patience, mourning by his grave.

But Meg saved Finch embarrassment by at once seeing
him and coming toward him with arms outstretched. She
still wore black but to-day she had brightened it by pinning a
little nosegay of pink artificial daisies on the breast of her
black lamb coat which had seen twelve seasons' wear.

" Merry Christmas! " she exclaimed, folding Finch to
her bosom. " And many, many of them! "

Finch hugged them both, then, after an appreciative glance
at the wreath on the grave, said: —

" Had n't you better come into the church? You 'll get
cold standing here."

" Yes, we 'll go at once. How do you like the wreath?
I think it 's marvelous the way they make these wreaths of
bronze leaves. They look so natural. But they 're terribly
expensive."

" It 's very nice, Meggie."

" I was saying to Patience, just as you came up, how
strange it is to think that when I die I shall have to lie here

among the Vaughans, instead of with the Whiteoaks, where I'd feel so much more at home."

"It seems strange."

"Do you think it might possibly be arranged that I should be buried among my own family?"

"Don't talk about it, Meggie."

Finch could not remember the time when death had not seemed real and terrible to him. The loss of both parents, when he was seven, had made an indelible impression on him. But Patience had the feeling that she could never die. Her mother too must live and live. She took Meg's hand and drew her toward the church. The last bell began to ring. People were mounting the icy steps — figures symbolic of the arduous Christian way. Finch hastened to the vestry. Patience called after him: —

"You'll find the surplices nice and clean, Uncle Finch. Mother and I washed and ironed them all."

"Good for you!"

As he passed the door he had a glimpse of Noah Binns ringing the bell, bending almost double to impart additional Christmas fervor to the act. Bell ringer, gravedigger, farm worker, he had been for many a year putting energy into only the first two of these callings. Now that he was in his seventies, he spared himself still more in farm work, yet demanded higher wages — and got them. He had a patronizing and resentful attitude toward the Whiteoak family. He firmly believed that they would like to put him out of his job of bell ringer and he had made up his mind to hang on to it as long as he could hang on to the bell rope.

Now his ferret eyes and Finch's large gray ones exchanged a look of mutual challenge.

"Hurry up," said Binns's eyes, "or I'll stop ringing before you get your danged surplice on."

Finch's eyes said — "If you let me down it will be the worse for you."

The church was filled by the scent of greenery that was twined about pulpit, font, and choir stalls. From his own body there came to Finch the clean smell of his freshly laundered surplice. Now he was in his seat near the steps of the chancel. There was no escape. He was in for reading the Lessons. Miss Pink, the organist, bent all her powers to the playing of the opening hymn. Finch stole a sly look at the congregation. For a brief moment his eyes rested on the family pews. There were the dear old uncles, with Archer fenced in between them and Adeline and Roma on the far side of Ernest. Alayne had not come. In the pew behind were Pheasant and her three sons. Across the aisle, in the Vaughan pew, Meg and Patience. All, down to Archer, knew the Christmas hymn by heart, so they were able to rivet their full attention on Finch. He began to feel horribly nervous. His mouth felt dry. He was sure his voice would come with a croak.

The calm tones of the Rector led the congregation through the intricacies of the service. Finch watched him standing or kneeling there, his brown beard streaked with silver, and thought of his simple acceptance of the Christian faith and his unostentatious adherence to it in his daily life. Finch felt calmed. After the singing of the *Venite Exultemus Domino* he moved with a kind of awkward dignity to his place behind the brass eagle. In a low voice he read: —

" Here beginneth the First Chapter of the Hebrews."

Meg's whisper, fierce in its intensity, came distinctly to him.

"Louder!"

No one regarded this admonishment of Meg's as out of place. Those of the congregation who were near enough to hear her thought it well that she should make an effort to keep Finch up to the family's standard of reading the Lessons. As for Finch, he colored deeply, then really let his voice out. It was a strong and moving voice. It had power in it. No one could complain now that what he read was not audible.

"Here beginneth the first Chapter of St. Paul's Epistle to the Hebrews . . . 'God, who at sundry times and in divers manners spake in time past unto the fathers by the prophets, hath in these last days spoken unto us by his Son.'" And so proceeded till he came to the question — "'For unto which of the angels said he at any time, Thou art my Son, this day have I begotten thee?'" Then his eyes rested for a moment on the congregation and he gathered the breast of his surplice in his hand and pulled at it as though he would rend it. He read on: —

"'. . . Thou, Lord, in the beginning hast laid the foundation of the earth; and the heavens are the works of thine hands: they shall perish; but thou remainest; and they all shall wax old as doth a garment; and as a vesture shalt thou fold them up, and they shall be changed: but thou art the same, and thy years shall not fail.'"

Surely Finch read the sombre words far too well. Surely his voice was too moving and the expression on his long face of too profound a melancholy. "As a vesture shalt thou fold them up!" It was not pleasant on a fine Christmas morning, thought Ernest. It was hardly decent. The little church had never heard the scriptures so read before. Even Mr. Fennel thought Finch was overdoing it.

But it was the way he tugged at his surplice that most worried the family. When he took his place behind the lectern to read the Second Lesson, his Uncle Nicholas clutched the lapel of his own coat, tugged at it, and shook his head so hard that his gray hair fell over his forehead. Finch wondered what was the matter with him. Then he perceived that his Uncle Ernest was doing the same. Startled, he clutched his surplice the tighter. He began to read in a loud nervous tone. Then he saw Meg. She was pulling at her fur collar as though she would pull it off! She was shaking her head! Now he understood. He released his surplice, controlled his voice. Suddenly he felt quite calm. He read the Second Lesson with credit and not too much feeling.

Pheasant's sons walked back with him across the fields. Rather they ran through the frosty air, drinking in its sweetness, rolling snowballs between their palms to hurl at each other. They were at Jalna as soon as the car which carried Nicholas and Ernest. Nicholas was somewhat disgruntled, for Ernest had insisted on his being bundled up in too many coats, mufflers, and rugs. He could not extricate himself from them. Twice he had tried to heave himself out of the seat and each time his heavy old body had sunk back on to the cushions. He had just got over a cold and Ernest was anxious about him.

"Dammit," growled Nicholas. "I feel like a feather bed. I'm stuck here. Tell the others. You must have dinner without me." He pushed out his lips beneath his gray moustache and blew angrily.

Wright now proffered his help. "Let me give you a hand, sir."

"No use trying, Wright. I'm stuck. Hullo, Finch! Tell them to have dinner without me — and the Tree without me."

Finch laughed and grasped him by the arms. Between them he and Wright got the old man out of the car and up the steps. The front door flew open and the children, still wearing their outdoor things, came tumbling out.

"Merry Christmas!" they shouted. "Merry Christmas, Uncle Nick!"

"You've wished me that three times already," growled Nicholas.

"It can't be wished too often, can it?" retorted Adeline.

All the way into the house Nicholas grumbled. He grumbled all the while he was being divested of his wraps.

He was more and more depressed about playing the part of Santa Claus. The saint might be old but he had no gouty knee to hamper him. He was hale and hearty.

The three dogs had pushed their way into the house. The five children tore upstairs to take off their things, then tore down again. The rich smell of roasting turkey and stuffing rose from the basement. Through the keyhole and crevices of the library door the pungent scent of the Tree stole forth.

"Why are Alayne and Pheasant trying to restrain the children?" Nicholas thought. "Let 'em make all the noise they can. It will take a lot of noise to fill the void made by the absence of Renny and Piers and Wakefield."

At last they were seated about the table, with the massive turkey in front of Ernest. Rags had put an edge on the carving knife that might have divided a feather pillow at one stroke. Ernest faced the task with admirable calm. He twitched up his cuffs and took the knife and fork in hand. Alayne, facing him, sat very erect, a fixed smile on her lips. She did not see Ernest, but Renny, at the head of the table, the carving knife and fork poised, his bright gaze moving from the turkey to the face of the one he was about to serve, well knowing the particular choice of each member of the family. Pheasant must not let herself think of that prison camp in Germany! No — she must keep the thought of Piers far back in her mind, remembering only the children and that this was their day. But not so long ago — though sometimes it seemed half a lifetime — Piers had been Santa Claus, pink and white and jovial. She clenched her hands beneath the table till self-control came, then she laughed and chaffed with Finch and Mooey. Finch was in high spirits. He had come through his ordeal without disgrace, even with some credit. Physically he was feeling better than in years. He and Pheasant and Mooey never stopped laughing and talking. Rags and his wife, she in a new black dress with snowy cuffs and apron, bustled about the table. Bright sunlight, streaming between the yellow velvet curtains, shone on the silver basket mounded with bright fruit, the gay crackers, the shining heads of the children.

But it touched something else. Nicholas bent forward to see. He could scarcely believe his eyes. Grouped about the centrepiece were three photographs framed in holly leaves. They were of Renny, Piers, and Wakefield.

"Well," growled Nicholas, "I'll be shot!"

He looked down at the richly mounded plate in front of him, at the mound of cranberry jelly Rags was offering him, in confusion and gloom.

"I don't like it at all," he muttered, but nobody heard him. He raised his voice and repeated — "I don't like it at all."

"What don't you like, Uncle Nick, dear?" asked Meg.

He pointed three times. "These memorial pictures. They fuss me. They take away my appetite. If they're left on the table I shall be sick."

"That is just the way I feel, Uncle Nick," said Meg, with a reproachful look at Alayne and Pheasant, whose idea it had been.

"I think it's a grand idea," said Finch. "It makes you feel that the chaps are almost with us in the flesh."

"I am sure they would be pleased," said Ernest.

"They'd hate it," muttered Nicholas. "'T would make 'em feel dead."

"Nonsense," said his brother.

"The chaps would be pleased," said Finch.

"They'd feel dead," persisted Nicholas.

Tears began to run down Pheasant's cheeks.

Alayne rose and took the pictures from the table. She carried them from the room with dignity, then with an impassive face returned to her place at the table. Nicholas emptied his wineglass. He felt better now. He joined in the lively talk. He drank a good deal and at last, when Finch and Meggie dressed him in his Santa Claus costume, they declared they had never seen it more becomingly worn. He forgot all about his gout. He was a noble, a magnificent Father Christmas. Everyone said so. At the last Adeline threw her arms about him and drew his head down to whisper : —

"You were splendid, Uncle Nick. Archer and Philip absolutely believed in you. Christmas is being almost as good as though Daddy were here."

So the year drew to its close. It was a mild winter. Yet there was enough snow to make it difficult for the birds to find food. Beneath Ernest's bedroom window there was a feeding table for birds on which Mrs. Wragge, three times a day, placed large bowlfuls of cut-up fresh bread. On it clustered the sparrows, getting more than their share of the food. But there were sleek, slate-colored little juncos too, and many a time the lively flash of a blue jay. The two old men watched them with never-failing interest. There was great excitement on the morning when a cardinal and his mate appeared. Shy at first, they soon grew bolder, till their coral-colored beaks pecked as intrepidly on the table as any sparrows. But when the pheasants trailed up out of the ravine the little birds gave way to them. Sparrows and juncos perched in the old hawthorn in which the table was built, to watch the great birds devour their bread, but a flash of blue and a flash of scarlet showed which way the blue jays and the cardinals had flown.

VIII

PIERS'S RETURN

THE winter months were mild enough but when spring came and there was no sign of spring it was a drag on the spirits of all save the youngest. In March and for part of April the countryside was covered by a shining layer of ice. People slipped and slithered as they walked. Fat Mrs. Wragge, carrying bread to the birds' table, fell and broke a bone in her leg which laid her up completely for a fortnight and sadly hampered her for another. To see her hobbling about the kitchen with her huge leg in a cast seemed the last straw to Alayne. Rags suffered from a continuous cold in the head. They were a pernicious pair, Alayne thought, yet she thanked God that they were there to get through the work somehow.

The ice was so smooth that even the dogs walked gingerly. As for the pheasants, they slipped and fell, sometimes on their breasts and sometimes on their tails, in a most droll and unbirdlike manner. This glassy monotony went on and on, week after week. It did not snow; it did not rain; it did not thaw. Winds blew down branches and blew them across the ice. The fringe of icicles hanging from the eave outside Ernest's bedroom window separated the colors in the sun rays as prisms.

In these spring months the two old men deteriorated so greatly that the others of the family began to doubt whether they would live to see Renny and Piers again. They lost appetite. They lost heart. They talked longingly of far-away days when they used to go to the South of France in the winter. They greatly missed Adeline's presence from the house. Alayne at last had had her way and Adeline had been sent as a boarder to a girls' school. Even the war news ceased to interest Nicholas and Ernest. When Adeline came home for the Easter holidays, she brought new life to them. She was so joyful to be at Jalna again, so full of stories of her escapades at school (exaggerated to make them laugh), such a sight for sore eyes as she galloped by on her sturdy bay cob, Timothy! But soon the holidays were over and again the brothers sank back in melancholy.

Then one day came news which electrified the family. There had been an exchange of prisoners of war and Piers was among those expected to arrive in Canada early in May. Pheasant, who bore the news, was almost beside herself with excitement. What she had hoped for, prayed for, at times despaired of, was going to happen! The relief was almost more than she could bear. But she had not much time for thinking. There was so much to be done. The house must be shining from end to end. She must have new clothes. Everything must be beautiful for the welcome of her mate. It was more than four years since she had seen him. He had been taken prisoner so soon after going to the front. What would those years have done to him? She did not let herself think. There was no time for thought. Polishing furniture, cleaning silver, making herself a new blouse, buying herself a new suit and hat, buying new clothes for the children. She kept her feet on the ground by making the money fly.

Sometimes she felt inundated by the flood of memories, anticipations, and apprehensions that swept over her. Sometimes her mind was a blank while she polished and sewed. Then came the day when she went to the hairdresser and when she bought a box of French face powder and a bottle of nail enamel, which last she never brought herself to the point of using. Then, on top of that, the day when his train arrived, eight hours late.

Finch and Maurice had persuaded her not to go to the railway station. Better welcome him in their own house with a good meal waiting. But they took the two small boys with them, wearing their Sunday suits and carrying a packet of sandwiches, in case the train should be delayed. Pheasant was thankful to have them off her hands. How she put in the day she did not know. By evening she felt exhausted by waiting. Her legs ached from walking the floor. Yet, when she heard the car coming through the mild May twilight, she ran swiftly to open the door. Then panic possessed her. She could not open it. Her throat was so dry she could not have uttered a sound. Nooky threw the door wide open.

She saw Piers carefully descend from the car, the golden light from the afterglow full on his face.

" We had a terribly long wait," cried Nooky. " We thought he 'd never come. But he 's here! "

This was her own Piers, limping swiftly toward her. His face was tanned by the sea voyage, his blue eyes were shining into hers. He crushed her against his breast.

" Home again — home again — little Pheasant! " he said, his voice husky. " By God, I can't believe it! "

If she had gone to the station she could have hung on to herself but here, in their own home, hearing his familiar voice in the familiar surroundings, she broke down and sobbed in an anguish of relief — relief, and regret for the years of their life which they had lost.

She had forgotten how stalwart he was. In these years she had lived among boys and old men or seen Finch's lanky figure. But what a chest Piers had! What shoulders! What a strong column of a neck!

" By God," he again exclaimed, staring about him, " it 's just the same! I can't believe in it."

" And me," she got out, through her tears, " what about me? Am I very changed? "

He held her off and looked at her. " Changed! You look just like you did the day I married you."

" We're changed!" cried Philip. " Daddy didn't know us."

" What do you think of Mooey?" asked Pheasant.

Piers looked speculatively at the youth. " He's just what I expected. He hasn't changed — except to grow tall."

" It's wonderful," said Finch. " Your part of the family is united again. Piers from the war. Mooey from Ireland. It's what you've been longing for, all these years, Pheasant. I'll bet you are happy, aren't you?"

" Happy!" The word was too much for her. She broke into sobs.

" None of that," said Piers, in a gruff voice. " That's no way to welcome a fellow. All right . . . all right . . . we'll go away again, won't we, Mooey?"

" You shall stay just where you are!" cried Pheasant, laughing through her sobs. She threw her arms around both of them and clasped them fiercely to her. " You'll never, never get away from me again."

Piers, a little shaken on his artificial leg, clasped Pheasant and Mooey to him, while Mooey, with eyes shining, clasped both parents. The sight was more than Nook and Philip could stand. They hurled themselves against the interlaced trio with the impetus of players in a Rugby match. There was a moment when it seemed that all five would go to the floor. Finch watched them, his face set in a happy grin, his eyes wet with tears.

They righted themselves, released each other; Piers went upstairs to wash and Pheasant went to the kitchen to prepare the supper. Finch followed her, while Maurice kept the two small boys in the sitting room. Finch said: —

" Doesn't he look fine? Even though he's a good deal thinner, he still looks pretty solid and handsome. I never expected to see him so solid and handsome. Did you?"

" No, I did n't. And I never expected to feel like this."
Again she fell to weeping.

Finch put his arms about her and patted her on the back.
" It 's natural, I guess. I feel like crying myself."

In a few moments she was calm and set about making an
omelette. Finch beat the eggs. He beat them so hard that
flecks of egg fluff flew in all directions but Pheasant did not
notice. Now her whole being was concentrated on the
omelette. If it did not rise properly, or if it rose and fell,
she could not bear it. She could not bear it. She would
cry again! She heard him moving about in the room upstairs. Is he really there? Oh, it can't be true! He can't
be home again! And all the while she concentrated on the
omelette.

Piers sluiced the soapy water over hands and face. The
soap was fine and scented. The towel was fine and damask.
There were pink bath salts in a jar. There was the shining
white enamel bath. The luxury of it was unbelievable.
His mind flew back to the crowded room in the prison camp,
the harshness, the only half-washed-away grime, the complete lack of privacy, the smells. He held the clean towel to
his nostrils and drew a deep breath. Those at home would
never understand. No words could make them understand.

He limped back to the bedroom. He looked down at the
inviting whiteness of the bed, the bedcoverings turned back
in a neat triangle, ready for the night. From it rose the
scent of lavender. The window of the room stood open.
The cool night air, freighted with the smell of lilac, came in.
It had been a mild winter but it had been cruelly persistent.
All through March and April the weather had been that of a
mild winter. No blade of grass had pushed its way through
the ice that still sheathed the land. The ice had no longer
glittered in the sun but had been gray under a cloudy sky.
But, when May came, there had been hardly any time for
spring. Scarcely had the newly opened leaves of the lilac

showed their shape when the flower buds threw open the tiny petals and formed themselves into white plumes that clustered, one above another, in great clumps. This lilac tree had grown from a cutting taken from the old white lilac that grew outside the window of the grandmother's room at Jalna.

As Piers had buried his face in the damask towel, so now he put out his hand, drew in a plume of the lilac and hid his face in it. He closed his eyes. He would have liked to obliterate in the lilac's fragrant freshness all he had seen and endured since he had left home. He would have liked to become again the same man he had then been. But he could not be the same. He felt that he could have remained with his face buried in the white blossoms till they faded and died. A twitter of nesting birds came from the eave.

"Daddy! Daddy!" called out Philip from below.

"Daddy!" To be called by that name! It went to his heart. The little voice made him feel softhearted. He limped quickly to the stairs, then descended them with care. Philip, waiting below, kept his eyes averted from his father's leg as he had been told. He had had other warnings about Piers's return. Try as she would, Pheasant had not been able to refrain from sometimes saying in exasperation — "I don't know what Daddy will say to your behavior!" Many a time Maurice had ejaculated — "If Daddy does n't skin you alive, when he comes home, I shall be surprised." Even his great-uncles had declared that his father would warm his seat for him when he came home. So Philip had looked forward to his sire's return with mingled delight and foreboding. To Piers, descending the stair, he looked the very best sort of little boy, with his straight back, his waving fair hair and fine blue eyes. Piers smiled at him, took his hand, and led him into the dining room.

The omelette was on the table. It had risen to an amazing height and of an unbelievable lightness. It stood poised there, as though intimating that it could endure such height and such lightness for two minutes and no more. Piers stared at it and at the parsley wreathing it.

"What's that green stuff?" he demanded.

"Parsley, Daddy," laughed Philip. "Don't you know parsley when you see it?"

Piers picked up a spray, sniffed it, and thrust it into his mouth.

"Do you like it?" asked Nooky.

"I may get used to such things by and by."

The omelette was swiftly disposed of. Maurice and Nooky carried out the plates and returned with a plump, cold roast chicken on a platter. Piers stared unbelievingly.

"What's that?" he demanded suspiciously.

"Oh, Daddy, it's a chicken!"

"And that funny mixture in the bowl?"

"Salad!"

"Hothouse tomatoes, if you please," added Pheasant.

"Gosh, do you live this way all the time?"

"Heavens, no! Fetch the wine, Mooey, dear."

Maurice brought the bottle of Chianti. Even the children had half a glassful each. Piers's health was drunk and it was only by superhuman effort that Pheasant kept herself from crying again. After the chicken came a trifle, well soaked in sherry, and, after the table was cleared, coffee.

Piers asked innumerable questions about the family, about the farm hands, the orchards, the stock, the show horses. His curiosity was boundless but he disappointed the two small boys by having little to say about himself and his experiences. Soon they were sent to bed and presently Finch left. A soft spring rain was falling. The scent of lilacs was heavy.

Maurice went outside and stood in the porch. He inhaled the damp air. His mind detached itself from this scene of his father's homecoming and returned to the mossy dampness of the air of Glengorman. What had that stay in Ireland done to him? How was it that old Dermot Court seemed more near to him than his own father? Three years would pass before he might journey back and see that loved spot. His mother must go with him. She gave the reality of childhood to every scene. But she would not stay there with him. His life had been torn in half while it was yet tender. He heard Piers's low laugh. He felt shy of reentering the room. He went softly up the stairs.

It was past midnight before Piers and Pheasant followed him. They crept up the stairs softly, like lovers, holding hands. She went to the bathroom and prepared a hot bath for him. He lay soaking in it, half-dazed in an ecstasy of relaxation. On the old mahogany towel horse that was always so ready to topple over hung brand-new silk pyjamas, striped blue and white. Certainly Pheasant had made the money fly. And in the pocket of the jacket a linen handkerchief with scent on it!

He thought of how he had lain for a day and a night in a ditch with his foot blown off by a piece of shrapnel. He turned his mind fiercely away from all that had followed. Now one leg of the pyjamas dangled loose.

When Pheasant came back after closing the children's windows against the rain which now slanted on a fresh wind, she found Piers in bed, lying on his back, his hair brushed smooth, and wearing the sweet expression of a good boy after his bath. He smiled up at her.

" Come here," he said.

She came and knelt down by the bed. He took her hands in his and his eyes lost themselves in the twilight depths of hers. " Little Pheasant," he kept murmuring, stroking her hands.

She could not speak.

His expression changed. His lips stiffened into a look

of pain. He placed her right hand on the stump of his right leg.

"Is it going to make you feel different toward me?" he whispered.

"Oh, Piers, how can you?" Her voice was hoarse from emotion. "How can you have such a horrible thought? The only difference it can make is that I'll love you more!" She bent and pressed her trembling lips against the maimed limb. "My precious love!"

He said sternly — "I don't mean because of any hero stuff, I mean because of my value — as a man."

"That's what I mean too!" she cried, eagerly. "I mean as a man. You've been through a terrible ordeal. You're home again — safe! You're yourself! Oh, if you knew the things I've imagined! I've imagined you as a shrunken shadow of yourself. And here you are — solid and healthy and beautiful as ever! What does a leg matter? Nothing!"

He lay watching her preparations for the night — the careful hanging up of her new dress, the brushing of her dark hair, the slipping of her white arms into the sleeves of her nightgown, her brief prayers which were just a wordless upsurge of thanksgiving, her turning out of the light which somehow brought the sound of the rain into the room. But the sound of the rain was benignant. Its voice was the voice of renewal. Lilacs were not enough, all the richer pageantry of nature was to follow. The movement of Pheasant in his arms, the movement of the branches outside his window, swept Piers's mind clean. The night was long and toward its close he sank down, deeper and deeper, stilled by the benign sound of the rain, covered by the wings of sleep.

IX

DAYS OF SPRING

HE sat the next morning in an old gray flannel suit, on the little flagged terrace, basking in the warm May sunshine. Bacon and eggs, toast, marmalade, and three cups of tea were inside him. His pipe was in his mouth, the smoke from it resting in blue oases on the quiet air. Only one thing was lacking to him — his wire-haired terrier, Biddy. She had been killed by a car the summer before. When Piers had looked forward to his homecoming, he had always pictured himself as encircled by a rapturous Biddy who had never forgotten him. He had been told of her death in a letter but this morning he missed her afresh. In his long years of imprisonment he had felt the lack of a dog's companionship as one of the hardest things to bear. Now, in the May sunshine, he puffed pensively at his pipe.

Steps came from the house and Pheasant appeared, followed by her three sons. She stood smiling down at Piers.

" We have a present for you and we 're going to give it to you now because — it simply will not be quiet for another minute. Bring her out, boys! "

The two younger darted into the house and reappeared carrying a hamper in which something small and white was bestirring itself.

" Open and see, Daddy! " cried Philip.

Piers lifted the lid of the hamper which was now on his knees. A four-months-old wire-haired puppy was inside, clean and white as a new toy, black-nosed, pink-tongued, ready to bound out of the hamper in its infant vitality.

" What do you think of her? " cried Nooky.   " Mother

and Maurice clubbed together and bought her. And Philip and I clubbed together and bought her collar."

"We knew you'd miss Biddy so," said Pheasant.

"She spent the night at Auntie Meg's," put in Maurice. "I've just been over to fetch her. I'm afraid she was pretty naughty. She made three puddles on the floor and kept them awake half the night whimpering."

Piers said nothing. The puppy was in his arms, wildly licking his face, nibbling his nose, trying its best to turn itself inside out in its joy.

"Do you like her?" asked Philip.

"Like her!" exclaimed Piers. "Like her! Why, if you had scoured the country over, you couldn't possibly have found anything else I'd like half so well."

"What shall we name her? It's a she, you know."

"She's well bred," said Maurice. "You must see her pedigree."

"We'll find a name for her," answered Piers. He snuggled the puppy in his arms. He would not be parted from her for a moment. Her pliant, ecstatic little body was the final drop in his brimming cup of content. When, an hour later, they went in a body to Jalna, the puppy went too.

Finch and Alayne met them on the drive. They were waiting there to stop them from all going in together to see the uncles. It might be too exciting for them. Piers climbed out of the car, took Alayne by the hand, then kissed her cheek. She looked thinner, older, he thought. But he was glad to see her. God, how glad he was to see every single one of the family! As they stood talking on the drive, his eyes kept wandering from the faces of those clustered about him to stare at the old house, standing there serene, just as though nothing especial had been happening in the past four years. Then suddenly he saw Ernest's face at a window of the drawing-room. Ernest threw open the window and called in a hoarse voice quite unlike his own: —

" Piers! Piers — here we are! Come in at once!"

" Oh, go to them, darling!" said Pheasant.

Finch warned — " Don't tell them any horrors or get them too excited."

Piers stared. " Are they so delicate as all that?"

He limped hurriedly to the house. Yes, he thought as he stood before them, they did look fragile, very changed indeed. It took him a moment or so to feel at home with them. Poor old fellows — they 'd obviously suffered a lot.

" Well, well, well," said Nicholas, " so here you are! It 's a great day, Piers. It 's a great day for us."

" Sometimes we wondered if ever we 'd see you again," said Ernest, his blue eyes wet with tears.

Nicholas added, with a deep sigh — " If only Renny were back again! And Wakefield! We still have them to worry about."

" Don't you worry about Renny," said Piers. " Colonels generally come back."

" Many are killed or wounded," said Ernest.

" Yes, but they have a better chance. He 'll come back. Don't worry."

Ernest smiled. " You are right. We must just rejoice in the fact that you are safe."

Nicholas looked Piers over. " You look fine. If three years in a German prison camp would make me look like that, egad, I 'd try it!"

" And lose a leg?" laughed Piers.

Nicholas scowled at his gouty knee. " I 'd give this one up and be glad of it."

Ernest still held Piers's firm hand in his. " Dear boy, you walk better than I had hoped for."

" I 'll walk better when I get a better leg. Still, this one has served me pretty well."

" Sit down between us," said Nicholas, " and tell us about your life over there."

Piers's eyes drank in the familiarity of the room. The feel of the chair he drew up was as familiar as the feel of the hand that drew it. The suit worn by Nicholas was familiar. Surely that suit was ten years old!

"They've given me a puppy to take Biddy's place," he exclaimed. "Did you know? She's a little beauty. I'll bring her in and show you."

"Yes, but not now," said Nicholas. "Tell us about your life over there. The real truth, you know, not just what they'd let you tell in letters."

Ernest looked nervous. "Yes, yes. I hope it wasn't too bad."

Piers smiled from one face to the other. "We had a good deal of fun," he said. "Not always, of course. But funny things happened."

He did not tell of the heartbreaking boredom, the lack of the most simple comforts of life, the crowding, the dirt. He told of the concerts they had put on, the jokes they had played on each other, the ribald stories. For all that they had been men of the world, Nicholas and Ernest never had heard stories quite so ribald as the ones Piers told them. They laughed till their sides ached. Finch heard the laughter and joined them. His loud laugh that always, when he had laughed with too much abandon, took on a hysterical note, was added to theirs.

When he and Piers went outdoors again, Piers's mouth was down at the corners. "Poor old uncles," he said, "they'll not last much longer. No one told me they were like this."

"It's been gradual," Finch returned sadly. "I'd never noticed it quite as much as this morning when they were laughing so hard."

Piers had to go down to the basement to see the Wragges, the wife even fatter and the husband even thinner than when he had last seen them. While he was there a shout came

from Philip — " Auntie Meg and Patience are here, Daddy!
Come — quick! "

Meg folded the brother with whom she had had many a
quarrel, but still loved deeply, to her ample bosom.   Patience
kissed him shyly.

" How well you look! " said Meg.   " Rested and well!
But of course you 've led a quiet, regular life.   Patience and
I have been through a terrible time.   We 've been thrown
from post to pillar.   I hardly know what a good night's
sleep is.   You will find us sadly changed — living in a tiny
house and doing our own work, except for a woman who
comes in twice a week."

" You look like a million dollars."

She tried to smile wanly.

" I 'm glad to hear it.   But really, Piers, when I found I
must sell Vaughanlands, I made up my mind to go through
it with an iron resolve.   I made up my mind to trouble no
one with my worries."

" Pheasant tells me you got a mighty good price for it."

" How can she know its value! "   Meg was indignant.
" I sold it at a sacrifice.   But don't let 's talk of sordid
things.   Let us sit down and talk about you."

They sat down in the old lawn chairs, worn by the wind
and weather to a grayish brown.   Pheasant and Alayne had
gone into the house.   Now Patience, given a look by Meg,
went with Piers's sons toward the stables.   Meg sat between her brothers.

" I don't call selling a property for a good price, sordid,"
observed Piers.

" All money dealings seem sordid to me," said Meg.
" They have a way of bringing out the meaner side of human nature.   Not that I ever have allowed material things
to influence me."

Finch looked at her admiringly as she uttered these words
but Piers's eyes were fixed on a rotund little cloud just above

the treetops. He had a sore feeling inside him and he could not have explained just why it was. Then he recalled the faces of the two old uncles, their looks so aged since he had seen them last.

"The uncles don't look very well," he said.

"Ah, it was the winter," said Meg. "And the anxiety. But now that you are home and the summer coming, you'll see how they will pick up."

"I hope so." After a moment's silence, in which he absorbed the almost forgotten sweet humming of bees in a flowering currant bush, he exclaimed — "Gosh, it will seem strange to see someone else at Vaughanlands! What is this fellow, Clapperton, like?"

"Very nice indeed," said Meg. "You must go with me to call on him. He has all sorts of interesting schemes. A sunroom, a swimming pool, a rose garden with a sundial."

"Hmph."

"You won't say that when you meet him . . . Oh, Piers, it will be such a relief to have someone at Jalna who has experience of farming and knows how the farm horses should be cared for! Of course, you have been told about the Clydesdale mare."

"No. What was that?"

Meg poured out the story of Wright's dismissal, of the man whom Alayne and Finch had engaged and how he had caused the death of the Clydesdale. Piers gave a grunt of heartfelt anger at the tale of incompetence and disaster.

"It was the same with everyone," said Finch. "Everyone was having trouble."

"It is a mercy," declared Meg, "that Wright had the loyalty to stay on even though Alayne discharged him. I can't tell you how overbearing she has become, yet she has little control of her children."

"I miss Adeline," said Piers. "When are her holidays?"

"Early in June. She's growing to be a lovely girl. How she hates going to boarding school! But Alayne would have it. Poor little Archer and Roma were dying to stay home to-day because of your coming but Alayne would n't hear of it. Really she's becoming a tyrant. The servants don't like her. Wright hates her, for she thwarts him at every turn. The poor dogs are so cowed they scarcely dare enter the house. She has torn off the lovely embossed wallpaper that has been in the hall ever since the house was built and had the walls done in cream color. It's really shocking."

Piers's eyes became prominent. "I did n't notice! I was in such a hurry to see the uncles, I did n't notice. The woman must be mad. She'll have old redhead in a rage when he comes home."

"She can find money for everything she wants to do," said Meg, "but she's positively penurious when other things are suggested. No one but Rags and Cook and Wright would have stayed with her."

"You exaggerate," said Finch. "I think Alayne is very kind. Think of how much she must have endured in having Uncle Nick and Uncle Ernest here!"

"Endured!" cried Meg. "Think of what it has meant to her to have them as companions! Alayne knew nothing of the world when she came to Jalna."

"She came from New York."

"Oh, that!" said Meg.

"Here they come!" Piers waved his hand in welcome to his uncles, who now appeared in the porch, followed by Rags carrying an armful of cushions and traveling rugs.

"We're coming," said Ernest, "to enjoy the sunshine. It is the first day we have found it really warm enough for sitting on the lawn. How green the grass is!"

"And there's the puppy!" Nicholas clapped his hands

at it. "A good one too. I'd like a puppy of my own but I dare n't suggest it to Alayne."

Meg gave Piers a look.

"And I," added Ernest, "have wished many a time in the past winter for a Persian kitten. They're very amusing little things. But — of course — they make trouble." He sighed and sank into the chair Rags had arranged for him.

"This 'ouse, Mr. Piers," said Rags in a low tone, "ain't what it was in regard to pets. I don't object to them. My wife don't object. It's the mistress who objects."

Piers scarcely heard. He was playing with the puppy. Oh, the delicious gnawing of its tiny teeth on his fingers! Oh, the velvet softness of its hide! Oh, its ignorance of misery or of pain!

Meg was saying — "To-morrow I will take you to see Mr. Clapperton. I'm sure you'll like him."

Piers turned to Nicholas. "What do you think of him, Uncle Nick?"

"Think he's a horrid old fellow."

"Oh, Uncle Nick," cried Meg, "how can you say such a thing! I think he is very nice and so is his secretary, young Mr. Swift, who is cramming Mooey."

"Cramming Mooey!" repeated Piers. "I have n't been told of that."

"He's no better," said Nicholas. "A horrid young fellow."

The next afternoon Meg did take Piers to call on Mr. Clapperton. She had arranged for this by telephone as she wanted to make sure that the new owner of Vaughanlands would be at home. It was very strange to Piers to stop before that door, to ring the bell, to be met by a stranger.

The newcomer seemed a decent sort, in spite of what Uncle Nicholas had said. There was something innocent-looking about him. He had a wide-awake inquiring look in his eyes. Yet there was a hard little quirk at the corner of his mouth, like a wrought-iron handle on a door.

"Ah, Mrs. Vaughan," he said, "come in, come in. I have just been thinking of you, for I need your advice about several things."

They warmly shook hands and Meg introduced Piers.

"It must feel wonderful to you to be at home again." Mr. Clapperton was leading them into the room that once had been particularly Meg's own. Now bereft of its chintz and soft cushions, it looked uncompromising. Yet it looked luxurious. Everything looked luxurious to Piers. He felt like a chessman who had been swept from the chessboard, thrown into a desolate dustbin, a rubbish heap where he had lain for years, and now been somehow rescued, wiped clean, tidied up and once again placed on the board to play his part. At Jalna he could talk but here he was almost dumb. He disappointed Meg by his terse responses to Mr. Clapperton's questions.

But Mr. Clapperton was not rebuffed. He talked on and on about greenhouses, swimming pool, sunroom. It was very hard to get anything in the way of building done but he was satisfied to go slowly. To play with ideas delighted him — now that he had leisure for playing.

After Piers's half-washed companions in the prison camp, Mr. Clapperton looked miraculously clean. He looked as though from birth onward he had been miraculously clean. He began to talk of the new bathroom he was installing, "for I cannot bear to share my bathroom with anyone, Mrs. Vaughan. Not even my secretary, who is quite a fastidious young man."

In the next room a typewriter was clicking energetically.

"Oh, I can *quite* understand," agreed Meg, who, all her life, had been accustomed to sharing the one bathroom with the family.

"Is that your secretary typing?" asked Piers.

"Yes. That's Sidney."

"He's tutoring my boy. I was at the stables this morning when he came. I have n't met him."

"Ah, he's very brilliant. When the war is over and he finds his proper niche, I think he'll make a name for himself."

Piers gave a grunt.

"Now, Mrs. Vaughan, I want you to come outdoors and inspect some of the things I've planned to do on the estate." He spoke with relish.

It was late in the May afternoon. There was an inexpressible balminess, a golden gilding in the air. Bees suddenly had become active, humming above the buttercups, lolling in the blossoms of an elm locust. Piers, staring across the fields, forgot what Meg and Mr. Clapperton were saying. His eyes rested on the hazy blue distance. Then he saw a man ploughing and two men planting trees.

"You are fortunate," Meg was saying, "to be able to get men."

"Veterans of the war. I pay high wages. Can you see what they are doing, Mrs. Vaughan?"

"That one is ploughing, is n't he? But — what a long furrow!"

"It is n't a furrow!" Mr. Clapperton chuckled. "It's a street! I'm laying out a village. That's the surprise I've hinted at. Now you see for yourself."

"A *village!*" Meg was thunderstruck.

"Yes. A village!" He gave a delighted laugh. "You know how one has ideas in one's mind — things you'd love to do, if you just had the money. Well, my idea has always been a model village. A pretty little village. A real picture village. When I retired from business — with plenty of money — I looked about me for a site. I wanted a place in the real country but not too far from the city. I must have people for my village. Well, there is a great scarcity of small houses, is n't there? I expect to get only half a dozen built this year. But after the war it will grow like wildfire."

" Why did n't you tell me this at the first? " Meg asked in a trembling voice.

" Because, being a business man, my dear lady, I was afraid you might raise the price. Besides which I wanted to surprise you and everyone else. Childish of me but I 'm like that."

" Mr. Clapperton," said Meg, "if I had known you would start a village here, I should not have raised the price of the estate, I should have refused to sell. As a matter of fact you must n't do it."

" But why? " He looked astonished and hurt.

" Because my family will never forgive you, if you do. Once my husband sold some land to a builder who intended to put up a few bungalows but my eldest brother never rested till he had put a stop to it."

" Well, I 'm afraid he 'll have to put up with my village. It 's been a dream of mine for years. Just you wait till you see it, Mrs. Vaughan. You 'll be delighted with it and so will your family. It is n't going to be one of these ugly villages that looks like a bit of a city broken off and set down in the country. Mine will be as pretty as a picture. No two houses exactly alike. Trees along the streets. You see I 'm having them planted already. And when the time comes for a gasoline station! Well, just wait till you see what Sidney and I have planned! "

" Where are you going to find buyers for these houses? " asked Piers.

" I 'm not going to sell. Just rent. You should see the waiting list I have, of people who want to get out into the country but still be accessible to their work. I even have a name chosen for my village. You 'll never guess."

" Clappertown? " said Piers.

Mr. Clapperton leant backward in his astonishment. "However did you guess?"

"I'm good at that sort of thing. And you're probably going to name the streets after trees — Maple Avenue, Spruce Avenue, Chestnut Avenue — and plant only the sort of tree to suit the name."

"I hadn't thought of that. What a fine idea!"

"And when you reach the point of building a pub, you can call it The Clapperton Arms."

Mr. Clapperton laughed and flushed. "I see you have the right spirit," he said. "Honestly, Mrs. Vaughan, I don't believe you'll have any fault to find with my planning. Please come over here and let me tell you."

They went to where they could see the little streets being marked by the plough, the little trees planted neatly at the verge. Instinct told Meg and Piers that to reason with Mr. Clapperton was useless. He was realizing the dream of his life. Indeed he scarcely seemed to hear any objections they made.

Piers was so deeply content to be home again that he was not much disturbed by the proposed building scheme. If a new village were to appear on the scene, it might not do much harm. Anyhow it was better than the devastation he had witnessed in Europe. What he wanted was to hasten back to his own house, to be under the same roof with Pheasant, to play with his puppy. He did not want to worry about anything.

He found Pheasant working in her flower border.

"I've made up my mind to have more flowers this summer," she said, kissing him rapturously, "now that you're home!"

Under the embrace, she concealed the fact that she had been having a time of it with Philip. She had had hard work to keep from saying — "Just wait till your father comes back!"

Piers's name often had been held over Philip's head, by various members of the family, by Rags and by Wright. One look into Piers's face had shown Philip what sort of man he was. In his presence the little boy was nothing less than an angel. The entrance of Piers into his vicinity had an effect nothing short of marvelous. The moment before he might have been looking and behaving like a small terror but the sound of Piers's voice, his step, a glimpse of him coming his way, brought a look of sweet obedience into Philip's face.

More than once Pheasant had to turn her own face away to hide the laughter in her eyes. She could not bear to tell Piers of his badness, though Maurice urged her to. It was Maurice's earnest prayer that Piers would one day walk in on the scene of a fracas. But Philip seemed to have a sixth sense that warned him of his sire's approach. Now he came into the garden and slipped a small grubby hand into Piers's as though for protection. He raised his baby-blue eyes to Piers.

Piers smiled at Pheasant. "By George, he's like Grandfather! I believe he's going to look even more like him than I do."

"Same pugnacious spirit, too," she replied.

Piers squeezed the little hand. He was proud of Philip. And of Nooky too, but the feeling of antagonism that Maurice had roused in him when a child was still roused by the youth. Piers tried to conceal this beneath a hearty manner but Maurice was conscious of it, even acknowledged to himself that he had expected it and that it would not take much to make him reciprocate. Yet they had been but two days together.

"Where's the puppy? Where's Trixie?" he asked.

Maurice came out of the house with her.

"She's just been making a puddle," he said, "in the dining room."

" I hope you cleaned it up," said Pheasant.

" Indeed I did."

" My God," exclaimed Piers. " You 've got an Irish accent."

" He affects it occasionally," said Pheasant.

" Don't do it," said Piers. " Trixie and I don't like it. Do we, Trixie? " He picked up the puppy, who went wild with kissing him and trying to fall out of his arms at one and the same time.

Piers became suddenly serious. " Have you heard the news? " he asked.

" What news? "

" This man, Clapperton, is going to build a model village or some sort of monstrosity on Vaughanlands."

" No! " she cried, astonished. " Who told you? "

" Himself. He must be pretty rich."

" It 's a horrible idea," Pheasant exclaimed. " Has Meg been told? "

" Yes. She can't prevent it."

" Why did n't she have building restrictions put in the agreement? "

" Don't ask me! But she 's taking it without much fuss. Why not? Changes are in the air. Anyhow he 'll probably lose all his money in the scheme. It 's crazy."

" No, he won't," put in Maurice. " He has a wonderful business head. Everything he does prospers."

" So you knew about it all the while? " said Piers, staring at him.

" Yes. Sidney Swift told me. But nothing could be done about it, so I kept it to myself."

" A strange thing to do."

Maurice flushed. " I knew it would be a worry."

" Well, I 'm not going to worry about it," said Piers. " But just wait till Renny comes home! If he is n't the death of that old blighter, it will be a wonder."

Nothing indeed could disturb Piers for more than a moment. His serenity at being home once again was too deep. He woke each morning with a delicious, calm surprise at finding himself under his own roof, with the five hundred fertile acres of Jalna smiling in the May sunshine. The day was not long enough for all he had to do. He loosed the pent-up vitality of the imprisoned years on the waiting land. Wright did the ploughing and he the harrowing, the seeding. As he sat behind the massive bodies of the team, as a thousand times he had dreamed of doing, watched the dark tillage spread or thought of the grain sown, gladness filled him that he had survived with the strength to do a man's work. Sometimes Pheasant's image came between him and the fields. In the years of absence she had become strangely unreal, a symbol of love and womanhood rather than flesh and blood. But now she was a warm, breathing being again whose heart he felt beating against his, who could not keep her eyes off him, who treated him sometimes like the returned hero of the war and sometimes like a little lost child returned to her. Whichever way it was, it suited Piers.

Never a day passed when he did not go to Jalna to see his uncles. Fresh from his farm work, ruddy, tanned by the increasing heat of the sun, he brought new vigor to them. It was amazing to see how they improved. Day by day they looked less and less like men nearing their end. Just to watch Piers eat his tea, just to witness the amount of bread and jam he consumed, was enough to make them hungry. He never visited them without telling them some ridiculous story to make them laugh. He made them go to the stables to inspect the fine calves and foals and little pigs that were arriving with an unprecedented strength and gusto. Even the hens hatched large broods as though to show him what they could do.

The note of peevishness left Ernest's voice. He put on

weight. Nicholas growled and grumbled less. His gout troubled him less, so that he was able to walk about and enjoy the garden. Piers's return had given a new meaning to life at Jalna. Now it seemed possible that the torn fabric of that life might be mended, the course of its stream again might flow strongly.

No one felt this more deeply than Finch. No longer was he leaned on, as a last support. He took his place as a younger brother. He threw himself into the work with all his strength, which was not great at the outset, for he had been very tired at the end of his tour. But working with the horses, driving the truck in the early morning, planting the vegetable garden, gave him a new vitality. Many a time he thought he would like to go on living such a life, with music no more than a love to come home to rather than an over-bearing mistress, as it must be in the life of a concert pianist.

There was one person who rejected all physical labor and that was young Maurice. Always there were his studies to intervene. To judge by what he said, Sidney Swift was an exacting teacher, but often they were heard by Pheasant in lively conversation, not of a mathematical sort. Maurice often returned to Vaughanlands with Swift and sometimes they went to town together. Piers did not like the tutor and looked forward to the day when he would see the last of him.

X

GEMMEL AND MR. CLAPPERTON

GEMMEL GRIFFITH lay on the side of a grassy knoll, drinking in the warmth of the sun with all her being, letting her mind wander free. She was so cruelly hampered in her physical movements that the pleasure of her life lay in her reckless and untrammeled thoughts. They were what Garda's bodily activities were to her, Althea's painting to her. Garda expressed her emotions of longing or fear, or whatever they might be, by household work, by tearing along the country road on her bicycle, by gardening. Althea expressed the strange hidden self of her in those fiercely individual drawings. What Gemmel liked was life itself. Lying on the edge of it, cloistered, free of responsibility, she watched it flow by her with hungry interest in all that came within her range. Passionately she longed for Althea or Garda to have love affairs. Oh, to watch their joys or miseries! To counsel or comfort them! She felt capable of anything. Oh, how she could love or hate, be frantically jealous, tear her heart out or break someone else's! Her supple hands felt their way through moss and among the tiny blue violets, as she lay with closed eyes on the knoll.

Her sisters had taken her there in a wheelbarrow made of wicker that had been given them by Finch. It had stood in the old carriage house ever since he could remember. Before his grandmother had got past gardening, she had used it among her flower borders.

One day he had trundled it over to the fox farm, offering it in its lightness to the girls for their work. But it turned into a chariot for Gemmel. Lined with cushions, it enthroned her while her sisters labored behind. They had possessed it for more than two years now. Little paths wound everywhere to show where Gemmel had been. This knoll, just inside the grounds of Jalna, was one of her favorite spots.

Now she lay there, the sun dappling her pale face, thinking over all she knew. She knew so much, she thought, that her knowledge was a world in itself. Yet, measured by the scholarship of schools, she knew almost nothing. She could not for the life of her have named the boundaries of foreign countries, or their mountains, or what king succeeded Edward III. She could not have explained latitude or longitude. But she could have repeated tales of strange happenings among the hills of Wales. She knew fanciful and frightening stories of the doings of the monks in the ruined abbey whose ancient walls dominated the stony farm, hidden among those hills, where she had spent the greater part of her life. The abbey and the tales of life there represented all she knew of religion. She had never been inside a church, for her father had hated religion in all its forms. More than once she heard him say that he had retired to the house in Wales to get away from a world ruined by mechanism and religion.

The Fennels had several times called on the Griffiths. They had been invited to the Rectory but only Garda had gone. Only Garda had been induced to go to church. Althea could not have borne the gaze of so many strangers. Yet she was as interested as Gemmel in hearing of all that Garda had seen and heard there. Now Garda often went to the services but only in a spirit of curiosity. The three were in truth pagans and felt no need for religion in their lives. They believed in the supernatural and clung to certain peasant superstitions they had got from servants in Wales.

Gemmel lay on the knoll thinking of how much more profound was her understanding of life than was her sisters'. She so loved it. She felt impatient of Althea's super-

sensitiveness, of Garda's contented acceptance of things as
they were. Her hearing was acute and now she heard a
step on the grass. She called out, in an impatient tone:
" Come here! "

As the steps drew near she opened her eyes expecting to
see one of her sisters. But it was Finch Whiteoak. He
said smiling: —

" I don't know whether or not to come. Your invitation
is n't exactly warm."

" I thought you were one of the girls. But — as you
are n't — I 'm delighted." She raised herself on her elbows
and smiled back at him.

He dropped to the grass beside her. " Are the girls out
of favor then? "

" I get tired of the same company. And they bore me by
the way they behave. You 'd think they had a hundred
years ahead of them, the way they never make a move to
change things. That attitude may have been all right in
the old days but now, at the speed things move with, it 's all
wrong."

Was she just trying to appear knowing, Finch wondered.
He asked: —

" What do you want them to do? " Did she realize, he
wondered, that they always had her on their hands, always
had to consider her first?

She made an expressive gesture with her hands that looked
almost too supple, too capable, as though they had too completely taken on the work of her disabled members. She
said: —

" I want Althea to show her sketches, not hide them.
They 're clever, I tell you. I wish you could see the sketch
she made of you the other day. It was a wonderful likeness
— the sort of portrait that could only be made when — oh,
well — " She plucked at the grass and then added —
" When someone thinks a great deal about another."

"I 'd like to see it," he said, a little embarrassed. "Do you think she 'd show it to me?"

"Never! But I might contrive to let you see it. You 'll be surprised. It 's full of feeling, yet I suppose you think Althea is cold."

"No, I have never thought that. I 'm sure she feels too much. If you 'll forgive my saying so, I think you three sisters are sometimes bad for each other."

"I 'm sure we are," she agreed. "But it makes our lives so much more complicated and interesting. Oh, if you could know what Althea is! But you never will. No one ever will but me. As for Garda — what do you think of Sidney Swift?"

"What has he to do with Garda?"

"Well, he 's always coming to see her and talking to her about himself by the hour. Do you like him?"

"I think he is what my uncles would call a *philanderer*."

"You mean when he does n't come to see Garda he goes to see Patience Vaughan."

"He 's wasting his time there."

"He speaks of Patience as the ' little heiress.' "

"Good heavens, she won't inherit a fortune."

"I 'd call it a tidy sum if it were to be mine. Sidney is always talking of riches and what they will do."

"They can make you miserable," said Finch.

"He talks," went on Gemmel, " of Mr. Clapperton's wealth as though he were Mr. Clapperton's heir. Perhaps he is. I don't know. All I know is that I won't have him breaking poor little Garda's heart."

As she said this, Gemmel sat up straight, with a defiant air. Her attitude, the fierce tone in her voice, made her sisters appear suddenly as two fragile children whom she had all their life protected and would continue to protect. Her love for them seemed greater than the love between any man and woman could be. Her egotism was such that she appeared ready to face any living menace on their behalf.

"Don't you ever think of yourself, Gem?" he asked, for the first time calling her by her sisters' abbreviation of her name.

"Never!" she declared. "I don't count."

But, when he had left her and she was alone again on the knoll, one would have thought she counted herself very greatly, for she fell into a paroxysm of weeping, she sobbed in despair and tore up the violets by their roots. "I do love him," she whispered hoarsely, with her mouth pressed to the warm earth. "I love him. I love him. Oh, if only he were in trouble and I might comfort him! I'd hold him in my arms and stroke his head and I'd kiss him."

She cried till exhaustion calmed her. She lay quietly gazing at the sky between the gently moving leaves. It was all over for her, she thought. It had never begun and now it was over. As though from the window of a prison she looked down into sunny meadows at her sisters, walking with their lovers beside a swift-flowing river. She wanted to cry out to them to come and rescue her, to spare her some part of their joy.

She saw Althea coming and lay smiling up at her.

"You'll never guess," she said, "who has been talking to me."

"You've been crying," said Althea sternly. "What made you cry?"

"Just the sheer joy of being alive. Don't you ever feel that way?"

"Yes. To cry a little but not that way. Your eyes are all red and swollen. And your lips — oh, Gem, you shouldn't go on like that!"

"It was partly what I found out from him that made me cry."

"From whom?"

"Finch Whiteoak."

"Was he here?"

"Yes . . . oh, Althea —" she raised her wet eyes to her sister's — "he loves you! I'm sure he does! When he says your name his whole face changes. When I told him you had made a sketch of his head, you should have seen how his eyes lighted. You know those long dreamy eyes of his."

"You told him I made a sketch of him. Very well, Gem, it's the last drawing of mine you'll ever see!"

"Nonsense. Why not let him see that you care for him? You know you do."

"I wish I could make you understand that I care for no one — in that way — and never shall."

"But why? You're so beautiful."

"The whole idea is repulsive to me . . . I am my own and I can belong to no one."

"But you belong to Molly and Garda and me. I don't know anyone who belongs more to those they love."

"Gem, you're being just stupid. You know what I mean. Finch Whiteoak is no more to me than Mr. Clapperton. Do you know he has just brought us some strawberries, and practically asked himself to tea this afternoon? You and Garda can entertain him. I'll not be there."

"Of all the impossible people I have ever known, you are the most. Now here's a rich man and not old, coming with an offering of strawberries and to drink tea, and you say you won't see him!"

"I dislike him."

"But why? He's so kind."

"He wants to change everything. He can't let things alone. He calls himself an idealist but he's just stupid."

When Eugene Clapperton came to the fox farm that afternoon, Althea did remain hidden in her room. Free from her restraining presence, the two younger girls reached an undreamed-of state of intimacy with the new neighbor.

He made wide gestures with his hands as he told them of his plans for a perfect village — a village surrounded by trees, with no ugliness anywhere. It would be impossible to get more than four or five small houses built before the end of the war. Two were already well on the way to completion. Eugene Clapperton invited the sisters to come to inspect it and they accepted the invitation.

His attitude toward Gemmel had a gentle fatherliness in it that made her free and bold with him, like a spoilt child. It was well for her that Althea was not present to see her.

Althea refused to go to see the proposed village of Clappertown, as he already called it, but he came in his own car and carried off Gemmel and Garda.

" Oh, Gem," Garda had exclaimed, " are you going to stop titivating? One would think you were going to a party."

With one of her swift movements, Gemmel turned from her survey of herself in the looking-glass.

" Do I look pretty? " she asked.

" Oh, pretty enough. But what does it matter! Going off to visit a middle-aged man! "

" It 's a party to me and I will make the most of it. I wonder if Sidney will be there."

Garda's rosy cheeks became rosier.

" I don't expect so. He is awfully bored when Mr. Clapperton gets on the subject of his village. He says there is nothing idealistic about it — that it 's just a money-making scheme."

" Then he ought to be pleased with it, for he 's always talking about money."

" He hates cant."

Mr. Clapperton took the girls to that part of the estate where the two cottages were nearing completion. They were indeed pretty, though rather too close together and rather too much alike. Sidney Swift appeared out of one of them and led Garda inside to inspect it. The elder man, who had got out of the car, now returned to it and sat down in the seat beside Gemmel.

"May I call you Gem?" he asked. "I must say I like this new fashion of familiarity. Of course, I'm very much older than you."

Gemmel thought wildly — "He is in love with me! Oh, help, help — what shall I do?"

But she said composedly — "I should like to be called Gem, by you."

"Splendid," he said, and he laid his hand on her knee. He looked deeply thoughtful.

She looked at his hand, longing to shake it off. It was a forceful hand, with short sandy hairs across the back of it. His fingers pressed her knee. "You know," he said, "I'm worried about these poor little limbs of yours."

An electric shock went through her. How dared he! Oh, how dared he! She flung off his hand and turned a blazing face on him.

"I don't want anybody's pity," she said.

His eyes filled with tears. "Don't be annoyed with me. But I think it's such a crying shame you can't run about like other girls and I'm wondering if something can be done about it."

"Done about it!" she repeated, in a tense voice. "What do you mean done about it?"

"Well, there are very fine surgeons in this country," he said. "They do miraculous things. I'd like to know how long it is since you consulted a first-rate doctor."

Her heart was pounding. "I can't remember," she stammered. "After I had the fall, when I was a baby, they took me to one of the best doctors. My spine was injured, he said, and I'd always be a cripple. My mother died when I was very young and my stepmother just accepted what my father told her. He was a dear man but he drank a good deal and he did n't bother much about us children. He was n't fussy, you know."

"Fussy!" repeated Mr. Clapperton, on a note of contempt. "*Fussy!* If you 'd been *my* daughter I 'd have been scouring the earth to find a cure for you." He struck one clenched hand into the palm of the other. " And I 'll see to it that you have the opinion of the best specialist in this country — if you 'll agree. Think of the years that have passed since your accident and of the advance in science in that time! Why — there may be hope for you, my dear little girl. Will you let me help you? I mean, find out who the best man is and take you to him."

A throbbing was set free on the air, like the strong beat of a perfect heart. The movement of the trees was the weaving of banners of hope.

" Oh, I don't know what to say," she stammered, her nerves quivering in fear.

" Just say you 'll let me help you. That 's all I ask."

" But it frightens me. The thought of an operation."

" No, no, you must n't say that. There is nothing to be afraid of. Just think what it would be like to run about and have fun like other girls."

" It would be heavenly."

" Think what it would mean to your sisters. You would have a grand time together."

" We could n't afford it. It would cost too much."

" Don't worry about expense. Leave all that to me."

He spoke with benign indifference to cost. Again he patted her knee. She became calm. She would do what he wished. She would trust him.

" Don't you worry about the expense," he repeated. " I 'm not the man to do things by halves. You know I 'm an idealist, a dreamer. I dream of a perfect village, out here in the woods, and I 'm going to build it. I dream of a perfect girl and I 'm going to do what I can about that. My

only fear is that I may have raised hopes that can't be fulfilled.   That would be dreadful."

She gave a little excited laugh.   " Now that you 've
roused hope in me I don't believe I shall ever give up hoping.
Oh, Mr. Clapperton, how soon can we go to see a specialist?
What have I done to deserve so much from you?   Whatever will my sisters say ! "

XI
ADELINE AND THE ORGAN

ADELINE saw her trunk being lifted safely off the baggage car and out on the platform. She hastened along the platform toward it, her suitcase bumping against her legs, her tennis racket and a large paper parcel gripped tightly under one arm. Wright came running after her, and the stationmaster followed in leisurely fashion. She was the only passenger to alight from the train.

Wright caught up with her and touched his cap deferentially, but his tone was jocular as he said — " It 's about time you came home."

" Oh, Wright," she gasped. " Am I actually here? Oh, my goodness, what heaven! " She laughed up at him, her eyes shining.

For an instant he was taken aback by her beauty. She 'd been pretty right enough when she 'd been home for the Easter holidays but now — what had come over her? It was as though a shining veil, a radiance, had descended on her. There was a finish to her, a polish, a quivering first bloom that made Wright scratch his head and stare, that made the stationmaster stare too when he came up.

" I was just telling this young lady," said Wright, " that it 's high time she came home. It 's pretty tough on me running the place without her."

" I guess you don't like goin' away to school," said the stationmaster, taking the check for her trunk and staring down into her face.

" It 's a nice enough school," she returned, " but when you know that you 're needed at home it makes you restless."

Wright winked at the stationmaster. "Her and me," he said, "have run the stables together, since the boss went away."

"So I've heerd," said the stationmaster, and he gave Wright a look appreciative of Adeline's beauty.

"I hope you won't mind riding home in the wagon," said Wright. "I had to come to the mill for feed and there's no sense in wasting gasoline."

"I'm glad it's the wagon," she returned. She went to the great dappled-gray team and patted an iron flank. Two pairs of liquid dark eyes looked at her in benign recognition.

Wright placed her belongings beside the bulging meal-dusty bags, helped her to the seat and mounted beside her. He turned the team and they jogged on to the tree-shaded country road, where the sunlight fell through the dark flutter of the leaves.

Adeline looked from side to side, from the backs of the jogging horses to Wright's face, and she felt an extraordinary exaltation. She pulled off her hat to let the breeze cool her head and exclaimed: —

"How heavenly! How's everything been going, Wright?"

"Not too bad," he returned, "not too bad. I suppose you've heard about the boss."

She turned a startled face on him. "Has anything happened to my father?"

"Nothing to worry about, I guess. He's had an accident. That's all. He was going somewheres in a jeep and it ran into a hole and he was thrown out on his head. He was in hospital but they say he'll soon be home. Perhaps I shouldn't have told you."

"Are you sure he wasn't severely hurt?"

"Yes. He sent the cable himself."

She drew a deep sigh of relief. "Oh, Wright, won't it be marvelous when he's home again?"

" I 'll say it will."

" You know, it 's over four years since I saw him."

" Yeh. I bet you 'll hardly know him."

She gave Wright an indignant look. " I 'd know him if he was in the middle of a whole army. There 's no one a bit like him."

" Well, I bet he won't know you."

" Of course he will."

" You was a little child when he left. Now you 're — well, you 've changed a lot."

" I 've grown a lot, I know — and got better-looking, I hope. My nose used to be too large for a child's face, Uncle Ernest said."

" It 's just right now." Again the man studied her, saw how the quick blood moved under the delicate skin, how one movement of the lips would change the expression of the whole face, from dark to bright, from firm to gentle. Now he said, in a confidential tone : —

" I 've seen a two-year-old I 'd give my eyeteeth to buy. Oh, miss, I wish we could lay hands on two hundred dollars. That 's all the farmer is asking for him. He has no idea of what 's in him. I can tell you, he has the makings of one of the finest jumpers in the country, or I 'm no judge of horseflesh."

" You 're a judge of that, if anyone is," said Adeline. " Oh, I wish I could see him ! "

" You can. I 'll take you there to-morrow. He 's nothing to look at, in the ordinary way. He spent last winter outdoors and he 's grown a great rough coat. He 's so thin his back looks hollow. Unless you know a great deal about the formation of a horse, you would n't see any promise in him. But if I had him home to feed up and to care for properly for the next year we 'd have a winner or my name 's not Bob Wright."

" Oh, if only Daddy were home ! "

"Yes. But he ain't, and this farmer wants to sell now. I was wondering if you could get your Uncle Finch to lend us the money."

"I 'll try but I hear his money is gone."

"Then there 's your two old uncles. A hundred dollars apiece would n't mean much to them."

"It hurts them terribly to part with money, I 've heard."

"You hear a good deal, don't you?" he grinned.

"Well, don't you?"

"Sure, I do . . . What about young Mr. Maurice? He 's supposed to be rich."

"He does n't get anything but an allowance till he 's twenty-one. Besides he does n't like horses."

"I wish you and me could go shares in the colt. But I have only a hundred dollars saved up. If only you could lay your hands on another hundred, we could buy him to-morrow and we 'd never regret it, I 'll swear to that."

"I have just sixty cents," she said ruefully.

"Well, that won't go far. Anyhow you might see what you can do with them uncles of yours."

"Have you talked to Uncle Piers about it?"

"Yes, and it 's no good. He says this is no time to go in for show horses. But I know better. War or no war this colt is worth five times what 's being asked for him."

"Gosh, I 'm dying to see him. Is the farmer an old man?"

"No. Sort of young. He got married just about a year ago. He 's fixing his place up. That 's why he is anxious for cash."

"Two hundred dollars, eh? And you have one hundred. If I could get hold of another hundred, we 'd have equal shares in him."

"Sure."

In the joy of homecoming, of being hugged, kissed, patted on the back, Adeline forgot the colt for a space. All the faces she knew so well smiled on her. She seemed almost a heroine. Roma gazed at her in adoration. " Oh, Adeline, I wish I might go to school too! " Archer wore an air of pessimistic approval. He looked as though, if he chose, he could tell her things which would take that smile off her face.

Alayne was upset to think that the child should have been told of Renny's accident by Wright. It was like Wright to have repeated such a happening to Adeline in the first moment of meeting her, and in his own crude way. She had forgotten to tell him to leave the breaking of the bad news to her. She feared Adeline might be shocked to hear of an injury to Renny.

" Darling," she said, putting her arm about Adeline, " you must not worry about Daddy. He had a concussion but he will soon be all right again — at least, I hope so."

" I 'm not worrying," answered Adeline. " Wright told me there was nothing to worry about."

The child's brow was as smooth as silk, her lips smiling. How little feeling she seemed to have!

" Well, I worried myself ill," said Alayne.

" I 'm sure you did," returned Adeline cheerfully.

Alayne took her arm from the child's shoulders.

The right moment had to be found for approaching the old uncles on the subject of purchasing the two-year-old. Adeline had already had a decisive refusal from Finch, who, like Piers, saw no sense in buying show horses at this time.

She chose the moment when they were sitting together in the light shade of the old silver birch tree, on the bark of which the initials of their parents, carved there nearly a hundred years before, were still faintly visible. Ernest had a volume of Shakespeare in his hand. Nicholas was placidly drawing on his pipe. The shadows on the lawn were lengthening and in and out of them hopped Archer's tame rabbit. Both men raised their eyes with a welcoming look, as Adeline came lightly across the grass. Nicholas stretched out a long arm and drew her to him. He said to his brother: —

"Is n't her resemblance to the portrait of Mamma extraordinary?"

"If anything she 's more — " Ernest looked expressively at the young face.

"You never saw Mamma at fourteen."

"Well," Ernest said to Adeline, "you look nice and healthy."

"I am. I 've never anything wrong with me."

"You 'll live to be a hundred like your great-grandmother," said Nicholas.

She laughed. "It seems a long while to live. But I don't mind. I think it 's good to be alive, don't you?"

"Sometimes . . . sometimes," answered Ernest. "Yes. I 've generally thought so."

She beamed ingratiatingly at him. "What book are you reading, Uncle Ernest?" she asked.

"*Othello.* I don't suppose you know that play of Shakespeare's. It 's not suitable for school study."

"We 've had *Romeo and Juliet.* It 's awfully boring. I like *Midsummer Night's Dream* though. It has n't all that love-making."

"I hear," said Ernest, "that *Othello* is to be performed in the town before long. I should very much like to see it but I find sitting through one of Shakespeare's plays too much of an ordeal for me at my age. But when you are quite grown up you must see *Othello.* It 's a great tragedy that hinges on the loss of a handkerchief. Desdemona is murdered by Othello because she loses the handkerchief he gave her."

"Goodness!" exclaimed Adeline, her mind on the colt. "I 'm always losing handkerchiefs."

"You don't understand, Adeline. This handkerchief was a love token."

"She's not a bit interested in love, are you, Adeline?" said Nicholas.

"Not a bit," she returned. "But I am interested in a grand two-year-old Wright has been telling me about. He's going to be a wonder."

"I suppose you know," Ernest continued, "that I am writing a book on Shakespeare."

"Yes. I know, Uncle Ernest."

"I should have had it completed by now, but for the war. The war, you know, dulls one's intellect, makes one stupid. I suppose it's the dreary round of reading the newspapers, listening to the radio. It takes the edge off one's mind."

"Yes. I know."

"Now I hope to have the book completed within the next year or so. But there's still a good deal of work to do on it."

"I'm sure there is, Uncle Ernest."

"What about this two-year-old?" asked Nicholas.

She turned to him with her soul in her eyes.

"Oh, Uncle Nick, Wright is so excited about him! And so am I. All we need is another hundred dollars and — "

"If you are thinking of me as a partner in this," said Nicholas, "you may put the idea right out of your head. Nothing can interest me in such a scheme. Another horse to worry over! Wait till your father comes home. Let him buy it if he wants to."

"It will be too late!"

"I am in complete accord with your Uncle Nicholas," said Ernest. "Nothing would induce me to put money into a horse. Piers is quite against it and his head is screwed on right."

Adeline had now nothing to do but to tell Wright of her failure. But, even though they could not raise the money to buy the colt, they rode over to the farmer's the following afternoon to see it.

Adeline had a sense of disappointment when she saw the shaggy, somewhat forlorn-looking beast, with mud caked on his flanks and burs clotted in his mane and tail. But Wright's eloquence soon roused her to the fever heat of enthusiasm.

"If only I could get hold of him," said the groom, "I'd make him into a wonder within the year!"

"Is there nothing we can do?" exclaimed Adeline.

"Nothing I know of unless we rob a bank."

"Is there nothing we could trade for him?"

"The man wants cash."

They were standing outside the farmhouse beneath a pair of giant elm locusts in flower, while the young wife of the farmer made them a cup of tea. She came now, with it on a tray.

"I'm sorry you won't come in and have something to eat," she said.

"Thank you," said Adeline, "but we must be getting home."

"This tea hits the right spot," put in Wright.

"My mother always says there's nothing like a cup of tea," said the young wife.

"We're great tea drinkers at Jalna," agreed Adeline. "You have a pretty place here."

"We think it's real pretty. Would you like to come in and see the parlor?"

"You go along, miss," said Wright. "I'll wait here with the horses."

Adeline followed the farmer's wife into the house and expressed the admiration she honestly felt for the red-papered room, furnished with mission oak upholstered in bright green velours.

"There's only one thing we need," said the farmer's wife, "and that's a piano or an organ. I was always used to one at home and I miss it terrible. I get homesick for it. Jim says he'll get me one when he can afford it, but dear knows when that will be."

Adeline's mind was a murky whirlpool of seething thoughts, shot through by phosphorescent gleams. She said slowly: —

"I have an organ of my own that was left to me by my great-grandmother but I never play on it. I'm not musical, you see. The only piece I know straight through is 'God Save the King.' I'd give this organ as a hundred dollars on the colt if your husband wants to get one for you. It's worth far more than a hundred. My great-grandmother bought it years and years ago, when things were made well. It's got shirred silk on its front and places for candles. You could have a lovely time playing on that organ. You'd never be homesick any more." Heartfelt conviction beamed from Adeline's eyes.

The farmer was dragged in by his wife. Half against his will, half willingly, he agreed to the exchange. But first he went out to Wright and asked him if the young lady had the power so to dispose of her property. Wright, completely mystified, declared that she was a spoilt child who could do whatever she wanted, and that if she said the organ was hers to swap, it certainly was.

"But what organ is it?" he demanded, as soon as he and Adeline were mounted on their eager, homeward-hastening horses.

"Have you never seen it? It's in that little room in the basement, between the cook's bedroom and the wine cellar. It's been there all my life. Everybody's forgotten about it. Aunt Augusta had a fancy to learn to play the organ when she was a girl, and Great-grandmother bought it for her. Nobody wants it. Oh, Wright, isn't it glorious that

I had this idea and we are going to get that darling colt?"

But Wright wore a dubious frown. "We might find ourselves in trouble over this. I ain't going to help steal any organ to help buy any colt, and that's flat."

Adeline's eyes were dark with the earnestness in her. "Well, you are a duffer. The organ's mine. I asked my father once if I could have it and he said sure, when I was older."

"But you ain't musical."

"I liked the looks of the organ and I thought the time might come when I'd want to trade it for a horse."

"How'd we get it out of the basement without anybody finding out? The missus would never fall in with that scheme."

"She'd never know. Rags will help us with it. We'll do it early in the morning before anyone is about. We'll just slide it out of the basement door into the truck and you'll drive it over to the farmer."

"How about when the folks see the colt at Jalna? The missus'd be for firing me again."

"We'll say you raised the money somehow and the colt's yours."

"That there colt's got to be fed."

"There's lots of pasture and you brought a wagonload of feed from the mill yesterday. Say, Wright, what's the matter with you? Aren't you glad?"

"Sure I'm glad." He grinned at her to prove it. "But I'm sort of scared."

"I'm not!"

"You're a terror. That's what you are."

She gave her horse a flick of encouragement. He needed no more to break into a gallop. Wright galloping behind, they skirted the fluttering surface of the lake. Joyful birds darted about them. Adeline's heart was joyful. She could hardly endure the waiting till to-morrow.

To-morrow came and at six sharp the truck was waiting outside the basement. Long dew-drenched shadows lay across the lawn. The house was still but as though watchful. It had seen many odd comings and goings. The Wragges, husband and wife, were in the basement and opened the door to Wright. He entered, grinning and a little sheepish. Adeline was waiting in the room where the organ was. She had a cloth with furniture polish and had rubbed the rosewood surface of the organ till it shone.

"Ha," exclaimed Wright, "is that it?"

"Yes," said Adeline. "Isn't it pretty?"

"It sure is. My gosh, if the boss finds this out he may not like it!"

"This 'ere room," said Rags, "is never entered except by me. I keep the key."

"Do you think you'll need my help?" asked his wife.

"We certainly shall. That horgan is 'eavier than it looks. You don't want me to bust myself lifting it, do you?"

"You'll never bust yourself workin'," said his wife.

Wright had brought a small hand truck and on to it they heaved the organ. He trundled it along the passage to the door. He had laid boards on the four steps and up these he and the Wragges began to push the instrument.

"Push harder," said Adeline, "it's hardly moving."

Mrs. Wragge was panting like a steam engine. The lacing of her stays broke and she uttered a sigh of relief. Her bulky form, her husband's thin one, Wright's sturdy frame, struggled with the weight of the organ. Slowly it ascended into the outer air, arduously they strove to heave it into the waiting truck.

"This ain't no job for a woman," declared Mrs. Wragge, her hair falling over her face.

"If I haven't busted myself it will be a wonder," said Rags.

Wright kept swearing steadily under his breath.

" I 'll help," said Adeline.   " I bet I can lift more than Rags can."   She pressed in among them and thrust her fierce young strength into the lifting.

It made an appreciable difference.   Perhaps it was that which finally shot the organ into the truck.   She laughed in delight.

" Sh ! " ordered Wright violently.   " Do you want your ma looking out of the window ? "

Adeline watched the truck move slowly out of sight along the drive.   She could scarcely endure the waiting to see the colt.   But two hours passed before Wright returned.

" Is everything all right ? " she asked.

" Fine.   We got the organ into the parlor and Mrs. Carter sat right down at it and played the ' Bluebells of Scotland.' It sounded swell.   They 're tickled with their part of the bargain, I can tell you.   Now I 'm going for the colt.   Want to come ? "

Wright had got a somewhat reluctant permission from Alayne to keep the colt, supposed to be his alone, at Jalna. There was, as he said, plenty of pasture and he would buy oats and meal for it from his own pocket.   She did not believe he would and she thought he showed a good deal of effrontery in making such a request.   But what could she do ?

With the hired man driving the horse van and Wright and herself trotting far enough behind to escape its dust, Adeline was as happy on that June morning as a human being could well be.   She was happier than Wright, for he had some qualms over what he had done.

When they reached the farm they had to go into the parlor and see how well the organ looked standing between the two windows, with a pink china vase and a photograph of the Carters' wedding group standing on the top.   At Adeline's earnest request Mrs. Carter played the " Bluebells of Scotland."   She followed this with " My Bonny Lies Over the Ocean," and would have continued with other pieces but her husband reminded her that it was half-past nine and there was the horse to be got into the van.

They found him in the barnyard and, after a good deal of coaxing, he was persuaded to enter the van. They had not reached the end of the lane when a great commotion took place inside, followed by a heavy thud. The van stopped. The groom and the child, with white faces, galloped up. The hired man, Bob, peered into the little window of the van.

" God Almighty! " he cried. " He 's down on his back! He 's turned a somerset! "

What had happened seemed impossible to believe. The colt had indeed, by some extraordinary convulsion, turned completely over and lay on his back, his head toward the rear of the van.

The farmer ran up and looked in.

" His back 'll be broke," he said.

" Sure," agreed Bob. " There 's nothing to do but shoot him. Got a gun? "

" Hold on," said Wright. " Hold on. What the hell are you talking about a gun for? Get me a rope, mister."

The farmer ran to a shed and came panting back with a heavy rope. His wife came pounding after him, distressed for fear the horse would die and the organ would be taken away from her. Wright had the door of the van open.

The horse, looking monstrous, lay on his back, his heavy hoofs dangling. His mud-caked belly looked disproportionately large, his teeth showed in a hideous grimace, his half-shut eyes were dull. Mrs. Carter thought — " And I got a beautiful organ for *that!* If he dies they will take the organ away! " She said to Adeline: —

" Come along with me, dear. We 'll go into the house and shut the door."

She tried to draw her away but Adeline threw her an angry look. " I won't leave him," she said fiercely.

" His back 's broke," said the farmer. " I can tell by the way he lies."

Adeline was stroking the colt's head. She was whispering — " Our Father which art in Heaven; don't let his back be broken . . . Hallowed be Thy name; don't let his back be broken . . . Lead us not into temptation but deliver us from evil; don't let his back be broken."

Wright tied the rope about the colt's neck, so that it would not slip.

" Now," he said to Carter and Bob, " we 'll pull him out and see what happens."

The three men pulled with all their might. The great supine bulk moved slowly out of the van. A pale tongue protruded at the side of the mouth. Out of the van and on to the ground the horse moved with the listlessness of the first primeval monster that stirred in early slime.

" Give him a kick," said Bob, " and see if he notices."

Wright knelt by the colt's head. He patted it reassuringly. Suddenly a convulsion stirred its frame. Its hoofs clove the air like thunderbolts. It champed its teeth, rolled over, and was on its feet, looking speculatively at those about it, as though it wondered what they would do to it next.

" Is it all right? " asked Mrs. Carter.

" Sure," said Wright, untying the rope.

" By ginger, I 've never seen anything like it."

" Nor me. I 've worked twenty-five years with horses, and I never saw a horse turn a somerset in a van before. He was scared to death."

" He 'll never go into it again," said Bob.

But Wright talked a little to the colt, took him by the forelock and led him, without mishap, back into the van. He said to Adeline : —

" I 've got to stay on the van to watch him. You 'll have to lead my horse. So mind what you 're about and don't get into any trouble on the way home."

Mounted on her own horse and leading Wright's bony mare, Adeline felt her heart sing as they returned to Jalna. The lumbering van ahead was a lovely sight to her. She doubted not felicity, in every shape and form, in the future. They turned into the gate at the back of the estate, far from the house.

When the colt was led into a loose box and had been given a bucket of fresh water and a feed of oats, Adeline threw both arms about Wright and hugged him with all her strength.

" Oh, I 'm so happy," she breathed.

He looked down frowning into her upturned face, where the eager blood showed its movement beneath the skin with every emotion. He took her wrists and disengaged himself from her.

" You had n't ought to do that," he said.

" Do what? "

" Hug me."

" Why? "

" Because you 're too old."

" Too old? "

" Yes. It ain't suitable."

She laughed. " Why, I could hug that post, I 'm so happy."

" Go ahead and hug the post," he returned sulkily. " That 's all right." He went along the passage to the harness room to get the clippers.

" You 're an old meany! " she shouted after him. " Old meany! Old meany! " She would have liked to throw something after him. But she was not really angry. When Wright began to clean the colt's rough coat, then to clip him, she looked on in an ecstasy of interest.

" Do you know, Wright," she said, " I prayed that the colt's back would n't be broken."

" So did I," answered Wright.

She was taken aback. " *You?* *You* prayed? "

" You don't suppose you 're the only one who can pray, do you? "

" What did you say? "

" That 's my own business. I did n't say much. Just sort of thought it."

She watched fascinated as the skillful clippers ran smoothly across the colt's rump, and clots of shaggy hair fell to the floor. She said: —

" I had n't thought of you praying, Wright, though you do sometimes go to church."

He straightened himself and gave his quizzical look. " When I first came to Jalna I never went to church. Then one day the boss said to me — " I don't like a man working for me who never goes inside the church. So if you can't make up your mind to go to service once a month, you can get to hell out of here."

" I think that was sensible."

" You do, uh? Well — I was mad enough to leave that very day. But I liked the place and I liked him. So I 've stayed ever since. I like Mr. Fennel too. He 's got a kind heart and he 's sensible — for a clergyman."

Freed from his unkempt coat, shining like a chestnut, his mane and tail combed, even his hoofs washed, the colt stood bright-eyed as though in wonder at himself. Adeline and Wright studied him blissfully. They had in him an endless subject for happy speculation.

When at last she turned toward the house, she realized that she was very hot and very dirty. She skirted the lawn, passed through the little wicket gate that led to the ravine, and descended the steep path.

Down there it was shady and cool. The stream, still moving with something of the vigor of spring, pushed its way among a verdant growth of honeysuckle, flags, and watercress. Near the rustic bridge there was a sandy pool in which minute minnows lived a complete and volatile life.

Adeline undressed and stepped into the pool. It was very cold. Slowly she sank into the water, forming a silent " whew " with her lips. She had brought a cake of a much advertised soap in great favor with Wright, that had a repulsive scent of carbolic, and with this she scrubbed herself, then lay down in the pool with her head on the mossy rim and allowed the stream to carry away the soapy lather. She picked a spray of watercress and ate it. She lay so still that the minnows lost their fear of her and darted alongside her relaxed limbs.

She heard a whistle and the sound of steps. She recognized the whistle as belonging to Maurice. She leaped beneath the bridge where her clothes already were, and crouched there smiling to herself.

Maurice saw the hideous pink of the cake of soap. He had a stick in his hand and leaning across the rail of the bridge, he tried to impale the soap on it. Adeline could hear him give little grunts of annoyance at his failure and she could scarcely restrain her laughter. Finally the soap slid quite out of sight in a tangle of watercress. Maurice gave up the attempt and went on his way across the bridge.

A spasm of hunger contracted Adeline's stomach. She scrambled out of the water, sat in a patch of sunlight for three minutes to dry herself, discovered that she was cold and all out in gooseflesh, frowned at the discomfort of hunger and cold, scrambled into her clothes, ran across the bridge and up the steep path to the house, for lunch.

It was a pity, she thought, that she could not relate all the events of the morning but there was so much in her life that she could not tell.

been a beautiful young man, and that, if he had lived, he

XII

ROMA IN THE MOONLIGHT

THE young moon, no more than a week old, was very bright
in the clear dark-blue sky, but the branches of the pines often
hid it in their blackness, so that the night seemed dark. But
then again the branches would weave, the moon would throw
its light on the quiet night.

Roma had brought the book for a walk. She had had
it in her possession for some time but this evening she had
had the desire to walk out into the woods with it where no
one would be near her. She had crossed the bridge and
climbed up the far side of the ravine into the little wood of
oaks and pines that shut the sight of the fox farm from
Jalna.

The book was *Last Poems,* written by her father, Eden
Whiteoak. There had been three books of his poems standing together on a shelf in the library. She liked this one
best because of its pretty color, the shape of the lettering on
it, and the title — *Last Poems.* As they were the last he had
written, it seemed to bring the book nearer to her. She had
taken it from the shelves and hidden it in her room. Now
to-night she had wanted to carry it on a walk.

She knew little of Eden. Alayne sometimes felt, now
that Roma was old enough to understand, that she should
tell the child something of the peculiar situation which once
had existed at Jalna but — what to say, and what to leave
unsaid! Surely some other member of the family would
one day tell Roma what she should know, before insensate
gossip reached her ears. But who was to tell her? Renny
was far away. It would have been impossible to Finch.
Nicholas was the one to have done it but he thought the

child too young to be troubled by such thoughts as might arise from the knowledge of what had taken place. Ernest more than once had remarked to Roma that her father had been a beautiful young man and that, if he had lived, he might have done great things with his talent. When she was older she must read his poems.

It had remained for Alma Patch, a girl from the village who used to come by the day to help with the children, to enlighten Roma. Alma was married now and had a weak-minded child of two, but she still could be persuaded at times to lend a hand with the work at Jalna. She was weak and thin but she would scrub floors, wash clothes, or stand all day on a ladder picking cherries. Always she brought her child with her, and he stayed close beside her all the while she worked. Once when she had taken him by train to town he had fallen out of the window on to the rails. The train had been stopped and crew and passengers had alighted in panic, expecting to find a mangled little body. But Oswald had got to his feet and was running unhurt after the train, howling for his mother. To her this escape was an everlasting pride. She was always telling the story of it and keeping it fresh in her son's mind by frequent reference. "Ossie, Ossie," she would reiterate, in a peculiar singsong and in the baby talk he understood — "Ossie — the chain yan down the chack — the chain yan down the chack!"

It was she who told Roma all she knew of Eden.

"Why surely you know," Alma had said, "that your pa was married to Mrs. Whiteoak that is!"

Roma had stared in bewilderment. "Then, is she my mother? Are Adeline and I sisters?"

"You *are* a silly girl! Of course you and Adeline ain't sisters. You're cousins, because her pa and your pa were brothers."

"But if my father was married to Auntie Alayne —"

"They did n't have no children. Then your pa ran off with a Miss Ware that was staying with Mrs. Vaughan, and your Auntie Alayne divorced him. I suppose you know what divorce is."

"It 's getting *un*married."

"Then your Auntie Alayne stayed in New York for a while and then she up and married Colonel Whiteoak, and they had Adeline and Archer."

"But where do I come in?"

"Well, you was born away off in Italy or France or some-wheres, and your pa and ma died and you came here when you was about the size of Ossie." She snatched up her infant and hugged him. "Ossie — Ossie — the chain yan down the chack!"

Many a time Roma had pondered on this conversation. Indeed seldom was she alone that she did not speculate on the strangeness of the grownups' behavior and her own peculiar situation. But she did not speak of this to anyone. Whether or not her mother or father had done something wrong she could not understand, but she felt something melancholy in her beginning. She clung to the thought of Eden's being a poet and she liked the book she now carried so well that she hesitated beneath the trees in the moonlight to examine it, as though she had not done so a hundred times already. She admired the delicate green of the cover, the way his name, Eden Whiteoak, stood out in fine gold letters, the little wreath of gold flowers. She would keep this book always and perhaps later she would take his two other books from the library and keep them too.

She heard a step, looked round, and saw Finch coming through the wood.

"Hullo," he said. "You here, Roma?"

She smiled, hiding the book.

How fair she looked in the moonlight! But she was a queer little thing. One never knew what she was thinking.

He took her hand in his. "Coming with me to the fox farm?" he asked.

"They won't want a child there," she answered.

"I'm not going to stay. I'm just going to ask after Gemmel."

"Is she ill?"

"No. But she's in a hospital. She's been having an examination — X-rays, you know — and that sort of thing, by a specialist. They think there's a possibility that she may be cured."

"That would be nice . . . Did you see the owl?"

"Yes. I don't like them. They're always after some poor little beggar of a mouse or small bird. They're un-canny. They frighten me."

"I like them . . . There's Althea Griffith. She'll try not to meet us. She always hurries away. Do you see her turning back?"

Finch began to run after Althea. He called out — "I want to ask after your sister. That's all."

As he caught up to her he looked at her half-admiringly, half-fascinated by her invincible shyness.

She spoke quietly. "The specialist says she should have been operated on years ago. They've known — skillful surgeons, I mean — how to do this particular operation for years. But away in the mountains in Wales, we'd never had any hope of such a thing. We'd just accepted what the doctors said when she was a baby."

"Will they operate now?"

"Oh, yes. They've every hope she'll be walking in a few months."

"Aren't you terribly excited? Aren't you and Garda happy?"

She clasped her hands under her chin and stood rigid as she answered — "I don't know. We're dazed."

"I'm sure you are. But when you can think calmly —"

"That's what I'm doing," she interrupted. "I'm out here trying to think calmly. You've no idea how hard it is to do. If Gem learns to walk, we shall have to begin an entirely new life. The whole pattern of our existence has been fitted round the fact that she's always stationary. She's the pivot."

"But if you three can go about together in the future, you'll be awfully happy, won't you? I have a picture in my mind of Gemmel running."

"So have I, and it frightens me." Althea relaxed suddenly and stood leaning against the rough trunk of an old oak, as though tired.

"How is Gemmel bearing the strain?"

"Quite coolly. Almost impersonally — as though someone else's fate, not hers, were to be decided. But I know her. Underneath she's on fire."

Althea had said so much, freely and without the strange cloak of shyness that disguised her real self. Now she looked at Finch startled and began to retreat from him. She remembered with terror what Gemmel had said of his feeling for her, that Gemmel had told him of the sketch she had made of him.

"Don't go," he said.

"I must. I have things to do. Good night." She almost fled along the path away from him. He felt angry at her. What was the matter with her? He could have loved her he thought, at that moment, if she had not had that atmosphere of impenetrability enveloping her. Suffering as she was, he longed to hurt her. He stood looking after her resentfully till, in her white dress, she looked no wider than a moonbeam.

"She's shy," said Roma.

"How clever of you to discover it! Come on, let's go home."

"She always acts like that."

" Does she really? "

" I don't believe the doctors will cure Gemmel, do you? "

" Yes. I 'm sure they will." They were descending the path holding hands. He asked — " What is that book? "

She held it up so the moonlight fell on it.

Finch's jaw dropped. He stammered — " Why, Roma, why — where did you get it? "

" In the library."

" Did someone give it to you? "

" No. I took it. I thought I had a right to."

" Well. I suppose you have." He leant against the railing of the bridge, looking down into the stream. He could see the sickroom and Eden on the bed, terribly emaciated. The book had just come from the publishers. He had put it into Eden's hands, hoping for some gleam of pleasure. But Eden had only said — " How very nice," and handed it back to him. Then he had said, quite loudly — " Don't leave me alone! I don't want to be alone." But a week had passed before Eden died.

" Have you read the poems, Roma? " he asked.

" Some of them. I wanted to bring the book on a walk. You won't tell, will you? "

" Never. Look here, Roma, I 'll tell you what we 'll do. Some day we 'll bring one of Eden's books out to the woods and we 'll read the poems aloud. We 'll take turns. Should you like that? "

" Oh, yes," she answered, placidly.

When they reached the lawn before the house, Finch left her and turned aside through the shrubbery. She went slowly into the porch, reluctant to go to bed. Archer was there, also on his way to bed, his hair erect above his high forehead. He had collected certain belongings to carry upstairs, among them a box in which he had had a butterfly imprisoned. The box was broken and the butterfly gone.

"It's your fault," he said with concentrated passion. "I left my butterfly for you to look after and you threw it on the grass and the dogs got it!"

"You did not," she returned. "You just showed it to me. Then you went off and left it. How do you know the dogs got it?"

He showed her the box. "There — do you see the teeth marks? And there's a bit of the butterfly's wings sticking to the lid. It's the last time I'll ever trust you to look after anything of mine."

"You didn't tell me to look after it."

"I did."

"You didn't."

They ascended the stairs quarreling. Archer said — "You're always against me. Whatever I try to do, you're always against me. If someone was to throw a rock at me you'd find two bigger rocks and throw them at me."

"Get out of my way," she said, as they climbed the second flight of stairs. "Don't keep joggling me."

"I will." He moved closer to her.

She took the book she carried and gave him a smart rap on the head with it. He burst into angry tears. In the first place, he was disturbed about his butterfly. In the second he did not want to go to bed.

She turned into her room, not giving him so much as a glance. He went into his own room, gasping and gulping, making the most of every sob. He began to undress. Every now and again he would call out: —

"If anybody threw a rock at me you'd throw two bigger ones!"

She was perfectly silent.

She sat down by the table where Eden, as a youth, had written his first poetry. His name was carved on it, just his Christian name — Eden. She traced the letters with her forefinger. Some day, she thought, she would cut her own name beneath it. It would look nice, as both names had four letters.

The moonlight shone in brightly, making Roma beautiful in her fairness. She had laid the book on the table and sat looking at it. " I will never give it up," she thought, " to anyone."

There was silence in Archer's room, then suddenly he came running into hers, stark naked. He was laughing. He leaped on her bed and began springing up and down.

" Roma, Roma, sitting all alone-a ! " he chanted.

She looked at him disparagingly. " If I were as skinny as you," she said, " I 'd never take my clothes off. I 'd sleep in them."

He gave a few more jumps but she had taken the spring out of him. He got off the bed and came and bent his white body over the table.

" What book is this ? " he asked peremptorily, like a professor.

" It 's mine."

" It is not. It 's Eden Whiteoak's. Don't you see his name on it ? " He looked at her slyly. " I 'll bet you don't know who he was."

" Yes, I do."

" Who then ? "

" My father."

" I bet you don't know who he was married to once." Archer's face looked pinched with shrewdness.

" I do so."

" He was married to my mother ! "

" I know who told you."

" Who ? "

" Alma. I 've known it a long while."

" My mother," Archer said, dictatorially, " did n't want him. She put him right out of the house. Then she married my father and had me. She had *me*, do you understand?"

"Having you was the silliest thing she ever did."

Again he was deflated. He could think of nothing to say.

"She did n't put him out of the house," went on Roma. "He ran away, of his own accord, with someone much nicer and much prettier and they had *me*."

Alayne's step could be heard on the stairs. The children looked at each other guiltily.

"Archer," she said, coming into the room, "how often have I told you not to run about like that! When you undress you are to put your pyjamas on at once." She came to the table and picked up the book. A stab of shock and pain went through her. How she had once loved Eden's poetry! How long ago! Ah, a different life — a different world — she had been a girl then! Well, almost a girl, only twenty-eight and he twenty-three! She had stood by this same table, from which his carved name stared up at her, and stroked his bright hair, smiled down into his eager face and bent and kissed him. How long ago! Another life. Another world. A world sunk under the waves of time, only now and again re-created in memory by some small floating object, such as this book.

"Who gave you leave to take this from the library?" she asked, her eyes on Roma's pale face.

"No one."

"You should not have taken it without permission. You must be very careful of it." As she turned away she asked — "Why did you want the book?"

"I don't know."

"Now that 's just being stupid, Roma. Of course, you know why you want it."

"No — I don't."

"Have you read any of the poems?"

"Yes — a few."

" Which ones? "

" I can't remember."

How, Alayne wondered, had Eden begot this uninteresting child! He, with his swift intelligence, his responsiveness! But there was Minny Ware — she had been shallow enough. Alayne took Archer's hand. " Come," she said, " it's getting chilly." She saw the tumbled bed and exclaimed: —

" I should think you would be ashamed to make your bed so badly. One would think you had been jumping on it."

The children stared at her in silence.

Alayne sighed and led Archer to his own room. Roma could hear him steadily talking, trying with all his powers to drag out the good-nights, to hang on to his mother a little longer. But at last she went, calling out — " Good night, Roma! " as she reached the head of the stairs. She was scarcely at the bottom when Archer turned his light on again.

" Good night, Roma! " he sang out. " Come and kiss me good night."

" No. Go to sleep."

He began to groan and moan, making dreadful noises.

Alayne called from below — " Archer, do you want me to punish you? "

" No-o," he whined, though he had no fear of her. Now he called softly — " Good night, Roma," repeating the words till she replied with a " Good night " to him.

She sat by the table in the moonlight, motionless except that now and again she turned a page of the book. She did so with an air of serene possessiveness, as though its contents were well known to her and beloved. So she remained till the moon sank.

XIII
RENNY'S RETURN

A MONTH later, at five o'clock in the morning, Renny Whiteoak alighted from a car at his own gate and turned into the
deep shade of the driveway. He had come on an early
train, had got a lift from the railway station and, unknown
to his family, was almost at the door. They were not expecting him for another fortnight. It pleased him that he
would surprise them, find them doing everyday things, instead of waiting in an excited group to welcome him. He
would take even the old house off its guard. It would be
dozing away, in the rich comfort of its Virginia creeper,
never expecting him. Well, he had been away an un-
conscionable time. Yet it had passed quickly, in confusion,
in noise, in mass movements of men. Here there was peace.

What a plunge it was into the shade of the evergreens!
How fresh, how still the early morning air! A red squirrel ran the length of a bough and sat swaying on its
tip, gazing down at him. Another squirrel darted across
his path and up the mossy trunk of a hemlock, in a flying leap
joined the first squirrel and the two peered down, talking
about him. And it was only five in the morning!

He stepped through a gap in the trees and on to the lawn
that wore a silver carpet of dew. Near his feet there was
a throng of tiny mushrooms that had sprung up overnight.
He stood looking down at them, deliberately savoring the
moment when he would raise his eyes to the house, anticipat-
ing the recognition it would give him. Out of the earth rose
the essence of the land he knew. Out of the hushed white
branches of the old silver birch came a long-drawn sigh of
recognition.

A robin, running across the dewy grass, caught an earthworm, drew it out to full length, to far more than full length; it snapped like the string of an instrument. Renny waited till both halves were devoured, then slowly raised his eyes to the house. His eyes moved over it, from eave to basement, from shuttered windows to vine-embowered porch. It had not changed. It rose solid and intact. By God, he never wanted to leave it again!

He would stay at home and think easy and comfortable thoughts. He would forget the victimized world he had been living in for more than four years. He would forget the planes that swept like a flock of vultures; the palpitating entanglement of mechanism that ground that earth. He felt that he hated everything mechanical. He would like to walk on his two legs or ride a horse for the rest of his days. He felt that he would like to see the land ploughed, harrowed, sown with seed, by man's labor alone, as in the old days at Jalna. His ears were weary of the throbbing of engines.

An early morning breeze swept through the leaves of the Virginia creeper. They vibrated, and the vibration seemed to spread throughout the fabric of the house. It seemed to say: " So you are home again, wanderer. And high time it is. My roof has waited all these nights and days to receive you; now bend your head under it and leave me no more."

He smiled and moved beneath the window of his wife's room. He picked up a handful of gravel from the drive and threw it lightly against the pane. He waited, his face upturned. She must have sprung up at the first rattle of the tiny stones for there she was at the window, throwing wide the sash, leaning across the sill to look down. She saw him standing below, his face raised to the window, wearing his uniform, as he had worn his riding clothes, with that air as though they had been invented for him and he alone could so well grace them.

She was in a pale blue nightdress, her fair plaits, now

more silver than fair, hanging over her shoulders. Some instinct must have told her who had thrown the gravel, for she looked less surprised than stunned by the sudden realization, in the flesh, of all she had yearned for in the long years. She had yearned for him, as the husband whose flesh was the barrier between her and the world, and all the harm evil gods could do her. She had yearned for him as the lover. She had not prayed for his return. She was, in truth, almost completely a skeptic and did not actually believe in the evil gods she sometimes conjured up, but thought all that happened was only chance. So, as chance had flung them passionately together, she would cling with passion to him, till the end.

"You are back," she said softly. "I'll come down and let you in."

She cast one glance at herself in the mirror before she flew down the stairs. Would he find her much changed? It could not be helped — the white hair — but he had loved the gold of it. Her hands fumbled with the key. She seemed to have forgotten how to unlock the door. There — now it came! He pushed it wide open. She was in his arms. She succumbed as to a wave that swept her away. She let herself go as she had not let herself go for four and a half years. It had not been possible to let go. All her energy had been concentrated on hanging on. But now — she sank in his arms, her head thrown back, her legs too weak to hold her up. He looked down into her face. She surrendered to the intensity of his gaze.

"You aren't changed!" he exclaimed. "You aren't changed at all! My sweet one. My own girl."

He pressed his lips to hers.

The sun was just high enough to send a splash of color through the stained-glass window. It was purple and it fell on her head. But when he carried her into the library and sat down with her on his knees, he saw the white in her hair.

"I told you!" she exclaimed. "I told you in a letter. Don't look like that or I shall think it makes a difference."

He took one of her plaits and kissed it. "It makes no difference," he said, "but — I did n't want it to change."

She sat up and examined his weather-beaten features, the aquiline nose, the mouth, hard but with such felicity in the expressions of love, the changeful brown eyes. His hair — why, there was not a single gray streak in it! It scarcely seemed fair that hers should change and his retain its stubborn dark red. He looked younger than she! And he was years and years older.

"The war," she said, almost coolly, "seems to have treated you well."

He gave the arch grin, so like his grandmother's. "Oh, I wear well," he said.

"But that awful time at Dunkirk — that accident in the jeep."

"I 'm over all that. But not fit for service. Feel that." He placed her fingers on the ridge of a scar on his crown.

"Oh, your poor dear head!" she cried, and drew it down and kissed it.

She had so many questions to ask, and he the same.

"Shall we ever find time for all the things we want to say!" she exclaimed.

He looked at his watch. "A quarter to six! I think I 'll go to see the uncles and the children."

"Not the children — not yet! Please. But go to the uncles if you think it is n't too early." She wanted to dress and, more particularly, to do something to her face.

"They want to be waked. They can sleep all the afternoon."

He caught her to his breast and kissed her again. They clung together motionless in the joy of reunion. Then —
"Lead me up the stairs with my eyes shut," he cried. "Let me open them and find myself in your room."

He closed his eyes tightly and she led him out of the room and up the stairs. In her room she said: —

"Open them quickly! It was horrible — as though you were blind."

He laughed, his eyes flew open. "My God!" he exclaimed. "It's like a miracle. I've dreamed this sort of thing. Oh, Alayne, we're together again! Yes — together." He moved about the room looking at her belongings — her toilet things on the dressing table. "I'm glad you haven't changed anything."

"I've nothing new!"

"Well," he said, "I'll go to Uncle Ernest first."

"You know that Adeline sleeps in your room."

"Yes. I shall tiptoe past."

"I'll have her moved from there to-day."

He creaked cautiously in his heavy boots down the passage to Ernest's door. Softly, he opened it and went into the room.

The old man lay on his back, his delicate profile with the high-bridged nose upturned, his hands folded on the coverlet.

"Uncle Ernest," said Renny, bending over him.

Ernest opened his eyes. He put up his hands as though to ward off his nephew. He gasped, in a hoarse voice — "You are his ghost! You have come to tell me — that he —"

It was almost like *Hamlet*. An observer might have thought that Ernest did it too well, that he must assuredly have heard Renny's laugh in the next room, have been prepared with this bit of play-acting.

"Don't be frightened, Uncle Ernest. I'm solid enough." He sat down on the side of the bed, took the old gentleman in his arms and kissed him.

"Dear boy. What a start you gave me! And how splendid you look!"

" You look pretty well yourself."

" Ah, many a time I wondered if I would last till you came home! Thank God, I have."

" Uncle Ernie, you could n't have used me like that — not been here to welcome me. It would n't have been home without you."

" No, no, I could n't have done that." Ernest's voice quavered but he hung on to himself. " Oh, how glad I am that you 're home! We 've needed you."

A thumping came from the floor of the adjoining room.

" There 's Nicholas!" exclaimed Ernest. " He hears us. You 'll have to go to him or he 'll have the whole family awake. I wish I might have had you to myself for a bit. I shall ring for my breakfast early this morning."

Renny hurried to Nicholas. He was sitting up in bed very disheveled. He held both arms wide and clasped Renny to him. Tears ran down his deeply lined cheeks. He could not speak.

Renny straightened himself, then sat down beside the bed. He said — " Well, Uncle Nick, I 'm home again. It feels wonderful."

" It is wonderful. It 's a miracle. First Piers — now you. All we need now is Wakefield. But how thankful I am! My knee is pretty bad or I should be prancing about the room for joy." He wiped his tears on the sleeve of his pyjamas. " Of course, you 've seen Alayne. How thankful she must be! Poor Piers has lost a leg. It 's very sad. Now tell me how you managed to get here so early. I heard you laugh in Ernest's room. I was already half-awake. I thought — ' No one but Renny laughs like that. He 's here!' And I thumped with my stick. Give me your hand. Let me hold your hand."

Ernest came in, wearing his dressing gown.

" You must be very hungry, dear boy," he said. " My own stomach is literally caving in from excitement. Yet

Wragge would resent it bitterly if I were to ring for any breakfast at this hour."

" Bad to eat when you 're excited," said his brother.

" But very weakening to go empty. I think I shall get a biscuit from my room." He left and returned nibbling a biscuit. " The biscuits have got very flabby," he said. " Most unappetizing. I don't suppose you have breakfasted, Renny."

" No. But I 'm not hungry."

" Now, tell us all about your journey," said Nicholas.

They plied him with questions.

At half-past six he said — " I think I shall go and see Adeline."

" I shall go with you," said Ernest.

They went to Renny's bedroom where she slept. He opened the door softly and stole to the side of the bed. She lay in the abandon of healthy sleep, her arms thrown wide. He bent and kissed her. Her eyes flew open. She looked up at him, dazed. Then a joyous smile curved her lips.

" Daddy ! " she cried, and was out of bed in one leap and on him.

Finch, Roma, and Archer had been woken by the unusual sounds. They came running down the stairs full of excitement. All trooped into Nicholas's room from where he had been loudly calling them to come. Alayne, joining them, thought —" Already he is surrounded by family. It will be a wonder if I can have him to myself once more to-day."

Rags appeared in the doorway and all but fainted. " The last time I laid eyes on you, sir," he said, while they gripped hands, " was at Dunkirk and you 'ad a bloody bandage on your 'ead. Seems as though it 's always your 'ead that gets 'urt, sir."

" A good thing it 's tough," said Renny.

Nicholas asked — " Have you had any ill effects from this last injury?"

" Well, Uncle, my memory was bad for a time, and now and again I still feel a bit dazed for a moment. But that 's wearing off."

" Poor head," said Adeline, stroking it with a possessive air. Her eyes devoured him.

" We thought," Archer said, " that you 'd likely get killed. We were pretty sure you 'd get killed."

There was a storm of denial.

" I wonder, Wragge," put in Ernest, " if I could have my breakfast tray now. All this excitement on an empty stomach is very bad for me."

Wragge did n't look pleased with the thought of a breakfast tray.

" Tell your wife," said Renny, " that I shall come down in a few minutes to see her. After that you and I can have a chat."

" I think, Wragge," said Ernest, " that I 'd better have an egg — in addition to my porridge."

" Very well, sir."

" Children," said Alayne, " you must go and dress."

" What a lovely early start we have," said Adeline. " What a day of celebration! Daddy, don't you think I 've grown enormously?"

" It 's disgraceful," he said, and drew her to his side.

Down in the basement he shook hands with fat Mrs. Wragge. She beamed at him and promised herself a morning of cooking his favorite dishes. Suddenly he exclaimed — "Where are the dogs?"

Rags had just descended the stairs. He gave a deprecating shrug. " Ow, sir," he said, " you 'll find a great difference where the dogs is concerned."

Renny frowned. " I know. Dear old Merlin 's gone."

"Yes. 'E's gone. And very sad it was. I knew it would be a blow to you."

"But where are the others?"

Rags opened the door leading into a small room that was sometimes used for an extra maid. An English sheep dog, like a mountain of animated hair, came trotting out, his eyes hidden in his hair, his bobtail lost in his hair, yet the whole somehow abounding in expression. After him came a broad-chested wrinkle-nosed bulldog and, in and out between their bulk, a little cairn terrier.

"Hullo, dogs!" shouted Renny. "Hullo, dogs! Do you know me? Of course, you do! Look at them, Cook! By George, it's grand to see them!" He squatted on his heels, the cairn in his arms nibbling his chin, licking his cheek. The other two shouldered each other to sniff him, to wag their welcome.

"Ain't it wonderful how they remember 'im?" Rags asked of his wife.

"It ain't so much they remember him as they know he loves them. They know by the way you touch them."

"Why were they sleeping in there?" asked Renny. The Wragges looked at each other.

"They're mostly kept out of the upstairs now, sir," said Rags, with portentous solemnity.

"But why?"

"Ow, we're getting too grand to 'ave dawgs up there. They bring in too much dirt. Did n't you notice the 'all, sir? It's been done over in cream color?"

"*Cream color!* What do you mean?"

"Did n't you notice the wallpaper was tore off and the woodwork and all was in *ivory* paint?"

"Good God, no! I — went upstairs with my eyes shut and came down — well, I must be blind!"

He left them abruptly and mounted the basement stairs,

the dogs pressing forward with him. Alayne had just arrived in the hall.

He looked about him, with a disapproving grin.

" Well," he said. " You 've made quite a change here."

Her lips felt stiff but she tried to smile naturally.

" I had to have it done. The old wallpaper was disgraceful."

She had used a provocative word.

" That wallpaper," he said, " was bought by my grandmother, nearly a hundred years ago. It came from France. You could n't buy its like to-day."

" I know," she said, a little impatiently, " but a hundred years is a long time. It had got very soiled."

" It could have been cleaned."

" Indeed it could not. Renny, just think of the children who have gone up and down those stairs putting their grubby little hands on the wall."

" *Your* children — " he placed a devastating accent on the *your* — " may have put their grubby paws on the wall. Certainly we never were allowed to. We 'd have got them smacked if we 'd tried it. Did you ever feel the gold leaves and scrolls on that paper? They felt solid. I 'll bet the men had a time to get it off."

" Yes. They did. But surely you must acknowledge that the hall looks larger, airier, more cheerful."

" Not to me."

" The ivory color seems to bring out the beauty of the rugs. I had n't realized before what fine ones they are."

" I had."

" Everyone remarks how the beauty of the banister, the carving of the newel post, stand out as never before."

" Hmph." His eye caught a strange new ivory-colored something against the wall. " What 's that? " he demanded.

" A radiator! " She faced him, half-defiant, half-proud.

" Renny, I have had an oil heater put in! I paid for it out of my own money. What a joy it has been! An even temperature, real warmth, all over the house — for the first time."

" *We* were never cold."

" It has done away with the awful old stove that used to be put up in the hall every winter."

He looked aghast. " The stove, Alayne! The stove! You don't use the *stove* any more? "

" Everyone says what an improvement I've made and, as I have said before, I did it out of my own money."

" Well — I could have shown you better ways of spending your money. And let me tell you this, I never came into the hall out of the cold and saw the old stove almost red-hot, with the dogs curled up about it, but I thought it one of the coziest sights I'd ever seen." He turned to Finch, just coming down the stairs. " Look here, Finch, I've heard of soldiers who came home and found themselves not wanted. By Judas, I begin to think that's the way it is with me! Everything I like best has been changed." He spoke with half a laugh but there was temper in his tone. " The dogs are shut in the basement. The paper torn from the walls. A cold-blooded heating system installed. The old stove turned into junk." He gave a flourish of his hand toward his grandmother's room behind the stairs. " I'll bet Gran's room has been brought up to date. I'll bet there's a streamlined bedstead in it and a dressing table with three mirrors."

Alayne would not let herself get upset. She put her arm about him and said — " Darling, nothing is changed in that room. Would you like to look in? "

" No. No."

The old woman with her caustic tongue, her mordant vigor, had given him all the maternal tenderness he had known. She and his aunt, Lady Buckley, whose dignity and restraint had seldom unbent and whose attitude toward him had been critical. He would not look into that room.

He let himself be drawn by Alayne and by the onward rush of the children into the dining room, where breakfast, unusually early, was laid. Rags was so excited that he forgot first the butter, then the marmalade. He hurried down to the kitchen for each of these, execrating his bad memory as he went. He was well aware of Renny's chagrin over the changes at Jalna and he placed first the butter, then the marmalade, before him, with an air of doing what he could to soften the blows that had been dealt him.

Alayne had been prepared for a certain amount of discontent over the innovations. Her idea was to make him forget these things in the general pleasure of homecoming. Finch ably came to her help and few could have felt disgruntled in the presence of the children, they were so bubbling with happy talk.

Renny's air became more resigned. The three dogs clustered about him while he fed them scraps of buttered toast.

"I suppose the dogs just got in because you did," said Archer.

"Right you are, Archie."

Finch chose to laugh hilariously at this and Alayne brought herself to smile.

"The dogs are so glad to see you," said Adeline. "They never forget, do you, pets?"

Renny fixed his eyes on his daughter's face. He said — "Do you know, Adeline, my spaniel, dear old Merlin, promised me that he would live till I came back. And I think he would have if —"

Alayne interrupted — "It was impossible. He was so miserable. We all agreed he could n't go on."

"I did n't agree," said Adeline.

"I did n't agree either," put in Archer.

" You were n't consulted," said Alayne, with asperity.

Renny turned to Finch. " Were you at home? "

" No. I was on a tour. But I guess he had to be done away with."

" He promised me," repeated Renny, "to keep well — to live — till I came back."

" I remember," said Roma. " Uncle Nicholas took you to one side and asked you something, and you lifted Merlin by his forepaws and you said, ' Merlin has promised me to keep well till I come home.' "

Renny's face lit up. He put out his hand and took one of Roma's in it. " Fancy her remembering that! " he exclaimed. His face contracted.

Good God — thought Finch — he 's going to cry!

" Now children," said Alayne, rising, " I think we have finished. Girls, you had better make your beds at once."

The telephone rang in the next room. It was Piers. News was already about that the master of Jalna had returned. In less than half an hour Piers, Pheasant, and their sons, Meg and her daughter, had joined the family circle. It was a day of light, fluttering breezes. Above the treetops the sky swept up and up, into infinite harebell blueness. The dominant color in the flower border was the blue of the larkspurs. Blue jays flitted among the trees. Alayne had put on a blue dress.

Ernest and Nicholas established themselves in their own chairs on the lawn. The rest of the family collected round them. Renny sprawled in a deep garden chair, the cairn terrier on his knee, the bulldog and the bobtail sheep dog at his feet. Already he had complained bitterly of the state of the latter's coat. " Ah, Jock," he had mourned, " you would not be the neglected bundle of rags you are if I had been at home! No wonder your mistress wants you kept out of sight."

Adeline was humiliated. " If only you knew how often

I have combed him! And Wright has too. But he has *such* a propensity for burs."

"When was he last combed?"

"Yesterday. No — I believe it was two days ago."

"More like two weeks ago. Never mind, Jock, you 'll not be neglected now." Jock gazed up at him with an adoring, sanctimonious expression on his woolly face.

Alayne stood in the porch contemplating the family group. It was twenty years since she had come to Jalna as Eden's bride. And there they sat, as they had sat then, close together in the invincible bond of their kinship! There were missing from the group old Adeline, Eden, and Wakefield. What would Eden be if he were living to-day? The grandmother had died. Eden had died. But seven young ones had sprung into being. What strong-featured individualists these young ones would develop into! Just as their elders. She had to acknowledge that Archer, in spite of his resemblance to her gentle scholarly father, fitted well into the group. Even Nooky was developing the Court nose. Her eyes came to rest on Renny. Was it possible that she beheld him sitting safe, with his dogs, his family! For the thousandth time she admired the way he held his head, the set of his shoulders, that look which, when he was mounted, made him seem a part of the horse. He looked not much older than Piers, for Piers had grown heavy and those years in the prison camp had done something to him. Alayne crossed the grass and joined the group, coming to Renny's side and sitting on the broad arm of his chair. He put an arm about her but not quite tenderly, for he remembered the wallpaper, the radiators, and the banished stove. The various irritations he had suffered in the moment of homecoming caused him to look with added dolor on Piers's affliction. He said: —

"It 's a strange thing to see you, Piers, with one of your legs missing."

A shock went through Alayne. How *could* he speak, with such dreadful openness, of what she had never yet referred to in Piers's presence?

Piers answered a little huffily — " I have a mighty good artificial leg. I got a new one after I came home. The first was just a makeshift. I get about very well."

" Indeed he does! " cried Pheasant. " There is almost nothing he can't do. Just wait till you see him sitting up on the harrow! He can do *anything*."

Renny pessimistically surveyed his brother. " It 's well," he said, " to feel so. That puppy you have climbing all over you — you seem very fond of it."

" Why not? It was a present to take the place of Biddy. You knew she was run over by a car."

" To take the place of Biddy! " repeated Renny, on a note of astonishment. " Do you mean to say that you would let this puppy take her place? But then — you never were very fond of her or she of you. She was always following me home."

Piers stared truculently at him but said nothing. Renny turned to Meg. " It seems strange," he said, " to think of you in that little house where Mrs. Stroud lived — a widow — in a little house."

" It is very strange and sad," she answered, taking his hand. " But not so bad as it might be. I have Patience — and the house looks quite nice since I have turned both halves of it into one, as it was originally."

" Meg got a very tidy sum for Vaughanlands," said Piers.

A gleam came into Renny's eyes. " She did! Good. I asked you in a letter, Meg, but you did n't answer."

" You must meet Mr. Clapperton," said Meg. " He is a perfect dear. So kind! So generous! "

" Indeed! So far I have n't liked what I 've heard of him."

" What have you heard? "

"That he bought Vaughanlands."

A vibration went through the older members of the family. If Renny did not like the idea of Mr. Clapperton at Vaughanlands, what would his feelings be when he heard of the proposed model village? A model village, named Clappertown, at his very door! No one dared tell him of it.

Meg continued — "His kindness to poor Gemmel Griffith is simply wonderful."

"Gemmel? She's the cripple, is n't she?"

"Yes. The poor girl never could walk. She just crept about the house — a terrible responsibility for her sisters."

"The oldest one, Molly," put in Patience, "is on the stage in New York. She's lovely."

"The really lovely one," said Finch, "is Althea."

"She's shy," added Roma. "She runs the other way if you meet her."

"Well, what has this fellow done that's so generous?" asked Renny.

Meg continued — "He took that poor, crippled girl to a specialist. She's had a most delicate operation on her spine, and before very long will be able to walk. She's now in a nursing home. Mr. Clapperton is paying for everything."

"He sounds damned officious."

Alayne's eyes met Finch's. They laughed, almost hysterically.

"But don't you think it was very kind and generous?" asked Meg. "It will change the girl's whole life — and her sisters' too."

"She seemed to me very happy as she was. I'd have let her alone. There are enough girls running around."

He turned to Nicholas — "What do you think of him, Uncle Nick?"

Nicholas blew out his cheeks. "I think," he said, "that he is a horrid old fellow and his secretary, Mooey's tutor, is a horrid *young* fellow."

"I quite agree as to Swift," said Piers.   "I can't stand him.   I don't like the ideas he's putting into Mooey's head."

Maurice flushed.   "He is a good teacher," he said.

"That's the main point," said Renny.   "How are you getting on?"

Pheasant broke in — "He has tried some of the exams and passed with honors.   They were child's play for him."

"It's math and science that get me down," said Maurice, "but I expect to get through them next year."

"My God," exclaimed Piers, "have we to endure that whippersnapper, Swift, about the place for almost another year?"

"Daddy — Daddy," interrupted Adeline, "when are you coming to the stables?   Wright has everything shining for you.   He's dying to see you.   Do come — please!"

"Are you sure," asked Renny, "that he has not had the whole interior done over in a pale ivory and central heating installed?"

"Positive.   Do come!"   She tugged at his arm.

He rose.   "All right.   Who is coming with me?"

Even Alayne, knowing the family's predilection for each other's society, was surprised to see them rise in a body, with the sole exception of Nicholas.

"Do you think you should attempt it?" she asked Ernest. "You haven't walked so far in a long while."

"He can rest in my office," said Renny.   "Take my arm, Uncle Ernest."

Nicholas said ruefully — "I'd go like a shot, if it were n't for my knee."

"Fetch his wheel chair, Finch," said Renny.   "We'll take him over."

Finch darted off for the chair.

"Hurrah," cried Archer.   "Uncle Nicholas is having his last trip to the stables!"

"It's not his last," said Adeline, indignantly. "He'll go lots of times — now that Daddy's home."

With many heavings and gruntings, Nicholas was installed in the wheel chair. Finch labored behind it while Ernest leant on Renny's arm.

Renny asked — "Aren't you coming, Alayne?"

"I cannot possibly," she answered. "I have a thousand things to do. Who do you suppose does the work in that big house?"

"The Wragges."

"They couldn't possibly do it all. Adeline, don't forget that all your things are to be carried upstairs from Daddy's room, and the beds to be made."

"I'll not forget. Hurry up, everybody!"

"Do come with us, Alayne," Renny said coaxingly.

"My dear, I cannot."

She stood watching them go. She smiled ironically at the strangely decorative procession they made. What was there about them? A freedom of movement, a letting of themselves go, combined with a valid Victorian dignity, as of beings important to the universe. There was Nicholas, a hilarious smile on his face, carried away by the excitement of this unexpected jaunt. There was Finch, a mousy-fair lock dangling over his eyes as he bent his back to the pushing of the wheel chair. There was Piers with the harsh years of the prison camp behind him, hardy, upright, though with a limp. There was Pheasant, her hand swinging in his. Meg and Patience on either side of Nicholas's chair. Young Maurice with his quick grace; the five children. There was Ernest, taking careful steps, guided by Renny. There was *he!* Fourteen of them in all, he in the centre, the pivot of their circle. Oh, to form one of that invincible procession, since her life moved in the stream with theirs! Oh, to be one of them! But she could not — not after twenty years!

All day she would watch them doing things together. Talking, arguing, eating together. Looking into each other's eyes, putting out a hand to touch each other. The young ones shouldering their way into the circle, to become stronger in its strength. All the long day she would look on but — at night she would have him to herself. She would redeem the loneliness of the years of separation.

XIV

THE WHEELBARROW, THE ORGAN, AND
THE MODEL VILLAGE

THE three dogs lived as though in fear of losing sight of
Renny. In and out, up and down, they padded after him.
The little cairn constantly got in the way of the many moving legs, darted aside, darted back, raised a face so appealing
that Renny must bend down to pet and reassure it. When
he sat down the bulldog sat by him, resting its massive head
against his leg, gazing at his very boots with adoration.
Through a dense fringe of hair, the sheep dog watched his
every movement. But he greatly missed Merlin, his blind
spaniel, that dog between which and himself communion of
touch had reached such sensitive expression. Now in the
morning, with the three at his heels, he prowled about the
various outbuildings behind the house. The shed where
flowerpots, garden shears, and lawn mower were kept, where
bulbs of gladioli and dahlia in their time were stored, where
strings of onions hung from the cobwebbed roof; the carriage house where his grandmother's old phaeton stood in
dim twilight and the carriage his grandfather had had sent
out from England, with its massive lamps, its interior trimmings of velvet and ivory, its sagging cushions on which
many little Whiteoaks had bounced. Then there was the
tool shed. He noticed how hammers and chisels lay scattered uncared for, and he frowned. Archer, Nooky, and
Philip, he guessed, had worked their will here. Well, they
would be sorry if he got after them. But this was only his
second day at home. He would prowl about peaceably, enjoying the dear, familiar sights and smells.

As he again passed the door of the carriage house it

dawned on him that something was missing from there. He opened the door and went in, trying to think what it was. It required some moments of scrutiny, then he discovered that his grandmother's garden wheelbarrow of wickerwork, light but strong, was gone. He looked in every corner for it. Then, coming out into the sunlight, he saw Finch crossing the yard.

" Hullo," he called out, " do you know what has become of Gran's wicker wheelbarrow? "

Finch stopped short. His jaw dropped. He stammered — " Well, no — I mean, yes — I 'm not quite sure."

Renny's eyebrows shot up. " What the devil do you mean? Have the kids broken it? "

" No. The fact is I lent it to the Griffith girls. They wheeled Gemmel about in it. She could n't walk, you see, and it was nice and light."

" Hmph. Well, she can walk now or soon will, from what I hear. You should n't have given it for such a use. It 's not strong enough. I value it, if you don't. I want you to fetch it home to-day. Why, both Gran and Meggie thought a great deal of that wheelbarrow."

" All right," said Finch. He hesitated and then continued — " There is something else missing. I think I ought to tell you. I have n't said anything about it to Alayne. It 's the organ that was in the basement. It 's disappeared."

" The organ! Aunt Augusta's organ! But how could it disappear? "

" I don't know but it has. I 've asked Rags and Cook but they had n't even missed it."

" Not *missed* it! Anything the size of an organ! "

" So they said."

" By Judas, there have been queer goings-on here! "

He strode to the steps leading to the basement. He descended them, the dogs rushing after him, panting, as though he were in full flight from them. In the kitchen he confronted husband and wife, she baking bread, he cleaning brass.

"Where is the organ?" he demanded.

The cook stared at him out of fat little eyes, the mass of dough in front of her, the smudge of flour on her red cheek, giving her an air of innocence. Rags, on the other hand, surrounded by tarnished brass trays, candlesticks, and urns, his fingers stained by the brass-cleaning mixture, looked a picture of guilt.

"I've been asked that before," said the cook truculently, "and what I say is — I've never missed it."

"Rags, *you* know where that organ is."

"So 'elp me — I don't, sir."

Renny went to the door of the room where the organ had been, threw it open and entered, the dogs shouldering each other to enter simultaneously. Finch followed. "I missed it about a fortnight ago. I remembered some old music books that used to lie on the organ and I had a sudden curiosity to see them. They were here all right but the organ had vanished."

Rags remarked from the passage — "I've always said that there outside door ain't properly barred. Any sneak thief could break through."

"And sneak out with the organ in his pocket! Do you expect me to believe such a story?"

"Well, as you know, sir, there's a great scarcity of musical instruments."

Renny fixed a penetrating gaze on him. "Tell me, Rags," he said, "who stole that organ. It never was taken out of this room without your knowledge."

There was a terrible silence, broken only by the sound of Mrs. Wragge thumping the dough.

"Come clean, Rags," said Renny.

Rags visibly curled up in his distress. "'Ow, Colonel Whiteoak, don't ask me!"

" I do ask you. I don't want to fire you, on my second day home."

" There are plenty who 'd be glad to take me on."

" I know there are. But you don't want to go to them, any more than I want a strange couple at Jalna. Who stole the organ? "

" Sir," said Rags desperately, " will you give me till noon to answer that question? "

" Yes. Come along, dogs. Finch, please see to it that the wheelbarrow is brought home. Gran's wheelbarrow — Aunt Augusta's organ! What next? " He strode into the room that formerly had been the coal cellar and where now stood the uncompromising bulk of the oil heater. The walls had been whitewashed, the floor cleaned, not a coal was to be seen. He stood gripping his chin, staring about wit a bewildered feeling. Was this the coal cellar? Was this home? He gave an ironic smile at his own concern, then, followed by his escort, made his way out of the house and along the grassy paths.

Standing among the raspberry canes was Alma Patch, plucking the dark red fruit, her small son, dirty of face, playing near by. When he saw Renny and the dogs he ran to his mother and clutched her draggled skirt.

" Hullo, Alma," said Renny. " So you 've got married and had a baby since I last saw you! "

She wiped her fruit-stained fingers on her skirt and Renny shook hands with her.

" Quite a fine boy," he said, for young things were always attractive to him.

" Oh, he 's just grand." Alma snatched up her child to show him off. " Ossie — Ossie — tell the gentleman about the train! Did you know he fell off a train, sir? And not hurt one little bit."

" I did indeed. My sister, Mrs. Vaughan, told me all about it in a letter. Took a whole page to it."

Alma beamed in delight. "Did she? My, just think of that! Ossie, tell the gentleman about the train."

Ossie brought out, in a singsong — "The chain yan down the chack. The chain yan down the chack."

Alma hugged and kissed him. "Yes, the chain yan down the chack and Ossie had n't a single mark on him! Was n't it wonderful, sir?"

"It was indeed. The raspberries look nice, Alma." He picked a handful from the canes and ate them. "By George, they taste better than ever."

"I suppose, sir," said Alma, "you 've met the new gentleman, Mr. Clapperton. He 's so kind. Ossie never tells him about the train but what Mr. Clapperton gives him a nickel, don't he, Ossie?"

"A very bad habit, bribing children," said the master of Jalna hastily. "Give him a smack on the head, if he does n't tell it. What about the train, Ossie?"

"Yan down the chack," said Ossie, squinting up hopefully.

"That 's right." Renny moved through the orchard. There was promise of a good crop of apples but the trees badly needed pruning. Certainly their trunks had not been whitewashed this year and there was a bough swathed in the sinister web of the caterpillars. He longed for the day when farm help would be plentiful.

He came out on to the church road and crossed into the churchyard. All was peaceful and unchanged here. The church stood solid and with an air of serenity. And there was Noah Binns digging a grave, standing waist-deep in it. He greeted Renny with a two-toothed smile. When Renny had last seen him, five black teeth had ornamented it.

"Been losing more teeth, eh, Noah?"

"Yeh. But I manage to chew most anything."

"Good. Digging a grave, I see."

"Yeh. It 's fur Chalk, him that was blacksmith here once."

Renny drew back astonished. "Chalk! Why — I'm sorry for that. I haven't heard of it. Chalk! Many a horse he shod for me and shod well."

"Never liked him," said Noah, driving his spade into the ground. "He was full of foolish ideas. One of 'em was that all men are good at heart. Looks like it, the way the world goes on, don't it?"

"He was a good man, Noah. Why, he shod my first pony for me. He was a young fellow then."

"Well, he was old enough when he died."

"When is the funeral?"

"At three o'clock — this earth's so hard with the drought I can hardly get me spade into it."

"I'll be here."

"A funeral on yer second day home! I wouldn't waste time on Bill Chalk's funeral if I was you. Him and his forge! Well, it's a gasoline station now. Things has changed. This year's a bad one — drought and blight. There's a blight on the world. It won't surprise me if I live to see its end."

"It will have to get a move on, if you're to see its end."

Noah Binns glowered up at him out of the grave.

"I've seed the end of a good deal," he said. "Blight, drought, bombs — they'll put an end to the world and danged if I'll care."

Renny turned away and walked quickly to the plot where, inside an ornamental iron fence, were the graves of his parents, his grandparents, his stepmother, his brother, and several infant Whiteoaks. His eyes traveled slowly across the green mounds. He read the names on the granite plinth and the names repeated at the head of each grave. He brought to life, in imagination, those whom he could remember — his father's blond face with that look of well-being, that indolent but rather arrogant good humor; his stepmother with her lovely long white neck, her large blue eyes that were always following his father's movements, happy only in his nearness. Both had died while he was at the last war. Eden — and at the thought of him, Renny's brows came together in pain. He should not have let Eden die! Eden might, with better care — but what more could they have done for him? Eden was bound to die. Tragedy was in the air when he had come home to die. Yet none had loved life better.

And those little graves, those of his stepmother's babies — he remembered how he, a careless boy, had dandled them during their brief stay and how she had wept at their going. And his grandmother; others in that plot might be but bone and dust but he could not think of her so. Surely if she were unearthed and brought to light, those carven features would still be set in the mould of humor, pride, and power.

His own features with their marked resemblance to hers softened to a smile. He turned and retraced his steps among the graves, past Noah Binns to the gate. He would not visit Maurice Vaughan's grave — not to-day. He had lost a lifelong friend. He did not want to dwell on that thought.

Noah sat, with dangling legs, on the edge of the dark opening in the earth, eating a sandwich, drinking cold tea from a bottle. He called out: —

"Know what I heard tell?"

"What?"

"Next winter's goin' to be the worst ever. Snow's comin' in November and it'll lie heavy on us till March. Rabbits is goin' to girdle the fruit trees. There's to be no fuel, and misery in all the land." The bottle fell from his hand and the tea was spilt into the grave.

"Oh, my tea," he groaned. "Spilt into Bill Chalk's grave!"

"Serves you right," laughed Renny. "Get in after it and I'll cover you up."

He went back to Jalna across the fields and turned into the path that led to the stables. He found Wright waiting for him outside the door. He wore a somewhat hangdog expression and said, as he moved forward a step: —

"Rags says you've been asking about the organ, sir."

"You bet I have," returned Renny. "I want to know where it is."

Wright hung his head. Then slowly he got out — "Miss Adeline and me are the guilty parties but we'd like to show you something first — before we tell about it."

He led the way to the paddock, to which the colt had that morning been brought from a distant field. Adeline was standing by the gate waiting for them. The colt, with a wisp of grass in his mouth, fixed his gaze inquiringly on the newcomer. The past weeks of good care had already done much for him. He was filling out, his coat growing sleek, but the fineness of his bony structure was plainly visible. He was still very thin and his stark alert head was as though carved out of bronze.

Renny looked him over, then turned to Wright.

"What has this colt to do with the organ?" he demanded.

Wright did not answer but stood with hanging head. Seeing Wright, to whom she had looked for protection, incapable of speech, Adeline too hung her head, the pair presenting a picture of complete though inexplicable guilt, to the penetrating gaze fixed on them. The colt drew nearer, and from deep in his interior there came a low whinny.

"Has this colt anything to do with the organ?" repeated Renny. "Come now, what has he to do with it?"

Wright could not speak, so Adeline, as though taking her life in her hands, made the plunge. Pointing over her shoulder with her thumb, as she had seen Wright do, she said: —

"The organ's half of him."

Renny stared at the colt as though expecting to see a keyboard and pedals develop along one side of him. "What do you mean, the organ's half of him? Come here."

She came close to him and he put a compelling hand on her shoulder. " Make a clean breast of this," he said.

Now the words tumbled out. " Oh, Daddy, you can see how beautiful he is — and a farmer had him and we wanted him terribly. Wright could see wonderful possibilities in him but Wright had only a hundred dollars and no one in our house would put the other hundred in. So I remembered the organ and you said once I might have it and the farmer's wife wanted an organ more than anything on earth, so I traded the organ for a half share in the colt. And Mr. Crowdy and Mr. Chase have seen him and they say they 've never seen a youngster more full of promise."

Renny turned to Wright. " So," he said, " you have led my daughter into pretty goings-on. You have helped her to steal her great-aunt's organ and to trade it for a share in a half-starved colt who may amount to nothing. It 's small wonder that she wrote to me that you and she were running the place together."

Wright looked crushed but Adeline spoke up bravely. " It was all my doing, Daddy. Wright did n't know I 'd made the bargain till it was settled."

Renny replied sarcastically — " And I suppose you got the organ from the basement and carried it to the farmer's wife all by yourself. A likely story. You need n't tell me Rags was n't in this, for he was."

" Oh, Rags was splendid," said Adeline, " he nearly broke his back carrying the organ up the steps and Cook helped too. We all were pushing."

Renny turned to Wright. " Of course you consulted Mrs. Whiteoak about this."

Wright answered sulkily — " I could n't. She 'd fired me once already."

" Already fired you! "

" Yes, sir. But I would n't go."

" By Judas, this is a house to come back to! Why did she fire you? "

" Oh, sir, that 's quite a story," said Wright miserably. " It 'd take some time to tell."

" I have plenty of time. Go ahead."

" Daddy, may I just ask you one thing? " said Adeline, standing up very straight. " Would you please have a really good look at the colt before we go into that other story? And it was all my fault too because Wright never knew how bad my knee was. Oh, please have a good look at the colt first."

Renny opened the gate into the paddock and entered. All three stood about the colt, he gazing at them out of proud full eyes, as though deep in his breast he knew what he could do. Adeline and Wright were his friends but he looked long at the newcomer, as though speculatively. Renny examined him from nostrils to rump, then, turning to Wright with one of his sudden changes of expression, he said : —

" Two hundred dollars they asked, eh? "

" Yes, sir."

" One hundred and the organ," put in Adeline.

Renny grinned. " I believe," he said, " that he has it in him to be a wonderful lepper." He had picked up the word in Ireland and continued to use it, though it grated distressingly on Alayne's ears.

" I thought you 'd agree to that, sir. Later on this colt 's going to be worth a lot of money."

" I grant you that he 's a good-looking fellow," said Renny, " and may make his mark. But, as for the organ — you come along with me, Adeline." He turned away, she meekly following.

Presently she slipped her hand into his and walked so, without either speaking. At last she spoke in a small voice.

" Daddy, what are you going to do to me? "

This she would never have asked but that she saw forgiveness in his eyes as he looked down at her. She threw all the innocence, sweetness, and goodness she could command into her look.

"You are a rogue," he said sternly, "and deserve to have a stick taken to your back but this time I forgive you. Though if your Aunt Augusta knew I don't think *she* would forgive you."

"I believe she would, Daddy, for Uncle Finch says she was a very understanding woman."

They had crossed a field where a cluster of Jersey cows had sought the shade, and where a flock of geese grazed by the stream. Beyond lay Vaughanlands. Renny threw his leg over a rail fence and thus elevated he surveyed the loved landscape. Adeline climbed to his side and perched there. The warm breeze fanned their faces, the sun was dazzling. Renny saw its shimmer on three strange roofs. He stared and stared again. He could scarcely believe his eyes.

"Why —" he stammered — "what houses are those?"

Here was something, she guessed, to draw his attention from her misdeeds. She fixed her bright eyes on his face. "Those," she said, "are the beginnings of Clappertown."

"Clappertown," he repeated, his color rising. "What do you mean, Clappertown?"

"Why, Daddy, that's the name of the model village Mr. Clapperton plans to build." Genuine enthusiasm came into her voice. "He's going to do wonderful things. For instance he's going to have a community swimming pool and we shall be allowed to use it. There's to be nothing ugly in the village — just pretty little houses and a special kind of people. Mr. Clapperton is going to keep everything refined. That's the word he used." She stopped. She could not go on, seeing the look on her father's face. He began to get off the fence.

"Why wasn't I told this before?" he asked.

"I expect no one dared. Where are you going, Daddy?"

"To tell him he can't do any building here."

"Oh, please let me come."

"No. I want to be alone with him."

"I do so want to hear what is said."

"You wait here till I come back."

She watched him stride across the field. How glorious, she thought, to have him home again, even though he did stir things up. She watched him with possessive pride. No other girl she knew had a father to compare to him.

Renny had a closer inspection of the cottages before going to the large house. He inspected them with such concentrated hate as brick and mortar might well have become aware of. Indeed the widowed lady who occupied the nearest one, looking out of her window and seeing his nearness and the threatening expression of his face, hurried to her door and locked it. Like a rabbit in its burrow she peered out at him, while like a fox he stared in at her till he turned away and went to Eugene Clapperton's door. He used the old knocker instead of the new electric bell.

Mr. Clapperton himself opened the door. He was dapper and self-possessed as always. He gave his visitor an inquiring look, though realizing at the first glance who he was. He did not in the least like his looks.

"I am Renny Whiteoak," he said. "I've been home two days and I've just discovered your would-be village. Good God, do you think I'll stand for that? Let me tell you that two bungalows were once built on this property, and I never rested till I had them pulled down."

Mr. Clapperton spoke in a conciliatory tone. "Come in, Colonel Whiteoak, come in, and let's talk over this matter agreeably."

"Agreeably!" his visitor repeated. "If you think I can be agreeable about a thing like this, you're mistaken. I'll stay here, thanks."

Mr. Clapperton liked him less and less. He was a disagreeable, a formidable-looking fellow. But he still spoke to him with forced friendliness.

"I'm sure you don't understand, Mr. Whiteoak. There is a great difference between shoddy bungalows and the type of dwelling I am erecting. I am an idealist. For many years it has been my dream to build and to own a model village. Just a *very* small one, you know, but perfect in its way, where people of refined taste and small means can enjoy lovely surroundings — There is to be a swimming pool — "

"I know, I know," interrupted Renny. "And *my* family is to be allowed to swim in it! Are you under the impression that *we* want a swimming pool? If we had wanted it we should not have waited for *you* to build us one."

Eugene Clapperton's anger rose. "Well, sir," he said, "I don't need your permission to go ahead with my plan. And what's more, you can't stop me. There were no building restrictions in the deeds of the property."

"If I had been at home when the sale was made there would have been."

"I dare say, but you were n't."

Renny spoke more quietly. "The properties about here," he said, "were acquired a hundred years and more ago, in order that those who valued privacy and their heritage of British tradition might enjoy both here. Do you want to be the one to spoil all that?"

"No, I don't. I came into the country because I like privacy. I can't see that I'm spoiling anything by founding a model village."

"You may found it, Mr. Clapperton, but you can't tell how it will go on. You won't live forever. Will your heirs care a damn who lives in your pretty village? Well, I'll just say this — it's the silliest scheme I've ever heard of. It's worthy of some sentimental old lady, with no grain of horse sense in her."

This was too much for Mr. Clapperton. He exclaimed

hotly — "I will build this village without any interference from you and I will run it, in my own way, without interference from you. From what I hear you have a very overbearing attitude in these parts, but it won't work with me."

At this instant Renny's dogs, who were well acquainted with Vaughanlands, ran pell-mell into the house, the bulldog almost knocking Mr. Clapperton off his feet.

"Get out!" he shouted, and kicked at them.

"I should advise you," said Renny, "not to kick my dogs. I don't want to shake you but in that case I'd be forced to."

"Then take them out of here," snapped Mr. Clapperton.

Renny whistled to the dogs. Soon his tall figure disappeared through the shrubbery.

"What a change," he thought bitterly. "When I left for the war, Maurice Vaughan was living here. It was a second home to me. Now he's gone and this blighter Clapperton is in his place with his fantastic schemes! It's unbelievable."

At home he found lunch waiting. During his absence this lighter meal had been substituted for the old-fashioned one-o'clock dinner. Now dinner was at night. He helped himself somewhat grimly to salad and remarked: —

"A pretty mess Meg has made — selling Vaughanlands to a crank like this Clapperton."

"We knew," said Ernest, "that you would be greatly disturbed by his project."

"Disturbed!" exclaimed his nephew. "I all but shook the weasand out of him."

A thrill went about the table. "Not actually!" cried Alayne in horror.

"Well, no. But I had a mind to."

She drew a sigh of relief. "How did you find out?" she asked.

"I saw the cottages. Adeline told me what he is up to. I went to see him."

" I suppose you had words with him," said Ernest.

" Yes.   Hot ones."

" Now there will be bad feeling."

" Certainly there is on my side, and he gave me a nasty look as I left."

" Horrid old fellow," put in Nicholas.

His brother looked at him critically.   " Watercress," he said, " down the front of your waistcoat."

Nicholas peered down his front.   He collected the sprays of cress with a trembling old hand and laconically poked them in under his moustache.   Archer giggled hysterically.

Renny gave a scrap of scone to each of the dogs in turn. For an instant the pink interior of the sheep dog's mouth was visible, then the morsel disappeared into his hairy face. Only his eyes gleaming through his fringe showed his eagerness for more.   The bulldog chewed ostentatiously on his back teeth.   He raised himself against his master's knee and looked over the table.   Delicately as a lady the little cairn accepted his share.

" How nice it is," said Roma, glancing out of the sides of her eyes at Alayne, "to see the dogs again."

" I guess the war seemed long to them," said Archer.

" Will you children please eat your lunch and not talk," said Alayne.

" This affair of the model village is very distressing," said Ernest.

Alayne wished the subject might be dropped.   She said — " As the building is inevitable, I believe the less we say about it the better."

" It is not inevitable," returned Renny, " and it 's not going to take place."

" What shall you do? " asked Finch, rousing himself from a reverie.

" Yes," said Ernest, " I should like to hear what you plan to do."

"I'd like," said Nicholas, "to duck that horrid old fellow in the horse pond."

"May God strike him dead," said Archer.

"Archer, leave the table and go to your room," ordered Alayne.

He rose and, rigidly straight with tow head erect, marched from the room.

"My fault," growled Nicholas.

"He'd finished anyway," said Roma, her eyes again slanting toward Alayne.

"That does not alter the disgrace," said Alayne.

"It alters the feeling in your stomach," said Adeline.

Finch gave a snort of laughter.

"You two girls also may go to your room," said Alayne. They left.

"I like children," said Ernest, "but it is much more peaceful without them."

"My father," said Nicholas, "would knock me down as quick as look at me."

"Come, come," said Ernest, "if our father knocked you down, you deserved it."

"I can't remember what I did but I do remember being knocked down. What is the moral, Finch? You've been knocked down, have n't you?"

"You bet I have." Finch flushed. "But I never tried to find a moral for it."

"If you can find a moral for your sufferings," observed Ernest, helping himself to more raspberries, "they are easier to bear."

"I do hope," Alayne said to Renny, "that you will have no disagreeableness with Mr. Clapperton. You certainly are helpless in the matter."

He frowned. "I know. I know. But give me time. In any case I'll make a struggle. I've not given up hope."

Considering all, he looked cheerful. At the end of the

meal he went and stood beneath the portrait of his grandmother. " I wonder, Gran," he said, " what you would have
thought of this Clapperton."

" Just what I think," said Nicholas. " A horrid — "

Ernest interrupted — " Do think of something new to say
about him, Nick. Reiteration grows so tiresome."

XV

ALMOST A PROPOSAL

When Renny Whiteoak had disappeared from sight, Eugene Clapperton turned, with anger manifest in every movement of his body, and entered the room where his secretary was typing. Young Swift continued to type, displaying no more expression than the machine itself.

"I suppose," remarked Mr. Clapperton sarcastically, "that you heard nothing of the little interview I had with Colonel Whiteoak."

"Nothing," answered Swift, turning in his chair to face his employer. "What was it about?"

"Surely you heard something."

"No. How could I when I was typing?"

"We were speaking loudly. He has a very penetrating voice."

Swift preserved an irritating silence.

Mr. Clapperton clenched his hands and said through his teeth — "It is unbearable that that man should interfere with me. I bought the property, did n't I? I paid for it, did n't I? I 've poured out money like water on improving the property, have n't I? I have an ideal I 'm trying to realize. Now comes this man and insults me — offers to lay hands on me!"

"Really!" Swift had heard all but it was against his nature to acknowledge it.

"Yes. I knew I 'd dislike him but I never guessed how much. And his sister is so nice. I look on her as a friend. And his two old uncles! They are courtliness itself. And his wife! A charming woman. How she endures him I can't imagine. The whole family is agreeable, with the exception of him."

" I certainly don't like Maurice's father."

" He is quite pleasant toward me. Now we are on the subject of likes and dislikes, Sidney, I must say I'd be very pleased if you'd make up to young Miss Vaughan."

" Patience, you mean? "

" Yes. She's a sweet girl and she'll have a tidy little fortune. I'd like to see you marry into the Whiteoak family. I don't approve of you going with Garda Griffith. I've been intending to speak of this for some time."

" She's a mighty nice girl."

" All three sisters are. When I think what my coming here has meant to them! I've completely changed their lives. I've rescued poor little Gemmel from misery and frustration. They're all so grateful — it's pathetic."

He was undoubtedly moved. He took several rapid turns about the room, then abruptly left it. Swift heard him cross the verandah, then had a glimpse of him going in the direction of the fox farm.

" So grateful to him! And how touching their gratitude is! " thought Swift. " The next thing will be that he'll marry one of them. I'll bet it's Garda he's after. Of course, it is! The old blighter! A young girl like Garda. A child! And I'm to marry Patience! *If* she'll have me. And leave my dear little Garda to him. What he wants is to push me out and never leave me a penny of his money — after all the times he's hinted — more than hinted — that he'll leave me everything! I wish he *had* got a shaking."

He in his turn fretted up and down the room. The covetous thought of Mr. Clapperton's money was never far from his mind. In the anticipation of inheriting it, he had borne a good deal. He would find it bitter indeed to be cut off from this hope by the marriage of his employer. He admired Patience but she was too cool, too critical, to capture his affection. Little Garda had that power, though it was not in him to be loyal to any woman. But Eugene Clapperton — Eugene and Garda — he ground his teeth at the thought of it.

Althea was preparing a tray for Gemmel when the knock sounded on the door.

" It 's *him*," whispered Garda. The magic pronoun was all that was needed to set them in a glow of eager welcome.

" She will have to wait for her lunch till he has gone," said Althea. " Go to the door, Garda."

Althea nerved herself to remain in the room. She smiled at him and offered her hand. He clasped it warmly in his.

" And how is everything with my dear little girls? " he asked.

" Splendid," answered Garda. " Gem had a good night. This morning she took three steps. It 's wonderful to see her. But she gets so excited."

" I hope you two hold her up carefully."

" Indeed we do. We 're more anxious than she is. She 's ready to try anything."

His face beamed. " Ready to try anything," he repeated. " She 's a little heroine. May I go up? "

He had been to see her every day in the hospital. Now that she was home again his possessive air in the three sisters was marked. With them he had shared anxiety, suspense, and the wonder of a cure that seemed miraculous. Garda led him upstairs to the room where, dressed in a light blue dressing gown, Gemmel lay on a couch. She looked up at them with a smile.

" Good afternoon, my dear." Eugene Clapperton took her hand and raised it to his lips. " I hear good accounts of you. You had a restful night and you have taken three steps."

" I would have taken a dozen," she said, " if those sisters of mine had not been so nervous."

"Ah, but we must be careful of you. You are a very precious person. Is n't she, Garda?"

"She 'll soon be a very independent person," returned Garda. She was conscious that he wanted to be left alone with Gemmel. So, after a moment's lingering in the room, she went downstairs to her housework.

"What sweet girls your sisters are!" said Eugene Clapperton. "They are devoted to you. But — are n't we all?"

She regarded him with a strange mixture of gratitude and wariness. "What you have done for me is beyond my understanding," she said. "You have the kindest, most generous heart in the world."

"Enough of that," he interrupted. "You know very well that I don't want gratitude from you. Only friendship and a little — yes, for the *present,* a little love." He gave an embarrassed laugh.

"We all love you!" she exclaimed. "We love you — like a — "

He interrupted — "Don't say like a father, Gem. Don't say that."

"Never. We love you like our best, our dearest friend."

He settled himself in a chair by her side. "Tell me," he said, "what you feel like when you stand on your two feet like other people, when you look right into people's faces, instead of up at them."

"It is such a new experience, it will take me a while to get used to it. Then, there are those who are supporting me. When they let go of me, stop being fussy over me, then I shall realize it."

"But you are happy, Gem?"

He again took her hand, and stroked it. "You know it 's my nature to want everyone about me to be happy. Even to be happier because of my existence. I 'm an idealist. I dream of happiness in a miserable world. But this morning I had a shock. Colonel Whiteoak called on me. He made himself very disagreeable about my village. He was insulting. I don't think I've ever met a more detestable man." A hard look came into his eyes. "But insults have no effect on me. I'll go on with my building. I'll make him look small in this community."

She smiled, she could not help it.

"You may smile," he exclaimed. "But just give me time. Give Clappertown time. We'll make him look small. When I get an idea in my head, Gem, I can think of little else. I have had the ideal village as my goal. My only other thoughts have been of you. But, by jingo, you've pretty nearly liquidated the village sometimes, you little scamp."

Life had offered Gemmel Griffith so little. It had not even given her the power of standing upright. She had always been forced to raise her eyes to other people, as though she were a being of inferior order, but now, now she could rise on her own two legs and soon would be able to walk. And here was this wealthy man, the man who had poured out his good money for her recovery, calling her a little scamp with an air there was no mistaking. She was divided between terror and a delightful sense of power. She had a sudden, half-mad desire to domineer over Eugene Clapperton, even while her heart was overflowing in gratitude to him. But gratitude was really against her nature. She had never been grateful to her sisters. The thought of being grateful for the rest of her days to Eugene Clapperton made her angry. She wished she could do something tremendous for him — pay him off and have done with it.

"Call me Eugene," he was saying. "I'd love to hear my name on your lips."

"Eugene," she repeated obediently and prayed that Garda might come with her tray. "It's a pretty name," she added, reaching for succor in that direction. "Do tell me how you came to get it."

He liked to talk of himself. He told her how his mother

had liked the name Eugene, and his father had liked the name Robert; so he had been called Eugene Robert. He never took his eyes from her face. She thought — " Has this look in his eyes something to do with my being like other women now? I 've never seen the look before — I do wish Garda would come."

" And your name," he was saying. " How did you get your dear name? "

" Oh, my mother was determined to give us unusual names. That was all. Much better, I think, to have been Elizabeth and Ann and Jane."

" My little Gem," he whispered hoarsely.

Garda came in with the tray. A little frown from Gemmel detained her and, looking at his watch and seeing how late it was, Mr. Clapperton left, promising to call again the next day.

" Don't give me my tray. I could n't eat a bite."

Garda looked frightened. " Are you ill, Gem? "

" No. Not ill. But — " She flung out her arm, then laid it across her eyes — " I 'm so disturbed. Mr. Clapperton has been trying to tell me he loves me."

" Really! Oh, Gem! How thrilling! You 've always been on the lookout for lovers for Althea and me, and now — almost before — " She hesitated.

" Go on."

" Almost before you 're quite well, you have one of your own."

" I know how Althea feels."

" Shy, you mean? "

She uncovered her eyes. " No, not shy. Just terrified."

" But he 's so kind. Think what he 's done for you. And for us through you. If you spent the rest of your life trying to repay him you scarcely could do it."

" I know."

" He 's done a miracle for us."

" Yes. Like Christ. And I 'd be willing to think of him like that."

" Do you think he wants to marry you? "

" I suspect it. Picture me getting married! "

" Gem, he 's terribly rich. He must be or he could n't do the things he does."

" I love worldly possessions. I 've always hankered for them."

" You could have *everything,* Gem."

" So could you and Althea. That is what excites me . . . Oh, why did this happen? And before I can take two steps alone! " She broke into sobs, covering her face with her hands.

Garda knelt beside the sofa and took her sister in her arms. " You need n't see him, if you don't want to. He 's often said he does n't ask for gratitude. Come, let me dry your eyes."

Gemmel controlled herself. " Give me the tray," she said.

" That 's a good girl. You must eat and grow strong. And, when all is said and done, it 's rather nice to think that you 've captivated a rich widower — with positively no effort. Think what you could do if you *tried.*" She arranged the tray in front of her sister.

Gemmel laughed through her tears and began hungrily to eat. " I 'll write and tell Molly. What fun to tell her! You must leave that to me."

" Now you talk like yourself. Be a good girl and eat up every crumb."

Remembering some dish she had left on the stove she hastened downstairs. Closing the door of the kitchen behind her she faced Althea.

" What do you suppose? "

" What? "

" Mr. Clapperton has been being sweet on Gem."

" She imagines it. You know what Gem is for imagining things. What did he say to her? "

" I did n't ask her."

" Then you don't really know."

" I could tell by the way she looked. She was excited. Oh, Althea, if she really and truly recovers, and if she would marry Mr. Clapperton, what a different life we 'd have! "

" I ask nothing better than the life I have."

" With Gem an invalid? "

" Gem never was an invalid. She 's always been well — except that she could n't walk. I 've never thought of her as a burden."

" Neither have I."

" I 've loved caring for her. She 's been like my child. Just like my little child."

" I know. I know. But think of her as *well* and *rich* — with nothing impossible to her."

" Is she eating her lunch? "

" Yes."

" I shall take her a glass of wine."

" All right. I 'll get the cigarettes."

They went up to Gemmel's room, doing their best to look natural. Certainly she now did. She lighted a cigarette and looked through the wine toward the window. " Eugene's wine," she said.

" Goodness," said Althea, " do you call him *Eugene?* "

" I may as well begin."

Althea said solemnly — " Gem, I want you to put the thought of that man out of your head."

" *What!* Never think of my benefactor? "

" Never, except *as* a benefactor."

" Althea, would *you* marry him if he asked you? "

" I 'd die first," she answered passionately.

" Ah, he 's not Finch, is he? "

Althea turned away her face.

" Gardie, would you marry him? "

" Marry him? Let him give me the chance."

" Just for greed? "

" I 'm not thinking only of myself. Picture what I could do for you and Althea."

" That 's just it, is n't it? " She lay, launching one tremulous smoke ring after another on the air, for no one could make them the way she could.

The screams of one of the Jalna dogs, in anguish of spirit as he chased a rabbit but could not overtake it, came through the open window, then died away leaving only the vague sweet murmurings of late summer.

XVI
GRANDMOTHER'S ROOM

ADELINE came to where Renny sat in the porch, the rain trickling noisily from the eave, the east wind blowing the long tendrils of Virginia creeper that, because of its luxuriant covering of the porch, could find no foothold. She put her arms round him from behind and kissed him with demonstrative affection.

"There's something I want most terribly to do," she said. "I've been wanting to do it ever since you came home."

His eyes turned toward hers that were so close. "Then why haven't you asked before? You are not usually so diffident."

"But this is something very special. I'm sort of afraid to ask."

"Out with it. If I refuse, I refuse."

She drew a deep breath. "Very well. It's this. All the while you were away I slept in your room. I wanted to sleep there more than anywhere. But now you're home I have to share a room with Roma. I want a room of my own and you'll never guess what room I want."

He stared. "What room?"

"I want Granny's room. I want Granny's room for my own — if you'll let me."

He drew her in front of him and set her on his knee.

"Are you actually telling me that you have the wish to sleep alone, in that queer old room? You couldn't change things about, you know."

"I don't want to change them about. I want it just as it is."

" And you have the cheek to ask for it?   What do you suppose the uncles will say? "

" Must it be as they say? "

" Well, she was their mother."

" But it's your house."

" No.   It must be as they say.   We'll go and ask them what they think of the idea.   Come along."

He sprang up, eager to tell his uncles what Adeline had suggested.   He was full of pride in her.

They left the front door open behind them.   The wet cool air flooded the house.   The dogs followed them up the stairs.   The door of Nicholas's room stood wide.   Ernest was in there with him and they were going through old letters.

" Come in, come in," said Nicholas, pulling off his spectacles.   " Come in and sit down.   Ernest and I are destroying old letters.   The time has come to go over them.   Some of them had better not be read by posterity, eh, Ernest? "   He picked up the little cairn and set him on his knee.

" Get off those letters, Jock, you brute," said Ernest, pushing the sheep dog from the neatly arranged piles on the floor near his chair.

" Now here is a letter," said Nicholas, " written to me by my mother, after she had first met Mary Wakefield and found that Philip wanted to marry her.   Not the sort of letter that Piers or Finch or Wake should read."

" Let me have it," said Renny, holding out his hand, " I'd like to read a letter from her."

" You'll destroy it afterward? "

" Yes."

Nicholas handed it over.   " What a racy vocabulary my mother had! "

" Now here is a letter . . ." said Ernest.

" Adeline and I would like to interrupt you, just for a

moment," put in Renny. "We have a proposition to make."

The two old men looked at him inquiringly, Ernest still clutching a handful of Jock's topknot, for the sheep dog wanted to sit nowhere but on the pile of letters.

"What sort of proposition?" asked Nicholas, pulling one of Adeline's curls. "I hope it's a proposition to make less noise over my head in the early morning."

"That's just it," she cried eagerly. "There will be much less noise — if only you'll let me do it."

"Do what?"

"Tell him, Daddy."

Renny grinned at his uncle. "She wants to sleep in Gran's room. Have it for her own. That's what she wants."

"Not really?"

"Yes. And for my part I think it a good idea."

Ernest held his chin in his hand pondering. He gripped his own chin and Jock's topknot and thought deeply. "My mother's room," he said, and repeated — "My mother's room."

"She'd sleep there," exclaimed Nicholas, "in that old, painted leather bed, with that old furniture — "

"She'd ruin it," interrupted Ernest, "in no time!"

"No, I'd not, Uncle Ernest," cried Adeline. "I'd take the very best care of it. I'd polish it and it would n't be shut away and dusty, the way it is now. Only once a fortnight does Mrs. Wragge go in and draw a dustcloth across the tables. And I'm Great-grandmother's namesake and I'm the image of her. I believe she'd be pleased, don't you?"

"The room is getting a musty smell," said Renny.

"My mother's room smelling of must," said Ernest.

"How old are you, Adeline?" asked Nicholas.

"Fourteen. And tall for my age."

"I'll not have Archer in there, racketing about."

"I pity him if he does," she exclaimed.

"It seems a nice idea to me," said Renny. "I believe the old lady would be tickled to death by it."

Nicholas and Ernest looked at each other. To them the room was a shrine, though in truth the old goddess had been a sardonic one. It was almost twenty years since their mother had died. In that room there was no air to breathe. Since old Adeline's vital presence had been taken from it, loneliness was its fate. It mourned, outside the life of the family. But, with this loved child continuity would be established, the river of life would flow on. The stretching of her young body on that painted bed would be the laying of a red rose on a neglected shrine. *Neglected?* Yes, neglected, because, what with increasing years, the distance away of their own rooms, the length of the winter, the worry over their nephews at the war, they had not entered their mother's room as often as they felt they should. There was something very melancholy in the atmosphere of the room. The faded hangings, the stuffed figure of her parrot on his perch, his staring glass eye seemingly fixed on his reflection in the dim looking-glass, all were melancholy.

But if young Adeline were to occupy the room, how different all would be! She would fly in and out like the summer breeze. Her clear high voice would shatter the deathly stillness. Surely, as Renny said, their mother would have wished it. Surely seventeen years was long enough for a room to go unused. As the brothers looked into each other's eyes they saw the same thought reflected there. Ernest waited for Nicholas to speak first.

"Well," he growled, pulling at his gray moustache. "Well, it's hard to know what to say."

"But, Uncle Nick, I'd take such care of the room! And I'm getting older all the time."

"So am I — worse luck," said Nicholas.

"And I am away at school the greater part of the year. In the summer holidays I am outdoors all the time. I couldn't do much damage, could I?"

"You are a good pleader," said Nicholas. "I've a mind —"

"Then you will!" she cried, throwing her arms about him. "I knew you would."

"What do you say, Ernest?"

"I agree. I think it is even suitable. The child is Mamma's namesake. She is the very image of her. Mamma lives again in her, you may say. I am quite willing that Adeline should have the room."

Adeline kissed him fervently.

"See that you are worthy of the room," Ernest continued, as though his mother had been a saint and not a rather deplorable old woman with a racy tongue and a violent temper.

"I will. I will," she promised.

Renny looked out the window. "It's pouring with rain," he said. "Alayne and Archer are in town at the dentist's. The stage seems set for moving into your new quarters. Let's get at it, Adeline."

It seemed too good to be true. With passionate eagerness she tore the bedclothes from her own bed and carried them down to her grandmother's room. Renny threw wide the window and let in the fresh damp air, till Nicholas hobbled in and ordered him to shut it. Nicholas and Ernest established themselves in two chairs and directed proceedings. They were exhilarated by the changing about. Certainly this was better than going over old letters. They had forgotten the dogs and now, upstairs, Jock was stretched among the letters, Bill, the bulldog, was supplying some deficiency in his diet with one of them, while the little cairn had overturned the waste-paper basket in search of a bit of cake Nicholas had dropped in it the day before.

"The child must not have that embroidered bedspread," said Ernest. "Fold it up, Renny, and lay it in the drawer of the wardrobe."

Renny did as he was told, then asked — " What about the things in the dressing table? "

" They also can be laid in the wardrobe. Her toilet articles — those old ivory brushes are quite lovely, and some day Adeline shall have them but it would not be suitable now — I shall keep them in my room if Nicholas approves."

" All right," said his brother. " Open the drawers, Renny, let 's see what is in the drawers."

" I know without looking," said Ernest.

Out came her scarves, her gloves, her ornate beribboned caps, her lace collars, the velvet bag in which she used to keep her handkerchief and a few Scotch mints. These inanimate objects so brought back her vigorous presence that it seemed her voice must be heard. Ernest put his fingers into the bag, and there was a peppermint! " Good God! " he exclaimed, and held it up.

" After all these years! " exclaimed Nicholas.

" It 's very moist and clammy." Ernest held it up waveringly. " What shall I do with it? "

He had a feeling that perhaps he ought to eat it rather than throw it away. But he could not bear to eat it. The decision was not left for him to make. The spongy morsel that once had been the peppermint slipped from his fingers to the floor. The little cairn terrier, trotting in, snatched it up and swallowed it as though it were just nothing to him. Nicholas burst out laughing. Ernest could not help feeling relieved.

Some instinct warned Adeline not to display too great a curiosity toward her predecessor's possessions. She fixed her energies on the arranging of her own bed linen on the bed wherein old Adeline had conceived four children, given birth to them, and watched her loved Philip die. No memories disturbed the child's joy in establishing herself here. When she had asked permission to do so she had had small hope of its being granted. Now here she was, smoothing her sheets on that coveted couch, plumping the pillows to rest her empty young head where that head, so full of memories, bitter and dear, so full of the passions and emotions of a long life, had lain.

All was put in order for her. The uncles returned to their rooms. Her father and the dogs went out and now, the rain having ceased, she opened the window, brought the carpet sweeper, passed it violently a number of times across the rug, then used quite half a bottle of polish in rubbing up the furniture. All the while she sang, in a fairly good voice, though noticeably off key, the color deepening in her cheeks, even her hair seeming to take some part in the activity. She felt that a new era in her life was beginning. She felt full of good promise. The day was all too short for what she had to do. She saw, stretching before her, a life teeming with pleasant things to do, once she could finish with school. Always would she sleep in that room, always have horses to ride, dogs to love, puppies to nurse. Always, always would there be her father. The rest of the family would be there too, for she loved them all dearly and never would part with one of them, but her father rose above them all, like the figurehead of a ship.

She still was in the room putting the finishing touches on it when Alayne and Archer returned. Archer had been a trying companion, with his endless questions and restless body. Alayne was tired. From the draft in the hall she at once perceived that door and window of the grandmother's room were open. When she saw what was going on she was astounded.

" Adeline, whatever are you doing? " she cried, looking as though she were witnessing some calamity.

Adeline thought — " Why need she look like that? " She said — " I 've moved in. Daddy and the uncles have given me this room for my own."

Archer advanced toward her with his mouth wide open.

" Look," he said, " my tooth." With his mouth stretched so, he enunciated horribly.

" I 've never heard of anything so ridiculous," said Alayne. " This is no sort of room for a young girl. Who said you could have it? "

" Daddy and the uncles. I 've wanted it — ever since Daddy came home. Now it 's to be my own always."

" Look! " cried Archer. " My tooth! It 's been filled."

" I should have been consulted," said Alayne. " I cannot understand how your father could consent to such an arrangement. But, if he did consent, he should have had the room emptied out and thoroughly cleaned."

" It has been cleaned. I 've done it."

" You! You don't know the first thing about such a job. You have just stirred up the dust and smeared everything with furniture polish. It 's disgusting. Where are all the clothes that were in the drawers? "

" Stored in the wardrobe."

" And you are to sleep in the room with them? "

" I don't mind. I like them. I 've carried down all my clothes and laid them in the drawers neatly, too. Look." She opened a drawer.

" And were the drawers washed out first? "

" No, Mummie."

Alayne uttered an exclamation of disgust.

Archer placed himself directly in front of Adeline, his mouth still open, his jaws aching. " Look," he got out, " my tooth! "

" Well," said Alayne, " I 'll say nothing more. I was not consulted. You took good care to wait till my back was turned. Come, Archer."

He gave a scream. He could not shut his mouth. He had held it wide open so long he had got a crick in his jaw. He made terrifying sounds when Alayne touched him. In terror she ran into the hall, calling for Renny. He was just entering the side door. " Archer's jaw is dislocated! " she cried.

Renny sat down and took his son between his knees. He took hold of his jaw and pressed it back into place. " There," he said.

" Is it all right? " asked Alayne in a quavering voice. " Had n't we better send for the doctor? "

" How does it feel, Archer? " asked Renny.

He stretched his mouth wide. " Look at my tooth," he said, forgetting all about his jaw.

" Oh, what a day! " Alayne rose to go upstairs. Renny put his arm about her and half-carried her. She felt tired out.

" Poor little girl," he comforted. " The trouble with you is that you take things too seriously."

" I know. I 've taken this family too seriously — right from the first."

He looked down into her pale face. " What do you mean? " he asked.

" It would take me twenty years to explain."

He laughed. " Don't try, my darling. Just relax and be happy."

She did make up her mind to trouble herself no more over the grandmother's room. Let them do as they liked with it. Let Adeline live amidst the moth-eaten garments of a centenarian, if it pleased her. Alayne had a hot bath, put on one of her prettiest dresses for dinner, and listened, with what equanimity she could, to the old uncles' praises of Adeline, Adeline's ecstasies over her new quarters, and Renny's frequently voiced satisfaction in the entire situation. As often happened, Finch was the only one who agreed with Alayne, but he did so by no more than an amused smile when their eyes met. Still it was a support.

Roma had been having a piano lesson from Miss Pink and had remained to eat high tea with her. When she returned and found that Adeline had removed from their room, she was delighted, for she wanted the room to herself. Not that she did not enjoy Adeline's companionship, but she liked the privacy of a room she could call her own, of which she could lock the door, in which she could arrange for her own pleasure, and hers alone, those treasures she cherished.

In the twilight the two young girls went to Adeline's new room and continued the work of settling in. With laughing and temerity they handled things which formerly they had not dared touch. An observer who had loved old Adeline would have been driven to remember her sardonic humor in order to bear with this peremptory and youthful fingering of her intimate belongings. Roma lounged on the bed, fanning herself with a feathered fan with carved ivory sticks. Adeline dressed herself in a purple velvet tea gown and placed an ornate lace cap on her head. She lifted the stuffed figure of the parrot from his perch and set it on the arm of the old lady's wing chair. She seated herself and, assuming a cracked voice, peered at the bird, exclaiming — "Pretty Boney, pretty Boney! Have a cracker, Boney!"

Roma fell back on the bed in an ecstasy of delight.

So they amused themselves till, hearing voices in the hall, they pushed the things back into the wardrobe, in a panic. Piers knocked on the door. Adeline, with dignity, opened it.

"Hullo," he said, "I hear you've been allowed to have this room. It's an honor, I can tell you."

"I know, Uncle Piers. I know it's an honor," she answered rather breathlessly.

"Now understand," he said, his chin firm, "you are never, on any account, to meddle with my grandmother's belongings. Later on they must be packed in boxes and carried to the attic. In the meantime none of you children are to touch them."

With their eyes held by his, they promised.

"That's right," he said. "And if ever I find you've meddled with them — why, you'll be sorry."

"Yes, Uncle Piers," they agreed in unison.

XVII

THE THEFT

RENNY had given much thought to Mr. Clapperton and to
the closely looming village of Clappertown. In fact he
thought of little else. In these early days of his return, when
he had expected to be completely happy, Mr. Clapperton's
presence at Vaughanlands hung over him like a well-groomed
cloud. He and Piers talked of him by the hour but Piers
could offer no counsel save resignation. The resignation of
all the family to the catastrophe was a mystery to Renny. He
felt that something might be done about it, if only he could
discover that something. But no amount of pondering
brought revelation.

In the meantime a new little house was brightly springing
into view. In spite of the obstacles to wartime building,
Eugene Clapperton seemed able to get both materials and
builders. Renny would perch on the boundary fence and
watch the tiny settlement with malevolent interest. The
little trees in the little street were growing fast. The baby
in the nearest house was screaming louder. The radio in
the next little house never stopped grinding out raucous
music. He pictured how, as the city grew, more and more
people would be inclined to come here, till at last there would
be no privacy and no peace. He loved the old village of
Weddles. It was enough.

He had other things to worry about besides his neighbor's
activities. All his expenses had risen, yet his income was
considerably less than it had been. Piers must have his
share from the farmlands or he could not live. What a
blessing that Mooey was to inherit Cousin Dermot's fortune

and what a pity he had not possession of it now. With help
so scarce, the farm brought in less than before the war.
With the big horse shows no longer held, the stables were
only a loss. The Wragges had demanded higher wages
and they were incorrigibly extravagant. It cost an excessive
amount to run the table. Then there were Adeline's school
fees. It was an expensive school and there always were
extras. Now he had promised Roma that she should go to
school with Adeline. It was no more than fair, he thought.
Alayne deplored this added outlay but in her heart she was
deeply glad that Roma would be out of the house for the
greater part of the year. Though Roma was so quiet,
Alayne always was conscious of her presence. She seemed
always to be coming upon Roma unexpectedly. Both would
start. Then the child would fade away but soon Alayne
would come upon her again, looking at a book in the library
— not reading but just handling it. Or she might find her
peeping into a cabinet in the drawing-room or stealing a
little biscuit or a lump of sugar from the sideboard. She
was not an outdoor child like Adeline.

Between brooding on Mr. Clapperton's village and worrying over money matters, Renny was absent-minded in
these hot August days. On this particular morning he
had promised to write a check for the grocer, whose account had been rendered several times. However, he went
off without doing it. Alayne sent Archer running after
him.

" Daddy! " shouted Archer. " You forgot to leave a
check for Mummie. You promised and you forgot."

Renny halted on the driveway. " Tell her I'll write it
when I come back."

" She told me to say she wants it now."

" By Judas! " he exclaimed irritably, and flung back
toward the house.

Alayne met him in the hall. " I am very sorry to bring

you back," she said, with a certain crispness in her voice, " but I have promised the grocer to pay him to-day. He calls about eleven o'clock. You promised to write the check before you went out."

" I know, I know!" He seated himself at the writing table in the sitting room and took a book of blank checks from the drawer. He added — " I can tell you that money is very scarce at the moment."

" When was it anything else? "

With his eyes on the check he was writing, he said — " Alayne, these are exceptional times. It will be different after the war."

" It will never be different while so much money is spent on the stables. Even Piers says that the show horses should be sold."

" Oh, we 've gone over all that! " he exclaimed.

" It 's useless, I know, to reason with you about certain things."

He handed her the check.

" I 'm sorry," she said, " but Mrs. Wragge tells me you 've forgotten to give them their wages."

He struck his forehead. " What 's the matter with me? " he exclaimed. " I never used to be so absent-minded." He wrote a second check and put it in her hand.

" Please let me see the checks," said Archer.

" They are of no interest to you," said Alayne.

" I want to see how much you pay the grocer and how much you pay Cook."

" That is not your affair, dear. Run out and play."

" I 'm tired."

" Then read your book."

Archer took up the book without enthusiasm and trotted after Renny. Striding across the lawn, Renny asked — " What is the name of your book? "

" Why, it 's *Robin Hood*. It 's a lovely story. Don't

you remember Mummie bought it for me the day I went
to the dentist?"

"I'd forgotten."

Archer stared up at him inquisitively. "Why is your
memory so poor?" he asked.

"Perhaps because of the bash I got on the head."

"I'm glad my memory is good. My grandfather, Professor Archer, had a wonderful memory. He never forgot
anything."

"Probably he'd never had a bash on the head."

"May I come with you?"

"No. I'm going to see Mr. Clapperton. But you may
come as far as his gate." He took the little boy's hand. The
dogs trotted importantly alongside. At a small gate in the
boundary fence, Renny left them and followed the old
familiar path to the familiar door. He knocked. It seemed
to him that the knock sounded hollow through the house.
He thought of Maurice Vaughan, his friend who had lived
there, his untidy hair, his smile that had so lighted his rather
heavy face, the pipe always in his hand. He thought of
his sister Meg's warm presence, of Patience as a child running to meet him. He was shown into the presence of
Mr. Clapperton, who greeted him with a frosty smile. He
half-rose from the desk at which he was seated, then sank
back, his expression so arrogant as to seem to inquire —
"And what can I do for you, my good man?"

Renny greeted him with determined cheerfulness and,
when he was invited to, sat down. He said: —

"I came here this morning to see if we could talk over
this affair in a more friendly spirit." His grin, as he looked
into Mr. Clapperton's pale eyes, would have done credit to
the wolf before he devoured Red Ridinghood's grandmother.

"I am always ready to discuss any affair with a neighbor,
in that spirit, Colonel Whiteoak. But I must say you
weren't very friendly when you last called."

"I know I was n't. That's why I 've come back."

"If you 've come here with any idea of making me change my mind, you are wasting your time."

"I only want to put your own case clearly before you. Will you object to that?"

"No."

Renny Whiteoak regarded him almost kindly. "I think," he said, "that you bought this property with the intention of settling down here for the rest of your life."

"I did."

"And you found the neighborhood kindly disposed toward you?"

"Till you appeared on the scene — yes."

Renny gave a short, triumphant laugh. "There," he exclaimed, "you have hit the nail on the head at once! Till *I* came on the scene!"

"What do you mean?"

"I mean that I have a lot of influence here. I mean that, if you carry out this scheme of yours, in opposition to me, you won't have a friend in the neighborhood. Not one member of my family will tolerate you."

Eugene Clapperton's color rose. "There are others."

"Who?"

"The Rector, for one."

"Good God! The Rector has baptized, married, or buried some one or other of all the family. My grandfather built the church. This is a small close community. You are nothing to anyone in it."

"You are mistaken, Colonel Whiteoak. The three young girls at the fox farm have a deep feeling for me. And I for them. I am the only person who had the initiative and the generosity to help that poor crippled girl."

Renny Whiteoak stared speechless.

"Between you and me," Eugene Clapperton burst out, "I hope, when she's fully recovered, to make her my wife. Of course, this is in strict confidence."

"By Judas!" was all the master of Jalna could say.

"So you see I have a stake in the community, and a very large one."

"Marry the girl or not, you can't build that village. I'll make it impossible to live in."

"What do you mean, sir?"

"How would you like a fine healthy piggery built right at the boundary line — not fifty feet from the nearest house? I own the fields all down one side of your village. I'll fill them with piggeries. I'll build an incinerator and smoke you out."

Eugene Clapperton raised his voice so high that it cracked. "You seem to forget," he cried, "that there is such a thing as the law to protect peaceable citizens of this country. Well — I'll get the protection of the law if you begin to threaten me or make nuisances for my tenants."

"The law couldn't do a thing to stop me."

Eugene Clapperton smiled sarcastically. "We'll see. You may find yourself with a heavy fine to pay. I guess that would put a crimp in you. Now, money is not scarce with me. I've plenty of it. I can afford to have the best lawyers to protect my interests. Just take a look at this, will you?" He placed his fingers on a pile of new bank notes that lay on the desk. "There's a thousand dollars in that pile. It is to pay my workmen's wages and for current expenses for which I require cash. I don't want to boast, Colonel Whiteoak, but that's a very small sum to me."

Renny stood up grinning. "I think I'll go," he said. "The impulse to kick your behind is becoming irresistible."

Mr. Clapperton drew back. Renny advanced a step. He intended nothing more forceful than a touch on Mr. Clapperton's chest to emphasize his next words, which, to judge by his expression, were to be of a jocular nature. But the look, the gesture, were intimidating to the other. He wheeled and left the room with a white face.

He went into the dining room where Sidney Swift was

sitting by the paper-strewn table. He raised his eyes as his employer entered.

"What's wrong?" he asked.

"That man — that redheaded devil! I just had to leave the room. He was threatening me again. Go to him, Sidney, and order him out of the house. Tell him to get out!" He walked nervously about the room.

Swift rose and, looking through the window, saw Renny Whiteoak cross the lawn.

"He's gone," he said.

Eugene Clapperton came to his side and peered also.

"I won't stand it!" he exclaimed. "I'll have him arrested for breach of the peace. If he ever lays a finger on me — "

"Oh, he won't do that."

"He won't, won't he? I wish you could have seen his face. I tell you he put his hand out toward me. I pity him if he ever touches me. He's threatened to — twice. You can testify to that, Sidney. Get me a drink. I feel all in."

Swift went to the sideboard. "Whiskey and soda?" he asked.

"No. Get the flask of brandy out of my desk. Lock the French window. He must have gone out that way. I wouldn't put it past that man to come back and make more trouble. He's a reckless, dangerous brute. Sidney, bring me my diary, too. I was writing in it when he came. I'll make an entry saying he threatened me. It might come in useful if I brought a suit against him."

"It certainly would," said Swift.

By the time he returned with the flask, Eugene Clapperton was impatient. "Well, you were a long time," he said peevishly. Swift saw that his hands were trembling.

"The flask was not in the desk," he returned coolly. "It was in the little cabinet in the corner." He got a glass from

the sideboard. " Better have a good stiff one," he added.
" Yes."

Eugene Clapperton again went to the window and peered
out. " Did you lock the French window? " he asked.

" Yes." He himself took a little brandy.

As he sat sipping the stimulant, Eugene Clapperton's color
returned. " What do you suppose that man said? " he
asked.

" Goodness knows."

" He said that, if I opposed him, I 'd not have a single
friend in the neighborhood."

" I don't dispute it."

This was one of the moments, and there were a good many
of them, when Mr. Clapperton disliked his young secretary.
Now he exclaimed angrily : —

" It 's perfect nonsense. I 've as many friends as he has.
I 'll make him look small before I 've finished with him.
He threatened to build a piggery right beside the village.
And an incinerator to smoke my tenants out."

Swift smiled. " I should n't put it past him."

" I wish," exclaimed Mr. Clapperton, " that he 'd got a
bullet through him over there."

Swift set down his glass. He said — " I 'm due at my
pupil's place shortly. Will it be all right if I leave now? "

" I should think," said Eugene Clapperton, with some
severity, " that you would not like to go to teach a youth
like Maurice, smelling of brandy."

" He does n't mind."

" Go along then. I think I shall walk over to the fox
farm. I get a great deal of pleasure from the society of
those girls, Sidney. They are friends who would not change
for anything he could say or do."

" I am sure they would n't."

" They mean more to me — especially one of them — than
I 've ever let on. I don't suppose you 've guessed anything

like that." A dull pink crept into Eugene Clapperton's cheeks. " I 'll bet you 've never guessed that, Sidney."

Swift gave a short laugh that was without mirth. " Oh, I 've suspected it."

" Can you guess which one? "

" Darned if I can."

" Try."

" You 'd better tell me."

" I 'm not going to tell you. Not just yet. Run along. Don't stay too late, Sidney. I may need you."

Swift ran upstairs, changed his shoes, and soon was pedaling along the country road on his bicycle. Mr. Clapperton returned to the small room where he had interviewed Renny Whiteoak. From the drawer of his desk he took a small mirror and a comb. He combed his hair though it was tidy enough, took a good look at himself and was not without complacency. Certainly he was a contrast to that red-headed Whiteoak who was apparently always on his uppers, always short of funds, who had cast an obviously envious glance at the pile of bank notes on the desk. Mr. Clapperton turned smiling to put away the bank notes. " I 'm darned careless to leave money lying about like that," he said aloud. " You 'd think, the way I act, that a thousand dollars was something you could pick up on the street, like a stick of chewing gum."

But the complacency left his face, the smile left his face, as he looked at the place where the pile of bank notes had been. They were not there! They were gone. He stared at the top of the desk dumbfounded.

He thought, Now let me keep cool, I must n't get rattled. The money *was* here. It *is* here. I must have put it in one of the drawers without thinking. He tore open one drawer after another. He turned out their contents, handled and rehandled the papers till there was complete confusion among them. Perhaps he had carried the notes into the dining room. He'd been excited — but no — he'd backed right away from Renny Whiteoak without going to the desk.

I must not get rattled, he thought, but he was rattled. He walked in a circle about the room. The money was gone. He had drawn Renny Whiteoak's attention to it — that proved it had been there on the desk during the interview. Now it was gone. It had been on the desk. He'd seen it, pointed to it. *But now it was gone.*

Suddenly he stood stock-still, petrified by the thought that had broken on him. Why — Renny Whiteoak, that hard-faced, hard-up rascal, had stolen the money! Just walked off with it, jammed into the pockets of his jacket, like a highwayman, like a thug, believing he could get away with it, believing Eugene Clapperton was so rich, so soft, he would do nothing about it. But he would do something about it. He'd raise hell about it.

He took the receiver from the telephone and rang up Piers's house. He left a message for Sidney Swift to return home at once. As he waited for him, the thought suddenly presented itself that Swift might have taken the money. Surely he had been longer than was necessary in finding the flask of brandy. But he put the thought from him. The young man was his own cousin, come of honest people. He had always appeared trustworthy. Still — the temptation might have been too strong for him, knowing how suspicion would inevitably be directed toward Renny Whiteoak.

Mr. Clapperton fretted from place to place. He would not stop searching. When Swift appeared he faced him abruptly.

" Whatever's wrong? " demanded the young man.

" There has been a serious theft." Eugene Clapperton fixed him with cold gray eyes.

" Theft? "

" Yes. A thousand dollars has been taken from the top of my desk."

" Gosh! Are you sure? "

" I could n't be more so. It was lying there in new twenty-dollar bills when Colonel Whiteoak was with me. Did n't you see it when you were searching for the brandy? "

" I 'd swear it was n't there then."

His expression was so open, so fearless, that Eugene Clapperton gave up all suspicion of him. He said solemnly — " Sidney, that man took the money. He crammed it in his pockets and hurried out through the French window."

" If he did he 's crazy. He 'd know he 'd be the first one suspected."

" Why? "

" Well — who else? "

" What about you? "

" Do you suspect me? " He stared almost truculently at his cousin.

" Of course not. But he might think I should."

" Are you sure you 've looked everywhere? "

" Sure. But I 'm willing to begin all over again. Let us have a systematic search."

They searched every corner of the desk, every inch of the room. When they had finished, Swift said — " You 'd better call in the police."

" No. Not yet. I want to hear what he says about it."

" Better not accuse him openly. I believe it 's a dangerous thing to do unless you have lots of evidence. He might bring a suit against you for defamation of character."

" I won't accuse him. Get him on the phone for me, please."

Swift did so and Eugene Clapperton, in a hard voice, asked : —

" Is that Colonel Whiteoak? "

" Yes," answered a voice, the very sound of which filled him with fury.

"Well, Colonel Whiteoak, I've something disagreeable to report."

"Oh. Are those prospective piggeries of mine already making a stink?"

"This is a serious matter, sir."

"Out with it then."

Mr. Clapperton cleared his throat. "Colonel Whiteoak, there was a pile of new twenty-dollar bills on my desk, amounting to one thousand dollars, when you were with me. Do you remember?"

"I do."

Mr. Clapperton's voice became a little shrill. "Colonel Whiteoak, that thousand dollars has been taken from my desk. It's been stolen."

There was laughter in Renny's voice as he answered: "Really? Well, that will scarcely excite you — such a small, insignificant sum."

"It is not small or insignificant. This is a very serious matter, sir."

"What are you going to do about it? Do you suspect anyone?"

"Only one person has been in that room outside of my secretary and myself."

"Who?"

"You, Colonel Whiteoak."

There was silence at the other end of the telephone for a space. Then Renny asked quietly: —

"Are you accusing me of taking that money?"

"No — no, but I thought I'd like to know what you had to say about it. I thought perhaps —"

At the other end the receiver was hung up. Eugene Clapperton waited, listened, slammed his own receiver on the hook. He twisted his fingers together. Swift could see that he was in a rage.

"What did he say, Eugene?" he asked.

" He *laughed* — as though a thousand dollars was nothing. He hung up. I'll show him whether it's nothing or not. He asked me if I accused him — then he hung up while I was still talking."

" You'll not get anything out of him."

" Do you mean that, if he took the money, I won't get it back? "

" I don't believe you will unless you can prove it and arrest him."

" What better proof do I need? I'll get a detective on the job at once." He unlocked the French window and threw it open. He drew a deep breath of the fresh air. He watched while Swift mechanically continued the search, looking again and again in the same places. He exclaimed irritably — " I wish I had my hands on that man! I'd knock his ugly red head against the wall."

Renny Whiteoak appeared in the French window.

" Did you want to see me? " he inquired.

" No — no — oh, no — that is — " Eugene Clapperton stood stammering, the color receding from his face, leaving fine reddish veins exposed on the grayness of the skin. He drew backward a pace, as Renny came into the room.

Sidney Swift's eyes were dancing. He said — " I guess there's been some sort of mistake. I guess Eugene's excited."

Mr. Clapperton, with the desk a bulwark between himself and Renny Whiteoak, said more calmly : —

" A thousand dollars has been stolen from this room, sir. Do you expect me to take that lying down? Would you take it lying down? "

" What have I to do with it? "

" I thought perhaps you could help me locate it."

" Why? "

" Well, it was here when you were here and — gone when you were gone."

Swift was looking warningly at his employer.

Renny Whiteoak exclaimed — " You are accusing me of stealing the money."

" No — I thought you might have a suggestion to offer."

" I have. Phone for the police. But let me tell you this — when this affair is cleared up it will be better for you to move away. And another thing — if I *were* going to make a thief of myself — it would take more than your God-damned thousand dollars to induce me."

The day was sultry. He was very warm. He pulled his handkerchief from his pocket and wiped his forehead. He saw Eugene Clapperton and Sidney Swift staring at something lying on the rug — staring almost with horror. His gaze followed theirs. He saw, lying flat and crisp and terribly visible, as though a spotlight were turned on it, a new twenty-dollar bank note. He stared at it bewildered. He raised his eyes to the faces of his companions, as though seeking enlightenment from them.

" Good acting," observed Mr. Clapperton. " Very good. Very convincing. You make me almost surprised myself. Very good acting."

" Why — " exclaimed Renny — " the thing was in my pocket! "

" Yes — so it was. So it was. How surprising! "

Renny bent forward and picked up the bank note. He turned it over and examined it. Then again he raised his dark bewildered eyes to Mr. Clapperton's. " How did it get into my pocket? " he asked.

" Look through your pockets," suggested Mr. Clapperton, " and perhaps you 'll find the rest of the money."

" You think I took it! " shouted Renny.

" What else could anybody think? "

" It was put in my pocket to incriminate me."

" By whom? "

He answered lamely — " I don't know." He laid the

bank note on the desk. Mr. Clapperton looked at it icily and then remarked : —

"That's one of them but where are the other forty-nine?"

Sidney Swift had been looking keenly at Renny. Now he asked — "Did you lay your jacket off after you left here, Colonel Whiteoak?"

"No. It has never been off my back."

Now, however, he took it off, turned the pockets inside out, shook it. With it still in his hand he pulled himself together. "The money must have been put in my pocket to involve me," he said. "There is no other explanation."

"Do you believe," asked Mr. Clapperton, "that that is possible?"

"I don't see how it could have been. I went straight home from here."

"What do you expect me to do in such a case?"

"Damned if I know."

"What would you do if you were in my place?"

"Think the fellow — that is, me — crazy."

"That won't bring the money back."

Again Renny mopped his forehead with his handkerchief but now the sweat that sprang on it was cold.

"Colonel Whiteoak," asked Swift, "have you ever had any lapses of memory?"

"Don't start any silly talk about lapses of memory," said Mr. Clapperton. "This either was a theft or it was n't."

"Do I look like a thief?" shouted Renny. "Have my family been thieves? By God, I don't think you're used to associating with gentlemen."

"That's an outworn word, sir."

"Not in my family."

"I'd very much like to repeat my question," said Swift. "I'd like to know if Colonel Whiteoak has had any previous lapses of memory."

"*Previous,*" sneered Mr. Clapperton. "*Previous. This is no lapse of memory.*"

Renny ignored him. "I had several insignificant lapses of memory," he said, "after my concussion."

Then it came to him, with startling clearness, how that very morning he had been thinking very hard of something — he could not remember what — while he was dressing, and had found himself in the dining room, without remembering having come down the stairs. The floor of the room where he now faced his accusers rocked with him — the little room where he and Maurice Vaughan had often had such jolly times together.

"I believe," said Swift, "that this is just another of them."

His cousin looked at him with hate. "I wish," he said, "that you 'd mind your own business."

"I thought you 'd asked me to help solve this thing."

"I did. But I did n't ask you to babble like an idiot."

Renny put on his jacket. He addressed Eugene Clapperton with dignity. "I want you," he said, "to engage a detective. Arrest me if you like. In the meantime I 'm going home." He moved, with the purposeful swiftness that characterized him, out through the French window and across the lawn.

His mind was in great confusion. He hardly knew what he was doing. The blond harvest fields that lay about him were so many blurred patches of yellow. His one clear thought was to hasten home. His one clear intention was to tell Alayne what had happened to him. Perhaps she could do something. Perhaps she could tell him whether he had shown any strange symptoms of forgetfulness since his return.

The front door was standing open. He passed through the hall and up the stairs, calling her name as he went. She answered quietly, for she was used to his sudden excitements. He found her in her room with one of Archer's socks drawn over her hand, her darning needle poised. The look on his face startled her.

" What has happened? " she asked. " Is it Archer? Is he hurt? "

" No." He drew a chair close and sat down by her side. " It 's I who am hurt — damaged. By God, I don't know what is to become of me."

" Hurt! " she repeated half-angrily, for what she saw in his face looked like temper to her. " You look all right. Where are you hurt? "

" Poor girl," he said, putting his hand on her knee, " I hate to tell you this."

Suddenly she was frightened. She sprang up. " Tell me. What is wrong? "

" Clapperton says I stole a thousand dollars from him and I 'm inclined to think I did. I 've no recollection of it. But you 've remarked how forgetful I am. I 'd a couple of lapses of memory after my concussion. Whether he is going to have me arrested, I don't know."

" Do explain this more clearly," she said, trying to swallow, for her mouth felt dry as paper. " Begin at the beginning and tell it clearly."

" Sit down," he said, and drew her to the side of the bed. They sat down together. He drew the child's sock from her hand, then held her hand to his lips.

" Oh, Alayne," he exclaimed, " this is such an idiotic thing but it 's frightening too. I could almost laugh at it but it 's deadly serious."

" *Will* you tell me what it is? What do you suppose my feelings are while you keep me in suspense? "

" I went to have a reasonable talk with Clapperton. About the village, you know. But you can't talk reasonably with that man. We were soon having words and I thought it better to leave before I was driven to lay hands on him. I had n't been long at home when he rang me up to say that a pile of bank notes amounting to a thousand dollars was missing. It had been lying on his desk while he talked. He 'd drawn my attention to it. Over the phone he all but openly accused me of stealing the money. He — "

" How dare he? " she interrupted, swept by anger. " The fool! How dare he? "

" Just listen, darling." He held her hand tightly as though he were a drowning man. " Just listen to what happened next. The car was standing in the drive. I jumped into it and was facing him in no time. Lord, it was funny for a moment! He was just saying he 'd like to knock my ugly red head against the wall when I walked in. He changed his tune, I can tell you. That Swift fellow was there and I must say he behaved more decently than Clapperton. As we talked I got pretty warm. I pulled out my handkerchief to mop my face and what do you suppose came out of my pocket with it? "

She just stared.

" A clean, crisp, twenty-dollar bill, obviously one of those that had been lying on his desk. It fell to the floor and we all stood glaring down at it."

" Oh no! " she exclaimed. " Not out of your pocket! "

" Oh, yes — right out of my pocket. Just like a conjuring trick."

" Then someone put it there," she cried fiercely.

" That 's what I said, at the first. But there was no chance of that. The jacket was never off my back. No one had been near me."

" What happened then? "

" Clapperton was tickled pink. You can imagine my feelings. Then Swift asked me if I 'd had any losses of memory. Clapperton said, ' Don't start any silly talk about loss of memory — this was either a theft or it was n't.' "

" A theft! " cried Alayne. " What a horrible man! "

" Yes. But there I stood, looking like a thief if ever a man did."

" What happened then? "

" I told him to put the police on the case — then I came home."

Her eyes searched his face. A sickening fear entered her mind but she asked calmly enough — " Renny, when you look back to your first interview with him this morning, is your mind quite clear as to all that has happened since? Do you have any feeling of haziness anywhere? Just go back over every moment."

He knitted his brow. " Yes. It 's all perfectly clear."

" Why did he accuse you? Had you been alone in the room with the money? "

" Yes. He 'd left in a huff. I believe he thought I was going to hit him but I 'd no such intention."

" Oh, that temper of yours! "

" I 'd no thought of hitting him."

" But you were angry? "

" Yes. He 'd been throwing in my teeth how little a thousand dollars meant to him and how much to me."

" I have begged you to stay away from him."

" I know you have."

" If you were angry, Renny, your mind was not quite clear."

" My mind is never clearer than when my temper is up."

" Darling, think back carefully. Have you ever had any sense of confusion in your mind since coming home? "

He made a gesture of irritation. " I don't know. I don't think so. But I 've had a lot to think of. I 've been worried about money."

" There was that check you forgot this morning. You 've been very forgetful about household accounts but that 's nothing new, goodness knows."

He sat in the silence of chagrin for a space, then he ex-claimed — "Alayne, after I had dressed this morning, I found myself in the dining room. I had no recollection of coming down the stairs."

"That is nothing!" she exclaimed, though her heart be-gan to thud painfully.

"It might be nothing if this had n't happened. But now — it's very significant." He tapped his head where the concussion had been. "I'm damaged here. By God, I'd as soon be a thief, as bound for an institution for the — "

She would not let him say the word. She flung her arms about his neck and kissed him. He pressed her to him al-most fiercely but his voice was tender. "Sweet girl," he said. "You won't let me go nutty, will you?"

She laughed, while her tears wet his face.

"No one is more sane than you," she said. "I won't hear you say such things."

He put her from him and stood up. "I must tell the uncles," he said.

She was aghast. "Oh, no, I don't think they should be told."

"They'd be sure to find out. This affair will be common property or I don't know Clapperton. I'll tell you what. I'll phone Meg and Piers and ask them to lunch. We'll talk it over together."

Again she protested but he was not to be dissuaded. She heard him go downstairs with energy. She heard his voice raised over the telephone, as he summoned the family to conclave. He was excited. He could scarcely bear to wait for their coming. He walked nervously from room to room, listening for the first sound of a car.

XVIII

CONCLAVE

For the sake of Ernest's digestion, Alayne had persuaded Renny not to disclose his reason for summoning the family, till after lunch. But the tone in which he had invited Meg and Piers was enough to make them feel considerable concern. Piers had communicated this to Pheasant, and her little face was anxious as she cast inquiring looks at the head of the table. Nicholas and Ernest were conscious of a disturbance in the atmosphere but their minds were chiefly occupied by the fact that the food was not nearly so good as usual. The soup was thin and flavorless, the cold lamb was tough. The salad cream was curdled. The blueberry tart was burnt. Certainly it was one of Mrs. Wragge's " off days," when it seemed as though a desire to spite the family possessed her. Finch was wrapped in thought concerning a concert tour which was being arranged for him and from which he shrank. He would have to work very hard in preparation for it, and he did not feel in himself the energy or power for hard work. The children had, at Alayne's suggestion, carried a picnic lunch to the woods. Both she and Renny ate little. Piers came to the conclusion that they had had a quarrel yet, when they spoke to each other, there was tenderness in their voices. No, it could not be a quarrel. Perhaps there was bad news of Wakefield.

After lunch they moved into the library and Renny himself carried in a tray on which were a decanter of Scotch, a syphon of soda, and a bottle of homemade grape wine.

" You 'll need something," he said, " to buck you up — when you hear what I have to tell you."

" What 's wrong? " exclaimed Nicholas, trying to start

up from the chair into which he had heavily dropped, and failing. "Is it Wake?"

"Don't tell me the boy is killed!" Ernest pressed his hand to his heart, the color fleeing from his face, his eyes suddenly large and very blue.

"No. Wakefield's all right. It's I who had better have been killed."

"Renny, what *are* you saying?" cried Meg.

Alayne stood with her back against the folding doors that had been closed so that Rags, clearing the table, could not overhear. Renny was being cruel, she thought, deliberately dramatizing a situation that, God knew, needed no dramatizing. But they could stand it. It was their way not to spare each other. Such blows on the spirit as this last remark only seemed to quicken every instinct of family preservation. Alayne felt deeply distressed but, at the same time, strangely interested in observing how this scene progressed, in a foregone pattern.

"I am saying," he went on, putting his hand to his head, "that I'm damaged here. My memory is playing me tricks."

"What tricks?" demanded Piers, staring at him.

"I'll tell you. I called at Vaughanlands this morning to talk to Clapperton about his building scheme. We had words and he left the room. Then I left. When he came back into the room he discovered that a thousand dollars, in new twenty-dollar bills, was missing from his desk. He rang me up and accused me of taking it."

"What's that?" said Nicholas. "Tell it again. I don't understand."

Renny repeated what had happened.

"I always said," declared Nicholas, "that he is a horrid fellow."

"You must bring an action for libel against him," said Ernest.

Meg cried — "And he's been so nice! Whatever has come over him?"

"Wait till you hear the rest," said Renny. "I went straight back to Vaughanlands. This time Clapperton's secretary was with him. We exchanged some heated remarks. I took my handkerchief from my pocket to wipe my forehead. I was blazing hot. *A twenty-dollar bill* came with the handkerchief and fell onto the floor. Incriminating evidence, eh?"

"Renny," put in Finch hoarsely, "you're not going to tell us that you'd taken the money without knowing what you did!"

"Just that."

"But you *couldn't!*" cried Meg. "Not you!"

"Why not I?"

"You've always had such a clear head."

"I suffered a bad concussion in France."

"But you've quite recovered."

"Physically, yes. But I had a couple of short lapses of memory when I was in the hospital."

"How bad were they?" asked Piers sharply.

"They were supposed to be very slight. Nothing to worry about. But, by Judas, I've plenty to worry about now."

"Renny, Renny," complained Nicholas. "Come and sit beside me and tell me this over again. You all talk so fast I can't follow you."

Renny went and sat close beside him. He said, "It appears, Uncle Nick, that I took the thousand dollars from Eugene Clapperton without knowing I was doing it — in a state of amnesia, you know. I can't remember what I did with it but evidently I left twenty dollars in my pocket with my handkerchief."

Nicholas's deep-set eyes were sombre. "This is a bad affair," he said. "Your memory gone — well, well."

Ernest said — "I find my own memory quite unreliable. I remember things that happened fifty years ago better than things that happened last year."

"I've shown signs lately of something wrong," said Renny. "This morning I couldn't remember coming downstairs. I was dressing. Then I found myself at the breakfast table — a blank in between."

"That's nothing," cried Finch. "I've often done that sort of thing."

"Later I forgot to give Alayne a check I'd promised her, didn't I, Alayne?"

"That's nothing new," she said.

"I forgot to pay the Wragges their wages. I forgot to send the vet a check for his account."

"That doesn't impress me," said Piers. "You always have forgotten to pay the vet. And not only that, how often have I had to prod you into remembering to pay me?"

Renny repeated angrily — "*Prod* me, eh?"

"Well — remind you — if you prefer that. However, you never did like paying accounts, you know."

Renny turned his head to look at him squarely. "I expect you'll go on to say that I'd have stolen from you if I'd had the chance."

"I've never had anything to steal."

Meg cried — "Piers, how dare you insinuate that our eldest brother would have taken money from you! He who has been generosity itself! He who has overpaid you — if anything! He who has given your wife and family shelter!"

"Look what *you've* done to him — by bringing this swine Clapperton into our midst."

Finch gave a hysterical laugh.

"I've always said," growled Nicholas, "that it was a mistake selling Vaughanlands to that fellow."

Now Ernest spoke. "I think," he said, "that the thing to do is for *you* to see a doctor."

"And end my days in an institution, eh?"

"No, no, dear boy. If you had to be — " He hesitated, searching his mind for a word.

"Locked up?" suggested Renny.

"No, no. We'll say *restrained*. We'd do it at Jalna."

Renny grinned. "Padded room, strait jacket — all that sort of thing, eh?"

"I don't believe," said Piers, "that there is anything wrong with you."

"Then how did the money get in my pocket?"

"Perhaps it was a kind of magnetism," said Meg. "Perhaps he unconsciously *drew* the money to him."

"Then where is all the rest of it?" asked Piers.

"God only knows," said Renny.

Piers was sitting beside a writing table where stood a papier-mâché letter holder, in which Renny kept receipts for household accounts. Piers always had liked the Chinese scene depicted on the letter holder and now he picked it up to examine it, as he had done a hundred times. He lifted it and the receipts fell out, lay scattered on the table. With an exclamation of annoyance he began to pick them up.

"I always say," reproved Ernest, "that it's better not to play with things."

Piers had stopped gathering up the receipts. He sat rigid, as though frozen into immobility.

"What's the matter?" demanded Renny sharply.

Piers hastily swept the receipts together.

Renny sprang to his side. Piers covered the papers with his hand.

"Let's see what's under your hand!"

"What are you getting up in the air about?"

"I know what is under your hand! There's no use in your trying to hide it." He caught Piers's wrist and lifted his hand, loosening the papers.

"Now what's the matter?" growled Nicholas.

" Look! " Renny dramatically pointed to where, among the receipts, lay a crisp twenty-dollar bill.

Every eye was directed toward it, as though a viper had uncurled itself on the table.

Renny sank into a chair and buried his face in his hands. There was a frozen silence. Then he raised sombre eyes.

" I wish," he said slowly, " that I 'd had a bullet through my head, rather than have come to this."

Meg came and stroked his head. " Don't say that, dear. It does n't matter what you do — we 're thankful to have you back."

" It matters to me. I 'm ruined. My reputation —"

" Now, listen," said Piers, " you 'll get over this. It is a beastly thing to face, I grant you, but we 'll face it together. I 'll take this money to Clapperton myself and have a talk with him."

" He does n't believe in a memory lapse," said Renny. " It was Swift who suggested that."

Meg was still stroking his head. " Lie down on the sofa a little," she said, " and I 'll cover you with the afghan."

" Let him alone," said Piers. " Let him think. Renny, try with all your might to go back over the morning and see if you can reconstruct everything that you did, from the moment you got up."

" I remember," put in Ernest, " a case of loss of memory in London, in the nineties. It was in all the papers. A man forgot he was married and —"

" Please don't interrupt, Uncle Ernest," said Piers. " I 'm trying to help Renny to reconstruct his movements. It 's just possible that he may be able to recall some act that will bring everything back."

" Quite so," replied Ernest. " It was with that idea in mind that I was about to tell —"

Nicholas interrupted — " Let me see that bank note."

Piers put it in his hand. Nicholas exclaimed : —

" And that horrid old fellow had fifty of these lying on his desk ! "

" Yes," answered Renny.

" And you are pretty sure you took them ? "

" I must have."

" Then where are the others ? "

" I don't know."

Meg said — " It seems foolish to return this one little bill to him."

" Here, Renny," said Nicholas, " take it, hold it in your hand. It may help you to remember."

Obediently, like a sick man, Renny took the bill, closed his eyes and sat motionless while his family looked compellingly, sympathetically, into those weather-beaten features which, in all their knowledge of him, had never before worn the expression of mute bewilderment which they now wore. Alayne could not endure it. The scene was too painful. She slipped quietly from the room, her going almost unnoticed.

He drew a deep sigh and opened his eyes. " I can't remember anything more than I have told you," he said. He laid the bill on the table.

" Perhaps later on you will be able to," Piers said cheerfully. " In the meantime I think we ought to have a search for the rest of the money. Will you turn out your pockets, Renny ? "

Obediently he emptied his pockets, not now like a sick man but like a criminal resigning himself to a search. He brought out his intimate belongings — his cigarette case, his lighter, his pencil, a shabby notebook held together by an elastic band, his wallet which, when opened, disclosed a few bills of small denomination, some silver and copper coins, the penknife that had been his father's. This his hand closed on, as though he would not be parted from it.

Ernest kept nervously pulling at the lobe of his ear.

Nicholas blew out his breath under his shaggy moustache. Pheasant wore the look of a child, present at a scene that it had no right to witness. Finch, unutterably miserable, kept his eyes fixed on the carpet.

"Nothing there," said Piers. "I think we ought to search your bedroom, Renny. You may have hidden the money in one of your drawers or in your cupboard."

"All right," said Renny, returning the articles one by one to his pockets.

"If we find the money," continued Piers, "I shall take it to Clapperton. If we find no more than this bill I shall take it to him and ask him what he's going to do. Is that all right, Renny?"

"Yes."

"What if he demands the payment of it all?" asked Ernest.

"He can't prove that Renny took it all!" cried Meg. "The first bill might have got into Renny's pocket by accident. We need not tell about the second. I don't mean we'd keep it. We'd give it to the Red Cross."

"I took the money," said Renny.

"Do you remember taking it?" asked Piers sharply.

"I remember nothing."

"You had better stay here while Finch and I go to your room." Piers spoke to him as to one who was unable to take part in the search — a sick man, a criminal — it did not matter which.

"Very well."

"Come along, Finch."

Finch followed him miserably. Up in Renny's room he said, in a shaking voice — "This is awful, Piers. I can't believe in it. To think of Renny — "

"Have you noticed anything strange in his behavior?"

"Don't ask me. If I begin to think about it I'll be sure I have."

" My God, what a family! "

Finch muttered — " I know he 's been worried about money."

Piers sighed. " That 's nothing new."

Doggedly he began to turn out the drawers. " Get busy," he ordered, " and search the cupboard."

But the most thorough search revealed nothing. They even looked under the mattress and shook the rug. When they returned to the library they heard Meg and Pheasant discussing in desultory fashion the bottling of peaches. Renny and the two old men sat silent. Ernest kept pulling at the lobe of his ear.

" Nothing up there," said Piers.

" You had better go and see Clapperton if you are going," observed Renny in an expressionless voice.

" I suppose it would be a pretty hard pull to pay back the thousand dollars? "

" Oh, he can't — he can't ! " cried Meg.

Piers turned to her. " Will you do it for him then? "

Her face fell. " Oh, I did n't mean that."

" You can well afford to."

" How do you know what I can afford? " she returned hotly.

Piers turned to Finch with a peculiarly sweet smile.

" Finch," he said, " if Meg were to repay you the fifteen thousand dollars you lent her for the mortgage on Vaughanlands, would you pay this thousand for Renny? "

" Would I? There 's nothing I 'd like better."

" Then it 's all settled. Meg will pay you and you 'll pay Clapperton."

" Will you, Meggie? " Finch asked eagerly.

" Oh Finch," she exclaimed, her eyes full of tears, " never did I think that you would bring up that debt against me — now that Maurice is gone and I am a widow, left to fight her battles alone."

" Listen to her," said Piers.

" If there is anyone I despise," said Meg, " it is the person who brings up old, unhappy far-off things."

Renny said — " I will pay Clapperton myself. I 'll sell some of the horses, if necessary."

" But I don't see why he should be paid," declared Meg. " You did n't know you were taking the money. You are not responsible. I think you should see a doctor — a psycho-analyst — and have a certificate from him that you are not responsible."

Renny gave a harsh laugh. " Thanks. I had rather pay the money to Clapperton."

Piers rose. " The first thing to do is to see him. I 'll go straight over. Coming, Finch? "

" I 'd rather not."

Ernest said — " Be polite to him. It will pay in the end."

" This is what comes," added Nicholas, " of selling Vaughanlands to a man we knew nothing about."

Mr. Clapperton was not in his house but Piers found him superintending building operations in his village. He greeted Piers coldly.

" Well," said Piers, " I 've come to ask you what you are going to do."

" I am waiting to see what your brother will do. I suppose he has told you that he took a thousand dollars off my desk."

" If he took it, he was not conscious of what he was doing. You know he had a bad injury to his head in France."

" That does n't bring the money back."

" No. But it might be well for you to remember that while you were piling up the dollars at home my brother and I have been doing our duty overseas and suffering for it."

" There was nothing I could have done over there. I have bought my share of war bonds. I 've given generously to the Red Cross."

"But not at the risk of your life."

"What do you expect me to do?" demanded Mr. Clapperton angrily. "Tell your brother to keep the money, with my blessing?"

"It would be the decent thing to do. You came here, a stranger, in his absence. You have depreciated the value of his property by your building. I believe it is worry over this village of yours that has brought on the amnesia."

Mr. Clapperton gave a groan of complete exasperation. He said — "I am not putting this case in the hands of the police. Your brother can pay me back or not — as he pleases. But if he doesn't, it's just plain dishonesty. I wonder what the countryside will think of that — if it leaks out."

"In short, you mean that you will see that it *does* leak out."

"Take that as you will."

Piers's eyes were prominent and very blue, as he returned: —

"You'll get your money, sir. And I'm willing to bet you an equal amount that your village will never be built."

"I don't want any bets with you." Eugene Clapperton stalked away. At that moment he hated all the Whiteoaks and almost wished he had never acquired the property adjoining Jalna.

Two days later he received by post a check from Renny Whiteoak for nine hundred and eighty dollars. On the intervening day Renny had discovered another twenty-dollar bank note, lying among his neckties in the small left-hand drawer of his chest of drawers. This drawer had already been carefully searched by Piers and Finch.

XIX

A CHANGED LIFE

In the three weeks that followed, a change came over the household at Jalna. A change came in the very air they breathed. At various times it had been deeply disturbed but this was a new quality. It was a quality of uncertainty. The head of the house was unsure of himself. He distrusted himself. He dreaded with primitive fear what he might do next. Each morning it came to him with a startled shock that his memory, his mind, was damaged. And this shock so clouded his mind that not all the long day was it clear again. Sometimes there arose in him a ferocious wish to tear himself free from this desolation. He would force himself to animated talk and laughter but this lively mood was so contradicted by the misery in his eyes, the drawn look about his mouth, that it was more depressing to the family than his dark mood.

During those three weeks, eight more of the twenty-dollar notes were recovered by him. He found them in the strangest places. It was uncanny the diversity of places in which he found them, and every time he found one there followed a day of gloom at Jalna. If only, Alayne and Finch often said to each other, the uncles need not have known! But they knew all and were affected by all. Every time he discovered one of the notes he hastened to inform them and to speculate wildly as to what madness would overtake him next. Constantly he begged the others to watch him, to keep him in sight, to give him no opportunity for these lapses. Yet, after a day of being constantly observed, he would probably find one of the notes next morning in some horribly whimsical place.

Though he had repaid the full amount of the theft to Eugene Clapperton, he did not look on these recovered notes as rightfully his. He would hand them over to Alayne's keeping with an air of longing to be rid of them that cut her to the heart. He spent much of his time searching for the place where the money was hidden. Over and over again he would search through cupboards and drawers where already he had searched many times. He never gave up hope, or perhaps was driven on by the weary mechanical urge of his tormented mind. He kept the house in disorder by his searching, for what he took out of drawers he returned but carelessly. One day he would take all the books from the bookshelves where Alayne, who had bought many books since her marriage, had them arranged to her taste. He would be convinced that he had hidden the notes among, or in, the books. He would open them, ruffle their leaves, and at last replace them in disorder. Perhaps, only three days later, he would again go through them, again leave them in confusion. On one occasion he turned his grandmother's room literally inside out, it suddenly being his conviction that he had hidden the money there. Doggedly, but with heavy heart, Alayne put it to rights again. Yet she would not let herself despair. She had so longed for his return from the war that she could not believe that now her peace of mind, her happiness in him, was to be shattered. Lying awake at night she would go over and over in her mind the happenings of the past weeks. She did not yet allow herself to think of the disappearance of the money as a calamity, but each week it more nearly approached that dimension.

He got the idea that he rose in his sleep, went to the hiding place of the bank notes, abstracted one, and then secreted it where he would find it on the morrow. Ernest had at one time been a sleepwalker, now Renny felt that he himself was leading a double life of night and day. On a sultry evening in late August he came to Alayne's room and, after a speculative look at the bed, said: —

"I want you to let me sleep here for a time."

She had been brushing her long hair. Now she turned and faced him, brush in hand. "But why?" she asked anxiously, fearing always some new symptom of strangeness.

"I am sure that it is at night I do these things. I want you to watch me."

She went to him and took him by the arms. "Darling," she said, "I do wish you 'd get it out of your head that you are a sleepwalker. That is an entirely different thing from memory lapses."

"Everything is wrong with my brain," he said tersely, his sombre eyes fixed on hers.

"I won't hear you say it!" she cried.

"But I know it — and so do you."

"Oh, if only you would see a doctor."

"Time enough for that." He turned away his head.

He tightened his arms about her. "May I sleep here?" he asked.

"I 'll love to have you. We shall sleep better together."

"The bed is not very wide."

"It is wide enough."

That night, with her arms about him, he had the most peaceful night he had known in weeks. But Alayne slept little. In spite of herself, the thought that he would rise in the darkness and go to the hidden hoard played cruelly on her nerves. Every time he moved a quiver ran through them, her heart quickened its beat. In the morning she looked pale and wan. But she could bear it! She could bear anything to help him.

In the afternoon Piers had a telephone call from her, asking him to come to her at once.

He found her waiting in the drawing-room where the shutters were drawn against the heat of the sun. Outside a hot wind was blowing. Piers's ruddy face was anxious.

" What 's up? " he demanded.

She pressed her knuckles against her eyes, her mouth quivered.

" Alayne — tell me! " He touched her on the shoulder.

" You must make Renny see a doctor," she got out, in a voice strangled by sobs.

" What has he done now? "

She uncovered her distraught face, controlling herself.

" Last night he slept in my room. He wanted me to be near — in case he walked in his sleep. I could swear he never left the bed. All the morning I knew just where he was. After lunch he went with Adeline to watch Wright schooling the new colt. Just before I phoned you I went to get myself a clean handkerchief and there — there among them — was one of those horrible bank notes! "

Piers stared in dismay. " Right in your drawer, eh? So — he 's begun to give them away."

" When he put it there I can't imagine. But I am driven to think he did it in the night."

" Perhaps he put it there yesterday."

" No. I know positively that it was not in that drawer when I went to bed."

" Are you going to tell him? "

" I don't know what to do. That 's why I sent for you."

Piers was pleased that she had confided in him rather than in Finch. " I should n't tell him," he said. " It might be the last straw."

" Perhaps it would make him agree to consult a specialist."

" I don't think so. Anyhow, what could a specialist do for him? This thing is in himself. Its cure is in himself."

" But we can't go on like this, Piers. It is ruining all our

lives. Oh, I shall be thankful when those girls go away to
school! They don't understand the change in him. They
don't understand the ceaseless searchings. He tells them
he is searching for an important letter he has mislaid, but
they are puzzled. I think Adeline is unhappy. I've never
known her so quiet."

"What I'm hoping," said Piers, "is that when all the
bills have turned up, he'll be better."

"The things he does are heartbreaking. I found a memo-
randum yesterday on his desk, giving the dates when he had
found each of the bills and just where. He thinks of little
else. He's afraid of what he will do next. Oh, Piers, I'd
a thousand times rather he had left a leg over there, as you
have, than have suffered such an injury as this."

"He'll get over it."

"I don't see what reason you have for thinking so."

"Well, he's physically very fit. He's at home, where he
wants to be. It's nature's wish to heal us." There was a
silence, then he added — "Alayne, there's something I
think I ought to tell you. People are beginning to talk.
Clapperton and that secretary of his have not kept this affair
to themselves — as decent men would have done."

"Oh, how cruel! We must never let him know."

"He does know. Rags has dropped a hint. Noah Binns
made some sly remark. Yesterday Renny said to me —
'You've got to read the Lessons in church next Sunday. I
can't stand up there in front of people reading the Scriptures
and everyone thinking I'm a thief — or completely nutty.'
I tried to reason him out of it but he wouldn't listen. You
know what he is when he gets an idea in that red head of
his."

"Oh, his poor head!" moaned Alayne.

"Who can wonder if he thinks everyone is looking at him
in suspicion. God, I don't know what I'd do if I were in his
place!"

" You'd get medical advice," said Alayne, " and he must." She did not hear the step in the hall.

Renny's voice exclaimed from the doorway — " So — you're discussing me as usual! "

Piers faced him sternly. " Well, we're driven to it, aren't we? You don't get any better and you refuse to see a doctor. Do you expect Alayne to chatter about the newest fashions? Do you expect me to keep my mind on my work? "

" Do you honestly think," asked Renny, his dark eyes on Piers, " that a neurologist could help me remember what I did with that money? The truth now! "

" He might help you. Even if it took him months."

Renny said quietly — " I have tried to remember till my brain has all but cracked. If it is probed into by some cursed quack — it will be the last straw." He pressed his fingers to that part of his head that had suffered the concussion. " It is here that I'm damaged. If you keep on harassing me about it, you'll drive me to wish I'd been finished over there." He wheeled and left the room. They heard him run up the stairs.

Piers came and put his arms about Alayne. His strong hand beat gently on her back. " There's one thing," he said, " we must not do, and that is to get hopeless about this. We've got to keep *our* courage up. Some day we shall find the money — or he'll suddenly remember where he hid it. You must lean on me, Alayne. We'll bring old redhead through this — safe and sound."

XX

OTHELLO

ADELINE was fast developing into something more than a child. She was growing tall and, beneath her thin summer clothes, charming curves of her young growth could be glimpsed. But her mind was troubled. The delight in Renny's companionship which she had so long strained toward was turning to bewilderment and sometimes to fear. What was wrong she could not guess. She did guess that the letter for which he was always searching had something to do with the change in him, but surely no letter was so important that its loss could so alter him. He had been so lively, so happy to have her with him when he had first come home, but now, more than once, she had seen him turn aside rather than meet her. At other times he would hold her close, looking down into her eyes with that strange shadowed look in his. Once when she had come up behind his chair he had caught her hands in his and held them against his head. He had said, in a muffled voice, unlike his : —

" Keep your hands there, Adeline. Perhaps it will help me."

She had held his head between her hands and asked — " Does your head hurt, Daddy? "

He had been silent a moment and then answered : —

" Yes."

Another time, when he had met her in the pine wood, he had said abruptly — " When you see me coming into the wood alone, follow me. Watch what I am doing. Don't leave me alone."

These words had been like a cold hand laid on her heart.

It was only when he was watching Wright school the new colt that he was his old self. At those times Adeline delighted in being with him. But when Spartan was led away the shadowed look returned to his eyes. He would sigh deeply, run his hand across his head, on which the dark red hair grew thick and strong, and turn away with an air of weariness. He had sold several horses to raise money for expenses, and at a poor price. But he did not seem to mind. Often he was taciturn or irritable. Roma and Archer kept out of his way.

In these days Adeline drew nearer to Maurice. On his part he found a new pleasure in her company. When he had returned to Jalna he had thought of her as a healthy romping schoolgirl, no more. But now she became interesting to him. They took long walks together. He found her more indulgent to the egotism of his young manhood than was Patience. She had a better mind, he thought, than Patience had — or Garda Griffith. Her face, when it was animated, fascinated him. When it was quiet, with that new sadness, it held him in wonder. He tried to draw her on to confide in him, to tell him what troubled her.

One afternoon, as they sat together beneath a wild cherry tree at the edge of the wood, he said: —

"You're growing up, Adeline."

"I ought to," she answered tersely. "I'm fourteen."

"You look more, to-day."

"That's funny. I mean — growing suddenly older in a day."

Maurice gave a little laugh. "Well, I suppose it's been going on all the summer, but I noticed it particularly when I saw you coming toward me on the path."

She ran her hand over the moss on which they sat, smoothing it. "It's funny," she said, "how all the grass has died under this tree and moss has grown instead."

"It's pretty. Like green velvet. Look, here's a yellow

leaf lying on it.   Summer is going.   You'll soon be back at
school.   I shall miss you."

"Will you?"   She looked gratified.   "I shall miss you
too, Maurice.   I get tired of hordes of girls.   They're
boring.   They talk of movie stars and having boy friends."

"Well, I'm a boy, are n't I?"

"Not in that way.   It's silly."

"But we're friends."

"We're cousins.   It's different."

Maurice stretched out on the moss and looked up into
her eyes.

"Do you know, Adeline," he said, "I'm eighteen and
I've never had a sweetheart."

"You show your good sense," she said.   "It's silly."

"You're enough of a sweetheart for me," he returned
laughing.   He rolled on to his back and stared up into the
tree where little black cherries hung thick.

She laughed too.   "I'm a funny sort of sweetheart."

"I don't think you're funny.   I think you're very
pretty."

She was embarrassed by his praise.   She picked up a
cherry from the moss and put it into her mouth.   She
said: —

"Archer is not allowed to come near this tree.   He eats
the cherries and they give him a pain.   But he comes just
the same.   He's always making himself sick on fruit."

"Kids are a beastly nuisance.   Philip is.   He won't do
anything Mother or I tell him but he's as smooth as silk to
Father.   Just a little cherub.   Father thinks he's perfect.
Yet I can do nothing right."

"You don't want to be thought a little cherub, do you?"

Maurice did not smile.   "My father has always been
down on me," he said.

"Has he?" she exclaimed, in astonishment.   "I never
knew that.   Why was he down on you?"

" I don't know. Yes — I do, in a way. When I was a kid he despised me for being afraid of horses. Now that I 'm grown-up — well, I guess we 're just uncongenial."

" What a pity! My father and I get along marvelously well. At least we used to."

Maurice looked at her curiously. He asked — " Do you think he 's quite well? "

" What do you mean, quite well? "

" Oh, nothing. But he had that concussion — it must have been pretty bad."

" That 's all over. But he worries about an important letter he 's lost."

" Oh." Maurice went on — " If it were n't for my mother I should be unhappy at home."

" She 's awfully sweet. I love Auntie Pheasant."

" When I go back to Ireland I 'm going to take her with me for a long visit. She 's never traveled. I wish you could come too, Adeline."

Her face was alight at the very thought. " Oh, don't I wish I could! I had the best time of my life when I went to Ireland with Daddy."

" Then why don't you come? I 'm sure your father would let you. Let 's see. You 'd be seventeen then."

She threw herself on the moss beside him and rolled there in blissful anticipation. " Oh, Maurice, how marvelous it would be! I 'd meet Pat Crawshay again."

" You certainly would. He 's never forgotten you."

" He was sweet."

" He 's my best friend. My only friend."

" I thought Sidney Swift was your friend too."

" Oh, yes, he is. But he 's older. We get on well but my father is scarcely civil to him. It makes it difficult for me because Sidney is so much at the house."

" He has a funny way of looking at one," Adeline said dreamily.

"He admires you. He thinks you're a little beauty. Perhaps I shouldn't have told you that."

The vivid color sprang to her cheeks. "That's silly," she said. "I don't think I'm a bit pretty. Roma's pretty."

"Roma's a kid."

After a silence he said — "Next week Sidney and I are going to see *Othello*. Paul Robeson, the Negro actor, is going to play the part. Sidney says he's first-rate."

"How marvelous!" she said, fervently. "Don't I wish I could!"

"You wouldn't like a Shakespearean play. They're too old for you."

"You make me tired! They're not too old for me! Uncle Finch has told me about seeing *Hamlet* and *King Lear* and *Richard the Second* in London. They're not too old."

"Then, you're too young."

"We take Shakespeare at school! *Midsummer Night's Dream* — *Romeo and Juliet* — but it's silly. Too much love-making. Oh, how I wish I could go with you! Do let me! Please, Maurice."

"Upon my word, Adeline," he said, "I'd like to take you but I don't think the play is suitable."

"Why?" she demanded, sitting up and staring at him. "I know more than you think. I'm not a baby."

"But this is real tragedy."

"I suppose you think I'm afraid of seeing people killed. I'm not a bit. Have you seen the play?"

"No. But — a husband strangles his wife because he's jealous. It's pretty awful."

"What had she done?"

"He believed she'd given away a handkerchief that he greatly valued. To a beast named Iago."

"It seems a little thing to kill a woman for."

"He was crazed by jealousy."

" Did he love his wife? "

" Madly.   That 's why he killed her."

"Goodness."   Adeline sat lost in thought.   Then she asked — " Did she love him? "

" With all her heart.   She was faithful to him."

" *Faithful,* eh? "   Adeline pondered on the word. " Then what became of him? "

" He ran a dagger into his heart."

She whistled, then added — " But Shakespeare nearly always killed his people off, did n't he? "

" In the tragedies, yes."

" I 'd love to see it."

" Your mother would never let you."

" But she wants me to be intellectual."

" She 'd never agree to your seeing this play."

A dancing sparkle lit Adeline's eyes.   "Mummie need n't know."

" How the dickens would you expect to manage that? "

" We could pretend you were taking me to the movies."

" No, no.   I could n't do that."

She scrambled to her knees, facing him, with flushed cheeks.

" Maurice, if you don't take me I 'll think you 're the meanest boy that ever lived!   You must take me!   You must!   Oh, if you knew how much I want to go, you 'd never refuse me!   I 'm dying to see Paul Robeson act.   I 've heard records of his singing.   And I do so want to see him in *Othello*.   No one has taken me anywhere in these holidays.   Mummie does n't like me to see those horrible war films.   But she did speak of my seeing one about a dog — ' Lassie Come Home,' I think is the name of it.   You could say you were taking me to it."

" I 'm to do the lying, eh? "

" It would be just a little lie, Mooey.   And you told me, only the other day, that you don't in the least mind telling a lie if it makes anyone happier. Just think how happy one tiny lie would make me!"

Maurice pulled up a small cushion of moss, examined it, and carefully replaced it. "It's a good thing," he said slowly, "that I have n't mentioned at home that Swift and I are going to *Othello*."

She went to him, moving with body upright but on her knees. She flung herself on him.

"Oh, Mooey, what an angel you are! As long as I live I 'll never forget that you did this for me. For the rest of my life I 'll do whatever you ask me to."

He put his arms about her. "See that you remember that promise," he said.

An hour later when he and his tutor were seated with their books before them, Maurice said: —

"My young cousin, Adeline, has coaxed me into taking her to see *Othello*. Do you mind if she comes with us?"

Swift smiled amiably. "Of course I don't mind. I 'd like to see a young girl's reaction to the situation."

"I should n't have promised her," said Maurice. "I 'm afraid it is n't the sort of play she should see."

"For God's sake," exclaimed Swift, "don't be so Edwardian! Adeline is no baby. Considering what the world is, the sooner she develops the better. It will be fascinating to watch her."

"It 's got to be kept dark. I 'm to say I 'm taking her to a movie. So don't forget and spill the beans."

"I shall not forget."

"You spoke the other day of our reading *Othello* before we see it. I 'd like to begin it to-day."

Swift was silent a moment, then he said — "I had rather read it with you after you 've seen it. You 'll appreciate it much more."

"But the other day you said just the opposite."

"I 'm always contradicting myself," said Swift testily.

" I wish you would n't remind me of it. It 's amazing that you 've never read the play. But after all, I 'd rather you would hear the wonder of the lines straight from the actors' lips and read them afterward." He leaned back in his chair and, with dreamy eyes, recited : —

> " 'T is true; there 's magic in the web of it:
> A sibyl, that had number'd in the world
> The sun to course two hundred compasses,
> In her prophetic fury sew'd the work;
> The worms were hallow'd that did breed the silk;
> And it was dyed in mummy which the skilful
> Conserved of maidens' hearts."

" The play is all about love, is n't it ? " said Maurice.

" About love and nothing else," returned Swift, smiling. " It will be good for Adeline to see what high emotion can be. For God's sake, don't let her awakening be in terms of moving pictures ! "

They saw Piers standing in the doorway. " Hard at work, eh ? " he said, sarcastically.

" Just getting down to it," smiled Swift.

In the kitchen where Pheasant was washing salad, Piers remarked — " I 'm glad I 'm not paying that tutor. I think he 's no good as a teacher, and I think he 's bad for Mooey. He ought to have a manly, middle-aged tutor."

" Mooey thinks Sidney Swift is very clever. He likes him."

" I 'm sure he does." Piers spoke with ironic heartiness. " He 's just the sort of fellow Mooey would admire — and imitate." He took out his pipe and filled it. Then he added — " Well, Mooey is n't very congenial to me now. I don't know how it will be with us when Swift gets through with him."

" I 'm afraid Mooey is like me."

" He 's not a bit like you. You are congenial to me, are n't you ? "

"If Mooey had been a girl, it would have been different."

Piers lighted his pipe and threw the burnt match on the floor.

"It would not have been in the least different," he said. "What were you like as a girl? Were you afraid of horses? No. You'd ride anything on four legs. You rode in a horse show not many months before Mooey was born."

"Perhaps that's why he hates riding."

Piers ignored this. He continued — "Were you always moping about with a book under your arm? No. Were you self-opinionated and la-di-da? No. If you had been any of these things I'd never have married you."

"You couldn't have helped yourself," said Pheasant. "I'd have married you."

A few days later Maurice remarked casually to his mother — "Swift and I are going to town to see a show of some sort on Monday night. I'm taking Adeline with me. She hasn't been about much in her holidays and she goes back to school on Wednesday."

"That will be nice for her." Pheasant was pleased by his thoughtfulness. "You must be careful to choose a nice film. Her mother is very particular about what she sees."

Maurice gave a little grunt.

"I do wish," Pheasant went on, "that I could go to *Othello*. It's to be here next week, you know. But good seats are so expensive."

Maurice bit his knuckle, not looking at her. Then he said — "I'll take you. We'll go toward the end of the week."

"Oh, Mooey, I wasn't hinting," she cried.

"I know you weren't, Mummie. But my allowance is quite decent and there aren't many ways of spending it out here. Do you think Father would like to go?"

"No, no. Shakespeare bores him. But how lovely it will be for us to go together!" She flung both arms about him. "Mooey, whatever girl gets you is going to be lucky."

"No girl is going to get me in a hurry," he laughed. "I guess I'll wait for Adeline."

"That would be a lovely match. Everyone would be pleased. The way she's coming on I don't think you'd have many years to wait."

In these days Adeline was living in a dream. Hour by hour she ticked off the days, straining toward the great night. She had lied to Alayne. She had tried hard not to lie. It had hurt her to lie with her mother's candid blue eyes on her. But she was cornered. She had been forced to say what film Maurice had asked her to see before Alayne would give her consent. Alayne was satisfied by the choice.

Once the lie was told, Adeline put it out of her mind. She would make it up to her mother by perfect behavior to the last day of the holidays. She took extra care in making her bed. She ran errands cheerfully. She even darned Archer's socks, which was a trial to her.

She led Ernest on to talk of *Othello*.

"I think the best Othello I ever saw," he said, "was Matheson Lang. What a voice! What grandeur he added to Shakespeare's words! Dear child, I was enraptured."

"They say Paul Robeson has a wonderful voice."

"I dare say but — I don't want to see him in the part. No Negro could be convincing to me as the Moor. An Englishman, with his face blackened, looks the part much more. You see I've been to Morocco."

"You've had a wonderful life, Uncle Ernest." Her eyes were full of admiration.

Ernest was gratified. "Yes, indeed I have, Adeline. I have had wide experience. Life on two continents. Travel. A keen interest in art, through many years. Art in all its forms. It's a great solace in one's old age."

"When I'm older will you let me read your book on Shakespeare?"

"I shall be delighted to, Adeline. I hope to finish it within the next year or so."

"Have you come to *Othello* yet?"

Ernest could not help looking pleased with himself. "One of my best chapters is on *Othello*. This is the point I emphasized — that no matter how great the passion two lovers have for each other, nothing can make them one. They are two separate beings to the end. And that is their tragedy. This is beyond you. But some day you'll understand, dear child."

She was silent, trying to survey with her inner eye the mysterious future that lay before her.

Hour by hour she pressed forward to the night of *Othello*. She began to feel that here was a turning point in her life. For one thing it would be the first play of Shakespeare's she had seen. For another it was the first occasion when she had gone out in the evening without her mother or one of her uncles. She was being carefully brought up. She wished it were just she and Maurice who were going. She thought she did not like Sidney Swift.

Yet, when on the night of the play she climbed into the car, he smiled at her in such a friendly, intimate way that she changed her mind. It might be good fun having him along. Renny and Alayne stood on the steps to see them off. Adeline suddenly felt as though she were going a long way from them, as though she were leaving on a voyage. Perhaps it was because she had lied about where she was going. She did wish she hadn't been obliged to do that.

"Good-bye," said Alayne, "and I do hope you'll enjoy yourselves."

"I wish you were coming with us, Mrs. Whiteoak," said Swift.

Adeline thought, He doesn't know Mooey and I are deceiving her.

"Film plays don't interest me," answered Alayne.

" What is the play? " Renny asked absently.

Maurice and Adeline each waited for the other to answer. She felt her cheeks burning.

" ' Lassie Come Home,' " returned Swift, smiling.

He does know, thought Adeline, and he does n't a bit mind lying!

" See that you don't miss that last train, Mooey," called out Renny as the car moved down the drive.

It was not far to the station and they had not long to wait. Seated in the train between the two young men, Adeline abandoned herself to the rich anticipated pleasure of the night. The train was crowded, most of the passengers being soldiers. Even the aisles were full of them. When they looked at Adeline she looked back, without timidity and without boldness. Maurice and Swift talked a little to each other across her. Sometimes they gave her a smiling look. It was so obvious that to her this was a great occasion.

In the city there was the ride in the tram, then they were in the brightly lighted lobby of the theatre. Maurice already had the tickets. Adeline had a feeling that he had paid for Swift's ticket, which seemed hardly fair. Swift was older and a tutor. He should have bought his own ticket. Adeline had heard that he was a sponge.

The theatre was filling fast. They had excellent seats. Maurice disliked any but the best. Now they were seated, with Adeline in the middle. She took off her little hat, laid it on her lap, and looked happily about her. Maurice leaned toward Swift and said: —

" My father and mother came here to a play the evening after they were married. They ran away, you know."

" Yes? " said Swift. " I wonder what was the play they saw."

" It was a Russian musical show. *Chauve Souris,* they called it."

" I 'll bet she had a great thrill out of it."

" Not more than I 'm having out of this," put in Adeline.

Swift looked down into her face. " It 's thrill enough for me," he said, " just to watch you." He could not keep his eyes off her but she was unconscious of this. She was watching the orchestra take their places. Now they were playing " God Save the King." The audience rose. Adeline stood at attention, her eyes steady, her hands at her sides.

Now the curtain was up. The street in Venice was discovered. Roderigo and Iago were plotting. Now the stalwart figure of the Moor appeared. His simplicity, his dignity, the grandeur of his voice went straight to Adeline's heart. She was fiercely on his side. She could not understand how any man could be as wicked as Iago. In the first interval she asked : —

" But how *can* he be so wicked? "

" He 's scarcely human," returned Swift. " He 's almost disembodied cruelty, delighting in suffering." He could not keep his thoughts from Adeline. As the play went on, he imagined he saw her emerging from childhood to womanhood before his eyes. He pictured her as a flower bud forced open by the fierce passions of the play. Did she understand the half of its implications, he wondered. Maurice's cheeks burned. He wished, with all his heart, he had not brought her. She was the only child in the audience. In the intermission people were staring at her. He felt angry at Swift for letting him bring her. He threw him an accusing look as they were smoking a cigarette in the foyer. They had left Adeline in her seat.

" If I 'd had any idea — " Maurice said grimly.

" Idea of what? "

" You know what I mean."

" If you mean that some of the expressions used are n't fit for a *nice* young girl to hear, you can stop worrying.

Adeline is too excited about the play to notice them and would n't understand if she did."

" I hope not."

When they were back in their seats, Maurice asked Adeline if she were still enjoying the play.

" Oh, yes, even more. But I don't understand how Othello can be so cruel to Desdemona. He's so splendid and he really loves her."

" I suppose jealousy made him brutal."

The curtain rose. Adeline gave her passionate attention to the players. As the climax in its horror drew near, Swift was aware that Adeline's body was rigid. It strained upward, as though she would rise and fly to the stage and take part in the scene. When the massive Moor in his sumptuous robe drew near the bed on which Desdemona slept, and said : —

> " I 'll not shed her blood ;
> Nor scar that whiter skin of hers than snow,
> And smooth as monumental alabaster.
> Yet she must die, else she 'll betray more men.
> Put out the light, and then put out the light" . . .

Swift groped for Adeline's hand in the dark, found it, and held it close. Again his mind was on her rather than on the play and he felt a cruel pleasure in her pain. Yet he longed to comfort her — to kiss her — hold her in his arms.

When the final curtain fell she seemed too dazed to realize that all was over. Maurice had to find her hat, which had fallen to the floor. Even the cool night air did not change her. They went to a restaurant and ordered sandwiches and coffee. Adeline shaded her eyes with her hand. She could not eat but drank the coffee. Now and again Swift glanced at her. He and Maurice discussed the play in low tones. On the homeward journey in the train, she sat silent looking out into the night, seeing there the tragedy re-enacted. The young men were silent too. Maurice was troubled by seeing how deeply Adeline had been stirred. Swift was sensually savoring his own emotion, thinking that never before had he felt like this toward a girl.

At the gate of Jalna, Swift said — "If you'd like to get on, Maurice, I'll take Adeline to the door and then take the path through the ravine, home."

"Is that all right, Adeline?" asked Maurice.

"I don't need anyone to take me."

"Yes, you do," said Swift. "It's very dark."

They got out of the car and watched Maurice drive away. The countryside was deeply quiet. The moon, past its prime, had risen but still was hidden behind the trees. The great hemlocks and balsams that bordered the drive made it a black tunnel. Swift took Adeline's hand and led her into it.

"I don't want to lose you," he said, trying to appear natural.

Her fingers clung to his but she said — "I couldn't possibly get lost here. I know it like I know the palm of my hand."

"I've been looking at your hands to-night and I think they're the loveliest I've ever seen."

She was pleased. "I got them from my great-grandmother. She lived to be a hundred and two."

"I hope you don't do that." There was a tremor in his voice. "I can't bear the thought of age in connection with you. I want you to live to your perfect maturity — then no more."

"That's a funny wish."

They were halfway along the drive. "Shall we stop here for a bit and talk? It seems a shame to go indoors after such an evening. You did enjoy it, didn't you, Adeline?"

She drew her hand from his and laid it against the trunk

of a hemlock.   She said — " I 'll never feel the same again.
Everything will seem different."

" You really saw to-night," he said, " how glorious and
how terrible love can be.   Have you thought much about
love ? "

" No.   I 'm too young."

He gave a little laugh.   " Well, I 'm not so young but it
seems to me I 've never really thought about it till to-night."

" But you 'd seen that play before ! "

" It was n't the play."

There was a silence, vibrant with the mysterious sounds
of the night.

" I wish I could explain you to yourself," he said, " and
explain the effect you have on me."   He thought a moment,
then he went on — " I can imagine a time when the soul
wandered through every part of the human body and every
part expressed the feeling of the soul.   But now that time
has disappeared and it 's only the rare person who shows
obedience to the soul — even to the finger tips — like a kind
of rhythm running through every movement.   You are one
of those people.   Do you understand what I mean ? "

" A little."

" The faces of most young girls and most women are
empty.   If you looked behind them you 'd find nothing.
But yours is different.   I can't find out what 's there.   Not
yet.   Is this queer sort of talk?   But, oh, Adeline, I want
to find out!   I want to be the first to show you love."

He took her in his arms and pressed his lips to her cheek.
He put his hand on the back of her head and forced her face
toward his.   Now his passionate kisses were on her lips.
For a moment she was too confused, too astonished to struggle.   Then a sickening consciousness of the difference between this embrace and any that ever had been given her by
the family, galvanized her.   She became a fury of resistance.
Swift was startled, enraged by her strength.   She was like a

strong boy. In the darkness he felt blind anger and desire. They wrestled, clasped together, like some nocturnal animal moving beneath the trees.

Freeing her lips she cried out — " Don't! Don't! "

He exclaimed — " Don't you be a little fool! "

Renny, who had been unwilling to go to bed till Adeline was safely home, had wandered some distance from the house. Hearing the engine of the car he had hastened back to meet her. The padding of his steps across the lawn was unheard by the two. He pushed through the heavy boughs of the evergreens and was upon them, all his being alight with fury for the protection of his child.

He caught Swift by the collar and jerked him away from Adeline.

" Take this," he said, almost quietly, and began to strike Swift repeatedly.

" Oh, Daddy! " gasped Adeline. " Oh, Daddy! " She did not know whether she cried out in relief at his coming or terror that he would kill Swift. It was so dark she could see nothing, but could just hear the thud of blows and Swift's exclamations of rage and pain. He was helpless in Renny's hands.

As Renny pushed him between the evergreens to the lawn, the moon rose above the treetops and sent a flood of silver light over house and lawn. It showed Swift standing with distorted face, one side of it covered with blood. Renny stood near by him, his attitude still threatening. In a strangled voice, Swift got out : —

" You God-damned brute! I 'll get even with you for this! "

" What? " exclaimed Renny, advancing a step. " What? Get even with *me?* If I broke every bone in your body, it would be no more than you deserve. Now, get out! "

Swift turned, and crossed the lawn toward the road. He took out his handkerchief and mopped the blood from his face. He kept muttering in helpless rage as he went.

Adeline, in terrified fascination, had followed the men to the lawn. Renny turned to her.

"Come," he said.

She moved toward him as though she would cast herself into his arms but he held her off.

"I want to talk to you," he said. "Come into the house."

He saw that she had dropped her little evening bag and he picked it up. Alayne had given it to her on her last birthday. It was the first thing of the sort she had possessed and she had cherished it. But now, seeing it lying on the ground, she felt nothing and would have gone into the house and left it there.

She followed Renny meekly, feeling dazed. They went quietly into the hall where the light still burned. The rest of the house slept in darkness. He led the way to the grandmother's room, which Adeline now occupied, and turned on the light there. It looked strange to the child. Even her father's face seemed the face of a stranger as he looked searchingly into her eyes and said: —

"It's lucky for you that you struggled against that man."

She stared up at him speechless.

Anger against her flared into his eyes. "Why don't you say something?" he demanded. "What did you do to encourage him? Men don't behave like that without some encouragement. Did you let him make love to you? What were you talking about? What did he say to you?"

Her eyes looked large and tragic against her white face. "I don't know."

"Yes, you do! What had he been saying to you?"

"He'd — been talking about — "

"Yes? Go on."

"About my soul."

"Your *soul!* Good God! What else?"

"About the play and about how terribly Othello loved Desdemona . . . I think . . . I'm not sure."

"Othello! That man took you to see *Othello?*"

She had forgotten the deception, the lie. She hung her head. "Yes."

He sprang forward and took her by the shoulders. "You said you were going to a moving picture, and all the while you knew it was to be *Othello?*"

"Yes."

"Was Maurice there?"

"Yes."

"You lied to your mother and to me. You went to a play you knew we'd not let you see. You spooned with that fellow in the dark — "

"No!" she shouted hoarsely. "I didn't do that!"

He looked wildly about the room. His grandmother's gold-headed ebony stick stood in a corner. Adeline had liked to see it there. Renny strode to it, grasped it, and returned to her.

"No, no, Daddy!" she cried, in terror.

Three times he brought down the stick on her back.

The door was thrown open and Alayne stood there in her nightdress. She threw herself on him. She thought: "He has gone out of his mind! Perhaps he will kill us." Who would come to her help? There were the two old men on the floor above and, far away on the top floor, Finch. Below in the basement there was Wragge. And Renny was so strong. With all her power she clung to him.

But he stood quietly now. He said, in a calm voice: —

"You don't understand, Alayne."

"What is wrong?" she asked piteously.

"It's this girl — our daughter," he answered harshly. "She's lied to us to-night. She did not go to a moving picture as she said she was, but went with Swift to see

Othello. Othello, mind you! I waited up for her. I came on them in the darkness — in the black darkness of the drive — struggling together. It is well for her, I told her, that she was resisting him."

An immense wave of relief swept over Alayne. His manner, his look, showed that he was sane. Nothing else seemed to matter. She took the ebony stick from his hand and replaced it in its corner. He stood quiet, his eyes fixed on Adeline. She had a white, stricken look.

Alayne spoke with authority. " Go to your room, Adeline. It's very late for you. I'll come up in a few minutes."

Adeline raised her eyes to Renny's face.

" Go up to bed," he said.

She left the room, closing the door behind her.

Scarcely was the door shut when Alayne broke out: " Oh, how could you, Renny? How could you?"

" I had to," he muttered. " I'll make her more careful in the future."

" But what were they doing?"

" It was dark, I tell you, and she was saying, ' Don't — don't!' How can I tell what led up to that?"

" Do you know how long they had been there?"

" Perhaps a quarter of an hour. I heard the car. I was down on the bridge. I came up and heard their voices."

" Did she seem frightened?"

" Yes."

" But why are you so angry with her?"

He said violently — " Do you expect me to pat my daughter on the back when she has lied about where she spent the evening? How do I know what encouragement she gave that man? You have seen *Othello.* You saw it with me — as a married woman. What do you think of the lines — of the scenes — for a young girl's entertainment? She saw a *Negro* in the part! What do you think of that?"

"I think Adeline is an innocent child. I'm as sorry as you are that—"

"As sorry as I am!" he broke in. "If you were nearly as sorry as I am, you would n't stand there—as cool as a cucumber. I tell you, I'll take a stick to her back every time she steps off the beeline I shall lay down for her!"

"We can't have scenes like this. I have faith in Adeline. She has a strong nature."

"What do you know of the life of to-day?"

"I know something of human nature," she answered steadily. "I've been married to two Whiteoaks and lived in your family for twenty years."

"That has nothing to do with this case," he said. He laid his hands on the footboard of the bed and stared at the head with its painted flowers and fruit. A sudden picture of his grandmother lying in the bed came before him. A smile crossed his face.

Alayne looked down at his hands. She exclaimed in horror—"What is that on your hand?"

He looked at his left hand.

"No! The other one!"

He spread it out. "That! It's blood."

She had been pale but now every vestige of color left her face. She did not speak but just looked at him in horror.

"That swine Swift's blood. I'll wager he'll keep away from here in future."

"Oh." Her breath escaped in a sharp exhalation.

He turned toward her. "What did you think? That it was Adeline's blood?"

"I don't know what I thought," she answered, controlling herself, "but I want you to go this instant and wash it off."

"Very well."

"Do you know what we did?" she exclaimed. "We forgot that Adeline sleeps in this room now and sent her upstairs to bed! I scarcely knew what I was saying."

"It is small wonder if our minds are confused," he said. "Where do you suppose she has gone?"

"I'll find her and bring her back to her room."

"No petting, mind. She's in disgrace."

Alayne ignored this and left the room. He also left, going down the basement stairs as though it were noonday and not the middle of the night.

Alayne saw Adeline sitting on the top step of the stairs, her forehead against her knees. Alayne laid her hand on the newel post. She felt weak and shaken. She called softly:—

"Adeline, come down. When your father and I sent you upstairs we forgot that you sleep in Grandmother's room. You must come back and go to bed."

Adeline rose obediently and descended the stairs. When her face was on a level with her mother's, Alayne looked into it with a pang. It was so pale, so frightened. Poor child, she had had a shock. Alayne laid her hand on her daughter's shoulder.

"You see what a night you have brought on us all," she said.

Adeline's face was contorted as though she were about to cry but she did not dare to begin to cry. She was afraid of what she might do.

"Adeline, promise me that never — never in your life — will you do such a thing again."

"I promise." Stifling a sob she pushed past Alayne and ran into her room, shutting the door behind her.

Alayne thought — "If only she had thrown herself into my arms! But never shall we be near each other." Her thoughts flew back to herself at Adeline's age, the well-ordered life of an only child with her loving parents, the confidence between herself and her mother, the long talks, the complete understanding, the gentleness of her father. Now, in this house, she had given birth to children she could not understand. She loved a man whose nature was as mysterious to her as a storm-swept cavern by the sea. She climbed the stairs slowly and went to her room.

In the little washroom in the basement, Renny turned the rasping taps on and off. As he dried his hands on the rough towel he exclaimed aloud — "By God, I wish I'd given him more! I let him off too easy. I've a mind to go over to Vaughanlands and pull him out of bed and thrash him again."

A scuffling step sounded on the brick floor of the passage. Rags appeared in the doorway in his pyjamas. Through a rent in the jacket his thin shoulder protruded.

"Was you wanting anything, sir?" he inquired, with an inquisitive look.

Renny let the water run from the basin and threw the towel into it. "No. Did I wake you?"

"Well, I'm not sure, sir. But it ain't usual for you to be washing down 'ere at this hour."

"Don't ever have a daughter, Rags."

"Trust me, sir."

"Boys are all right but girls —"

"There isn't a finer little lidy in the countryside than Miss Adeline, sir. I 'ope she 'asn't been doing anythink to annoy you, sir."

"Oh, not especially, but I hate to see her growing up, at this particular time."

"It's a lousy world, sir, and no mistake."

"Well, go back to bed, Rags. The night's well on."

"Couldn't I get you a drink of something?"

"No, no, go to bed."

Renny ascended the stairs. Outside Adeline's room he stopped and listened. There was no sound within. For a moment he had an impulse to go in and make her repeat to him the happenings of the evening from first to last. By some overpowering act of his own to cleanse her from Swift's touch. His own little girl. His anger welled up against young Maurice who had exposed her to this by his carelessness — his lying. Perhaps it all had been arranged between Swift and him. Who knew what Maurice really was?

He strode into the library and took the receiver from the telephone. He asked for the number he wanted. The bell buzzed several times, then Maurice's voice answered.

" Is that you, Maurice? "

" Yes, Uncle Renny."

" Still up, eh? "

" Yes. I was reading."

" Reading *Othello,* I suppose."

There was a moment's silence, then Maurice answered: —
" Yes."

Renny exclaimed, in a voice harsh with anger — " I won't trouble telling you what I think of you. Send your father to the phone."

" Uncle Renny, please let me explain."

" I don't want any of your explanations! " shouted Renny. " Send Piers to the phone."

" But he 's in bed asleep. It 's past two o'clock."

" What the hell do I care what time it is! Tell him I want to speak to him."

" But Uncle Renny — "

" If you don't send him to the phone I 'll drive over there and rouse him myself."

" Very well."

Renny sat motionless, a grim smile on his lips, waiting for Piers's voice. It came.

" Hullo, Renny. What 's the matter? "

" I wish you were here. I 'd like to talk to you."

" What 's wrong? "

" Everything."

Piers now spoke with false composure. " Please tell me what you want me to do. Do you want me at Jalna? "

Renny unleashed the anger in his voice. "No. I just want you to thrash your eldest son for me."

"What has he done?"

"He did n't tell you?"

"No."

"Well, he took my daughter to see a Negro actor in *Othello* to-night. Rather a sensual play for a very young girl, is n't it? But he did n't tell me he was taking her. Nor you nor his mother, I 'll bet. He said he was taking her to a movie. Swift went with them. Maurice left Swift to bring Adeline to the house. I found them in the pitch-dark in the drive — struggling together. He 'd been trying to make love to her. This is what Maurice exposed my daughter to."

"What did you do?"

"Gave Swift something to remember and took Gran's stick to Adeline's back."

"Gosh!"

"Is that all you have to say?"

"You must n't take it too seriously, Renny."

"What — what?" shouted Renny.

"Hang on to yourself. What I mean is, Adeline will forget this — or almost forget it — if you 'll let her."

"My God, I wish you had a daughter — then you 'd know how I feel!"

"I have an eldest son who is a disappointment. He always was spineless, and living with that old man in Ireland did him no good. I 've always disliked Swift. He 'll never come into my house again. As for Maurice — I 'll tell him what I think of him."

"Tell him from me that he 's not to see Adeline — nor speak to her for the rest of the holidays."

"All right. You 'd better go to bed now, old man."

"I 'll not go to bed to-night. What would be the use? I could n't sleep."

" Tch! Was Adeline much upset? "

" Yes."

" Poor kid! She could n't know what was going to happen."

" Go and hold poor little Mooey's hand and tell him how sorry you are for him! "

" Don't imagine I'm not angry about this, Renny. If you were here you would n't be disappointed in what I'll say to him. Good night."

" Good night."

Renny turned out the lights and went upstairs. A light was still burning in Alayne's room. He tapped on the door.

" Come in."

She had put on a dressing gown, for the night had suddenly turned chill. She was shaking a tablet from a bottle.

" A sedative," she said. " Will you have one? "

" A dozen."

" Don't be foolish." She gave him one and a drink to take it in.

" I've been telephoning Piers," he said.

" Oh, no! " she exclaimed reproachfully. " Not at this hour! "

" Did you imagine that I should let Maurice have a comfortable night's sleep after what he did? "

" I suppose not." She sighed deeply. " What did Piers say? "

" He did n't say a great deal, but he'll give Maurice a piece of his mind."

" I could not have believed this of Maurice. I think Sidney Swift has been very bad for him."

" When Meg sold Vaughanlands to Clapperton, she did a bad day's work for us." The name " Clapperton " brought the theft like the touch of a cold hand on his heart. The corrugations on his forehead hardened. Alayne came to his

side, where he had seated himself in front of her dressing
table, and began to stroke them.

"I think I should go down to Adeline," she said, knowing he would not let her. "She may be crying."

"Let her cry."

"Oh, Renny, you should not have done what you did!
If my father had laid a hand on me, I'd have died. But I
can't imagine him doing such a thing."

"Can you imagine yourself giving him such cause?"
he asked sombrely.

For answer she sneezed.

"You are catching cold," he exclaimed, "and no wonder
— going about in your bare feet."

She put out her hand across him and opened the top drawer
of her dressing table to get a handkerchief.

She opened the drawer, looked in, and quickly shut it
again. "They are not in that drawer after all," she said.

"Why did you shut that drawer?" he demanded.

He put his hand on the knob to open it.

She did not answer but held the drawer shut.

"I know," he said, his voice hoarse with anger and hate
for himself. "I know. You don't need to tell me. I
saw it. It's another of those cursed twenty-dollar bills."

Her arm dropped to her side. She let him open the
drawer. Lying on top of the little pile of handkerchiefs in
the left-hand compartment was the crisp new note, the figures
"20" standing out on the greenish-yellow ground like a
menace, the face of the King like a calm rebuke.

Renny took it out and looked at it.

"In your room," he said. "I have put it here in your
room. Alayne, is this the first time you have found one of
the notes here?"

"There was one other," she answered, not looking at him,
"about ten days ago. I couldn't bear to tell you."

"Why don't you watch me more closely?" he broke out.

"Nobody watches me! I'm allowed to drift about in my derangement——"

"You are *not* deranged!" she interrupted. "I won't let you use that word."

"Tell me a word then. Give me a word, for God's sake, that will describe me!"

He looked so wild that she was frightened. She put her arms about him and clasped his head to her breast. She felt his hot tears on her breast.

"Oh, don't, don't, darling!" She was crying too. "I can't bear it."

He raised his eyes, wet with tears, to her face.

"It looks," he said, "as though you are to be the mother of a wanton and the wife of a——"

"Be careful! I will not hear you say such things!"

He closed his eyes, resting his head against her breast, listening to the beating of her heart. "Very well," he said, resignedly. "I won't say them."

"You know they're not true."

"Oh, Alayne, if only I could find where I've hidden that money!"

"You will. I know you will. Quite unexpectedly you'll come on it and everything will be cleared up."

"Everything but my mind," he returned bitterly.

She spoke with confidence. "Your mind will be clear too."

He drew away from her and took a notebook from his pocket. In it he entered, in his small firm handwriting, the fact that another of the notes had been found, and where, with the date. After that he went to his own room to undress. Alayne stole down to Adeline's door. It was locked. She asked——"Would you like me to come in, Adeline?"

The child's voice answered quietly——"No thanks, Mummie. I'm all right."

"Would you like something to eat, or a drink?"

" No thanks."

" Good night, then."

" Good night."

The first intangible essence of the day crept into Alayne's room, the first bird notes sounded among the late summer leaves before Renny slept, with Alayne's arm about him. Still she lay awake.

XXI

PIERS AND HIS SON

PIERS turned from the telephone and took up his crutches. Awkwardly he ascended the stairs and went toward Maurice's room, one leg of his pyjamas dangling empty. Pheasant intercepted him.

" Mooey says it was Renny on the phone."

" It was," answered Piers, moving on.

" Why could n't he have waited till morning, when he knows it 's hard for you going up and down the stairs without your leg? "

" Because he was in a rage, and no wonder."

" Whatever has happened? He 's not angry at Mooey, is he? "

" He certainly is." Piers went into his son's room and shut the door after him.

Maurice was sitting by a table on which there was a reading lamp, making a pretense of reading. He raised his eyes guardedly to Piers's face.

" Reading *Othello,* I see," remarked Piers, pleasantly.

" Yes. I am."

" Did n't get enough of it at the theatre, eh? "

Maurice was silent. A tremor of fear ran through him. He had been so afraid of Piers when he was a child. Now, standing there on his crutches, his healthy face flushed with anger, he was almost as intimidating as ever. He said: —

" You ought to be ashamed of yourself. I should think you would have had more sense than to take a child like Adeline to see such a play as *Othello.*"

" I did n't think it would hurt her."

" And you did n't think it would hurt her to be made love to by Swift? "

" How was I to know he would make love to her? "

" You should have taken her home yourself. You must have a pretty good idea of what sort of man he is. It was a damned stupid thing to do and I am ashamed of you."

" I 'm sorry." Maurice made the apology perfunctorily. Piers was more irritated than appeased by it.

He said —— " Being sorry won't help poor little Adeline. Her father took a stick to her back."

" No! " Maurice was aghast. " Surely not! "

"He did. And I won't say she did n't deserve it. But I will say you deserved it more."

" It was cruel. I don't see how Uncle Renny could do it."

" Well, you know, he is very like our grandmother and she was always ready to give us a rap with her stick. There was the gold-headed stick standing ready and Renny laid it on Adeline in the good old family tradition." Piers chuckled.

A rush of anger brought Maurice to his feet. He walked excitedly about the room with clenched hands.

" I hate such scenes! " he said hotly.

" The trouble with you is that you 're spoilt. That old man in Ireland completely spoilt you."

" I shall not be sorry to go back there."

" It 's just the place for you," returned Piers pleasantly. " An old ivy-covered mansion, on the point of tumbling down — a few tottering retainers to touch their forelocks to you — a friend or two like Swift, to sponge on you. Upon my word, Mooey, I don't know how I ever got you."

They stared at one another in their hostility. Then Piers added — " I won't have Swift about the place any longer. In the morning I 'll tell him to go."

" All right.   I don't care."

" Another thing.   You are to go to Jalna right after breakfast, and apologize to Renny."

Maurice bowed coldly.

" Renny says you are not to see Adeline again before she goes back to school.   Understand? "

" Yes."

" Now, go to bed.   Make up your mind to turn over a new leaf.   See if you can be a little more manly — a little less self-centred.   Good night."

He turned, leaning on his crutches, opened the door, and stumped back to Pheasant.

Maurice did not undress.   In his anger and his humiliation he threw himself on the bed, grinding his head into the pillow, clutching the bedclothes in his hands.   In the blackness behind his closed eyes his father's fresh-colored face with that ironic smile stood out.   Maurice had felt secure in his homecoming.   He had, as his support, the cherished years of his life at Glengorman.   He was almost a man.   He had patronized Pheasant and the little boys.   A father, returning after years in a German prison camp, surely was no longer one to intimidate.   He was proud of his father. They might even become friends.

Yet soon their relations were much as they had always been, excepting that a new resentment was added on either side — on Piers's side because Maurice now had the aloofness of a young man; on Maurice's, because that aloofness was so vulnerable.   He lay, with nerves tense, seething in his resentment.   Adeline's image rose before him, as her enchanted gaze was fixed upon the stage.

At last he slept and woke late to hear his young brothers scuffling in the next bedroom.   For an instant he was bewildered to find himself lying fully dressed on the bed. Then the happenings of the night returned to him, and with them the consciousness that his head ached and that he was very hot. And there was his father to face! And the apology to Renny. He got to his feet and pressed his fingers against his temples. The noise from the next room increased. He undressed and dressed again in loose flannel trousers and jersey. He went to the bathroom and laved his head and face with cold water. On the way back he looked in at the small boys while he dried his hair with a rough towel. Their room was in disorder. As Nooky put the sheets on the bed, Philip pulled them off. They whacked each other with the pillows. Philip's cheeks were bright pink, his fair hair waved upright. Nooky's face was a delicate pink all over and his fine straight hair fell over his forehead. Maurice regarded them pessimistically.

" Where 's Father? " he asked.

At that instant Piers's voice came from below.

" Boys! Come to the head of the stairs! "

Close to each other, as though for support, they went as they were bid. Philip's face assumed a look of sweet obedience.

Piers looked up at them. " I want you," he said, " to get on with your work. If I call you down here, you 'll be sorry."

" Yes, Daddy," said Philip, sweetly and cheerfully. Nooky hung his head, speechless.

Piers stood staring up at them. They turned humbly and re-entered the bedroom. Once there, Philip leaped on Nooky's back and they crashed as one body to the floor. There was a roar from below. They rose and, grasping the bedclothes, began to hurl them with passionate eagerness on to the bed.

Maurice turned from the scene with distaste. He went to his own room, brushed his hair, and, hearing Piers go out through the front door, went down to the dining room. The teapot had been left for him, and toast and marmalade. He wanted nothing but tea. He poured himself a cup and lighted a cigarette. Through the window he could see Pheasant working in the garden. There was quite a wind, and her hair was blowing back from her face.

His cigarette was just half-smoked when Piers came into the room through another door. Maurice felt himself start and his start was obvious to Piers. He came and sat down at the table facing Maurice.

Maurice thought — " Good Lord, is he going to begin again? "

Piers looked at him thoughtfully. He said: —

" Remember what I have told you. When you 've finished your breakfast you are to go and apologize to your Uncle Renny."

" Can't I do it by phone? "

" No. And you are not to speak to Adeline."

Maurice pushed his chair from the table. " I 've been told all this before."

Piers still looked thoughtfully at him. " There is something else I must tell you," he said. " There is to be no unpleasantness in the house over this affair. You are to be cheerful with me and I 'm to be cheerful with you."

Maurice stared at him suspiciously. What was he driving at?

" Your mother is not to be worried," Piers went on. " She 's had more than her share of anxiety in the past. Now she 's to be made as happy as possible. She 's going to have a child."

Maurice stared at Piers, dumbfounded.

Piers laughed. " Well — what 's so remarkable about that? Other women have babies. Why not she? "

The color deepened in Maurice's cheeks. " Of course — of course," he stammered, but could think of nothing else to say. He had a sense of shock, of outrage, of calculated injury to himself.

Piers laughed again but this time it was more of a chuckle. "Upon my word," he said, "one would think you were hearing of the facts of life for the first time."

"It 's just that — "

"Would n't you like a little sister?" Piers's voice now had a cajoling tone. "Come now, tell Daddy you 'd like a baby sister."

At that moment Maurice hated Piers. He rose stiffly. "I guess I 'd better be off."

The smile left Piers's face. He said — "I rang up Swift this morning and told him — that is, I told Clapperton to tell him — that his services as tutor will not be needed any longer. Swift is *indisposed,* Clapperton says."

"Oh. All right. Well, I guess I 'll go." He left the room, hurried out of the house by a door where he would not be seen by Pheasant, and turned in the direction of Jalna. Bitterness welled up in him. His mother . . . his mother . . . Oh, he could not bear to think of it! It was horrible. It was indecent. That brute — that cocksure, smiling brute — to do this to her — and laugh about it! If he had been asked to guess a thousand things that might have happened, surely this would be the last to enter his mind.

As he neared Jalna the humiliation of what he had to do, the dread of what Renny's reception of him might be, drove all other thoughts from his mind. The sweet, dry, playful breeze of late summer refreshed him. As he turned from the dusty road into a path leading across the fields, he noticed how extraordinarily dry everything was. The triumphant sun, after having given life to the season's growth, now was sucking it away, leaving dry, rustling leaves, parched grass, and only those wild flowers whose harsh fibrous stalks made them insensible to drought. So the goldenrod, the Michaelmas daisy, and the pale blue chicory flourished. Like the essence of the dry light air made palpable, thistledown and the fluff of milkweed floated high and low. Bees

sought in haste for the ever-decreasing honey. A myriad
crickets chirped and the insistent orchestra of the locusts
made the most of this last act before the falling of the final
curtain. An old crab-apple tree, standing alone in the field,
bore a luxuriant crop of little apples, with a silver bloom on
their red cheeks. Maurice began to feel less unhappy. He
saw Wright in the meadow adjoining and, climbing the fence,
intercepted him.

" Can you tell me where my uncle is? " he asked.

" Colonel Whiteoak? "

" Yes."

Wright pointed with his thumb toward the stables. " In
his office. He's searching for that there letter he lost, if
you know what I mean." Wright's broad face was heavy
with gloom.

" Oh, yes. Thank you. I'll go there." Maurice spoke
in his light, impersonal voice. Wright looked after him
glumly.

Maurice thought — " He's never had any respect for me
just because I don't like riding." He hastened to the stable,
eager to get the misery of the apology over with.

He found Renny in his little office, where the desk was
heaped with papers, every drawer emptied out, even the
wall cupboard disgorged of its contents. That morning he
had found one of the twenty-dollar notes in his ledger.

Maurice pulled himself together.

" Good morning, Uncle Renny."

Renny turned toward him absently. He scarcely seemed
to see him.

Maurice went on — " I've come to tell you how sorry
I am about last night. I'm terribly sorry about the whole
thing. I should have known better."

" Yes, yes, you should have known better. It was a
damned stupid thing to do. Don't ever do anything like

that again. You don't know what it might lead to." He stood staring at the littered desk.

"How tired he looks," thought Maurice, and suddenly instead of feeling afraid of Renny he felt sorry for him. He felt a warmth, a kindness, springing from him. If only his father had been like Renny, he felt he might have got on with him.

Renny said — "I suppose you 've heard something of how Clapperton's money disappeared."

"Yes," answered Maurice, coloring.

"By God, everyone has heard of that!"

"Are you looking for it here, Uncle Renny?"

"Yes. I — well, I had a sudden idea that it might be here. I 've emptied out everything, as you see, but — " he pressed his hand to his head — " my brain is so tired I think I may have overlooked it. Now I want you to go through the papers on this desk, very carefully, and make sure it is n't here. I 'll search the cupboard again."

Maurice, relieved at the turn the interview had taken, yet deeply embarrassed, began the search. Neither spoke. From the stable came the sound of a steady clatter of hoofs as a horse was led out, and, from a stall, a low whinny.

Maurice gave an exclamation. Renny turned sharply.

"Look, Uncle Renny." He had opened a little brass stamp box. In it, folded very small, was a bank note. It was folded so that the King's face looked out at them, the head nobly held, as in a frame.

Renny took the box and extracted the note. "That 's two this morning," he muttered. He sat down at the desk and drew his wallet and a notebook from his pocket. He placed the twenty-dollar bill in the wallet and made a neat entry in the notebook. He returned both to his pocket, then looked up at Maurice with a smile that was more like a grimace of pain.

"You have a crackpot for an uncle," he said. "I hope you're proud of him."

Maurice could think of nothing to say but stammered, "I'm terribly sorry, Uncle Renny."

"Yes. So are we all."

It was indeed terrible to Maurice to have this disgraceful and frightening thing, about which he and his mother had spoken in whispers, about which he and Swift had speculated in careful undertones, brought into the open and himself alone in this box of a room with the perpetrator — the victim — whatever you might call him. And he was n't asking for a special sympathy — just including himself in the family group who were sorry that this calamity had overtaken them. And that look in his eyes, that were so like Adeline's. Maurice had not noticed the resemblance before.

Renny rose abruptly. He went to the cupboard and took out a bottle with a little Scotch in it and poured himself a drink. "You'd be surprised," he said, "if you knew how these things unnerve me."

Maurice felt a rush of gratitude and love toward him. He had been so decent about last night. He was suffering.

Maurice asked — "Shall I tidy the papers, Uncle Renny?"

"No. I'll put them away." He set down the empty glass and looking at the litter on the desk, as though the sight of it were hateful to him, gathered it in handfuls and thrust it back into the drawers. "Now let's go out into the sun."

Outside he threw back his head and took a deep breath. The three dogs ran to greet him and he bent down, fondling them. "Good old boys! No — bad old boys! You have noses. Why don't you smell it out? What does all this fuss over me mean? Nothing! Get busy with your nose, Jock! Smell it out, Bill!" He caught up the little cairn and kissed it. "Why don't you help me, little rascal? No — you think of nothing but bunnies and mice."

Suddenly Maurice saw Adeline standing quite near them

on the path. He was startled by her pallor and by the bluish shadows beneath her eyes, but her lips were red, with a feverish look. She looked unusually tidy and her cotton dress was obviously fresh that morning. Renny did not see her but went on fondling the dogs, pulling Jock's topknot, scratching Bill behind the ears, while the cairn was vainly striving to lick his face.

Maurice and Adeline stood looking at each other. With a gesture of his hand toward Renny and a shake of the head Maurice tried to tell her that they were not to speak. She seemed to understand. She nodded gravely but drew a little nearer. Renny straightened himself and saw her.

" Well," he said, as though to himself, " I must be off." He turned toward the paddock where Wright could be seen schooling the colt.

Adeline moved quickly to him. She ran beside him looking up into his face. Then she slipped her hand into his and Maurice saw his fingers close on it. He saw them fall into step with an air of complete harmony.

XXII
RENNY AND HIS DAUGHTER

RENNY, with Adeline's hand in his, hesitated for only a short
while by the paddock to watch Wright's skillful handling
of the colt, then turned across a field to where a group of
young alders made a small shade by the stream. The stream
was very shallow because of the drought but still it was active,
hurrying over the pebbles as though to gain the shade of the
ravine. He dropped to the edge of the bank, his legs hanging over it. She sat close to him. She felt the sun on her
bare legs and arms. She saw the sun on his thin muscular
hand and she dared be happy, though with a tremulous happiness, as though at any moment the cloud of his anger would
darken her sky. He turned to look into her eyes. She
returned his look with the complete surrender of childhood.

" Adeline," he said, " I am afraid you will think I was
very hard on you last night."

" No, no," she said, in a muffled voice. " It was all
right."

" Parents don't do that sort of thing nowadays." He
tried to make her smile by smiling at her but her lips were
moulded in gravity.

She said, in Ernest's very tone — " If they did more of it,
there would n't be so much juvenile delinquency."

He could not endure that. He took her in his arms and
held her close for a moment. She thought — " Always,
always I shall remember this. I shall think — ' How much
happier I was then! ' Or I shall think — ' How much more
miserable I was then! ' I don't know which I am but — I
shall always remember."

"It infuriated me," he said, "that Swift should lay a hand on you."

Her eyes flashed. "But I was n't to blame, Daddy."

"Can you say that out of your very bones?"

"Yes."

"What do you feel about him now?"

"I hate him."

"Why?"

The question, thrown so vehemently at her, took from her the power of thought for a moment. She could not speak.

"Why?" he repeated.

Now she could think and answered with decision, "Because he led me into trouble with you."

He looked at her keenly. "That's a good answer."

After a silence, he asked — "Adeline, do I seem different to you from what I used to be?"

"A little."

"A little! You mean a lot. I'm terribly worried about something. I can't tell you the cause. But perhaps when you come home for the Christmas holidays, you'll find me a better companion."

"What I want is to be with you!" she exclaimed. "Always. To be at Jalna with you. Or, if I go anywhere — to have you come with me."

"Stick to that for the next seven years and I'll be a happy man."

"I will stick to it always." She pressed her face to his shoulder. "Daddy, will you let me help you search for the letter? I will never stop searching all day, not till I find it, I promise you."

"If I have n't found it when you come back from school, I'll tell you everything."

"Is it *really* a letter?"

"Don't ask questions. I can't explain it to you — not yet."

She did not leave his side all the morning. They came in to lunch hand in hand. There was a complete understanding between them, Alayne thought. Adeline might lie to him, might do things in direct opposition to his wishes, he might take a stick to her back as he had last night, still there would be complete understanding between them. The hot sunshine, the fresh air, had brought color to Adeline's cheeks, but Alayne looked ill. She had spent the morning going over Adeline's clothes, in preparation for school. She had discovered shoes that should have been taken to the shoemaker for mending long ago, stockings that should have been darned, tunics that should have been mended. Roma had an entirely new school outfit — an added expense — to say nothing of the doubling of the large fees. Roma was in a blissful daze. To be going off to school with Adeline was a felicity she had not hoped for. Archer showed no sign of missing either girl. His mind seemed concentrated on the fact that he was to be the only child at Jalna, with an unquestioned field for his egotism.

The last morning came, with the bustle of luggage being carried downstairs, the continual running up and down and in and out of the children, the unheeded advice, the tips from the uncles, the hugs, the glibly given promises. Adeline, thought Alayne, was made of hardy fibre. She looked, she seemed, as resilient as ever. But she did not see her as she stood alone saying good-bye to her room, her dear room, in which she had spent a night of the despair a child can know. Morning had brought a lifting of that despair, being restored to Renny's love had made her well, for indeed she had felt ill. But the night had left its mark on her. She carried a scar on her heart which all the joy of coming years would never quite erase. In her thoughts she did not separate the events of the night. *Othello* — the supper in the restaurant — the journey home — Swift's strange talk, his hot embrace — Renny's violence — were so closely woven as to be inseparable, making a confused, a chaotic pattern in her memory.

Now she stood on the platform of the country station as the train, with hissing and roaring, came to a stop. She wore her school tunic, her long black stockings and black shoes. She carried her coat, her box of tuck given by Mrs. Wragge, and her badminton racket. Her hair, flung back from her forehead, rippled like a pennant. Roma, similarly equipped, stood close beside her. Archer, clinging to his father's sleeve, hopped up and down in his excitement.

" Got your tickets safe? " demanded Renny.

" Yes." Roma patted her pocket. Adeline showed her ticket between her teeth.

" Right. Don't swallow it."

Heads of other children showed at the windows. Renny put the two aboard. Archer scrambled up the steps after them and had to be lifted down just as the train started. Adeline, peering out the window, saw them standing hand in hand on the platform. The train swept her away. Eager chattering schoolgirls surrounded her. They fired questions at her.

" Hello, Adeline! Who is your friend? "

" Is she your sister? "

" Is she the cousin you 've talked about? "

" What 's her name? Has she been to school before? "

" Did you have fun in the holidays? I had a super time."

" So did I! "

" So did I! "

Adeline smiled but she groaned inwardly. Girls — girls — and more girls — teachers — games — Scripture — exams! Another term!

XXIII

THE PROPOSAL

Two depressed gentlemen sat facing each other across the luncheon table at Vaughanlands the day after the notable performance of *Othello*. The face of each was so distasteful to the other that he could scarcely bear to look at it. Eugene Clapperton's face was sallow, his eyes tired and his thin lips compressed. He felt that his troubles, since coming to this place, were so unreasonable, so endless. He had come intending to be a friend to everyone, a beneficent influence in the community. His reward had been hostility from the Whiteoaks, the really dreadful upset over the theft, and now this attack on his young cousin. He sympathized with Sidney, yet he was disgusted with him. Sidney should have known better than to have been drawn into an exchange of hot words with Renny Whiteoak, who was a violent and dangerous man, if ever there was one. Sidney had not made clear to Eugene Clapperton just what had happened. It was all very muddled and doubtless he had lied. One thing was certain — he had got a severe beating. It had been a shock to go to his bedroom to call him and find him lying there with one eye completely closed, the other badly swollen, his lip cut, and a basin of bloodstained water on the washing stand. It had been a frightening climax to a series of depressing events. He wished Sidney had remained in bed. No one could enjoy a meal with that face opposite, with those disgusting noises Sidney made drawing in his soup from the spoon.

" I wish you 'd let me send for the doctor," he said.

" I don't want a doctor," mumbled Swift.

" You 're sure there are no bones broken? "

" Positive."

" That man should be arrested for assault. There is nothing I 'd like better than to see him brought into court. I let him off once.   It 's a shame to allow him to get away with this."

" He 's crazy."

" Will you agree to a charge being laid against him? "

" I do wish you 'd let me alone! " exclaimed Swift petulantly.   He laid down his spoon and made no further pretense of eating.

Eugene Clapperton leaned across the table, fixing the young man with a cold gray eye, and demanded: —

" Sidney, what did you do to make Colonel Whiteoak attack you? "

Swift exclaimed through his swollen lips — " I was kissing Adeline!   Is there any harm in that? "

The older man colored.   He rose and walked nervously about the room.   " You should n't have done that.   She 's not one of these common girls who will kiss any fellow. Her people are n't that sort of people.   They 're well-bred. I don't like the way this sounds, Sidney."

Swift felt like telling him to go to hell, but he only grunted.

Eugene Clapperton said — " I hate to look at you, Sidney. You 're a terrible sight."

Swift could have screamed, but was silent.

" I had a phone call from Piers Whiteoak this morning," went on his cousin.   " He does n't want you to continue with the tutoring."

" He 's fired me? "

" Yes."

" I don't give a damn."

Eugene Clapperton eyed him coldly.

" I should think you 'd be very much humiliated, Sidney. I 'm worried by all this upset."

"Don't worry about me. I can look after myself."

"So far you have not shown much disposition to do so."
Swift began to cry. "If you knew how miserable I
feel," he said, "you'd pity me, instead of finding fault."

"I do pity you but you have brought all this on yourself.
Now go and rest. I'll stroll over to the fox farm and
have a chat with the Griffiths. They always cheer me up."
He laid a comforting hand on Swift's shoulder, but he
wriggled beneath it like a spoilt boy.

"My goodness," continued Clapperton, "you are getting
a very black eye!"

He went off, leaving Swift in a ferment. For himself,
he felt better. By the time he reached the fox farm he was
almost cheerful. The path was springy beneath his feet.
The thick golden sunshine tinted everything its own hue.
It was a lazy golden world among the trees, the air vibrating
with the trill of insects whose movements were unseen and
whose voices only intensified the sense of remoteness.
Gemmel Griffith sat in a deck chair on the little lawn which
had been freshly mowed by Garda. The sweet scent of the
cut grass met Eugene Clapperton as her figure came into
view. The moment he saw her he was conscious of the
new posture she had gained since the operation. She sat
differently, with a new awareness of the power of her body,
of its responsibilities. Before that she had moved like a
fish in the sea, without responsibility, drifting, careless of
others. But now the lives of others pressed in on her. She
was forced to think of them in a new, personal way. She
had used to plan for her sisters, always leaving herself out.
But now she must plan for herself. Her body had been
given freedom but her spirit was now chained to the life of
movement and fact.

As she saw Eugene Clapperton's figure approaching, a
shiver ran through her. It was partly excitement at the
coming of the man who had done so much for her, partly

fear at the thought that he desired to do more. He had done enough! Let him stop there — at the barrier. She wanted no more.

He waved his hand and called out gayly : —

" Good afternoon! My, what a picture you make! If I were an artist I 'd paint you."

She held out her hand, turning her face upward in the old familiar movement. She greeted him shyly. He took her hand and sat down in an uncomfortable rustic chair made of cedar saplings.

" I hope I am not disturbing happy daydreams," he said, caressing her with his small light eyes.

" You are always welcome," she returned, with the old-fashioned dignity of her upbringing.

" That 's fine." He drew a little closer. " There was never a time when I needed your friendship more."

" Oh. I hope there is nothing wrong." Never, she thought, could she speak familiarly to him.

" I 'm worried. But I did n't come here to talk about myself. How many steps have you taken to-day? "

" Seventeen. And without much help from Garda. The doctor says I shall be walking about like anyone else in a few months."

" You 'll never be like anyone else. You 're unique."

" I suppose I am — in a way." She spoke pensively.

" In every way," he insisted. " I 'd like to show you off — let the world see you. How would you like to go to Victoria — have a look at the Rockies? Or go down to Quebec? "

" I 'd love it."

" When this war is over I 'm going to do some traveling. I 've always promised myself that. Also I must have a complete change. This is the darnedest place I 've ever known. It gets on my nerves. It 's Whiteoaks whatever way I turn. I 've got to have something new in my life."

"Must you wait till the war is over? Could n't you go away now?"

"It 's impossible. But I am worried. I 'll tell you what happened last night. Colonel Whiteoak gave Sidney a regular beating. You ought to see him. It 's disgraceful. But, mind you, I have sympathy for the man, much as I dislike him. He caught Sidney kissing his young daughter in the dark. He 'd taken her to a play before that. Sidney says it was quite innocent but evidently that redheaded ruffian did n't agree."

"Why, Adeline is only a child!" exclaimed Gemmel.

"Yes. That 's why I 'm sorry this happened."

"I 've always envied her." Gemmel drew the image of Adeline before her and gazed at it, rapt. "I don't know what there is about her but I 've envied her more than anyone I know."

He patted her knee. "You 've no cause to envy a living person now, Gem. You 're perfect."

She made a restive movement. "You say Renny Whiteoak struck Sidney! Sidney would hate that. He is so abominably careful of himself."

"Sidney is no coward." Eugene Clapperton spoke defensively. "Whiteoak is a very intimidating man. I hate the sight of him."

"He has been very kind to us."

"Kind to you? How? In what way?"

"This house is his. He has never taken a penny in rent for it in all these years."

Eugene Clapperton stared in astonishment. "No rent! Well — I never! No rent! Why should he let you live rent free?"

"I guess he is just naturally generous."

"I don't want his generosity for you. I 'd like to get you away from this house."

Garda appeared, carrying a wineglass in which there was a raw egg, with a little sherry on it.

" Time for your egg! " she exclaimed. " Good afternoon. Mr. Clapperton."

" Eugene," he corrected.

" Oh, yes — Eugene." She gave him her warm smile. " Now, take the egg, Gem."

Gemmel held the glass, where the golden egg yolk floated like a little globe in the transparent white. " Please look the other way," she said.

Obediently they looked up into the trees. She took the glass in both hands, put the rim to her lips, opened her mouth wide, and the golden globe disappeared.

" It 's down," she said.

Their eyes returned to her, expectant, as though strength had already been added to her from the egg. She returned the glass to Garda. " Don't go," she said.

" I must. I 'm in the middle of ironing." Her cheeks were hot, her palms red from her work.

When she had gone, Clapperton exclaimed : —

" Poor child! I wish I could see a better future for her. She has no chance here in the country, pinned down to the drudgery of housework."

" I know," Gemmel answered despondently.

" And Althea. She would get over that terrible shyness if she went about and saw new places and met new people. She 's crippled mentally as you were physically. I want to look after you three girlies. I want you to have a good time. But you, above all, Gem. I 've been waiting for months to ask you." He bent close and whispered in her ear — " Will you marry me, Gem, little girl? "

He was conferring another great favor on her. She heard that in his voice, read it in the slanting glimpse she had of his face. She had only to put out her hand and accept the blessings of security for Althea and Garda, who had devoted their lives to her. She could give them their chance to be what nature had designed them for — not slaves to her but free, out of reach of the restrictions of poverty. Even though she soon would be well and would no longer need their care, what could they do? They were not fitted to take a part in the struggle of the new world that was shaping about them. She could lift the burden of their support from the shoulders of Molly. All her fear, her shrinking, melted away from her, leaving her as impersonal as the egg in the wineglass. She felt herself ready to be disposed of, swallowed in one gulp by Eugene Clapperton. And she would make him so happy!

She was eager to get it over with. She tilted her head so that her eyes looked straight into his.

" Yes — I will," she answered in her sweet voice with its Welsh intonation.

He had greatly feared she would refuse him, she was so oddly aloof, with the shyness of a wild creature, and now her assent filled him with an exhilaration he had not felt in many years. He had even forgotten that he could feel it. As he gathered her in his arms it swept through him like a spring wind, blowing away the worries and irritations of the past months. His joy, his gratification, even included Althea and Garda. He would take the three sisters to be the young life of his home. Sidney must go. One of the girls could act as secretary. Above all, above all, here was Gem in his arms, her lovely dark head on his breast. Gem, restored to health, poised to take her first steps into real life, always under his guidance, her welfare the first object of his existence, always to do exactly as he told her, which naturally would be for her good.

XXIV

AFTER DARK

THE Griffiths sat close together in their living room three evenings later. They sat close, as though some outside force had threatened to separate them. Gemmel would have been almost unseen in the last of the twilight but for her quick gestures, the familiar turning of her head on her long graceful neck. Garda was more visible because she was in white. Althea's face and hands, because of the extreme fairness of her skin, showed most clearly.

"Everything is going to be different now," she said. "This little home, in the middle of this little wood, can never be the same."

"It will be empty," said Garda. "How strange! Are you sure Eugene wants Althea and me to move to Vaughan-lands?"

"He does," Gemmel answered positively. "He says so. There's plenty of room there."

"It will be heavenly," said Garda. "Eugene is so generous. He's a wonderful man. It will take the three of us the rest of our lives to repay him for what he has done and will do."

"I hate being grateful to a man," said Althea.

Garda laughed. "Then you are different from me. I find myself being grateful to men just for their existing. The world would be awful without them."

"It would make no difference to me," said Althea, "if they all were swept away."

"But you do like Eugene, don't you?" Gemmel asked anxiously. "If you don't, I will not go on with the engagement."

" What an idiotic thing to say! Of course I like Eugene.
I think he 's the most generous being I 've ever met. And I
want you to marry him and do all the things you 've longed
to do."

" Gem," put in Garda, " that was a funny thing to say,
for a woman who is in love. You should be ready to go on
with the marriage, even if Althea and I were dead set
against it."

Gem lighted a cigarette. The flame of the match illuminated her face for an instant. " I 'm not like other women!
I 've been dependent on you two for so long that I could n't
go against you. You 've been my physical legs till you 've
become my spiritual legs as well."

" I hate gratitude," said Althea. " It 's sickening from
you. Why should you be grateful to Eugene? He 's getting what they call in this country ' a great kick ' out of all
he does for you."

" I think Gem loves him for himself," said Garda.

" Let her come out with it then, as though she were in
earnest."

" I am in earnest," cried Gemmel, " I *do* love him."

" It would be horrible to marry without love," said
Garda.

" It would be horrible to marry with love." There was
a fierceness in Althea's voice. " I wouldn't marry — even if
I adored the ground the man walked on."

" It is easy for me to love," said Garda. " I believe I
could love two men at the same time."

" You 'd better be careful," Gemmel warned, " or you 'll
come to grief."

" She 's just the silly kind who does," said Althea.

Garda hugged her own body, laughing. " You can't make
me ashamed."

" There is just one man living whom I could marry," said
Althea, under cover of the deepening dark.

" A moment ago you said you would n't marry — not if you adored the ground the man walked on ! "

" Yes. I did say that. But I don't love this man. I merely mean that — oh, I 'm getting tangled up ! " She was filled with chagrin at what she had said — her sisters with astonishment.

" Tell me who he is," said Gemmel, " and I 'll get him for you."

" I know who he is," laughed Garda. " He is Finch Whiteoak."

" Never," Althea spoke in a whisper. " I might love Finch but I could n't marry him."

" Who is it then ? "

" I won't tell. Nothing can persuade me. So please don't ask."

" Will you tell us if we guess right ? " asked Garda.

" I say that nothing can persuade me. If you keep on trying, I 'll go to bed."

Garda's giggles were silenced by a knock on the door. The Griffiths always were startled by a knock. The silence among the Welsh hills had been almost unbroken.

Althea laid a restraining hand on the youngest sister. " Don't go to the door. The house is dark. Whoever it is will think we are out."

After a little Garda whispered — " It is Finch. He always drums with his fingers on the door while he waits."

" Do let him in," exclaimed Gemmel. " I want to tell him about my engagement."

Althea resigned herself. " Very well. Let him in."

Garda ran to the door. In a moment Finch's tall figure appeared, following her.

" Sitting in the dark ! " he exclaimed. " You do look mysterious." He dropped into a chair beside Gem.

Garda turned on the light. She said — " We were discussing a wonderful piece of news. May I tell him, Gem ? "

"Yes."

"Gem is engaged."

Finch stared for a moment in surprise.   Then he said —
"To Mr. Clapperton, I suppose."

She nodded, smiling up at him.   The darkness had sunk
back into the corners of the room.   The window curtains
stirred in the light breeze.   Finch took her slender, supple
hand in his.   "I hope you 'll be very happy," he said.

Garda answered for her.   "We are delighted.   Eugene
is so kind.   Don't you think it is a good match?"

"Yes.   But, you know, none of us likes him very well.
There 's no use in pretending that we do."

"It must make no difference in our friendship," said
Gemmel eagerly.   "Everything must be just as it was with
us."

He was silent.

"We are all to move to Vaughanlands," said Garda.

Finch turned to Althea.   "You too?"

"Yes.   He has promised me a room in the attic where I
can shut myself up when I choose."

"It sounds like a beautiful arrangement."

"The house will have three mistresses in place of none,"
said Garda.

"It will have the same old master," added Althea.

"Althea is in a detestable mood," said Gemmel, lighting
another cigarette.   "But I don't mind.   She 's just envious."   The sisters laughed and Finch had a moment's pity
for Eugene Clapperton.   Still, he was a hard old bird.   He
could look after himself.   But these three girls — always in
league with each other . . .   He asked: —

"What about Swift?"

"He is going," answered Garda.   "Is n't it a pity?"

"Not as far as I am concerned."

"But your brother was cruel to him.   Then your other
brother dismissed him.   And now Eugene thinks he can get

on without him. Poor fellow. He came to see us this morning and he has a patch over one eye."

"I think it improves him," said Althea. "It gives his face the character it lacked."

"What is he going to do?" asked Finch.

Garda shrugged, pretending it did not matter to her. "Dear knows. But he's so clever. He'll find something."

"I thought of him," said Finch, "as always attached to Clapperton. He seems almost like his son."

"Eugene is still fond of him," said Gemmel, "but he does n't want him in the house any longer."

Finch asked — "Who do you suppose arrived at Jalna this morning?"

"I can guess." Garda's face was alight at the mere thought of an arrival from the outer world. "Your brother Wakefield! How glad you all must be."

"You 're right. We heard yesterday that he was to come and he arrived before lunch."

"Has he left the Air Force?"

"Yes. He 's finished with that. He 's been at it too long. Four years of flying, with scarcely a break. He shows it. He 's very tired. He had a heart attack after the last raid he took part in. When he was a small boy he had a lot of trouble with his heart but he outgrew it. Now he must have a long rest."

All four were silent as they remembered Wakefield's engagement to Molly Griffith, now an actress in New York. That engagement had come to an unhappy end. The movement of the lives of those two stirred against the lives of the four in the room.

"Life takes a lot of courage," Gemmel said, after the silence.

"You certainly have had courage," said Finch.

"No, no, I 've never really lived. I 've existed in a little silk cocoon, woven by my sisters."

Garda's admiring eyes feasted on her. "Now you 're going to spread your wings," she said.

"And flutter as far as Vaughanlands! But it takes courage just the same."

Althea turned to Finch. "Gem does n't really want to get married."

"Indeed I do. You must n't think that others feel about it as you do."

"My marriage was a failure," said Finch.

There was a sense of fatality about him that fascinated the girls. He sat with his long hands clasped loosely between his knees. His light brown hair was fine and thick, there was something fine in the droop of his head.

"But it was an experience," said Garda.

"One I wish I had n't had."

Gemmel said — "Perhaps you play the better for it. It 's always being said that suffering is good for art."

"There was n't any suffering I could n't have imagined. Why should I experience it? Besides — it was suffocation rather than suffering."

He had never spoken to them of his marriage before. The sisters felt an exhilaration in his coming out of his own aloof atmosphere to talk openly to them of his private life. They tried to draw him on to say more — all but Althea. But he withdrew as suddenly as he had advanced. He was suddenly shy and before long he left. He had an unaccountable desire to kiss the sisters good-night, as though it were good-bye. First he bent over and kissed Gemmel. She did not mind. She seemed to like it. Her skin was silken and delicate, never having been exposed to extremes of weather. She was in complete possession of herself, Finch thought. No one could take anything away from her. Yet she was passionate, he was sure. To kiss Garda was like kissing fresh fruit — a peach, an apple, with its firm, round cheek. He took her hand as he kissed her and, for an instant, closed his eyes. She turned her head till her lips touched his cheek. " Good night," she murmured. He turned then toward Althea but she had disappeared.

Garda laughed. " You 'd never expect her to stay for that, would you? "

" Gardie," said Gemmel, " you have a horrible way of putting things."

" I hope I have n't offended her," said Finch.

" Not at all. She likes you better than you guess."

All the way through the stillness of the ravine, Finch felt the atmosphere of the sisters reaching after him. It was like shadowy hands stretched out after him. All sounds were stilled for the night, the birds silent, the frogs as quiet as the cool damp stones in the stream. Even its murmur was inaudible till he reached the bridge, for the season had been dry. He stood there a space listening. All his life he had tried to put a meaning into the murmuring of the stream. Ever since he was a small boy he had been sure it uttered a message meant for him alone. Now he thought — " I shall never know what it says till the time comes for me to die. Then I shall understand." He pictured himself near his end, clinging weakly to the railing over the bridge, leaning low above the water to hear. He felt unspeakably lonely.

He left the bridge and mounted the path at the other side of the ravine. Now he was free of the Griffiths and the atmosphere of Jalna reached out to receive him. There were lights in the rooms and the windows shone among the vines. The vines were the sleeping place of a score of young birds and their mothers. Earlier in the evening, when he had come out, he had disturbed them and they had rushed forth with sleepy flutterings, not knowing where to go or what to do. But the mothers had not been really afraid. They had collected the young ones on a telephone wire and in the hawthorn tree, quieting them with wise cheepings.

Even after that there had been frantic flutterings in the creeper and the last sleepyheads had tumbled into the open. There were but a few of them but they made a greater noise of fright than all the rest. The mothers sat on the wire and in the tree ignoring them, as if they had quite enough young without them and these last did not matter. But finally they all were safe on some perch and by the time Finch had crossed the lawn they were winging back into the sheltering vine.

Finch found Wakefield alone, sitting on the seat in the stone porch. It was wonderful to come back and find him sitting there. In the dark, when the strained look in Wake's eyes could not be seen, it was almost as though he had never been away. Finch dropped to the bench beside him and they exchanged a few casual remarks. Finch wanted to feel as they had felt when as boys they had lounged here together. Then he remembered how uncompanionable they had been, how Wake had irritated him by his artless assumption of superiority. It was later, when Finch had had a nervous breakdown, that they had been friends. Finch did not want to remember that time. Now it was Wake who was struggling against the effects of strain and exhaustion. But spiritually and physically Wake had been through hell in the past five years, thought Finch, and he put out his hand in the dark and touched him.

" Does it feel good to be home? " he asked.

" It's bliss. I should like to sit here — feeling everything — seeing nothing — for six months — then sleep for the next six months and wake up having forgotten all I'd ever experienced."

" You'll rest."

" I suppose I shall."

" It's put new life in the uncles, having you back."

" Uncle Nick looks pretty old."

" He looks far better than he did last spring, and when his face lights up — he looks fine."

"Yes . . . What's the matter with Renny?"

"You've noticed something?"

"God — how could I help? Is it trouble between him and Alayne? She looks depressed."

"We all are — depressed. But I hate to tell you, on your first night at home. There's nothing you can do about it."

"Tell me." Wakefield spoke impatiently.

Finch moved closer to him on the seat and in a low voice poured out the story of the theft.

"It's impossible," exclaimed Wakefield. "He could n't have done it. He could n't have taken the money, hidden it from himself and then keep on doling it out to himself in that insane way. It does n't make sense."

"Does an injured mind make sense? Does the war make sense? I have reached the point when nothing seems too crazy to be true. Do you remember how the spirit, Lorenzo, in Keats's 'Isabella,' said: —

"'I know what was, I feel full well what is,
    And I should rage, if spirits could go mad.'"

"Don't!" exclaimed Wakefield, moving uneasily in the shadow.

"I don't know what will happen to Renny, if this goes on. He's always searching — always trying to remember. It's very hard on Alayne."

"Has he consulted a doctor?"

"No. Nothing can persuade him to. He told me yesterday that he has lost eighteen pounds since this happened. He watches himself in a grim, detached sort of way. He thinks he's headed for — "

"For what?" Wakefield asked sharply, as Finch hesitated.

"I don't exactly know. But something disastrous. He's just watching and waiting. Something must happen. He can't go on like this."

"I should think that, when the money is all recovered, he 'll stop worrying."

"Perhaps. I hope so."

"How many of the bills have been found?"

"About fifteen. That leaves thirty-five."

"It 's ghastly. It can't go on. Why does n't Alayne do something?"

"What can she do? Nothing but wait, like the rest of us."

The door opened and Renny came into the porch, the light of the hall behind him. He stood clearly defined in his isolation. He was acquiescent in the doom he saw foretold for him. Yet he was master of himself as of the house. He was even cheerful and smiling.

"Hullo," he said. "I was wondering where you had taken yourself to. Having a confidential talk?"

"It 's good to be home," said Wake, "and just relax."

"It 's good to have you. We will not let you go away again in a hurry."

It was the same cry of the grandmother. "Don't let them go away. Keep them together. Don't let anything separate us." Wakefield chafed in his spirit, even while he passionately longed to submerge himself in the family.

"I should like," said Finch, "to be at Jalna for the rest of my life."

Renny came and sat beside him and laid his hand on his knee. "Good man," he exclaimed, "and so you shall."

"What about this concert tour Uncle Ernest was telling me of?" asked Wakefield.

"Well, of course, I must do that. But I 'll come back when it 's over."

"He 's practising hard," said Renny. "I like to hear him. I like those modern pieces. They sound even more muddleheaded than I am. Has Finch told you about me, Wake?"

"Yes." The word came out painfully. He hated to acknowledge that he knew.

"What do you think of it?"

"I think it will all come right."

"That's good. So do I — sometimes."

"I think you're as sound as a nut, Renny."

"Tell me that — when a week has passed — if you can."

"I'll have a search for that money, myself."

"I wish you would. And I wish you'd watch me. I've begged them all to watch me. Alayne, Finch, all of them, but they won't. They leave me to myself and the next thing I know I've been to the hiding place, brought out another note, and hidden it again in some ridiculous spot. One would think they did n't want to help me. But you will, won't you?"

"Of course, I will." Wakefield's heartiness of consent concealed the distress he felt. Renny, to be asking for help in such a pass! It was unbelievable.

As a drowning man desperately reaching out for aid, Renny said — "Begin to-morrow, Wake. You may well be the one to run me down. I can tell you, I'm a wily one. But you always have seen everything that went on. By heaven, I'm glad you've come home."

XXV

THE FINDING

WAKEFIELD accepted Renny's theory that a dual personality had been engendered in him by the concussion, as, when a small boy, he had accepted every longbow Renny had drawn. It even seemed to him plausible that Renny's personality should be split in two, the one a thief, the other an unwilling object of the thief's charity who continually sought to bring the thief to justice. Wakefield could believe anything, for a time at least. To Finch this theory was fantastic, yet he could offer nothing in its stead. So much and so helplessly did he brood on the mystery of it all that he found it hard to settle down to the practising for his concert tour. Sometimes he felt that he should go away for this preparation, where he might have peace of mind. But where could he go? Here was the piano he loved, as he would never love another. Here, bent above him at night, was the roof beneath which alone his being was complete. All other places left him but half a man. In his boyhood he often had longed to get away from the bonds of Jalna. Now, when he was away, he gladly felt these bonds drawing him back. Was it the land? The house? The spirit of his grandmother that gave him strength? Was it Renny? If Renny died — or if the dreadful thing that threatened him came to pass — would the bonds still hold? As he sat practising hour after hour in the shuttered coolness of the drawing-room, these thoughts came in on him.

Renny was deeply glad that Wakefield was home again. Now the last source of anxiety for his brothers was gone. He would concentrate all his powers on the solution of the mystery that enmeshed him. His restlessness at night disturbed Alayne's sleep. She lay always with an arm about him, so that if he rose to walk in his sleep she would know. But he never did. He noticed her paleness and returned to his own room. But, in his room, he made a trap for himself with cords drawn across the door, which would cause him to stumble or even fall, if he tried to go out. Nothing happened. The truth was that he slept little at night. He lay listening to the striking of the grandfather clock in the hall below, longing for the day. Morbid imaginings assailed him. Sometimes when he did fall asleep, he dreamed he was confined in a strait jacket and woke struggling to free himself, wet with the sweat of terror. His best sleep was in the daytime, when he would stretch himself on the sofa in the library, stationing Wakefield near by to watch him and to follow him, if he went out. The sound of the piano did not wake him. Sometimes Finch would come into the room and the two younger brothers would stand looking down into the high-colored bony face that seemed formed to withstand the stress of life's fiercest attack.

Sometimes he would wake and smile up at them. Then it was impossible to believe that anything was wrong with him. He would get up, light a cigarette, and tell Finch to continue with his practising.

"Come, Wake," he would say, "we'll see how he's getting on."

The two would sit at a little distance from the piano; Wakefield, with his head resting on his hand, Renny leaning back in his chair, his eyes fixed on Finch's hands. He was proud of their swift sure movements across the keyboard. When Finch had played Brahms's variations on a theme by Handel, Renny would smile at Wakefield and remark —
"Pretty good, eh?"

"What's that piece called?" he asked, when Finch had played Debussy's " La Cathédrale Engloutie."

Finch told him, and he remarked — " I wish you 'd play that to me every day."

At first Finch found the presence of his brothers a strain, but later he liked having them sitting quietly there. He began to think of the music as healing their scars of war. They had been hard and manly, he vulnerable. Now he felt he could heal them with his music.

Sometimes Nicholas and Ernest joined them and the five men seemed to overcome even that large room by their presence. There seemed no place for any women in the room. The present suffering, the vulnerability, the scars, the recollections of the past, all were masculine.

Piers seldom came to Jalna in these days. He always found something that needed doing about the farmlands. He was active despite the loss of his leg. He was proud to show what he could do. His muscular frame was hardening once more, after the years of inaction in the prison camp. But his chief reason for remaining away from Jalna was that he shrank from being for more than a short while with Renny, in his present state. He could meet him in the stables, on the land, talk to him of crops and the breeding of cattle, but to sit at Renny's table, to spend an evening with him, conscious all the while of his abstraction — that look in his eyes — was too much.

When one morning he met Alayne in the orchard, carrying a small basket of red apples she had gathered for the table, he was startled by the change in her. She looked wan. Her fair hair drooped lifelessly about her thin temples. Her lips were pale. He stood staring, making no attempt to conceal his scrutiny.

She smiled. " Well, I am not improving in my appearance, am I ? "

" You 'll be ill, if you go on like this."

" To tell the truth, Piers, I don't feel very well now."

" It 's a damned shame," he broke out. " That fellow has

got to see a doctor. If he won't do it willingly, he must be forced."

" He 's not an easy person to force, as you know."

" Can't he see what he 's doing to you ? "

" He does n't see anything clearly."

" Then he must be made to see."

Piers's steady blue eyes, his stalwart body, gave out masculine strength and support to Alayne. She had a blind desire to throw herself on his breast and cling there. For an instant she loved him, he who so often had been antagonistic to her. In imagination she clung to him, kissing him. She was so overwrought she scarcely knew what was real or what was unreal. Piers suddenly put his arms about her and kissed her.

" There, there," he said comfortingly. " It will come out all right."

" I know," she sobbed, and withdrew herself.

" I 'll see what I can do with old redhead. When did he find the last bill ? "

" Two days ago. Stuffed into the bowl of his meerschaum pipe which he had n't smoked for months."

" Tck. Whoever hides them is ingenious."

" Piers, do you believe it *is* Renny ? "

" I can't see who else it could be."

" Adeline comes home for her mid-term week end tomorrow. I did so hope the atmosphere would be cleared by now. She was very conscious of the change in Renny. I often saw her looking at him in a puzzled way — and the scene after *Othello !* He would not have been so upset if he had been normal."

" I think he would . . . Anyhow I 'll see him this morning and talk him into consulting a doctor. See if I don't."

Piers set off at once to find Renny. Standing over him as he sat on the swivel chair in his office in the stable he said —

" The time has come when you 've got to do something about the lost money. All your searching won't bring it back. You are ruining your health. You are ruining Alayne's life. I am your brother and I know what I am talking about. I am going with you to consult a psycopathist. He 'll make you wish you had gone to him at the first. He 'll take the quirk out of your memory. Do it for Alayne's sake. She is at breaking point. Come, now — say you will."

Renny raised his eyes to Piers's face. " If I have n't found the money at the end of a fortnight," he said, " I will do whatever you say."

" Make it a week."

" Very well. A week."

Piers was elated. He had expected a struggle, possibly failure. He said — " I can't tell you how glad I am — for all our sakes. It 's taken a load off my mind."

" I wish my mind were as easily relieved."

" Renny, I have worried about you more than you know. Now I feel that something is going to be done."

" What if the fellow says I 'm deranged? That I 'll get worse? "

" I would not believe him. You 're as sound as one of your own horses. Have n't you seen a horse suddenly begin to shy at some object he has previously ignored? He 's got to be treated carefully — led up to it — walked round — encouraged to look at it from every side. That 's what the psycopathist will do for you."

" My God, I 've looked at this thing from every side! "

" You can't cure yourself without help."

Renny made a sardonic grimace.

But in spite of himself he felt a little cheered. In a week he would cast off responsibility and let the family do with him what they willed. On the other hand, he clung desperately to the coming week, dreading what might befall him at its end.

He was glad to have the two young girls at home again.

He aroused himself from the cloud that oppressed him, to
chaff them, to make them laugh. Adeline's laugh was high,
gay. It seemed to come from all parts of her being, the
natural expression of their mirth. Roma's laugh was
scarcely more than an audible smile. When she smiled her
lips bent down at the outer corners, though the sensitive upper lip was raised. There was an oddness in her smile that
later would be fascinating.

A period of wet weather had set in after a long drought.
The last of the apples fell into the long wet orchard grass.
The red and gold maple leaves showed their last brightness
against the pewter-gray sky. The turkeys trailed among
the blackberry canes, searching for the last berries. "Everything is at its last," thought Renny, walking through the
orchard path with the three dogs following him, more in
stolid resolve not to lose sight of him than in pleasure. The
long grass brushed their faces, they found no scent of wild
creature.

At the end of the orchard, Michaelmas daisies glowed in
little mauve stars. A few oats had fallen there in the seeding time and now bore grain, hanging delicately from the
stock, not garnered. There was a miniature graveyard, the
resting place of all the dogs who had died at Jalna, since its
building. Twenty-eight little graves were there, each
marked with a low stone on which was carved a name. Once
they had been cared for but now many were so overgrown by
wild grasses, Michaelmas daisies, and goldenrod, as to be
lost. The oldest grave and the one with the tallest stone
was that of Nero, the great Newfoundland who had come
from Quebec with Renny's grandparents. Many a time he
had heard old Adeline tell of Nero's exploits. "Ha," she
would exclaim, " a greathearted dog if ever there was one!
He loved me and I loved him. The day he died I thought
my heart would break from the grief in me."

Renny thought of all the dogs buried there, how they had
padded over the farmlands, through the orchard, chased

their quarry, sometimes caught it but more often lost it. Had their fun. Been cherished. Never ill-treated — no, not one. Yes — wait! There was the Irish terrier, Barney, who had been stabbed to death by a Scotch laborer because the poor dog had run about wildly, frothing at the mouth. But he had only been overcome by exertion with heat, he had not been mad. Renny's brows drew together at the remembrance. Strange how painful memories hurt him more than ever in these days. He turned his eyes to the newest graves, those of his two clumber spaniels, Floss and Merlin. Never could he love another dog as he had loved those two. And they had taken with them some of his best years.

The living dogs waited expectant for him to go on. Now, when he moved, they became the leaders and he followed them to the road and along it to the church. It looked closed-in on itself, the stained-glass windows one uniform brownish color, the heavy door shut against the world. What had it to do with the world? Inside its walls one might hear the story of Noah and the Flood, but what had that to do with the clouds and rain of to-day? That was all very well when there were half a dozen people on the earth. If he had been Noah he would have taken Merlin and Floss into the Ark, and for horses his mare, Cora, and a beautiful high-jumper he had owned after the last war. Launceton, that was his name.

He was still smiling a little at the thought when he saw the Rector pruning a hedge in his garden. His gray beard and hair were curly in the damp air — the scent of the clipped cedar filled the air, the flat, sharply articulated leaves of it lay all about. The dogs slipped through the hedge and Mr. Fennel disappeared for a moment as he bent down to pat them. Then he put his hand over the hedge to greet Renny.

" Lovely rains we 've been having," he said.

" Yes. I suppose they 're needed."

" It 's a great benefit to the fall wheat."

" I guess it is."

" You 're no farmer, Renny."

" No. I leave that to Piers."

" You must miss the horse shows — both financially and for their pleasure."

" I miss nothing but my peace of mind," Renny returned sombrely.

Mr. Fennel made a sound of sympathy, then he asked : —

" Have you found any more of the notes lately? "

" Yes. They turn up steadily. But there are still more than half of them missing. I found one this morning in a drawer I constantly use. But the odd thing is that this note smells distinctly musty. It points out pretty clearly that they 're hidden somewhere outdoors and that these rains are dampening them."

" That is interesting. I believe you 're right."

" I 've wasted a lot of time searching in the house and stable. But imagine starting on five hundred acres! No. I shall never discover them."

" But, if they turn up, one by one, will you be satisfied? "

" How can I be? I shall not know what I may do next."

" Then why do you go on searching? "

" I must."

Mr. Fennel gently opened and closed the garden shears he held.

" Renny," he said, " I think we *must* do something."

" I 've promised Piers to consult a psycopathist next week. Nothing else will satisfy the family."

" I don't believe a psycopathist will help you."

" Neither do I, but I have promised."

Mr. Fennel ran his thumb along the cutting edge of the shears, as though to prepare for a fresh pruning. He said, almost laconically : —

" What do you say to doing away with useless effort? You have been dropping buckets into an empty well. Now let us go to a Well which is ever brimming to the top with help for us. But perhaps you have already done this. Forgive me for taking for granted that you have n't."

Renny turned away his face in embarrassment. "If you mean praying, I have n't. It would be impossible to me — in the personal way you mean."

Mr. Fennel studied the profile presented to him. From the front, Renny's face had seemed to him stationary, set in the mould in which inheritance, experience, and passion had formed it, unchangeable in its essence. But the side view appeared moving, full of possibilities, capable of expressing the soul.

"I suggest," said the Rector, "that we should go into the church and kneel together and ask divine help in solving this mysterious trouble."

With his profile still turned, Renny answered — "No, no, I could n't do that."

"Why?"

"I should feel a fool."

"Do you feel wise, as you stand here?"

"No, but I feel natural. The other would be unnatural to me."

"Unnatural to you who have assisted in the services in that church your grandfather built — where you were christened, confirmed?"

"Yes."

"Renny," the Rector put his hand across the hedge and tapped him on the breast, "I have asked your help many times. I have asked you for money for the church when I knew you had little to spare, and you never refused me. I ask you to do something that I desire more earnestly than anything I have asked before. Don't refuse. Come with me into the church for a few minutes."

Now Renny turned his eyes on him with a half-humorous look. "You make it impossible for me to refuse. But I certainly think I shall be a comic spectacle for the Almighty, if He happens to notice me."

"He will notice you," said Mr. Fennel, "and you will not be comic." He stuck the point of the shears into the ground, wiped his palms on the wet grass, and came through the gate to Renny.

Together they went into the church.

It was cool in there. There was no sun to shine through the stained-glass windows. They had retreated into themselves, holding, as it were, their bright colors close. Each section of colored glass was complete in itself, not merging into one glowing picture, but startlingly blue or crimson or gold. To Renny the interior of the church was as familiar as a room in his own house.

He stopped short as he heard the organ softly played.

"It is Finch," said the Rector. "He will make no difference."

They went up the aisle. At the chancel steps Mr. Fennel turned to Renny. "We will kneel here," he said.

They knelt side by side. Mr. Fennel bent his head, folded his hands, closed his eyes. Renny knelt upright, his dark gaze resting on the altar where there were blue asters from Meg's garden. The smell of cedar came from Mr. Fennel. He looked as tranquil as though this were an everyday occasion.

Finch had heard their entrance but had continued to play till they knelt. The sight amazed him. It even frightened him. He saw the solemnity of their attitudes. If it had been anyone but Renny . . . his wary yet subdued look went to Finch's heart. His hands sank from the keyboard. He bent his head but he kept his eyes fixed on Renny, so steadfast in his isolation. Mr. Fennel's voice was now audible. He prayed: —

"Our divine Father, we have come to Thee to-day most earnestly to ask Thy help for Thy servant, kneeling here beside me. For many weeks he has suffered anguish of spirit, from the fear that he is no longer aware of all that he does. Yet though he has struggled manfully to understand the strange predicament in which he finds himself he has failed. But where manhood fails, Godhead triumphs. So he has come to Thee to implore Thy help. Here in Thy house, we implore that help, for Thy Son's sake. Amen."

"Amen," muttered Renny, rigid, half-angry at what he was doing.

For a space there was silence as they remained kneeling. Then the faint, late summer song of a small bird came through the open window and the patter of a few raindrops sounded in the leaves. As in a procession the three men passed down the aisle, for Finch had joined them.

Outside the dogs were sitting mournfully waiting on the doorstep. They rose, shook themselves, and led the way down the walk. The Rector laid his hand on Renny's arm. "Thank you for doing what I asked," he said. "Now let us wait calmly and see what happens." He smiled in his beard and went back to his hedge cutting.

The brothers walked on together toward Jalna.

Renny gave an embarrassed laugh. "Don't tell Piers or Alayne about this," he said. "I did it to please the old boy."

"I don't see anything strange about it. If your religion means anything to you it ought to be good for *that*. I'm glad you did it."

"But you won't tell Piers or Alayne?"

Curiously there came to Finch's mind the picture of himself as a small boy, saying to Renny in a choking voice — "You won't tell the others you gave me a licking, will you, Renny?"

Now he answered — "Certainly I'll not tell them but I repeat that I'm glad you did it."

Finch directed his steps toward the accustomed path across the fields but Renny said — "Let's go round through the woods. They are looking lovely now."

"It will be pretty wet."

"A little damp won't hurt you."

They continued their way along the road, once standing aside to let an army truck, filled with soldiers, pass. They went through a farm gate and found themselves on the edge of the pine wood. Oaks and maples were there also, and, in the heart of the wood, an assembly of silver birches. But the pines predominated. There was a magnificent toughness in them. Each branch appeared complete and solitary in itself but the whole was cohesive and daring in outline, not subject to the seasons as were the oaks and maples. All the autumn these last had lorded it, in the majesty of their rich coloring, but now, since the heavy rains, half their brightness lay at their feet or drooped ready to fall. But the pines faced the winter with the same equanimity with which they had greeted the spring. Never were the boughs so dense as to conceal their noble trunks. The rust-colored pine needles lay thick on the ground but there was undergrowth too, brambles, wild raspberry canes, the vine of bittersweet and the venturesome wild-grape vine whose tiny fruit would pucker the mouth with its sourness.

Through the wood a bridle path had, for nearly a century, been the delight of galloping young Whiteoaks. Along its verge the undergrowth was thickest. Here, the weather for some reason seemed more cheerful. Men and dogs stretched their legs and breathed with greater freedom.

Jock, the sheep dog, pressed his shaggy body among the bushes, sniffing, while the others ran along the path in chase after a buck rabbit whose great leaps were to save him from destruction. Now Jock continued to snuffle, then uttered a cry of delight.

"What has he found, I wonder," said Finch, following him into the thicket.

"Here, Jock!" called Renny, striding along the bridle path.

But Finch pressed his way through the brambles that

seemed deliberately to impede him.　Jock was whining and
Finch heard a childish voice whisper — " Be quiet, Jock."
Then he saw a fair head and shoulders covered by a blue
jersey, bent beneath the undergrowth.　Roma was crouching
there.　Now she raised a white, frightened face to Finch.

" Sh," she breathed.　" Don't tell."

He stood staring down at her.　" What are you doing? "
he demanded.

She knelt, white and frightened but smiling now, pretending not to be afraid.

" I am playing a game," she whispered.

" A nice place for a game!　Why, you 're wet as a rat.
What sort of game? "

She was fondling Jock.　She drew him in front of her,
trying to hide something with his bulk.　" It 's too silly to
tell.　I 've been playing it for years."

Finch, remembering his childhood, was sorry to have
spied on her.　He said — " Don't tell me, if you don't want
to.　But you 'll catch a cold here.　Can't you finish the
game another time? "

" We have only the week end at home.　Was it Uncle
Renny who called Jock? "

" Yes."

She looked still more frightened.　" Please, Uncle Finch,
don't tell him I 'm here.　It 's — a secret."

Renny's voice came back to them.　" Finch!　Where are
you?　What 's the matter? "

" Do go, Uncle Finch," she implored.　" I shall get into
terrible trouble if you don't."

Renny was coming back.　He was whistling to Jock but
Roma held him fast.　He struggled, whining in his anxiety.
She held him tightly by a handful of hair and when, in a
panic, he tore himself away, a number of gray hairs were
left in her grasp.　He yelped in pain.

Finch turned to intercept Renny.　Whatever the child

was up to he would not give her away. He could hear her
scrabbling among the undergrowth as though she were hiding something. A sudden thought illuminated his mind.
He wheeled, turned back toward where she hid, wheeled
again, walking in a circle. Renny reached his side. He
demanded — " What the dickens is going on? "

" Nothing." Finch felt dazed.

" Well — you certainly look queer." With a decisive
sweep of the arm, Renny parted the bushes. Roma was
crouching there, a mysterious smile on her pale upturned
face.

" Roma! " Renny bent forward to discover what she
sought to conceal.

But now she no longer tried to hide anything. She stood
up straight and looked into his eyes; her hair, wet from the
rain-soaked undergrowth, lay flat on her forehead. She
said, in a low confidential voice : —

" I did it."

" Did what? "

" Took the money from Mr. Clapperton and gave it to
you."

Renny turned to Finch, as though to ask if he also had
heard.

" Yes? " said Finch. " You took the money? "

Roma nodded, in a determined way. " I wanted Uncle
Renny to have it. That old man had too much and Uncle
Renny not enough. I knew that, because I 'd heard talk.
So when Archer told me about Robin Hood and how he had
taken money from the rich and given it to people who needed
it, I thought why could n't I — so I did and the rest of it 's
here."

Renny crashed through the bushes to where she held up
an old teakettle. He took it from her in frantic haste and
lifted the lid. Inside there was a brown paper package tied
with a piece of tape. With fingers visibly trembling he un-

tied it and disclosed a roll of bank notes, all of the twenty-dollar denomination. He held them to his strong aquiline nose.

"They smell of mould," he said.

He turned to Finch. "I'm glad you're here, Finch. If you were n't, I'd think I was dreaming." Then he broke out — "The money! My God — I've found it! It's in my hand. And my mind's all right — " He struck himself on the forehead with his clenched hand — "I'm not demented! The money is found! Can you believe it? Oh, Roma, tell me all about it. Make it clear, for I feel dazed. How did you get hold of these bills?"

Finch put his arm about him. He looked so wild that Finch was afraid for him. Roma's face had lost the frightened look. It had an expression of secret pride.

"I took them," she said, "that morning you went to see Mr. Clapperton. I heard you tell Archer he could n't go with you. I was behind the big syringa bush. So I followed you and when you went into Mr. Clapperton's house, I went on to the verandah and I heard you being angry with each other and then I saw him go into the room at the back and I went down the hall and peeped in at you."

"Go on — go on." His eyes were avid on her face.

"Are you angry, Uncle Renny?"

"No, no, go on."

In her quick child's voice she continued — "I peeped in and I saw you go out by the French window and I saw all the money on the desk and I gathered it up and ran out without making a sound and I hid the bills under a big stone. All but one." She gave a little peal of laughter.

"Yes? Go on."

Finch wondered how Roma could talk, with those burning eyes fixed on hers. When he was a child he would have been hopelessly stammering, getting mixed up, not able to go on. But she continued — "I kept that in my hand and before we went in to lunch I crept up behind you — you were sitting on your heels taking a bur out of Jock — and I put my arms round you."

" I remember! My God, I remember!"

She laughed again at the remembrance of her cunning.

" I hugged you and I pushed the twenty-dollar bill into your pocket without you knowing. Was n't it a lovely surprise?"

" A beautiful surprise. Oh, Roma, Roma — what you did to your poor uncle that day!"

" That 's why I did it. I knew you were poor and Mr. Clapperton was rich. Even when I was listening I heard him talk that way. So I just took the money for you."

" And what then, Roma?" Renny held her with his eyes.

" Then, after lunch, I went back and took the bills from under the stone. I 'd almost forgotten where I 'd hid it. Would n't it have been awful if I 'd never found it? Because you 'd never have had it."

" Yes. Go on."

" But I found it and I knew where there was an old teakettle and I put all the money in it. Then I brought it here and hid it in the bushes and every time I wanted to I came and took out a bill and put it some place where I knew you 'd find it. Did n't I think of a lot of funny places?"

" You did indeed — God forgive you!"

" I have a mysterious mind. Even when I was going to school I did n't forget you. I hid some bills for you to find while I was away, and as soon as I came home I got out another to give you."

" The one that smelt musty!" he exclaimed.

The full import of his release from dreadful apprehension now swept over him. He caught Roma beneath the armpits, lifted her so that her face was on a level with his, then kissed her rapturously.

" Roma," he exclaimed, " you 've saved my reason by being here at this minute. If you knew what relief I feel! I 'm a new man." She kissed him back and he set her down and turned to Finch. " We must go straight home and tell Alayne. Poor girl — how happy she 'll be. But first I must count the bills." He ran through them, counting aloud. " All here! Nothing more to worry about. What 's the matter, Finch? Have n't you anything to say? Good God, if you 'd been through what I have, you 'd find plenty to say! "

" Roma did a terrible thing. She is old enough to know better."

" She thought she was doing a beautiful thing, did n't you, Roma? For my part, I can think of nothing but the relief. An iron band that was round my head has snapped. I am free. I am not headed for the madhouse."

" Very well," answered Finch. " Let 's accept this as a blessing. The money 's found. I 'll try to forget what you 've been through and be glad with you, Renny, but I could weep when I think of the past months."

" They 're gone. Done with. Let 's get back to Jalna. Won't the uncles be glad? Poor old boys! I 'm afraid they 've been pretty miserable." He plunged through the undergrowth and back to the path. In one hand he carried the teakettle. Roma clung to the other. He exclaimed: —

" What a triumph for Fennel! By George, I ought to go first to him and tell him. He 'd say that prayer did the trick, and perhaps it did. What do you think, Finch? "

" I don't know, Renny. But it 's beginning to rain. If we go straight to Jalna you can phone the Rector from there."

" Very well, I 'll do that. Hello, there are Piers's boys. Nooky — Philip — where are you going? Come here."

The small boys approached, each eating an apple. Rain was beginning to fall. They stood staring up at Renny, feeling something wild in him, but whether of anger or some other emotion they could not tell. They were half afraid of him. He had returned the notes to the kettle. Now he extracted two of them and pressed them into the hands of the little boys.

"Now," he said, "here is a present for you. Twenty dollars apiece, to celebrate this lucky day."

"For heaven's sake, Renny —" broke in Finch.

"No, but I want to. Boys, you are to run straight home, show your father what I have given you, and tell him and your mother and Mooey to come to Jalna, as fast as they possibly can. Do you hear?"

They were dazed. They stood with the bank notes in their hands just staring. The rain came down hard.

"Do you understand? You are to tell the others to come straight to Jalna?"

"And is all this money for us?" asked Nooky, helpless under the munificence of the gift.

"Every bit of it. Tell your father so. He is to come at once to Jalna. Now run."

They scampered along the path. They were panting when they reached the road. They were winded when they tore into the dining room where Pheasant was setting out the tea things.

"Boys, you *are* naughty," she cried. "How often have I told you not to come rushing in without wiping your shoes? Now you 've brought mud —"

"Where is Daddy?" they shouted.

"Sharpening the lawn mower. Tell him to come to tea. Then change your shoes and —"

They were off.

"Oh, the rudeness of them!" mourned Pheasant to herself. "And only a little while ago they were so sweet. It 's the school. I know it 's the school."

Evidently the mower had been sharpened, for there was

Mooey pushing it languidly across the lawn. The rain had ceased. What a pity Mooey always looked half-dead when he was made to do any work. It was so irritating to Piers. When Piers had a thing to do he went at it like a man. Mooey's expression was so lugubrious it made her laugh. Still, it was no fun mowing wet grass.

The little boys found Piers with three rats in a trap. Ordinarily this would have been a fascinating discovery but now they had no more than a glance for the captives.

" Daddy," they gasped, " look here what we've got! "

Piers stared pensively at the rats. Two of them were young. They crept over the wires, passing and repassing each other, searching for that fatal entrance by which they had come into the trap. The other rat was older and almost twice as large. In his efforts to escape he had wounded himself and now he lay with a resigned look, one pink paw, like a little hand, pressed to his side where a trickle of blood ran down.

" Daddy," shouted Philip, brandishing the twenty-dollar note, " see what Uncle Renny gave me! "

" I've got one too! " shouted Nook.

Piers's jaw dropped. He said — " Did he give you those? "

" Yes. And we're to keep it. And you're to go to Jalna as fast as you can."

Nook added — " And Mummie and Mooey are to go too. Uncle Renny was awfully excited."

Piers groaned and placed the rattrap on a shelf.

" Aren't you glad? " asked Nook.

" Glad! " he said. " Glad! Would you be *glad,* if your eldest brother was going haywire? "

He strode to where Maurice was feebly pushing the mower. He held up his hand. Maurice stopped the mower and looked sulkily at him.

" Mooey," said Piers, " we're going over to Jalna.

Your Uncle Renny is completely off his head. He has been giving twenty-dollar bills to the kids. God help me, I don't know what I should do."

Maurice leaned on the handle of the lawn mower and stared at Piers in consternation. " Must I go? " he asked.

" Yes. Get out the car while I go and tell your mother. No. I 'd better not tell her the truth. I shall just say we have to go to Jalna. Get out the car."

XXVI

ALAYNE HEARS THE GOOD NEWS

STANDING in the hall they could hear voices from the
drawing-room. Renny listened.

" It 's Alayne," he said, " and the uncles. Now you two
wait here while I go in and tell the news." He still held the
kettle in his hand. His face was lighted by a smile, almost
wild in its relief. His hair clung wet to his head. He flung
open the door and went into the room. Finch and Roma
hung back in the hall, he with a feeling rather of apprehension than joy, Roma's small face inscrutable.

Nicholas was chuckling over a copy of *Punch,* his gouty
leg resting on an ottoman. Ernest was rearranging the
articles in the cabinet of curios from India. Alayne was
sewing a patch on the elbow of Archer's pyjamas. All three
turned to look at Renny.

" Hullo," said Nicholas. " I see you 've come in out of
the rain. Sensible man. Sit down and let me read you
this sketch."

Ernest held a tiny jade monkey in his hand. " For some
reason," he observed, " I have always loved this little monkey.
I remember how, when I was not more than three — "

" Whatever have you in the kettle ? " interrupted Alayne,
but broke off at the expression on Renny's face.

He held it up. " Here is the loot," he said.

They just looked at him, not knowing what he meant.

At arm's length he displayed the kettle. " I have found
the lost money," he said. " In this old teakettle — look."

He thrust his hand inside and brought out the roll of bank
notes. He strode to Alayne and tossed them in her lap.
" There they are," he exclaimed. " Now you can breathe

free. Your husband is neither a thief nor a lunatic. Neither is he a sort of Jekyll and Hyde. He's a sane man and the happiest in this Dominion."

"What's he say?" demanded Nicholas. "What's this all about?"

"He says" — Ernest spoke tremblingly — "he has found the money — the bank notes that were taken from Mr. Clapperton." He replaced the jade monkey in the cabinet and advanced toward Renny with his hands held out. "I'm so glad, dear boy. I'm so glad. I'm so —" Tears began to run down his cheeks. He was afraid he was going to break down. He grasped the back of a chair for support and made gulping noises.

"Good!" Nicholas almost shouted in his joy. "Good! Now we have the laugh on that horrid old fellow. You say you found the money in that kettle. And where was the kettle? Sit here, beside me, and tell me everything. Well, well — if ever I was glad of anything, I'm glad of this. In a kettle, you say?"

Alayne stood up. She moved almost stiffly to Renny's side, letting the roll of bank notes fall to the floor. She looked into his face, her own white and drawn. "Is it true?" she whispered. "Do you remember everything now?"

"There's nothing to remember. I had absolutely nothing to do with taking the money. It was all a child's prank. No — not exactly a prank — the poor little thing wanted to be like Robin Hood — take from the rich — give to the poor."

"Not Archer!" gasped Alayne. "Don't tell me it was Archer who stole the money."

"Do you say one of the *children* took the money?" demanded Ernest.

"Yes. And hid it in this old kettle and doled it out — a note at a time. But the poor little thing thought she was being a kind of fairy godmother."

Alayne's face was rigid. " Then it was Adeline who did this horrible thing to us." She could scarcely articulate, her throat was so constricted. " It was Adeline."

Nicholas kicked the ottoman from him. Without assistance he got to his feet. He brought one fist into the palm of the other hand. " I want this explained so I can understand it," he thundered.

" Where is Adeline? " came from Alayne's white lips.

Renny smiled at her. " Adeline had nothing to do with it. I don't believe she has the imagination to invent such a scheme. It was Roma."

Alayne put her hand to her throat. " How did you find out? "

" She told me — herself. You mustn't be angry with her."

" Not angry! " Alayne gave a hysterical laugh. " Oh, no, I'm not angry."

The door opened. Piers, Pheasant, and Maurice, Meg and Patience, entered, with Finch and Roma close behind.

Probably, on the battlefield, Piers's face had shown no greater excitement, no greater apprehension, than it now did. With his new, stiff gait he came into the room, his eyes fixed on Renny. When he saw him smiling he was not relieved but stood, watching him warily, ready to humor him, to control him if necessary. Meg advanced fearlessly to Renny's side.

" Piers brought me with him," she said, " to hear the good news from your own lips. Renny, dear — I'm so glad." She laid her hand on his arm.

" Yes," said Piers. " Wonderful news."

" Think what it means to me," Renny exclaimed. " I'm a new man."

" Are you sure you know just what you have been doing all this afternoon? " Piers looked keenly into Renny's eyes. They were glittering from excitement.

" Know what I 've been doing! My God — I 've seen every move under a magnifying glass. Don't look at me like that, Piers. It shows what you 've had in your mind. But don't worry, I 'm as normal as any of you."

Again Nicholas struck has hands together. " I 'm an old man," he said, " and I think some consideration should be shown me. You all are talking, talking, talking, and no one has made things clear to me."

Ernest said — " You know that the lost money has been found, don't you? There it is — lying on the floor where Alayne dropped it."

Meg bent and picked up the roll of bank notes. " To think of it," she exclaimed. " And are they all here?"

" Every single one of them," answered Renny. " I 've counted them."

" God bless my soul," said Nicholas. " Where had you hidden them?"

" I had not hidden them. It was this little girl." He put his arm about Roma and drew her into the centre of the group. " She did it to help me."

" She stole the money from Clapperton!" shouted Nicholas, divided between horror and amusement.

" Yes. She followed me into his house, on that day when the notes were taken. She pinched them — for my sake, mind you — she did not keep a single one, she ran with them out of the house and hid them in this kettle in the woods. After that she put them where I should find them — just one happy surprise after another for me. Poor little thing — she did n't understand."

" Not understand," growled Nicholas. " Not understand what thieving meant — a girl of twelve!"

" I can't believe," said Ernest, " that she knew nothing of all the searching, the dreadful nervous strain — "

" She knew nothing."

" When I think of the nights," interrupted Piers, " when

I have woken, wondering what cloud was hanging over me — when I think of all Alayne has been through, and when I look at this smug youngster — "

Meg interrupted — " What about me? One would think that you and Alayne were the only sufferers. I can tell you there were nights when I never closed my eyes. Often I could n't eat, could I, Patience? "

" Oh, I know you are worn to skin and bone from worry," returned Piers.

" Are n't we all? " cried Ernest. He bent down to look into Roma's face. " Roma, you must have seen something of all the searching — the anxiety."

" I was at school."

" But before you went to school."

" I don't remember."

" Did you never confide in Adeline? "

" No, Uncle Ernest."

" My God," cried Renny, " don't you realize what finding the money means to me? I 'm a free man. My sky is clear. Nothing else matters. Nothing else matters."

Meg took him in her arms and kissed him. She enfolded him in her motherly embrace. He laid his head for a moment on her shoulder. He closed his eyes, trying to be fully conscious of what had happened but, when he closed his eyes, the old darkness of fear swept back to envelop him. He had suffered too long. He could not be entirely cured in an hour. What he wanted was to relax the tension of his nerves, to be surrounded by a calm rejoicing. It did not matter whether or no Roma had acted wrongly. He was astonished that the attention of the family should be centred on her, rather than on the fact that he was mentally whole. He straightened himself and opened his eyes. He saw Alayne standing tense and white, not white but gray, with a bluish cast. He went straight to her. " Just think of what this means to us," he said, in a low voice. "I'm a normal man, Alayne."

A moment passed before she could answer, then her voice came, harsh and unlike her own.

"I am thinking of what it *has* meant to us. I am thinking of the days of futile searching, when your mind was fastened on that one thing. I am thinking of the times when you found the separate notes, hidden here, there, and everywhere — with devilish ingenuity. I am thinking of our sleepless nights and your fear that you were losing your reason. And *my* fear. What kind of a life have we lived for months? Have we had an hour's peace? Look at your face. It has lines it never had before. Look at mine." She turned it up to him. "And that girl did it all to us by her devilish trick. She did it purposely to torture us. And now you ask me to think only of the relief!"

She broke into loud crying.

The others stared at her in shocked silence for a space. The color was drained from Renny's face. Roma looked at Alayne, fascinated.

"I think you ought to take her up to her room and make her lie down," said Piers.

"Give her a drop of brandy," said Nicholas.

Wakefield appeared in the doorway. "What's happened?" he cried, his eyes twitching.

Finch went to him. He muttered — "Shut up. It's all right. The money is found."

Renny was half-leading, half-carrying Alayne up the stairs. She stumbled beside him without speaking till they reached her room and the door was shut behind them. Then she threw herself on the bed and lay there, staring up at the ceiling. His instinct to comfort her made him throw a silk-lined quilt over her but she flung it off, as though in anger.

" I don't want anything over me," she said.

He went to his own room and returned with a little brandy in a glass. He raised her and patted her back while she drank it. " Come now, come now," he kept saying.

She raised her eyes, wide and blue, to his face.

" Can you expect me," she said, " to forget all you 've suffered and to give myself up to simple rejoicing ? "

She had left a mouthful of the brandy in the glass and he drank it.

" Alayne," he said, " such a burden has fallen from me, such a cloud has been lifted from my mind, that I can think of nothing else. You know, darling, I 've been a very unhappy man."

She raised herself on her elbow. " If a wife," she said, " met her husband outside the door of a prison where he had been tortured, would you expect her to be filled with joy at seeing him free again ? To look at the scars of his suffering and never give a thought to the torturer ? "

" Yes."

" You would expect that ? "

" Yes. I 'd expect her to be so glad to see him free that nothing else would matter. Also this is an entirely different case. Roma is no torturer. She 's a little girl who was playing a kind of game. She thought — "

Alayne interrupted fiercely — " Don't speak of that girl as innocent. Nothing will convince me that she has n't gloated all these months over the trouble she was making. From the hour she entered this house she hated me. I 've seen it in her eyes a thousand times."

" Now you 're talking rubbish. She was a baby of less than *three* when she came to Jalna. How could she hate you ? "

" She did. I could feel it."

He answered angrily — " You could feel it, for the simple

reason that you disliked her because she was Eden's child.
You 've never been just to her."

Color flooded Alayne's white face.   " What did I do that
was unjust?   Tell me one thing."

" I can't put my finger on any one thing," he answered
impatiently.   " But your dislike was there."

" Just as her hate for me was there."

" Roma does *not* hate you.   She hates no one."

" Well — I hate her ! "

" Because she 's Eden's child."

" Why must you go on repeating that ! "   Her voice broke
hysterically.

He got up and moved restlessly about the room.   Then
he said more calmly — " Let 's be reasonable.   Eden is dead.
Roma cannot help being his child.   She is ours now — to
care for — "

" She 's not mine to care for !   I won't have her in the
house.   Not a day longer."

" Alayne ! "   His brown eyes widened in astonishment.

" I mean it.   I won't see her growing up with our children.
She is full of deceit.   It 's her second nature.   You can't
make me believe she has n't reveled in her power over us.
I will not have her instilling her perversion into Adeline and
Archer."

" Just what do you mean? " he demanded.

" Let her go to your sister.   I repeat I will not have her
here.   I could n't breathe the air she breathes.   If you had
lost your reason — it would be her fault.   If I had lost
mine — "

He came and looked down on her.   " You 're too ready
to brood on the past, Alayne.   Think of the future.   It is
bright, if only you will let it be so.   There 's nothing I want
so much as to forget what has happened — if you 'd let me.
When I was coming home, with Finch and Roma, I thought
I 'd never been happier in my life.   I had found the lost

money. I knew there was no crick in my brain. I was ready to wipe everything else off the slate. Let me tell you something. I was talking to Mr. Fennel this afternoon and he persuaded me to go into the church with him and we knelt on the chancel steps and he prayed that everything would be made clear and, inside half an hour, it was. What do you think of that?" He smiled half-apologetically, half in wonder at a true miracle.

Alayne said — "And I suppose you and Mr. Fennel believe that divine guidance led you to the very spot where Roma was."

"Why not?"

"And I suppose you think she should be rewarded for what she has done. Oh, Renny, we're too different. We can't feel the same about anything."

"We can feel the same about our relief, can't we? Upon my soul — I think you might try."

She stretched out her hand, caught his, and kissed it. "I shall be as happy as you, if you will send Roma away. But I will never leave my room while she is under this roof. My nerves won't stand it." She buried her face in the pillow. Hoarse sobs tore her throat.

"Very well," he said resignedly. "I will ask Meg to take her for a while." He went to the door.

"Forever, I tell you! I won't have her here."

He went down the stairs and met Wragge in the hall. "I thought, sir," Wragge said, "I'd better lay the tea in the library, as there seems to be a conference going on in the drawing-room. Everything is ready, sir."

"Right. We'll be there directly." He went into the drawing-room and closed the door behind him. Wragge at once applied his ear to the keyhole.

Finch had told Wakefield what had happened. The two were standing in a corner together. Maurice and Patience were together by a window, their young faces embarrassed yet inquisitive. The two uncles, Meg, and Piers were in a group about Roma, who stood pale and composed, looking from one face to another as they questioned her.

" It seems clear," Ernest said, " that the child thought she was doing a benevolent thing."

" You know," Meg added, " it is just the sort of thing Eden might have done, half mischievous and half kind-hearted. I think Roma is very like dear Eden."

Piers said, with a grin — " If Eden ever had got his hands on those notes, he 'd never have parted with them."

Wakefield flushed and called out from where he stood : — " That 's a lie. Eden was the most generous chap I 've ever known."

" Good for you," Finch said, under his breath.

" I never saw any signs of generosity in him," said Piers.

Wakefield retorted with heat — " That is because you shut your eyes to all the good in him. I can never forget how he gave me the last money he ever earned."

" He knew he had no further use for it," said Piers.

" I am glad," Ernest said, " that Wakefield shows a spirit of gratitude. It is all too rare. On my part, I never forget a benefit given."

All eyes now turned to Renny, standing just inside the door.

" How is she ? " asked Nicholas. " Feeling better ? "

" She 's pretty well upset."

" No wonder. Poor girl, she 's been feeling wretched."

Meg exclaimed — " But why, in the name of heaven, can't she stop feeling wretched ! People who go on hugging their emotions to them are beyond me. Why can't she rejoice with the rest of us that the mystery is solved ? I feel ten years younger. Why should Alayne make a scene ? "

" She 's at the end of her tether," said Piers. " No one knows better than I do what she has been through."

" Well, I must say that sounds queer to me," returned his

sister. "As though you could know better than Renny, when he was the cause of it all."

"That is just why I know better. I saw it from the outside."

"Whether you see things from the inside or the outside, you always know better than anyone else." She smiled ironically.

"Whatever happens," said Piers, "you see things strictly from your own point of view. Other people's don't exist for you."

They stared at each other truculently, their fine clear eyes prominent. By the window their two children stood looking on, Patience hotly partisan for her mother, burning to say something on her side; Maurice embarrassed, yet faintly amused.

Renny spoke, with his hand on the doorknob. "Rags has laid tea in the library. We'd better go."

Ernest drew back. "In the library! I am afraid that won't suit me. Already I have a slight cold. I don't like to leave the fire. I don't think there is a fire in the library. I'm sure there isn't. Will you please see, Renny."

Renny strode across the hall. Returning to the doorway he said — "No, there's none."

"Then I can't go. Never mind. Never mind. It doesn't signify."

"What has happened to you, Uncle Ernest?" asked Piers. "No one is generally more keen for their tea than you."

"I found Alayne's weeping very upsetting."

"All the more reason for taking your tea."

Meg exclaimed — "Poor old dear! I'll carry your tea to you here. I'll bring my own as well. We shall have ours by the fire together — away from all dissension."

"I want my tea by the fire," said Nicholas.

"You have no cold." Ernest regarded him with mild asperity. "Just now you were complaining of the heat."

" I want my tea by the fire."

" We 'll carry it all in here," said Renny.   " Come along, Mooey and Patience.   Get busy."

They sprang to help.   Roma gave a little laugh of pleasure and ran after them.   Meg settled down to be waited on. Piers looked thoughtfully after Roma.   He said : —

" That 's the strangest kid I 've ever known.   She does n't realize in the least the enormity of what she has done.   I think she 's about six in her mind."

" You 're wrong," said Finch.   " Her mentality is nearer sixteen."

" I agree with Finch," Meg said.   " Roma is a very intelligent child.   She grows more like Eden in her looks.   I shan't be surprised if she becomes a poet."

Piers blew out his cheeks.   " Whatever she may become, she is a little troublemaker now.   She has nearly wrecked Renny's life — to say nothing of Alayne's."

" That is all over, thank God," said Ernest.   " When the tea comes in, Renny must tell us all that happened from the very beginning.   One's mind gets a little confused with all the talk."

Maurice and Patience appeared, carrying two trays.   The one on which sat the stout silver teapot with a silver robin perched on its lid was placed in front of Meg.   She said with a happy smile — " How natural it is for me to be pouring tea at Jalna again.   Tea always is a pleasant ceremony to me and I have a theory that it never should be poured except by one who really relishes it.   Alayne does n't even like tea. She drinks one cup but I 've heard her say many a time that she could very well do without it."

Renny asked — " Roma, where is Adeline? "

" With Wright in the stable.   There 's a little foal."

Renny put a cup of tea and a plate with bread and butter and a small cake on it into her hands.   He said — " Take them and run away somewhere.   We want to talk."   He opened the door for her and she passed under his arm with a docile glance up at him. He closed the door after her, came back and stood by the fire.

Nicholas had swallowed the first cup of tea and now, wiping his moustache with an appreciative "Ha!" he said:—

"Good idea to put the child out. Now we can talk. Renny, I can't tell you how glad I am. Many a time I thought you would lose your wits. Now we know you're sound. Come and give me your hand."

Renny came and shook the shapely old hand. His lip trembled. For a moment he felt unmanned. "I've worried a lot," he said.

Ernest, not to be outdone by his brother, said — "Some of the Courts were not quite right in the head. My mother had a young brother, Timothy —"

Piers interrupted — "This affair has been enough to send anyone bughouse. That kid is not to be let off scot-free. Something must be done about her."

"That is what I want to talk about," said Renny. "Alayne refuses to let her live on at Jalna."

"What?" exclaimed Nicholas, his hand cupping his ear. "What's that you say?"

"I say that Alayne cannot bear the thought of being in the same house with Roma. Alayne's nerves are at breaking point, poor girl."

"Whose house is it, I should like to know?" asked Meg. "Yours or hers? Roma has never been any trouble to Alayne. Roma would never be a trouble to anyone."

"Oh, yeah?" said Piers. "What about *this* affair?"

"She meant only good. You could see that in her little face."

"Alayne won't have her here," said Renny. "She says she will not leave her room while Roma is under the roof."

"This is a pretty to-do," said Nicholas.

" She 'll get over that feeling," Ernest added.   " A night's sleep does wonders in calming one down."

" She won't calm down," Renny said, " till Roma goes. Meggie, I am wondering if you will take Roma — for a time at least."

Meg's face fell.   " Take a child into my house, when I have all my own work to do!   Oh, I 'm afraid it would be too much for me."

Piers quoted laughing — " Roma would never be a trouble to anyone."

" If you feel like that," retorted his sister, " take her yourself."

" We have no room for her.   You have two extra bedrooms."

" As to the work, " said Renny, " Roma makes her own bed.   And does n't Patience help you? "

Patience, who did most of the work, now said — " I think we could manage very well, Mummie."

" Wherever she goes," said Renny, " I shall expect to pay for her keep."

" I 'm not thinking of cost," said Meg.   " Such a thought never entered my head.   But to please you — to help make things smooth for you — I 'll take her.   I know what Alayne is when she 's roused.   Roma shall come with me this very evening."

" Thank you, Meggie."   He gave her a warm look.

" It 's nothing," she declared.   " It 's nothing to what I would do for you.   You know, Renny, I feel that every one of us should do everything possible to make up to you for all you 've been through."

" I 'm afraid I have put you all through a good deal," he said ruefully.

Finch said — " Tell them about Mr. Fennel's part in finding the bank notes, Renny."

Briefly Renny repeated what had happened, not at all embarrassed by this suppliant picture of himself, but eager to give credit where credit was due.

" Well — I 'll be damned," said Nicholas.

" It is remarkable," declared Ernest, " and shows what efficacy there may be in prayer, even in these days. Does the Rector know of the sequel? "

" Not yet. I 'm going to phone him directly."

" He is such a dear," said Meg. " I 'm sure that, if anybody's prayers would be listened to, his would."

Wakefield said — " I 've known stranger things than that in the war."

" You say," said Nicholas, " that you got straight up from your knees and went and found Roma with the kettle."

" Yes."

" Where is the money? " asked Piers.

" I picked it up," said Meg. " It was on the floor. Here you are, Renny." She offered him the roll of bank notes.

" Thanks." He stuffed them into his pocket. Then he exclaimed — " By George, how am I to explain this to Clapperton? I don't want to tell him that Roma took the money."

Meg ordered a fresh pot of tea and they settled down to discuss, with fervor and many interruptions by Nicholas, this new complication.

XXVII

THE CHILDREN

RAGS moved with great agility from the door but still Roma knew he had been listening. She had caught him at it before, and he had caught her at it. Now they gave each other a wary glance. He remarked: —

"So you 've been sent from the room, miss. That was a good idea, for little pitchers 'ave long ears. Ever 'eard that saying?"

"It 's a wonder yours are n't a mile long," she returned composedly.

He turned to her abruptly. " Has that there money been found?"

"You know it has."

"And who found it, may I ask?"

"I did."

He came close, his face alight with curiosity. " Let me in on the whole thing, Miss Roma, and you 'll not be sorry."

She stood balancing her cup and saucer. " I 'm not allowed to tell," she said. " Please don't bother me."

"As though I 'd bother you! Tell or not, just as you please but — I bet you 're in for a lot of trouble."

"Did Auntie Alayne say so?"

"She don't like you."

"I know."

"What would you s'y to leavin' Jalna?"

"I would n't go. Uncle Renny would n't let me go. He likes me better than anyone, excepting Adeline."

"My eye! You 'ave a good opinion of yourself."

"I know things."

Rags gave her a look of grudging respect. " Do you think 'e likes you better than 'e likes 'is wife? "

" Yes. He told me so."

" You're a riddle and no mistake. 'Ere comes Miss Adeline, looking wetter than a rat." His expression changed to one of doting admiration as Adeline flung open the door at the back of the hall and appeared in her riding things. She came toward them eagerly.

" Shut the door, can't you? " said Rags.

She went and kicked it shut. She exclaimed — " I 've been riding Spartan! It 's the first time Wright would let me on him. He 's wonderful. He moves like Pegasus might move, if he 'd had a cocktail. Oh, what bliss! " She pushed her hair back from her forehead. " Where are you going with your tea, Roma? I 'm starving. I could eat seventeen currant buns with jam on them. What 's going on in there? "

" Family conclave," said Rags. " Get Miss Roma to tell you. She knows all about it."

Roma began to ascend the stairs.

" May n't I go in? " asked Adeline.

Rags puckered his face and gave a decisive shake of the head. " I should n't if I was you, Miss Adeline. There 's serious matters being discussed."

She looked anxious. " Is anything wrong? "

Roma said over her shoulder — " Come up to my room and I 'll tell you."

" All right." Then, in a cajoling tone — " Ragsie, *would* you bring me some tea? "

When she called him Ragsie, he would have died for her. Yet he muttered at the way he was overworked, as he rattled down the stairs to the basement.

Roma set her plate and cup of tea on the table that had been Eden's. She took care not to place either of them on the spot where Eden had carved his name. She took a piece of bread and butter and began to eat it. Adeline came in, pulling off her wet cardigan as she came. Standing in her white blouse and riding breeches she looked tall and very slim. Her beautifully marked brows were bent in an expression of concern. She asked: —

"What are you going to tell me, Roma?"

Roma continued to eat in silence. She could not decide how to begin her story.

"Is it something about the letter that was lost?"

"It was n't a letter."

"What was it then?"

"Money. A thousand dollars."

"*A thousand dollars!*" Adeline was astounded by the enormity of the sum. Then a wave of jealousy swept over her, jealousy that Roma should know what was so closely connected with Renny and what she herself had not known. "When did you find out?"

"I 've known all along."

"Who told you?" Now the jealousy hurt her cruelly.

"Nobody. I knew because I took the money. I took it from Mr. Clapperton and hid it in the woods. Uncle Renny thought *he* had taken it, and forgotten, but to-day I told him."

Questions came sharply from Adeline. It was hard to get the story clear from her cousin's answers but at last she understood, in a bewildered fashion. She was silent for a space, then: —

"It was frightfully dishonest," she said. "You might be sent to prison."

"I don't care. I wanted him to have the money."

"Was he glad to have it, do you think?"

"Oh, yes. He hugged me and kissed me."

"Goodness. It seems worse to me than lying about going to see *Othello,* and I got into a terrible row for that."

"Uncle Renny was glad about this."

"Was Mummie glad?"

A smile flickered across Roma's face. "No. She made a scene. She was furious at me but I don't care."

Rags came up the attic stairs with a tray. He panted ostentatiously as he entered the room. "Three flights of stairs," he said. "If I don't get my sciatica back at me it 'll be a wonder. No system can stand what mine 'as to put up with."

"Oh, Ragsie, what a superlative tea!" She began hungrily to eat.

The two girls were silent till he left the room. Then Adeline asked — "Where is Mummie?"

"In her room. Uncle Renny helped her up."

"*Helped* her! Could n't she walk?"

"She was too angry."

"Goodness, Roma, you make things sound strange."

"They are strange."

Steps sounded on the stairs. Patience and Maurice came in. She said — "Well, you have messed things up, Roma. You may be pleased with yourself but I think it 's pretty awful. Now you 're going to be a little blessing to Mother and me."

"A blessing?" repeated Roma, not understanding.

Maurice said, perching on the footboard of the bed — "Let her alone, Patty. She 's had enough said to her."

"That 's a benign attitude for you to take but she is n't going to live with *you*."

"I should n't mind if she did, and you won't be any trouble, will you, Roma?"

"Where am I going?" she asked, her eyes wide.

"You are coming to stay with us," answered Patience, "and you are to help me gather up your clothes. The suitcase you brought back from school will do for the present. We can get your other things later on."

"I don't want to."

" Mummie and I don't much want to either. But you 've brought it on us."

" Why ? "

Patience turned laughing to Maurice. " Is n't she priceless ? "

He stretched out a long arm and took a handful of Roma's fine fair hair, drawing her to him. He said — " Can't you realize that it will be better for everyone if you stay with Auntie Meg and Patience for a while ? "

" It 's Auntie Alayne who does n't want me," she said, twisting her hands together.

Patience exclaimed — " Is it any wonder ? You have nearly wrecked her reason with your little tricks. Come, get the suitcase."

" Her hair," said Maurice, fingering it, " is n't hair. It 's like down. I love the feel of it." However, he loosed it and she moved reluctantly toward the clothes cupboard. She said : —

" I will stay only a little while. I don't have to stay, do I, Adeline ? "

" You 're at the bottom of all this," said Adeline, " so I don't care what you do. Besides, you 're a thief."

" It was n't real stealing. I did n't keep the money."

" You did worse. You made my father search and search and search for it." Her dark eyes were brilliant with anger. " You made him suffer."

" But you should have seen how glad he was when he found it."

" Stop arguing," Patience said, " and give me your clothes." She set the suitcase in the middle of the floor.

" I won't go," said Roma, " till I ask Uncle Renny if I must."

Patience made an exasperated sound. " It was he who asked Mother to take you. You 'd not stay where you are not wanted, would you ? "

"You don't want me."

"Well, somebody's got to have you."

Roma raised her eyes to Maurice's. "May I go with you?"

He answered gently — "I'm afraid we have n't room for another child. Mummie is n't very well."

"I'd be at school most of the time."

"I think this is just a visit, Roma. You'll come back to Jalna after a little."

She succumbed and began to help with the packing. Rain streamed down the windowpanes and made a muffled thunder on the roof. Up here the scenes below had a sense of unreality. The children seemed shut in behind the walls of rain. Yet at last Roma's clothes were packed and she followed Patience resignedly out of the room.

"Good-bye," she said, from the doorway, and made the word sound final and rather tragic.

"Good-bye," returned Adeline briefly.

Maurice said — "You'll be seeing each other when you go back to school, won't you?"

"Yes," answered Adeline, and they sat in silence for a space. Then Adeline said sombrely — "I wish I might never see Roma again."

"I don't blame you. But Father says she is only about six, in her mind."

"Six! You should hear the things she says."

"What sort of things?"

"I can't remember. They're not things you can remember."

He came and sat down beside her. "You are the one I like, Adeline. Do you know, we have n't had a word together since *Othello*."

"Neither we have. It seems ages ago. Everything has gone wrong since that night."

"But you did enjoy it, did n't you?"

A rapture of remembrance lighted her face. "It was gorgeous."

"Swift acted like a fool. But he was just carried away by you, as you were carried away by the play. You have no idea what you looked like, Adeline."

A quick color moved into her cheeks. She asked: "Do you ever see him?"

"Very seldom. He's still at Vaughanlands. Have you heard that Gemmel Griffith is to marry Mr. Clapperton?"

"That old man!" She was aghast.

"He's not so old and he has lots of money. Garda is delighted. She told me so."

"Then she's a selfish pig."

"Oh, no. But it will be a great thing for all of them. They're going to move into Vaughanlands. I expect Swift will leave then."

"I hope he does." She took another buttered bun.

Maurice watched her with his indolent smile. He asked — "Can you spare me a cup of tea? I was too excited downstairs to take anything. I'll drink out of Roma's cup."

Adeline sprang up, eager to do something for Maurice. She rinsed Roma's cup in the ewer on the washing stand. She filled it from the teapot and offered him a bun. They sat smiling at each other, munching the buns, casting from them the remembrance of the past hour.

"This is fun," he said. "I wish you weren't going away so soon."

"So do I. I never shall like school."

"What do the girls talk about?"

"Boys. Imaginary love affairs. They haven't had any real ones. Different kinds of make-up — yet they're not allowed to use any. Movie stars — they know all about their silly marriages and about the films they are in, though we're hardly ever taken to the cinema. It all makes me sick.

I 've lived too much with real people to enjoy living with those girls."

" Do they like you? "

" I don't know. They say I 'm snooty."

" I dread going to University. I did all my studying with a tutor when I was in Ireland. I had only one friend and I wanted no other. I miss him."

" I know. He is Pat Crawshay."

" Sir Patrick Crawshay." Maurice dwelt on the name with affection. " He 's been a baronet since he was three. His father was killed in a hunting accident."

" I remember him. He had tow hair. We rode together when I went fox-hunting in Ireland."

" He has told me about that. When the hunt was over he asked you if you would kiss him good-bye and you warned him that you were pretty strong and you gave him a hug that nearly cracked his ribs."

Adeline gave a joyous chuckle. " I remember. He did n't like it a bit."

" Not like it! He liked it so well that he says he is coming over here to marry you when you are eighteen."

" What conceit! " She looked scornful but she was secretly pleased.

Maurice said, with a serious look in his dark blue eyes —
" I don't think I shall allow that, Adeline, even though Patrick is my best friend."

" Don't worry." She spoke with equal seriousness.
" I 'm never going to marry. I 'm going to live always at Jalna with Daddy. I shall never find a man I 'd love as well as I do him."

" You say that now. Just see what happens when you fall in love with a chap your own age."

" You 'll wait a long time to see that."

" I 'm willing to wait, Adeline."

Something in his voice confused her. She could no longer

think clearly or speak with decision. The soft thunder of the rain resounded on the roof. They sat silent, not looking at each other. Then Maurice bent toward her and ruffled her hair with his lips.

Piers's voice sounded from below. "Mooey! Come along. We're going."

"Good-bye," Maurice said abruptly and rose.

"Good-bye." Her air was laconic. She listened to his footsteps going lightly down the stairs.

After a little she heard the sound of Piers's car on the gravel drive. She was alone, in Roma's room. Roma was gone. Snatched up by the powerful world of the grownups and taken to another house. Adeline could not remember when Roma had come to Jalna. She seemed always to have been there. But never had she seemed like a sister. Perhaps it had been something in Roma herself, perhaps something in Alayne that had kept Roma an outsider. Now she was gone and Adeline had a sense of loss, of blankness. She wished Mooey might have remained. She shrank from meeting Alayne. She was afraid of what Alayne might say about Roma, even though she herself felt hot anger at what Roma had done. How could Renny have kissed her — been pleased with her? For the first time in her life Adeline felt jealous of Roma, and that at the moment of her disgrace and banishment.

Archer came running into the room. His eyes looked very large and intensely blue under his tall pale forehead. His hair stood on end. He shouted, as though Adeline were deaf: —

"Roma's gone! What do you think of that? Did you know? Who said you could have tea up here? Who carried it up? Roma's gone! Now I can jump on her bed if I want to. I'll jump on it now."

He leaped on to the bed and began jumping wildly up and down. "I'll come in here whenever I like. I'll come in

the middle of the night and jump up and down on the bed.
Why do you s'pose they sent her away?" He fell and lay
across the bed panting.

Adeline said — "You'll be the next to go. See if you
are n't."

He all but rolled off the bed in his astonishment. "Me?"
he cried. "They would n't dare! Who'd send me away,
I'd like to know."

"They'd have a family conference — like to-day — then
off you'd go."

"Where?"

"I don't know. *They'd* decide that."

He was on his feet, beginning to run out of the room, his
face distorted by suspicion and fear. "I'll see about this,"
he said, as he ran.

She was after him, caught him and held him fast. "Don't
be a little silly. I was pulling your leg."

He wriggled until he could look into her face.

"Honestly?" he demanded.

"Of course. They never could send you away because
there's no one on earth who would take you in."

He laughed happily. "Are n't you glad Roma's gone?
There'll be just us two and we'll do everything together,
shan't we, Adeline?"

Downstairs all was quiet. The uncles were tired out.
Nicholas lay sunk in his chair sleeping. A bubbling snore
vibrated his gray moustache. Ernest sat close by the fire,
resting his nerves with a game of patience. Winter was on
the way and now they could settle down peacefully to wait
for it.

XXVIII

THE CLEAR AIR

THE two cars had gone and he stood alone in the porch. It had been a great year for growth and the Virginia creeper, unsatisfied by all its conquest of the past ninety years, had reached out with new vigor to spread its lusty leaves on every prominence where it could find support. Time and again it had been pruned but not this year. Now the tendrils draped the porch, the new growth clinging to the old or hanging loose, so that those who went in or out had to push it aside. To-day rain dripped from it, ruddy fallen leaves carpeted the porch, still there were enough and to spare. His warm-colored tweeds, the red of his hair, the weather-beaten tone of his skin, fitted well with the autumn tints about him.

Never had a rain seemed so cleansing. He felt its benefi-cence through all his being. He stretched out his hand palm upward and when it was wet he laid it against his forehead. There was a blessing in it. He drew deep breaths of the damp air. His lungs seemed truly to expand for the first time in months. His heart beat with a new gladness in the mere fact of life. The fact of his sanity, his soundness, vibrated through him. Suddenly he laughed at the thought that he ever could have doubted it, been taken in, enmeshed by a child's game of make-believe. But what a pity he had had to send her away! He had seen by her little face that she had not wanted to go, even though Meg and Patience were so kind. Still it would be only temporary, he would see to that. Alayne would agree to her coming back to Jalna after a little. He must go up to Alayne, poor girl, and cheer her up. He must think of something nice to do for her.

But first he must telephone the Rector. He turned swiftly and went into the library.

Mr. Fennel's voice answered his ring.

"Hullo," said Renny, "I have something to tell you." He could not keep the joy out of his voice.

"You have found the money?"

"Come now, you might have let me tell you."

"The first syllable you spoke told me."

"I found it not more than half an hour after I left you. It was hidden in the woods. I'm coming over this evening to tell you all about it. I can't tell you over the phone."

"Of course not. I'll be glad to see you."

There was a silence, then Renny said with some embarrassment — "I must thank you for what you did for me."

"Don't thank me. Give thanks where it is due."

"Yes. Certainly. Well, I'll come over this evening. You'll see a new man in me. It's as though a load I'd been staggering under for months had been swept away. You'll be surprised when you hear how."

"I'm prepared for anything, Renny, since we prayed for help."

"Well — good-bye. I'll be over."

"Good-bye, and God bless you."

Renny hung up the receiver and sat a moment, resting his head on his hands. His most trivial act seemed to have a new importance, as though adumbrated against a clear sky. He felt marvelously self-conscious, as though everything he did were a marvel. The very room appeared more spacious, when of late its walls had drawn to press him in, to suffocate him. Now he would go up to Alayne. He mounted the stairs and went straight into her room. The windows were open and the rain was blowing on to the sills.

He went and sat on the bed beside her. He bent over her, looking into her tear-stained face.

"Roma's gone," he said. "I sent her to Meg's."

She opened her eyes wide in surprise.

"Gone," she repeated. "For how long?"

"To stay. Meg is going to keep her. As you feel so bitter against her, it seemed the best thing to do."

She half-rose, leaning on her elbow, her eyes searching his. "Don't you feel bitter?" she asked tensely.

"No. I'm just thankful to find that I'm — all right."

"What are you made of?" she exclaimed. "You have suffered hellishly. I have suffered. Yet you feel no bitterness at the one who caused it all."

"She didn't understand."

"Not understand that she was *thieving* and *lying*? Please don't ask me to believe that."

"Alayne, I don't ask you to believe anything except that I am sound and out from under that cloud. My God, surely that is enough to make you happy!" His voice broke.

She drew his head down to where her lips would rest between his brows. She said — "Darling, it will make me happy — later on. But just now I can't think of anything but of how you were made to suffer."

"Help me to forget. That's all I ask."

"I will, I will," she said, stroking his head. "And — Renny, thank you for sending Roma to Meg. I couldn't have forgotten with her in the house."

She knew that never, never could she forget or forgive what Roma had done. It was the culmination of the years of distrust she had felt toward her. She must pretend to forget, for Renny's sake, but she would never submit to having Roma at Jalna again.

"Do you know," he said, "you are looking very tired. Now I've got an idea."

"Tired!" she repeated. "That's putting it mildly. Any looks I have ever had, I've lost."

He denied this with a kiss. "Don't you want to know what my idea is?"

" Yes."

" It 's for you to go to New York for a visit. You have n't been there for years. Not since Adeline was four. Do you remember? "

Did she remember? She was not likely to forget the time she had left him, as she thought finally, and, after months in which she had more and more longed for him, he had gone there and brought her and her aunt triumphantly back.

" Yes," she breathed, " I remember."

" A change will do you good," he went on. " Your friends will like to have you visit them. That Miss Trent, you know, is always urging you to go."

The thought of going to New York, the thought of mingling again in that swift, intense life, made her pulses quicken. To get away from this backwater, away from all these relations — But she said — " No, not unless you will come with me."

" We can't afford that," he said. " You know very well we can't. Miss Trent could n't take me in. Hotels are abominably expensive. But I 'll tell you what I will do. I 'll go and spend a few days with you and bring you home. How would you like that? "

She could not resist. The prospect put new life into her. To leave this house where she had spent such days and nights of apprehension, seen Renny so suffer; to breathe new air; to mingle with the cosmopolitan crowds, far from this rain-soaked countryside; to see the newest plays; to be far from the uncles with their irritating habits of the aged; to be far from the children with their irritating habits of the young; five hundred miles from the Wragges, with whom she had struggled alone for nearly four years — oh, it was bliss! Even to be — and she scarcely could bring herself to acknowledge it — away for a little while from Renny, whose face, whose every act, had become the focus of her anguished observation. Away from him she could rest her mind from him, the weight of his presence would be lifted from her. Perhaps, at that distance, she would be able to achieve a saner feeling about Roma, no longer be swept by such a surge of bitter anger at the thought of her. She said, twining her arms about him : —

" I will go, if you will promise faithfully to come for me."

" I promise." He kissed her, but half-absently. He could not give his mind wholly to any thought but that of his release.

She wished she might stay in her room and not be forced to meet the family again that evening, but she knew Renny would expect her to be at the table and feel keen disappointment if she did not appear. He must not be disappointed. Also she felt a new energy in herself. The thought of change stirred her. She took pains with her dressing, putting on a light blue voile dress with bright flowers on it, and silver sandals.

The meal passed well. Nicholas and Ernest were tired and talked little, but they said again and again how nice she looked. Adeline too was quieter than usual, giving Alayne contemplative glances as though wondering about her. No place had been set for Roma. Finch and Wakefield talked determinedly of impersonal things. Renny seemed scarcely to know what they were saying but laughed and agreed with his brothers. Rags, for some reason, cast disapproving looks at Alayne. All were conscious of her new vitality.

" There is nothing to equal travel," said Ernest. " I never took a journey but it did me good."

" I guess," said Nicholas, " that I have taken my last."

" Nonsense, Uncle Nick." Renny spoke from where he stood by the sideboard. " When you 've had a few glasses of this good claret, you 'll not say that. It 's some I stored in the cellar before I went to the war. One of these days you 'll be setting out for old London."

The good claret did warm the old man's spirit. He did, before he left the table, talk of a visit to England, but Renny must go with him to look after him — or Finch. Finch would do.

"Now," said Renny, " we are to drink to Alayne's visit to New York. She's had a pretty monotonous time since the beginning of the war."

" The monotony broken only by worry," put in Ernest.

" Oh, no, Uncle Ernest," she objected.

" I say, yes. And I say you deserve a holiday."

" And may it be a happy one," said Renny, smiling at her and drinking.

" God bless her," added Nicholas, wiping his moustache. " Ha — that's good claret, a very good flavor."

" Thank you all," said Alayne, tears in her eyes. Really they could be sweet, when they wanted to, she thought. She would remember this evening. It was so different from what she had expected. She had feared objections to Roma's going, even expressions of pity for the child. But there was nothing of the sort. Roma had gone to Meggie's. And why not? they seemed to say. Meg was her aunt and would be kind to her.

Did Renny know what weariness was, she wondered, as she saw him set out for the Rectory that evening. But she was not sorry to see him go. She was too tired for talk. The uncles went early to bed while she and Wakefield sat in the drawing-room listening to Finch's desultory playing. He would play what came into his head, reaching out toward the concord of sounds as one might reach out to a tame bird. When it eluded him, he did not try to follow it but let it go, and turned to another. He sat with head bent, the firelight playing on his sensitive face. Alayne wondered about him, about his wife Sarah and about their child. He must be almost five years old. Did Finch ever think of him? Surely he would, under the influence of Sarah and her Russian husband, grow into a being alien to Finch. But one's own children — right beneath one's own roof — what would they grow into? Roma was definitely and most dreadfully herself, in spite of all influence. She must put Roma out of her head. The thought of Roma made her feel ill. She said: —

"Play Bach, will you please, Finch? I want to be held, so I can't think of anything but the music."

"I never think so freely as when I 'm listening to Bach," said Wakefield. "He unties the strings, unbuttons the buttons, and I let myself go."

"I can't remember anything straight through to-night."

"Then play just bits," said Alayne. "Drown the sound of the rain. It comes down heavier and heavier."

"Summer is gone," Wakefield said. "Why should we live in a climate where we freeze half the year? I wish my grandfather had built Jalna in New Zealand or South Africa."

"Then I 'd never have known it," said Alayne.

"And been all the better off, I should say." Finch got up and stretched his arms.

"No, no," begged Alayne. "Please go on. We 're sorry we talked, are n't we, Wakefield?"

"It did n't matter." But, now that there was silence, he sat down again and began to play.

All was quiet when Renny returned. He had stayed late at the Rectory. He had hoped to find the house so when he came back to it. He came quietly into the hall, locking the door after him. It had turned cold outside and he missed the glow of the old stove that had so long stood there. He missed the sight of the dogs stretched comfortably about it. Those unfriendly radiators Alayne had installed had taken as much from the spirit of the house as they had given it in physical comfort. He hung his hat on the hatrack, from which the carved head of a fox looked sharply down on him.

He ran his hand across his own head, in a peculiar sweeping gesture. He stood with his head poised, as though in relish of its liberation. He raised his eyes to the eyes of the fox — a hunted creature. He knew what it was to feel hunted by shadowy huntsmen, riding nightmares. But now he was free of all that. He was in control of his mind. He would think what thoughts he chose — pursue them or not, as he liked. He ran his hand caressingly over the glossy walnut grapes with their leaves that decorated the newel post. To-night he had an especial love for the house, and through its weather-mellowed bricks and staunch timbers he felt an especial intimacy come out to him.

He gently opened the door of Adeline's room and went in. It was pitch-dark except where the light from the hall fell on the mirror. In this luminous space the objects of the room were dimly seen. He went to the side of the bed and sat down on it. He could just make out the lines of her body, slender and severe beneath the covering, and her head dark on the pillow. He bent and put his lips to her cheek. She woke without fear and said — " Is that you, Daddy? "

" Yes," he answered, " but don't wake. I only wanted to make sure you were all right. Go to sleep."

" Lie down beside me."

" I must n't. My clothes are damp."

" Where have you been? "

" At Mr. Fennel's."

" Were you telling him how glad you are? "

" Yes."

" Do you believe there was a miracle? "

" Why not? "

Adeline, out of the teaching of recent confirmation classes, asked — " Was all this done to try your faith, do you think? "

" God knows . . . I certainly was tried."

" Daddy, I hate Roma."

" No, no, don't say that."

" For once, Mummie and I agree about feelings."

He was startled.   " That 's an odd remark for a child."

" I 'm not just a child any more."

" That 's true."

" Daddy, I don't believe there was a miracle.   I believe you found Roma just by chance.   She 's a little beast and enjoys being powerful."

" Adeline, do you hear the rain? "

" Yes."

" It sounds peaceful, does n't it?   That 's the way I feel. Peaceful."

" I 'm so glad.   I feel that way too.   I 'll not be angry at Roma — if you 're not."

" Good."   Again he kissed her.   " Now go to sleep."

She kissed his hand.   " I like the smell of you," she said.

A sudden, dark possessiveness of fatherhood came over him.   He would never willingly give her to any man.   Not for years and years.   He ran his hand along the outline of her body.   She was breathing deeply.   Soon she slept.   The breath from her youthful lungs mingled with the air of the room that for so long had been the stronghold, the snug retreat, of a very old woman.

He tiptoed out of the room, closing the door behind him.

He could not bring himself to go to bed.   He wandered from one room to another, in each one thinking the same thought — no more searching here — no more unexpected finding of another twenty-dollar bill, with the horrid start, the deeper conviction of his own strangeness that had accompanied each finding.   Suddenly he remembered the little notebook in which he had recorded the dates of the days when he had recovered the bills.   He took it out, sat down at the desk in the library, and made the final entry.   " Remainder of notes found in old teakettle, hidden by Roma," and the date.   He sat gazing at the entry, satisfaction

smoothing his features, till an observer might have thought
he intended to spend the rest of the night so.   But, at last,
he rose and went into the drawing-room where a handful of
coals made a dusky glow on the hearth.   He laid the notebook on these and, resting his arm on the mantelshelf, waited
for it to burn.   The coals were reluctant to destroy it.   The
neat black book lay on their glowing surface intact for some
time.   Then, abruptly its leather cover curled at the edge, a
flame thumbed the pages over which he so often had pored.
Soon it was burning, then was no more.   He gave a little
laugh, wheeled, and went out into the porch.

The rain had ceased but still fell from the leaves of the
Virginia creeper.   It had brought down a lot of them, he
noticed.   The clouds were breaking and the moon, dwindling
towards its last quarter, showed through the watery shafts.
The evergreens looked solid with their weight of moisture.
A silence had come on all living things of the countryside.
No more song of locust or note of cricket, no more rustling
of small birds hid in the creeper, no hoot of owl or sound
of scurrying to burrow.   Winter was coming.   To Renny
the old house seemed to say — " I don't mind the winter,
now that you 're all right, my boy.   In fact I like the winter,
with the fires going and the family gathered about the fires."
The house seemed to draw closer into itself, press closer to
the earth, resisting all but what passed beneath its roof.

He struck a match and looked at his watch.   To-morrow
would be Sunday.   No — to-day was Sunday.   He would
go to church with very different feelings from last Sunday.
It had been hard to go in these last months, but there was the
firm habit of churchgoing, handed down by his grandmother, and he would stick to it.   His grandmother !   What
would she have said about this affair and Roma's part in it?
He had thought less often of her in recent months than at
any time since her death.   Much less often than when he
had been at the war.   Now vividly he felt her presence, saw

her in her formidable Victorian clothes, her full skirts sup-
ported by petticoats, her bodice made firm by boned stays,
her caps with intricate trimmings, her cashmere stockings,
and her shoes, always made to order.   He missed her — yes,
he still missed her.   The tender recollections another man
would give to a mother's memory he gave to hers.   Not that
she had been tender to him.   Many a time hot words had
been exchanged between them, but they had loved each other,
each had been proud of the other.

He came into the house, not locking the door behind him.
He seldom locked doors, feeling always ready to defend what
was his, without barricading.   In the dining room he stood
before the portrait of old Adeline as a beautiful young
woman, and smiled up at her.

" Gran," he said, his voice low, " I 've been through the
hell of a time, but it 's all right now.   I 've a mind to get
tight to celebrate.   What do you say? "

The brown eyes smiled down at him.   It was certain that
whatever he did that night she would approve.   But suddenly
he yawned, a relaxed, beneficent yawn such as had not
stretched his jaws in months.   His eyes watered.   He was
sleepy.

In spite of the activities of the house he did not wake till
ten.   There was barely time to shave, to dress, to eat his
breakfast and go to morning service at eleven.   In truth
an hour was not enough for all that had to be done.   Nicholas
had decided to go to church that morning.   Ernest, in spite
of his ninety years, never missed a Sunday even when the
weather was inclement.   He still stood through the longest
Psalms but he no longer knelt on the worn red hassock.   He
must satisfy his sense of reverence by sitting with his forehead bent to the pew in front of him.

His gouty leg was the greatest obstacle to Nicholas's
churchgoing, but there were other obstacles.   He could no
longer see to read the service.   He knew it by heart cer-

tainly but he had a way of getting muddled in the responses
and producing the wrong one, in his still resonant voice,
sometimes timing the uttering of it wrongly. Sometimes
he dozed and snored. It tired Ernest to have Nicholas sitting beside him doing these things. Some time ago he had
reached the point where he encouraged Nicholas to stay at
home. Nicholas, on his part, found it very pleasant to relax
in his comfortable chair or to stump about with only Alayne
and himself in the house.

But this morning he made up his mind to go. It was no
ordinary Sunday and he must take his part in the celebration.
Wakefield, with great patience, helped him to dress. When
this was accomplished he made an impressive figure. His
head was indeed magnificent. Wakefield helped him down
the stairs and into the car. Ernest was already there, im-
maculate, nervous, looking at his watch. The children had
taken the way across the fields with Finch.

"Five minutes to eleven," Ernest said, frowning.
"Whatever is keeping Renny?"

"He slept late, and no wonder," returned Nicholas.

Wakefield said — "He'll be here in a jiffy."

"I need not have hurried so," growled Nicholas. "I'm
quite out of breath." He panted ostentatiously.

"You were a solid hour dressing." Ernest tried to restrain his impatience but again he looked at his watch. "I
remember," he said, "how my mother disliked being late
for church."

"Run in, Wake, like a good boy," said Nicholas, "and see
what is keeping him."

"Urge him to make haste," added Ernest.

Wakefield darted up the steps. It was five minutes past
eleven when Renny slid into the driver's seat. "Sorry," he
said, grinning over his shoulder at his uncles, "but I couldn't
find my collection."

The words "couldn't find" sent a chill to the hearts of

Ernest and Nicholas. Was it possible that Renny was again beginning to lose money? But he looked so cheerful they could not feel anxious. They even continued to feel a little annoyed with him.

The first hymn was over and Mr. Fennel was already reading the service when they entered. Every head turned to look at them as they progressed slowly down the aisle, Nicholas leaning heavily on Renny's arm. Renny established them in the family pew beside Adeline and Archer, then knelt at the end next the aisle. In the pew in front knelt Piers, Pheasant, and their three sons. Going to church was an irritation to Maurice. In Ireland he had gone or not as he pleased and usually he did not please. Now he wore the sulky expression he usually wore at church. But he was conscious of Adeline sitting directly behind him. He was sure she was looking at him. He wished he might have been sitting beside her. Nooky and Philip always looked so angelic during the service, it was hard to believe they could ever do wrong. Pheasant, casting a contemplative look at them, thought — " I wonder which of them the new baby will be like. I do hope it is a girl. I should so love to have a daughter. But it is said they are a greater problem to bring up than boys. Goodness knows, boys are problem enough. All but Nooky. He 's always so sweet and loving. How marvelous it is to think that Piers is home safe — that I am going to have another baby — that Moocy is back from Ireland — that Renny and Wake are back from the war — that the horrible mystery about the stealing of the money is cleared up. Surely no other person in the church has as much to be thankful for as I. I really ought to be pouring out my gratitude in prayer but it 's so difficult for me to concentrate on prayer and always has been. How very strange it seems to see Roma in the pew with Meg and Patience. That child looks perfectly imperturbable. I do hope my little girl won't have a circuitous, baffling nature.

How beautifully Piers's hair grows about his temple! I do hope she will have hair like Piers's. It would be lovely on a girl. Goodness, Uncle Nick has dropped his prayer book!"

Nicholas had indeed. Now Renny was recovering it for him and Ernest was giving him a reproving look. As the service progressed, Nicholas gave his brother still more cause for feeling ruffled. He found the pew narrow and heavily shifted his bulk in it. He loudly tooted his nose. When, after the reciting of the Lord's Prayer, Mr. Fennel said — "O Lord, show Thy mercy upon us," Nicholas, instead of joining with the rest of the congregation in saying, "And grant us Thy salvation," took the next words from Mr. Fennel's mouth and loudly declaimed — "O Lord, save the Queen." He did not even say the *King* but most emphatically the *Queen,* as was printed in his prayer book of Victoria's time.

Nooky and Philip began to giggle, which set off Archer. Piers quieted his two with a look but Archer could not stop despite a pinch on the leg from Adeline and a rap on the head from Ernest's prayer book. Renny signaled to Archer to come and sit by him. As the little boy clambered in front of the knees of his great-uncles, Nicholas demanded — "What's up? What has he done?" He took off his glasses and frowned down on the tow head. Renny laid a calming hand on Archer's shoulder and the giggles ceased.

Finch, standing in his surplice behind the brass eagle of the lectern, read the Lessons with such a feeling of content as he had not known for a long while. There, sitting in the pew before him, was Renny, himself again. That red head, fitting symbol of the family pride, erect, confident, seeming to shed the light of leadership on the tribe. This was one of the occasions on which Finch read too well — but this morning Mr. Fennel was not embarrassed by it.

Mr. Fennel's sermon was on "miracles in our time." His remarks were so heartfelt, so pointed, that every member of the small congregation felt something of the situation of the Whiteoaks in it, for by some means word had got about that the lost money had been found, that the eldest Whiteoak was no longer under a cloud. He himself looked self-conscious. Throughout the sermon he never took his eyes from the Rector's face.

When Piers collected the offertory, Renny watched with alert interest as the contributions from his family fell on to the plate. Nicholas had a time of it to find his. " Can't find it," he mumbled, then did find it and the two heavy fifty-cent pieces were dropped with a clatter. Now Piers, ruddy and solid, held the plate under Renny's nose. With an air of cool detachment he took from his pocket five clean but musty-smelling twenty-dollar bank notes and deposited them on the modest pile of silver. A shock vibrated through the three pews occupied by the Whiteoaks. A small smile flickered across Piers's lips. Then he moved stolidly along the aisle. Pew after pew was permitted one spellbound look at Renny's contribution. Then Piers and Peter Chalk, who kept the motor repair and gasoline station and who had this year been returned from the scene of war, minus his right hand, marched side by side to the steps of the chancel where the Rector awaited them. Miss Pink, though unaware of what had happened, drew jubilant strains from the still sweet-sounding old organ. The bulk of Piers Whiteoak and Peter Chalk was impassive.

As Mr. Fennel accepted the alms a benign expression lighted his bearded face. He turned sharply, his surplice swinging, and moved toward the altar.

Nicholas, tugging the end of his moustache, muttered, not inaudibly — " Too much. Too much."

Meg felt faint. She would be glad when the service was over and the family could meet in the churchyard.

XXIX

FROM CHURCHYARD TO VAUGHANLANDS

MEG with her daughter on one side of her and her niece on the other moved, with as great rapidity as was decorous, out of the church and toward the family plot where she could see other members of the family already drawn together. A sumach tree had sprung up just inside the hedge which surrounded the churchyard and had reached medium size, scarcely noticed, till its leaves had turned blood red and, by the last squally rain, been swept on to the Whiteoak plot. There they lay like a gorgeous carpet. Meg looked at them astonished and then at the naked tree, its thin black limbs wet with rain.

" However did that get in here? " she asked Piers, who was leaning against one of the iron supports of the fence surrounding the plot. His leg that had suffered amputation always pained after the fixed postures of church service. His brow was contracted as he turned to look at the tree.

" I 've no idea," he said. " The leaves are pretty though."

" I always dislike sumachs. They 're so untidy. I must tell Noah Binns to cut it down."

" Be here to see him do it or he 'll get the wrong tree."

" It 's lovely," said Roma.

Meg took Piers by the arm. " Is your leg hurting, dear? "

" A bit. It always does in church. It 's not being able to stretch it out."

" What a pity! Piers, was n't it ridiculous of Renny to put such a sum in the offertory. Did you see how many notes there were? "

" Five."

" Merciful heavens! I don't see how you bore it —

knowing how he needs money. I think I should have snatched it off the plate."

Piers laughed. "He did what it pleased him to do. He's had little enough pleasure for a long while. Why grudge him this?"

"I don't grudge it, if he wants to do it, but — it looked — like an act of contrition. I was so embarrassed. You should have seen Patience's face! But Roma never flickered an eyelid."

Meg turned to Renny, who now joined them, and said — "Oh, my dear, it was so like you to make that thank offering! But wasn't it a little too generous? You know, if you keep on the way you have begun, you will soon be rid of all the money."

"My feeling is," he returned, "that I did not give half enough."

"You should have prepared me," laughed Piers. "I almost dropped the collection plate."

"I am sure," Meg went on, "that Piers will agree with me when I say that what you gave to his boys was far too much. If you had given any such sum to Patience, I should insist on her returning it."

Piers looked uncomfortable but said nothing.

"Of course," she continued, "if Piers is willing to allow you to hand out twenty-dollar notes like pennies to his children, just at a time when you scarcely are accountable for what you do, I am powerless to prevent it, but I can only say I am astonished and mortified for him."

"Meg," said Piers, leaning hard on the iron fence, "you may keep your astonishment and your mortification for yourself. I feel neither."

"Don't quarrel," put in Renny.

"The trouble is," Meg said, "that Piers has become so used to taking favors from you, that he thinks nothing of them."

" The trouble with Meg is," retorted Piers, looking only at Renny, " that she is eternally trying to put me in an unfavorable light."

" How unjust," cried his sister. " Why, from the time you were a small boy, I have always shielded you — stood between you and justice."

" That 's right," said Piers, " make me out a criminal."

" Don't quarrel," repeated Renny. " I am perfectly accountable for what I do, and I 'll give away all the remainder of the money if I choose."

Nicholas now stumped up, leaning on Maurice's arm. Ernest, following with Patience, Pheasant, and the four children, exclaimed : —

" What a glorious day! It seems as though all nature were rejoicing with us. How very pretty those scarlet sumach leaves look, scattered over the graves."

" What I want to know," said Meg, " is how that tree got in here. I never saw it till to-day."

All eyes turned, somewhat accusingly, toward the naked tree.

" Neither have I," Ernest agreed. " How very extraordinary! "

" Birds eat seeds," said Archer, " and the seeds fall down in their droppings and a tree grows."

" Those are things," said Ernest, " that we don't talk about in public."

" Trees? " demanded Archer.

" No. Droppings."

" But birds are n't like us. They do it in public."

Pheasant and her two little boys giggled.

" What 's all this about? " asked Nicholas. " I did n't hear."

" Nothing of importance, Uncle Nick," answered Meg. " The important thing is that I am now going to take Roma to Vaughanlands, to tell Mr. Clapperton, with her own lips, that she took the money. That is what we decided yesterday, is n't it ? "

" Yes, yes. Bless me — it will be the talk of the countryside."

" Renny's name must be cleared," said Piers.

Ernest gave Roma a pat on the shoulder. " Well, there 's one thing certain," he said, " they can't put you in jail."

" What a good thing," said Pheasant, " that she goes back to school to-morrow."

Renny asked of Meg — " Is Roma settling down all right ? "

" She is settling down beautifully. She 's really a dear little thing and so unusual. I 'm sure she meant no harm by what she did. Alayne is always talking about child psychology — why does n't she apply it to Roma ? How is Alayne ? "

" Pretty well."

" Hm. She made quite a scene last night."

" She was at the end of her tether. Would you like me to drive you to Clapperton's ? Finch can drive the uncles home."

" Oh, yes. I 'd like that."

Cheerfully, considering the difficulty of her errand, Meg collected Roma and they set out along the country road where gleaming puddles reflected the blue of the sky and the last bright colors of autumn grouped themselves for a final show. The three spoke little till Renny stopped the car in front of Eugene Clapperton's door. Looking over his shoulder, he said : —

" I can't tell you how strange it seems to me to come to this house where I saw you and Maurice living happily together, and to realize you no longer own it and — that bounder Clapperton does."

" I 'm sure it must seem very strange to you," she said. " What sad changes took place during the wars. After the

first war you came home to find dear Papa in his grave —
to say nothing of our stepmother — and after this war you
returned to find me living in a small house and Maurice
gone."

" It 's a peculiar thing," he said, " that all I experienced in
these last years has not dimmed — not in the least dimmed —
what we went through here, at the time when Eden died.
It 's as though it were yesterday."

Meg drew a deep sigh. " Yes, as though it were yesterday."

" Did he die here? " asked Roma. " I always thought he
died at Jalna."

" Why, Roma, I don't see how you got that idea," exclaimed Meg. " Look! You see the window at the corner,
just above where the clematis grows? That 's the room, up
there." She gazed at the window as though she might again
see there the emaciated figure of a young man, in a light blue
dressing gown, looking longingly through the pane for a
sign of spring.

Roma peered up at the window. " Did he die in the
summer, Auntie Meg? "

" No. There was snow on the ground."

" Well do I remember," said Renny, " standing in the
snow by that spruce tree, waiting for Piers — to make him
go in to look at Eden."

" Was he dead then? " asked Roma.

" Yes."

" Why did n't Uncle Piers want to look at him? He must
have looked beautiful when he was dead. He was young
and he was a poet."

Meg and Renny exchanged looks of painful remembrance,
then she said — " Yes, he had a beautiful face. Come now,
dear, we must go in to see Mr. Clapperton. Don't forget
that you are to speak clearly and look right into his eyes.
Come."

Renny opened the door of the car for them. They got

out and went up the steps to the front door.   Meg had first
entered this house when, as a child of two years, she had
come to take tea with little Maurice Vaughan.

The door was opened by a maid who looked at them with
surprise.   She showed them into the living room and, in a
few minutes, Eugene Clapperton, with an air of being ready
for anything, came in.   His gray suit, his neat gray hair,
looked businesslike, but he wore soft, fleece-lined slippers, so
that his coming was noiseless.   He greeted Meg stiffly, ignoring the child.

" Good afternoon, Mr. Clapperton," she said, in her warm,
confidential voice.   " This is my little niece.   She and I
have come on important business.   Have n't we, Roma ? "

" Well, is that so ? " he said, giving the two a suspicious
look.

" Stand up, Roma," Meg said, " and tell Mr. Clapperton
why you have come."

Roma stood up, as though in school.   " I came," she said
clearly, " to tell that I took all that money and hid it and
yesterday Uncle Renny found me with it, in the woods.   I
had it hidden in an old kettle."

" Whatever is this fabrication ? " Eugene Clapperton demanded testily.

" It is no fabrication."   Meg spoke with some heat.
" This little girl followed my brother when he came to your
house, on the day when the bank notes were taken.   She
followed him right into the house and, when he left, she
slipped into the room where the money lay on the desk and
took it.   All these months she 's kept the secret but now it 's
discovered.   Mr. Clapperton, you know what queer things
children sometimes do."

" I don't know anything about children," he returned with
severity, his face reddening.

" She is such a good little girl," said Meg.   " It 's the
first naughty thing she 's ever done."

" If you can call a criminal act, *naughty*."

" Indeed it was scarcely even naughtiness.   She had been reading *Robin Hood* and she wanted to be like him, don't you see? "

" I know nothing of Robin Hood."

" How very strange !   Then I must tell you that he was a robber who stole from the rich and gave to the poor.   Roma set out to do just that, did n't you, dear? "

" Yes, Auntie Meg."

" She knew my brother, the one who owns Jalna, was in somewhat straitened circumstances financially.   He usually is, unfortunately."

" So I have heard," said Eugene Clapperton, not without satisfaction.

" She thought she would assist him by occasionally hiding one of the notes where he would find it.   We never suspected her, and she kept her secret perfectly."   Family pride kept Meg from disclosing the complete story of mystification and mental anguish to which Renny had been subjected.

She concluded — " Quite an achievement for a child of her age, was n't it? "

" It is well that you can regard what she has done in such a favorable light, Mrs. Vaughan."   He added, turning to Roma : —

" I hope you have promised never to do such a thing again."

" Yes.   I have."   She spoke without embarrassment. She still was standing.   Looking at Eugene Clapperton out of her slanting eyes, she asked — " May I go upstairs for a minute? "

" Why, yes," he stammered.   " Certainly, if you want to. Do you think you can find your way? "

She did not answer but over her shoulder gave a little smile at Meg.

Meg said when she had gone : —

" Roma is such an unusual child.   I know quite well why

she has gone upstairs. She wants to see the room her poor father died in. It was the corner room — just above us."

"Well — well — " Eugene Clapperton looked at the ceiling. Steps sounded over their heads. There she was, moving about in the room above. His anxious mind flew up to the dressing table and he wondered if he had left any valuables lying about.

Meg's face suddenly burned in anger. This man — this nincompoop — had given her not one single word of sympathy in exchange for her telling him that her poor young brother had died in the room above. But what could you expect of such people? She rose, and said: —

"I must be going as soon as Roma comes down."

He rose too. "I saw Colonel Whiteoak in the car. If you are agreeable to it, I think I'll go out and tell him I'm glad his reputation has been cleared."

Meg looked doubtful but she said — "Just as you like."

Roma was coming down the stairs.

"I saw the room," she said to Meg. "I guess it looks different."

Eugene Clapperton, with an air of formality and even self-importance, accompanied them to the car.

Renny Whiteoak's eyebrows shot up when he saw him. He had been standing by the car and now acknowledged Clapperton's greeting with a derisive grin. He opened the door of the car but kept his eyes on Clapperton's face.

"Everything explained to your satisfaction?" he asked.

"Yes. I'm very pleased that the affair has been cleared up. I'm glad I didn't take any action in the matter. Colonel Whiteoak, I'd like to forget our past differences and shake hands, if you're willing."

He advanced, holding out his hand. Renny Whiteoak looked at it as though he would refuse but, with a smile still flickering over his face, he suddenly gripped it with decision, as a distasteful duty performed.

Eugene Clapperton cleared his throat.　He said : —

"I hope neighborly relations will be resumed among us. I'm a sociable man and I enjoy a feeling of goodwill in my surroundings and I like to entertain my friends."　He did not wait for any response but hurried on — "I want to tell you that I am engaged to be married.　Perhaps you have heard a whisper of it.　I am to marry one of the Miss Griffiths — the second one — the one who was crippled — now a lovely girl and becoming more active every week.　We hope to be married in the early spring."

"Congratulations," Renny rapped out, his eyes on Eugene Clapperton's tie, as though he could not bring himself to look above it.

"Yes, indeed," added Meg.　"It will be so nice for both of you.　Will her sisters stay on at the fox farm?"

"No.　They will come here with her.　They are dear girls and I am only too glad to take them into my home.　We are grateful to you, Colonel Whiteoak, for the loan of the fox farm but we shall no longer require it.　Would you like to sell the property?"

"Yes.　Fifty thousand dollars."

"Ha, ha — that's a good joke.　It's not worth a penny more than ten thousand."

"Fifty thousand to you."

"Well, I see you don't want to sell.　Let's hope you can let it.　There's such a demand for those little houses I am building on my property I might ask what I please.　But I like to be moderate.　All through my life moderation has been my aim."

"It seems scarcely moderate," observed Meg, "to take three girls into your house at once."

Eugene Clapperton laughed in genuine pleasure.　"When it comes to human relations," he said, "I don't believe in moderation.　I believe in unlimited generosity and affection."

" I do hope you 'll be happy," said Meg.

As he watched the car disappear he straightened his shoulders with an air of relief and thought — " That man depresses me. I hate to be near him. I don't like any of them and that 's a fact. They don't like me. They 're envious and no wonder. But I 'll be civil to them for the sake of my three dear girls — above all, for my dearest girl. As soon as I have had lunch I 'll go straight to see her. How happy my life will be when I have her with me — with me continually and Sidney gone! I 'm sick of having him in the house. He is the most egotistical, self-centred person I 've ever met. Horribly ungrateful, too. He has all the qualities I dislike. I wonder I have endured him so long. He has made a convenience of me — that 's what he has."

The waiting till spring for his marriage seemed almost unendurable. Had it not been for the sake of Gem's health he never would have endured it. Over and over he would count the weeks — even the days — crossing them off on his calendar like a schoolgirl. This calendar, with the days crossed off in red ink, was a source of amusement to Swift. " Your Nemesis is drawing ever nearer, old boy," he would say to himself, as he fingered it.

XXX

A MORNING CALL

RENNY had wanted to carry flowers to her. It seemed the proper thing to do on this first call after her engagement was announced. It was curious to think how the Griffiths had come to the fox farm, three young girls in black with scarcely a penny among them and Gem a cripple, and how she was now able to walk and soon was to become the wife of a prosperous man, mistress of Vaughanlands. Yes, certainly, it was an occasion for flowers. But, when he had gone to the flower border, he had found all the dahlias sodden and dead from frost; even the tough-stemmed chrysanthemums were frozen. All that were left were the low bushy French marigolds, their foliage still extraordinarily green, their flowers vivid copper giving out their pungent scent. They had all the garden to themselves. He took out his knife and snipped off a sizable bunch. He was not quite pleased with it. He should have taken roses to her, or lilies of the valley or — considering what he was about to ask her — orchids. However at the verge of the ravine he found some Michaelmas daisies, tiny pale blue flowers on thin stems, and he added a few of these to the marigolds. Though they were wild they improved the bouquet, he thought, giving it a more girlish, more ethereal look.

The fox farm was very sheltered among the trees. The grass was greener here, the air less sharp. He had a moment's misgiving when he passed between the two round flower beds, on either side of the path to the door, lest there might be marigolds blooming there. But there were only purple petunias and bronze-colored nasturtiums. He was relieved and knocked at the door.

For the first time Gemmel herself opened it. It was amazing to see her standing there without support. For a moment he just stood and stared. Then, presenting his offering, he said: —

" A very humble nosegay, but the best I could find." She took the flowers, held them at arm's length, then close. " They 're lovely! The first marigolds I have had since I left Wales." She turned to a small framed drawing on the wall. " That was our house."

He examined the picture — the low stone house with austere hills rising beyond it and, on the nearest, the ruin of the ancient monastery.

" What a place to live! " he exclaimed. " Scarcely a tree in sight. I 'll wager the winds were terrific."

A wild smile flickered across Gemmel's lips.

" They were. The greatest longing I had was to walk on the hills in the wind. Now that I 'm better I hope to go back there some time and do what I longed to do."

They went into the living room. He watched her free movements with approval. " It 's wonderful," he said, " to see you like this. How does it feel? "

" I 'm like someone who has waded in a little pool, and is now plunged into the ocean."

" The ocean of matrimony too, I hear." His smile was a little sardonic. " You wasted no time."

" I had wasted too much already," she answered gravely.

" Well. My congratulations to Clapperton. And to you, on becoming mistress of Vaughanlands. It 's a lovely place."

" Yes. It is."

" I am sorry — " a frown corrugated his forehead — " that Clapperton seems bent on ruining it."

She stared and repeated — " *Ruining* it! "

" Yes. This harebrained scheme of a model village. It 's bound to ruin the property."

" I don't see why."

He gave a short laugh. " It 's all right now and probably very amusing. But think of the future! In the natural course of things, you will outlive your husband by many years. That village will grow. It will get completely out of hand. God knows what sort of people will live there. Your property will depreciate in value every year. You 'll end by being glad to sell it at any price. I 'm sorry about it for your sake."

Never had she thought of this aspect of her engagement to Eugene Clapperton. Great as was the difference in their ages, the thought of outliving him, of a free, independent life without him, had never entered her head. Now it shone through her consciousness like a cold silver thread. She would be eternally grateful to Eugene. She loved him — in a thankful way — but this thought of mental and physical freedom — she almost forgot Renny Whiteoak's presence in the contemplation of it.

He was saying — " I should like to think of your being proud of Vaughanlands for the rest of your days. I should like to think of you as my neighbor for the rest of mine. But, mark my words, you will live to have slums about you, if Mr. Clapperton goes on as he has begun."

" But, if it 's so foolish, why does he do it? I always think of him as shrewd."

Shrewd indeed, Renny thought. Damned shrewd. A grimace of distaste for Eugene Clapperton's kind of shrewdness made his face grim for a moment, then resolutely he forced his features into a benevolent smile. He said: —

" A man may be shrewd in some ways and still be hipped in others. Mr. Clapperton has this Quixotic idea of a perfect village. He thinks he will preside over it and keep it so. But the village will be like that Frankenstein monster. It will ruin Vaughanlands, it will ruin Jalna. I won't pretend that I am not afraid for Jalna. I 'm dreadfully afraid for it. I think my old grandmother would rise from her grave and curse him, if she knew what he was about. Perhaps she does know. Perhaps she has cursed him and his." Now he was laughing as though ashamed of his vehemence, but Gemmel had heard the talk of superstitious Welsh servants and the thought of the dead woman's curse was not unreal to her.

" But what can I do? " she asked. " Eugene won't listen to me."

Renny grinned. " You don't know your power. Ask him for the site of the village as a wedding present. Tell him that the thought of the village is abhorrent to you — that it 's affecting your health. You have never been married. You don't know yet what your power is. I tell you, a woman can do almost anything she likes with a man. You 're far cleverer than most girls. Don't weaken. Make him give up this plan, and the day will come when you 'll thank me, with all your heart, for this advice."

" I 'll do it," she exclaimed. " I 'll put a stop to this building. See if I don't."

" But you must be careful not to mention my name. Simply tell him you can't endure to see the property spoilt."

" I will." She spoke solemnly.

" Splendid! " Renny exclaimed, and quite simply took her in his arms and kissed her. " You 've made a friend for life. I 'll dance at your wedding."

" And you 'll be friends with Eugene? "

" Nothing can stop me. Not even he."

She was elated, but whether because of their compact or because of the embrace, it was impossible to say. His kiss had been spontaneous, lightly but firmly planted on her cheek. She had felt a magnetic power, from his arm and from his chest, encircling her. She sank into a chair as she saw her sisters entering the room, and reached for a cigarette.

The two shook hands with Renny, Althea turning her face from him. Garda said — " Is n't it wonderful to see

Gem walking about — standing up — sitting down — just as she pleases?"

"Wonderful. And yet so natural that I feel as though she always had."

"It will take me a long while to get used to it," said Garda. "Every morning when I wake I could shout for joy when I remember. Is it any wonder we all love Eugene?"

"I don't," said Althea.

"You are notoriously ungrateful."

Renny said — "That's right. Why should a woman be grateful? Let her take whatever comes her way, as her due."

Garda came and sat close beside him. "You can't prevent our being grateful to you," she said, "for letting us live here all these years."

For some reason that remark made the girls seem very vulnerable and lonely. He said brusquely : —

"I'm sorry you're going. I wish you might have stayed here forever. Do you know that this little house, as it stands, has always been lived in by women? And friends of mine. I bought it and had it carried here on rollers. I can remember just how it looked, trundling down the road. My fox terrier had got into it and kept running from one room to another, peering out of the windows. First Clara Lebraux and her daughter, Pauline, lived here and now you three. Always women."

"And always rent free," said Althea, looking out the window. "I hope your next tenant will be a man and pay his rent."

"Althea has a materialistic mind, though you wouldn't guess it," said Garda.

They sat clustered about him, finding his presence exhilarating, which Eugene Clapperton's was not. When he appeared that afternoon, Althea remained upstairs with her drawing board and Garda, in mackintosh and galoshes, went for a walk. Gemmel sat beside him on the sofa, outwardly gentle but inwardly poised for a struggle.

"You are such a dear, sweet girlie," he said, holding her thin fingers against his lips, speaking through them. "I don't know how I can wait till spring for you. To-day, as I walked here, I smelled that dank smell of leaves rotting and wet earth. My goodness, everything was lonely. I wished the winter was over. Six months till we marry! I don't see how I can wait."

"The time will soon pass."

"Of course, you 're not as anxious as I am." He spoke resignedly. "That 's natural. But I hope you 're a little anxious."

She did not answer but smiled into his small, pale eyes. "You 're glorious in that red dress, Gem. I 've never seen you in red before."

"Molly sent it to me from New York."

"It 's as good as sunshine on a day like this. My little sunshine!" He clasped her to him fervently. His dry lips, of a mauvish color, sought hers but found only her cheek. "You must n't be shy," he whispered. He savored the silence of the house. He said — "Do you know, this is the first time we 've been completely alone in the house. Just us two."

"Althea is upstairs," she said hurriedly, with the ridiculous feeling in her heart that Althea would hear her, if she cried out for help.

"Althea does n't count with me," he said. "She 's the most nondescript, colorless person I 've ever met. Not that I don't like her, mind you. I do like her and I 'm willing to treat her as a sister."

"You 'll find that Althea has plenty of character," she returned, a little sharply.

"That 's good. That 's fine. But you have character

enough for both. You 're quite a fiery little thing, or could be. We 'll get on. Don't you worry, little girl."

"There is only one thing I worry about," Gemmel spoke gravely.

"You worry? What about?" His jaw dropped in apprehension.

"About the village," Gemmel answered. "About Clappertown."

He brought his teeth together with a snap. "It 's enough to worry me into the grave," he said, "the way those Whiteoaks go on. What do you suppose they 've done? They 've built an incinerator — just a paltry rubbish burner, but how it smokes! — right against the boundary between their property and my tenants. They 've made an enclosure farther along and turned fifteen pigs loose in it. All four tenants have been to my house to complain of the smoke and the smell. It 's enough to drive me crazy. Of course, I 'll complain to the police but — to tell you the truth — I 'm half afraid of the eldest Whiteoak. I think he 's touched in the head. He 's a very queer man. Don't you think so?"

"Yes. He is rather odd."

"But why do you worry about the village, Gem?"

She stroked his head, as she never had stroked it before, with a lingering, persuasive touch. She might have been Delilah and he a thin-haired Samson. He drooped, he sank in his seat, as though his head felt heavy. "Oh, girlie," he murmured.

"I look on those people in those little houses," she said, "as snakes in our Eden."

"Snakes!" He sat bolt upright. "Surely not *snakes*, girlie." But he did like her calling her future home an Eden. It showed how her love for him was increasing.

"I never see those little houses," she continued, "without thinking how inappropriate they are and picturing what it will be like when there are streets of them. We shall have no privacy whatever."

She yearned for privacy with him! And she should have it or he 'd know the reason why.

" I 'll see to it," he said, with his jaw set, " that there is no trespassing on our part of the estate."

" I shall never be able to forget them. It won't be at all like living in the country. I was brought up among the Welsh mountains and I hate the thought of people all about me."

" But you 'd like to be the little lady of the manor, would n't you? "

" There could n't be a manor in this country," she said decisively. " The word has no meaning outside England. It 's feudal. It 's the demesne of a lord."

" Oh, well," he said, " I only used the word figuratively."

She clasped her hands between her knees and sat staring at the floor. A long silence fell between them. Then he asked: " What do you want me to do? "

" Nothing. Just what you like. You have done so much for me already that I could n't ask anything more."

He clutched her hand and squeezed it. " You can ask whatever you want. But, remember, this project of a model village has been a dream of mine for many years. I 'm a great dreamer, you know."

" Yes. I know."

" You believe me, don't you? "

" Of course. You have a benevolent nature. You go about doing good."

" Oh, girlie, girlie — " he all but broke down — " the only one I want to please is you! If you dislike the thought of the village, I won't build it." As Eugene Clapperton said these words he realized, in a great sweep of relief, what a load would be lifted from his own shoulders if he gave up the project.

Gemmel clasped him in her thin arms. A delicious sense of power made her feel buoyant as a fish in the sea.

"Oh, thank you, dear Eugene! Thank you."

He became too demonstrative in his infatuation and she withdrew a little, sliding to the other end of the sofa.

He laughed, embarrassed by his own fervor.

Then he said, seriously — "Now, Gem, I want you to make Colonel Whiteoak understand that you persuaded me to do this. I don't want him to get the idea that he intimidated me. Tell him, the first time you see him, that you persuaded me. Understand?"

"Yes, Eugene. I will."

XXXI
FINCH AND HIS SON

ALAYNE went to visit her friend, Rosamund Trent, in November. It was a time when the countryside was, to her mind, melancholy. New York would be a revivifying change, the theatrical season in full swing, clean pavements to walk on instead of muddy paths or wet grass, shops overflowing with luxurious commodities, restaurants with luxurious food, a renewal of old acquaintances. She was to be gone a month.

Finch had left some weeks earlier on a concert tour. Never before had he set out on a tour feeling so tired. The strain of long hours of practising, added to the tension of contemplating Renny's struggle against the web that enmeshed him, had taken much of his vitality from him. The long engulfment of the war had taken something he felt he never could regain. Perhaps it was the power of enjoying solitude. There seemed no more to be any real solitude. The world lay in a tangled heap and, until he could extricate himself, he would always be tired. He was not fearful of his own performance in his recitals. He knew that, no matter how tired he was, he always could, when the moment came, forget his weariness and put himself with abandon into his playing. But afterward he paid for it in hours of wakefulness when he should have been refreshing himself with sound sleep. He had sedative tablets which he took when driven to it. They were not habit-forming but he was afraid of them. He would look at his watch at three in the morning and say — " If I am not asleep in an hour I will take one." Then he would lie in the dark listening to the sounds of a strange city, trying, with all his might, to sleep. Then he would think — " I am trying too hard. It does n't matter whether I sleep or not. I will relax and care about nothing." He would stretch his body on the bed and relax, inch by inch, consciously, putting all thoughts out of his head. On this night a face appeared before his closed eyes, the face of a man he had seen in one of the front seats at his concert. The forehead had been noticeably large, now it was enormous. It pressed the eyes, nose, and mouth down, down and down, till they disappeared into the collar. The face, now all forehead, grew larger and larger. Finch threw himself to the other side of the bed. A streetcar rattled past the hotel.

Now, to quiet himself, he thought of Jalna and all those at home. He pictured each one of the family, from Nicholas down to Archer. For a space he was calm. He drew deep breaths. Then he noticed that they all had enormous foreheads that pressed their features, down and down, into their necks. Nicholas's gray moustache was swallowed, Renny's grin of triumph over finding the money. Rags, featureless, floated about with the tea tray. Someone — was it himself? — was playing the piano.

He flung to the other side of the bed. He felt suffocated by the heat of the bedroom. He had turned off the radiator and opened the window but still it was too warm. The overheating of the hotels was one of the trying things about a town. He found himself, as so often, envying Renny and Piers.

Resolutely he lay on his back. He pictured the little church at home, the first snowfall lying in the churchyard. He pictured the family plot, where those who had given themselves to so many emotions now lay at peace. The snow lay lightly on the graves. Too lightly, for it did nothing to restrain those within. A restless movement ran through their bones. In frantic haste his spirit fled from the place. He pressed his fingers to his temples. Was it possible that he was going to have one of those attacks of pain in his head and neck which once before had nearly wrecked him? He gently massaged the back of his neck. He looked at his watch. Just twenty minutes had passed since last he had looked at it. He could not go on like this. He took one of the tablets in a gulp of water and settled down to let it work its beneficent will. But he was so thoroughly awake that the tablet took some time to soothe him. In truth his imagination seemed more terribly alive. He felt himself playing Bach's Italian Concerto in F major. But he could not control the black keys. The white keys behaved themselves, doing his bidding, but the black keys raced away from under his fingers like ants. He wondered why the thought of ants was so intolerable to him. There was some painful scene in his memory connected with ants but he could not recall what it was. Now the black keys had run right away from the keyboard, scuttled down the legs of the piano, and were clambering up the legs of the bed. They were running this way and that over the bedspread. Finch stretched out his hand and turned on the light. He took another tablet, for he must be fit to play that night. He remembered that he was in Oregon and that the Pacific was near. That was a calming thought. He pictured the endless rolling of the waves. He tried to repeat poetry about the sea but the poems eluded him. One line from some forgotten poem went on and on in his brain — " Hateful is the dark blue sky." Over and over it was reiterated till he felt nothing, could see nothing but that dark blue arch burning above him. " Hateful is the dark blue sky." Not since boyhood had he remembered the words — beautiful and menacing. . . .

He woke at nine, relaxed but not rested. Thank God, he thought, I have only two more concerts to get through! He took a bath and had a pot of tea and some toast sent up to him — poor tea and poor toast. Scarcely had he swallowed it when a telegram was brought him. Something has happened at home, he thought, and tore it open in nervous haste.

Nothing had happened at Jalna. The telegram was signed by a lawyer in San Francisco and told of the death of Sarah, in a motor accident. Would Mr. Whiteoak come as soon as possible and take charge of his son, who at present was with Mr. Voynitsky. Finch read the telegram three times before he took in its meaning. Even then he could not bring himself to believe it. Sarah dead! Sarah — who had seemed impervious to the weakness of flesh! She had been like the figure of a woman cut from ivory or porcelain. He always had been so sure she would outlive him by many years. And she was dead. He could not believe it. He could see her in his aunt's house in Devon, her violin tucked under her chin, her glittering eyes fixed on him, as though he were the source of her music. And how she had sapped his vitality! But he lived and she was dead — killed suddenly, in a brutal crash. He groaned — picturing it — her blood on the pavement, her black plaits soaked in blood. He pictured her on the cliffs in Cornwall, gliding over the sheep-cropped grass with that strange gliding walk of hers. And she was dead! He pictured her as she had appeared in his bedroom in Ireland when her white arms had drawn him on to the bed with her, renewing their life together when he had thought himself free of her forever. And now he was free of her forever and could not believe it, did not want to be free of her at that price. How white her skin had been and how fine! It had never sunburned or tanned. Other women had looked weather-beaten, coarse, beside her. And now that skin was gray in death.

She who had never liked children had been like a tigress with her own. She never would let Finch share the child with her. The child was everything. Finch had sunk to second place. And now here was that Russian — Sarah's third husband — in possession of the child.   Finch lay back in his chair, oblivious of his surroundings, thinking of Sarah, the child, the Russian.

The telephone rang.   The leader of the orchestra wished to see him.   An appointment was made.   The telephone rang again.   The president of a women's club invited him to be the guest of the club at lunch.   Controlling the irritation in his voice, he politely refused.   The telephone rang again.   A newspaper reporter wanted an interview.   He couldn't give an interview to anyone!   He was too tired. Would he answer a few questions over the phone?   He would, and answered them so wildly that, when he hung up the receiver, he was hot with anger and humiliation.   The telephone rang again.   It was another newspaper reporter. Finch managed to answer a few questions with moderate politeness.   He got his hat and went out into the street.

Fortunately he had only two more engagements to fill. He felt incapable of filling them with success but somehow he did.   At the end he felt less tired than he had expected.   It was not playing the piano that tired him — it was the people he had to meet.   If the people could have been obliterated, excepting as audiences, he could have enjoyed a concert tour. But there always were the people — talking, eternally talking.   If only he might have talked to the few who interested him!   But inevitably they were pushed into the background by those who did not interest him.

Now it was over.   He had interviewed the lawyer in San Francisco and learned from him that all that was left of Sarah's fortune was to be held in trust for her child.   Finch was astonished by the dwindling of that fortune.   The lawyer shrugged.   He intimated that probably the Russian knew what had become of it.   Still it was a tidy sum for a boy to inherit.   In Sarah's will no provision was made for him till he came of age and into possession of the whole. The interest would mount up.

As the taxi moved in a cold gray fog towards the house where Sarah had lived, Finch had a feeling of utmost unreality. He could not picture Sarah in this place. He had seen her in many places but he could not picture her here. Why, he could not have said, but it was impossible to him. And now there was this Russian to be interviewed. Perhaps, when he had met him, he would be able to picture her here.

His mouth was dry when the taxi turned into the short drive that led to the Spanish-looking stucco house, half-covered by a climbing rose. A big-boned Swedish woman opened the door in answer to his ring. He asked for Mr. Voynitsky and was shown into a living room with many windows. Many windows did not succeed in making the very modern furniture look comfortable. A smallish man with a wide smile sprang up from a very deep chair and advanced to meet Finch.

"Good afternoon, Mr. Whiteoak," he said with a strong foreign accent. "I am very pleased to meet you."

They shook hands, his small compact hand gripping Finch's firmly.

"Won't you please sit down," he said, and at once offered Finch a cigarette. No? A cigar, then. No? Then, surely a drink. Finch wanted none of these.

Voynitsky lighted a cigarette. His wide smile that discovered small square teeth passed from his face and a look of melancholy took its place. He was oily, thought Finch, a villainous-looking little fellow, whatever he did. And Sarah had gone to bed with him! Well — in the dark he might be all right. Finch never had understood Sarah; meeting her third husband he understood her less than ever.

"This has been a terrible calamity," observed Voynitsky.

"Yes. Were you — in the car, when it happened?"

"Fortunately not. If I had been driving, never could I have forgiven myself. Sarah was herself driving. A truck came along very fast. She turned to one side. The pavement was wet. The car skidded. It struck a telegraph pole. Sarah was instantly killed."

The pupils of Finch's eyes dilated in horror.

" Was she alone? " he asked.

" No. The child was with her."

" He saw that! "

" He is too young to understand. He 's all right."

" He is with you here? "

" Yes, but I am giving up this house. You will like to have your little boy with you at once I am sure. He is a nice little boy. I am very fond of him. Yes — very fond. He is a little spoilt. Sarah could deny him nothing." Voynitsky began to bite his nails, as though in irritation at some recollection. Finch thought — " They did n't get on very well, not all the time." The little man may have got most of Sarah's money away from her but, when it came to quarreling, Sarah could hold her own.

" Yes," said Finch, " I will take him with me to-day."

" That is good, because I must sell this house at once. The associations here are too painful, you understand."

Finch looked about the room, trying to discover something that might remind him of Sarah. Her body had rested against these very cushions but no spiritual imprint of her remained in the room. She had gone out of it — a healthy young woman — and never come back. Now Finch wanted nothing so much as to leave this house — never see it or its owner again.

" I heard you play last night," Voynitsky was saying. " I was in the audience. I enjoyed your playing so much."

Finch muttered something incoherent. He was glad he had not known that Voynitsky was present.

" I should have liked," Voynitsky went on, " to have made myself known, to have thanked you at the end, but I thought it might be embarrassing for both of us. Allow me to thank you now." He showed both upper and lower teeth in his smile — like the winner of a beauty contest.

Oh, to have him at Jalna! Oh, to treat him rough! To take him by his oily hair and obliterate his oily smile in a snowdrift! To make him plough a field under Piers's direction — to put him on one of Renny's horses and make him go over hurdles — to make him dig holes in the ground and then chuck him into one of them!

"I am glad you enjoyed my playing," said Finch, "and I agree that it would have been embarrassing for us to have met last night."

"Sarah," said Voynitsky, "adored your playing. She herself played the violin well."

"Yes. Did she keep it up?"

"Not as she should. Happiness made her indolent, so I told her."

Both men were lost in their own thoughts for a space, then the Russian said: —

"I will bring your boy to you." He went briskly to a door at the end of the room and called to someone.

A moment later a thick-set, foreign-looking woman entered with the child by the hand. The room, the Russian, the nurse, the child, all were unreal to Finch. In this situation he scarcely could believe in himself. Here was a room in California. Here was Sarah's third husband. Here was a stolid woman with his own child by the hand. Here was his child! Here were he and his child looking into each other's eyes.

The tiny boy, in white shorts and light blue jersey, his thick straight hair worn in a fringe on the forehead, was self-possessed. He looked at Finch out of narrow, greenish eyes; his delicate lips were composed in a small smile.

Voynitsky showed every tooth at him. " Come, Dennis," he said, " and say hello to your papa."

The child came forward from the nurse's side. He held out a limp little hand, a hand that felt unbelievably small and fragile to Finch as he took it.

"How do you do," said Finch.

The child did not answer but stared, as though fascinated, into Finch's eyes.

"Say hello to Papa," urged Voynitsky.

"Hello to Papa," came in a small, shy voice.

"Listen to him!" laughed Voynitsky.

"Ain't he cute!" exclaimed the nurse.

Was it possible that this — his child — his own flesh — breathed and had his being in this atmosphere! Finch had a sudden, violent desire to snatch him away from it.

"Will you come with me?" he asked.

"Say, 'Sure I will, Papa,'" urged Voynitsky.

"Sure I will, Papa," came the little voice.

He introduced himself between Finch's knees and stared up into his face.

"Ain't he cute!" exclaimed the nurse.

"Will it be all right if I take him now?" asked Finch.

"Absolutely," declared Voynitsky, with a beaming smile.

"I'll get him ready," said the nurse. "His clothes is packed and he sure has plenty of them. Come, Baby."

He trotted off with her.

"What does he eat?" asked Finch.

"Anything, as far as I know. Oh, I forgot — no bananas — no chocolates. Anything else. He's no trouble."

"Is he highly strung? Nervous?"

"No, no. He can take whatever comes. Look at him — that accident — he does n't even remember."

"Does n't remember?"

"No. He just says Mummie's gone away."

"It was a terrible thing," Finch said, heavily.

"Yes, was n't it?"

They sat in silence. Finch felt that Voynitsky was yearning to be rid of him and the child, but he was polite. " Do have a drink," he urged.

To pass the time, Finch agreed. By the time their glasses were emptied, the nurse had returned with the little boy. He now wore coat and cap. Finch thought: —

" He's a pretty child." A feeling of fatherly pride rose in his heart.

The nurse was helping the taxi driver to carry out a large trunk. They were laughing together. The woman looked the stronger of the two.

" All those clothes for a youngster? " exclaimed the driver.

" Sure. He's a reg'lar little dook."

Voynitsky bent and kissed the child. " You will remember Dmitri, won't you? "

" Yes," came the composed little voice.

He trotted at Finch's side from the house. Finch lifted him into the taxi.

Voynitsky had pressed Finch's hand on parting, and said — " We both loved a remarkable woman. Never shall we see another like her. I am heartbroken, Mr. Whiteoak."

Finch was thankful to get away. He looked almost fearfully at the small being by his side. Already he had telegraphed Renny, telling him of Sarah's death, and had got a telegram in reply — BRING THE CHILD TO JALNA. It was what he had expected. Now he wondered how he could care for anything so young and fragile during the long journey. To be sure he knew something about children but this was Sarah's child, his brief past was an enigma. What if the child began to cry and kept on crying! It would be horrible. He might miss even Voynitsky — cry for him.

When Finch had got him and his trunk into the hotel bedroom he led him to the window and showed him the view over the harbor. Dennis stood with his eight little fingers in a row on the sill and looked out with gravity.   It was an old story to him.

" I guess you 've seen it often," said Finch.

" Yes.   Show me something different."   He spoke distinctly, in an extraordinarily sweet voice like Sarah's.

" I 'm afraid there 's nothing else to show you."

He turned and looked up critically into Finch's face. " Mummie always had something else," he said.

Sarah seemed to be in the room with them.   Finch was conscious of the scent of her black hair, so luxuriant, yet so fine and so ordered in its arrangement.   He could not believe she was dead.

As though conscious of his thought Dennis said : —

" But she went to sleep, right on the road, and a policeman brought me home.   Dmitri cried but I did n't."

" Do you like Dmitri ? " asked Finch.

" No."

" Neither do I."

" Why ? "

" I can't tell you.   I simply don't like him."

Dennis gave a sudden, clear little laugh.

" Let 's kill him," he said.   " You hit him.   Then I 'll hit him.   Then we 'll both hit him.   Then he 'll be dead."

" Did he ever hit you ? " asked Finch.

" He smacked my face.   Then I screamed.   Then Mummie screamed.   Then he screamed."   Again Dennis laughed, this time more loudly.

" Surely he did n't scream."

" Well, he said he was sorry.   I 'm hungry."

Finch felt an immense relief.   Here was something to do. He took Dennis to the dining room and ordered a careful meal for him.   After that he persuaded him to lie on the bed for a while.   He took him for a walk.   He bought him picture books and read aloud to him.   Then came another meal.   Then it was time to go to the railway station.   Dennis was not tired but Finch, five times his size, was dog-tired. He was even more tired when, after long days and nights of travel, he reached home. He might have relaxed on the train but for Dennis. Always he was watching Dennis. Once he fell asleep in his seat and, when he woke, found Dennis at the end of the railway carriage, waiting an opportunity to slip through the door. On the whole, no child could have been better behaved than he but he was always moving, kneeling up to look out the window, lying down to stare at the lights on the ceiling, lying precariously on the edge of the seat, squatting on his little haunches. The train seemed extraordinarily dirty. The little boy's hands often must be washed. As the melancholy-looking young man herded him along the aisle to the washroom, women gave them looks of curiosity. Young women tried to make up to Finch through his child, older women to give him sympathy through his child, till his invulnerable reserve discouraged them. Once Finch forgot that Dennis could not digest chocolate and let him eat chocolate pudding which, shortly after, Dennis brought up. Once each night Dennis woke Finch by crying, whether from indigestion or a bad dream Finch could not discover, but he lay awake listening for the crying. Those were the only tears. Finch would, several times a day, take Dennis on his knee and show him the pictures in his book. It was strange, he thought, how he who never had had a parental thought now had parenthood violently thrust upon him.

When they alighted from the train there was Renny to meet them, looking so well, so happy, it warmed Finch's heart to see him.

"Come right along," he said, "the car is waiting." He picked up Dennis and kissed him. With him on his arm he strode to the baggage room. The luggage was retrieved. Outside the air had the feel of winter. A few snowflakes floated on the sunny air. Finch followed in Renny's wake;

a weight of responsibility seemed to drop from his shoulders.
He wondered if the day would ever come when Renny would
not make him feel young and inexperienced. But he liked
it. He sniffed the sharp air. New life entered into him.
He helped the porter stow the luggage in the car and tipped
him.

"Too much," observed Renny. "You're not in the
States now."

He took the driver's seat and placed Dennis on Finch's
knee. "Has he enough on?" he asked. "It's cold."

"I think so. I don't know." And he asked the little
boy — "Are you cold?"

"No," came the small, self-possessed voice, "but I want
to go to the lavatory."

Renny gave an exclamation of impatience. "You are a
dud father! Why didn't you attend to that before you left
the train? Well, take him now and be quick about it." He
leant back and lighted a cigarette.

When the two returned, after this expedition, Renny
looked at Dennis critically and remarked — "Hair like
Eden's — eyes like Sarah's — nose like yours . . . a pity
about Sarah, wasn't it?"

"Yes," mumbled Finch. "But we'd better not talk
about it. He remembers."

"Poor little chap." Then, after some questions about the
journey, Renny asked — "How did she leave her money,
Finch?"

"Everything to Dennis. She hadn't a large fortune left.
I imagine that the Russian got most of it from her."

"Hm. What is he like?"

"Like nothing you've ever seen."

"Well, I am glad you have taken your child from him."

"He wasn't at all reluctant to part with him."

Renny smiled down at Dennis. "Now you are going to
live at Jalna," he said.

"Look here, Renny." Finch flushed in embarrassment. "What about Alayne? Will she mind having Dennis in the house?"

"She'll love having him. Alayne is very fond of you and she helped to make the match between you and Sarah. She'll love having him. And he'll be company for Archer. She is still in New York, you know."

"Why — I thought she'd be home by this time."

"So did I, but her friends persuaded her to stay on. I'm going down at the end of the week to bring her home."

Finch felt he had been away a long while. He had questions to ask about every member of the family. Dennis sat quietly looking out at the December fields, the uneasy green lake where gulls flung themselves above the gray water into the gray sky and sank again to the water, as though in mournful pleasure. The sun had disappeared. Purple clouds, heavy with snow, moved closer to field and lake. The car sped along the almost deserted road.

Finch lifted Dennis to his knee as they turned in at the gate. "Look," he said. "This is Jalna, where you're going to live."

"Oh. Was I ever here before?"

"Yes. When you were a baby."

"Shall I have someone to play with?"

"Yes. Other children, and dogs. Lots of dogs."

Dennis laughed in delight but when they went into the hall and the dogs rose from where they sprawled about the hot stove and made a loud barking, he clung to Finch's legs in terror. Renny picked him up and set him on his shoulder.

"Now you're safe," he said.

Finch exclaimed — "The stove! Why, Renny, you've got the stove back!"

Renny grinned triumphantly. "Yes. Doesn't it look cozy? The dogs like it. I like it. The uncles like it. I thought it a good time to install it again while Alayne is in

New York. She 'd have objected, you know. But she won't be able to say much, coming home after such a visit."

" Has she been told about Dennis? "

" Not yet. But she 'll love having him."

Nicholas's voice came from the library. " I 'm in here, Finch! Come right in and bring the child. How glad I am to see you! "

XXXII

A DEBT REPAID

A week later Alayne and Renny returned to Jalna from New York. They were accompanied by Rosamund Trent, a friend of Alayne's before her marriage to Eden, who, during all the years, had kept up a steady correspondence with her and for whom Alayne had a peculiar affection, though Miss Trent often irritated her. In the days when they had shared an apartment together Rosamund had mothered Alayne, poured out on her a passionate devotion, offered homage to Alayne's intellect. Alayne had relaxed under the mothering, tried her best to deserve the devotion, and realized the homage to be somewhat excessive. Rosamund Trent's exuberance was often trying but her kindness was inexhaustible. She had a deep pity for Alayne because of her marriage to the two Whiteoaks who had buried her in the Canadian countryside for the past twenty years, yet she had at the same time envy for Alayne because she lived a life that was rich in experience unknown to her or to her other friends. In Alayne's rare visits to New York, Rosamund Trent had done everything in her power to make Alayne happy, had in truth done her best to make Alayne sorry she had ever left New York. Always she had wanted to visit Alayne at Jalna and always Alayne had shrunk from such a visit. What could she do to make things exciting enough for Rosamund? What could she do to smooth over the eccentricities of Nicholas, the delinquencies of the Wragges, the presence of too many dogs, the unmanageableness of Renny? Yet perversely she felt pride in those contrasts to Rosamund's well-oiled existence. There had been, however, no pride in the one bathroom with its vocifer-

ous plumbing which served the whole family, no pride in the
old stove that, to her mind, disfigured the hall in cold weather,
no pride in the smell of horses that every so often got into
the house.   Rosamund would be a visitor she never would
be able to forget for a moment and she shrank from entertain-
ing her at Jalna.

Yet now she was at the door !

Rosamund had literally asked for an invitation.   And she
had made known to Alayne her reason for her eager desire
to visit Jalna.   Hearing it, Alayne had cast anxiety aside
and doubly welcomed her friend.   When Renny had arrived,
he warmly had seconded the invitation.   She was not the
sort of woman who attracted him, but she was Alayne's
friend and that was enough.

Rags opened the door with a bow and a deferential smile
of welcome.   Miss Trent looked him over with approval.
" What a nice face ! " she whispered to Alayne.   " The real
old family retainer type."   Rags overheard her and his smile
solidified into a look of such sweet servitude that even
Renny noticed it.   Alayne noticed nothing but the stove
in the middle of the hall, from where she had thought it was
banished forever.

Her accusing eyes sought Renny's.   " Has anything gone
wrong with the oil heating ? " she asked.

" Nothing."   He returned her look with an arch grin.
" But there's something so cheerful about the old stove.
The uncles like it.   The dogs like it.   It makes the hall
cozy.   Don't you agree, Miss Trent ? "

" I do indeed.   I haven't seen a coal stove since I used
to visit my grandfather's farm in Vermont when I was a
child."

Alayne felt mortified.   What was the use in trying to do
anything with this house — this family ?   But she controlled herself and turned to greet Nicholas and Ernest, who
were being given an arm down the stairs by Finch and

Wakefield. It was mid-morning and the two old gentlemen were making their first appearance of the day, having
taken particular care with their toilet, more especially Ernest,
who, fifteen years before, had had a great admiration for
Rosamund Trent.

That admiration was not lessened as he again met her.
Her fur-trimmed coat, her odd but very becoming hat, her
beautifully done hair which, in the interval, had become a
fine even gray, the perfection of her make-up — vivid as to
lips but not too vivid — filled him with a pleasurable anima-
tion.

" I never shall forget the time we crossed the ocean together," he exclaimed, grasping her hand.

" Nor I ! " She returned the grasp, her eyes glowing.

" I was there too," mumbled Nicholas, " though I don't
suppose you remember."

" As though I could forget ! " she cried. " I enjoyed
every minute of it. What a happy world ! " She turned
then to Finch. Both remembered how, on that voyage, she
had borrowed ten thousand dollars of his newly inherited
fortune to put into an antique business she had started, and
how she never had repaid it. The slump of the thirties had
made repayment impossible, but a flush overspread her
cheeks.

" You were such a sweet boy," she said.

He gave an embarrassed laugh.

Alayne said, " Rosamund, this is my youngest brother-in-
law, Wakefield."

Miss Trent looked into the handsome young face and declared — " He is very like you, Colonel Whiteoak."

" Thanks," said Renny, delighted.

" I escaped the red hair," said Wakefield.

Alayne was looking for Archer. She saw a little boy
descending the stairs but he did not run down to meet her
and he was only half Archer's size.

"Why — who — " Her astonishment made her almost speechless. "Whoever is this?"

Finch stared at her in consternation. "Is it possible," he asked, "that Renny has not told you?"

"Told me what?"

"About — Sarah."

"Renny has told me nothing."

Renny took the child into his arms and said — "This is Sarah's little boy. Sarah was killed in a motor accident, while Finch was in California. Finch brought him home to Jalna. Kiss Auntie Alayne, Dennis." He held the child close to Alayne. Dennis obediently clasped her neck and kissed her.

Her face, after its momentary eclipse behind his small person, appeared deeply flushed. Another child — a young child — in the house — and Sarah dead. It was cruel to have broken such news to her at a moment like this. She felt too confused to do more than turn and hold out her hand to Finch.

"You must have been terribly shocked," she got out.

"Yes." Still holding her hand, he said, "Renny told me he would tell you."

Renny was dividing his caresses among the dogs, having set down the child. He said — "I didn't see any sense in telling her before we came home."

Nicholas put in — "Well, well, it's all over with Sarah. She was a strange girl. Let's put her out of our minds. Tell us about New York, Alayne. You look amazingly well."

Rosamund Trent had thrown her arm about Alayne, as though to keep her from falling. "I think a little sherry would be good for her," she said.

Wakefield hurried to get it. The rest moved into the drawing-room, where a bright fire encircled birch logs on the hearth. Ernest conducted Miss Trent to a chair.

" No need to be upset," Renny said shortly, to Alayne.
" You could scarcely expect me to hear news like that
without a qualm."

On her other side Finch said — " Dennis is not to stay at
Jalna unless you want him, Alayne. I 'm looking for a nurse
for him. They 're terribly hard to find."

" Nonsense! " exclaimed Renny. " Of course we want
him. He 's company for Archer."

" Who is looking after him now? " she asked.

" Everyone gives a hand," said Renny. " He seems to
like it. He can dress himself. I 've had him on Wake's
old pony already. He 's going to make a rider."

" Where is Archer? "

" At school," answered Nicholas. " He played truant
yesterday. Wakefield warmed his seat for him."

Wakefield returned with glasses and a decanter of sherry
on a tray. He said cheerfully — " We don't want Archer
to waste his time like I did, do we? "

" Ha, ha, ha," laughed Renny. " So you gave him a
warming, eh? "

Alayne felt stiff with resentment. She drank her sherry
in silence. Rosamund Trent, as a connoisseur in antiques,
was admiring the graceful old pieces glowing in the firelight. Ernest was delighted to have her as a visitor. In
these dreary days of early winter, with the war still drag-
ging on, she would be an exhilarating companion. Finch
captured his son and turned him outdoors to play with
Archer's old tricycle. He thought that Alayne might have
given Dennis a warmer welcome. He always had stood by
her. It was true she had held out a sympathetic hand to
him when she was told of Sarah's death, but she had not been
sympathetic about Dennis's coming. A little child! A
very small boy! What was he in the house? Nothing.
Alayne had been too occupied in resenting the smacking

Wake had given Archer to think of Dennis as a poor little motherless boy, and himself as a widower.

The family outside Jalna were eager to meet Miss Trent. Piers and his family, Meg and hers, all came and all were favorable toward her. From Meg down to Dennis, they admired and liked her. She was so whole-souled, so appreciative of what they had, so generous toward what they had not, so friendly. Only Nicholas remained aloof from this concerted approval.

Alayne relaxed in the success of her friend. Now she was glad she had invited her to Jalna. The visit to New York had done Alayne good. She felt extraordinarily well and happy. She accepted the return of the old stove to the hall as one of those inevitable things that happened at Jalna. You might struggle to change it but you could not change it. To see Renny himself again, almost more than himself, was enough to make her happy. He had put on flesh in these last weeks. He looked the picture of a hard, weather-beaten huntsman, in love with life as he lived it, in his own limited sphere. He talked of what he would do with his horses, when the war was over. Soon it would be over. He let others talk and mourn over the problems of reconstruction. They were as helpless as he but had not the sense to realize it. He did not worry over matters he was not capable of controlling. Rosamund Trent from disliking him, from trying, as she once had done, to influence Alayne against him, came to admire him, to like him, perilously near to loving him.

She had been a week at Jalna. She had, as it were, got her bearings in the household, before she approached Finch on one of the chief objects of her visit. He was alone, sunk in a deep chair in the library with a book, when she came in. She wore that marvelously well-groomed air which so attracted Ernest, so made him wish he was thirty years younger, and so irritated Nicholas. Finch gathered himself out of the chair and gave her a vague smile. He did not want to be interrupted.

"Reading!" she exclaimed. "Then I won't come in." But she was in.

He offered her a chair and a cigarette.

"I'm glad to find you alone," she said. "I want to talk with you." She sat down and inhaled the smoke from her first puff.

"Oh." He looked inquiringly at her. He hoped she was not wanting to borrow more money from him.

"Your uncles are safe in the drawing-room," she said, and added with enthusiasm — "What old darlings they are!"

"Yes."

"Especially your Uncle Ernest. He's a real museum piece."

"I'm so used to him, you know, he does n't seem out of the way to me."

"I guess that 's true." She studied the rug for a moment of indecision and then came to the point, with dramatic emphasis. "My principal reason for making this visit is to pay my debt."

"Your debt," he repeated, bewildered.

She laughed gayly. "Certainly. My debt to you. Surely you have n't forgotten."

"No, I had n't forgotten. You say you want to *pay* it?"

"It 's about time, is n't it?"

He could not answer. No one who had borrowed money from him had ever paid it back. It was incredible that Rosamund Trent should. He stammered — "Well — I don't know."

But obviously she was in earnest. She was taking a check out of the white handbag she carried, and saying — "I 've made it out for fifteen thousand dollars. I know that the compound interest on ten thousand dollars for fifteen years would be terrific. I can't calculate it, can you?"

"Not possibly," he answered, looking at the check she had put into his hand, as though it were a viper. "You must n't think of such a thing."

"But I must pay interest."

"I'd forgotten all about it."

"I had n't! I've brooded on it. All through the depression, all through my financial recovery, I've brooded on it. When I knew you were married to a rich wife, I did n't worry so much, but, when I heard you were divorced, I'd wake in the middle of the night and think — 'That poor boy is wanting his money!' Of course, I know you are making enormous sums by your recitals but — a debt is a debt and, if you're anything like I am, you like people to pay you what they owe you."

"I was n't worrying."

"But I was! And now — after all these years — I can breathe freely again." She drew a deep breath to prove it, her beautifully controlled body gallantly responding.

"I don't want interest."

"Nonsense. Interest is due and must be paid. Remember you have a child to bring up. He's lovely. I wish he was mine."

Finch pocketed the check, very pleased to have it, yet somehow very uncomfortable in accepting it.

Ernest appeared in the doorway. He said — "Do come and talk to Nicholas and me. We're dreadfully bored by each other. If you don't come soon we shall be driven to quarrel."

Finch was glad to escape from the somewhat embarrassing situation. He was glad to have the unexpected check but found it difficult to accept. The debt was too old, its payment like a too extravagant present. Rosamund Trent, on the contrary, sprang up with buoyancy, taking Ernest's arm and walking him back to the drawing-room at a quick pace. Rags had just brought in a pot of chocolate and a plate of fancy biscuits. Nicholas, of late, ate lightly at table and grew hungry between meals. The mid-morning chocolate and biscuits were very pleasant to him, though he found the quality of the biscuits very inferior to those of years past.

" What's the matter with food? " he demanded. " Can you tell me, Miss Trent? "

He offered her chocolate and biscuits which she accepted, saying — " I should n't. I 'm putting on weight. But I can't resist. I 've been hungry ever since I came to Jalna."

" Now," said Nicholas, peremptorily, " tell me what you think of that biscuit."

" It 's very nice."

" Nice! It 's no better than a mixture of flannel and starch soaked in water. We used to make good biscuits in this country but the makers have learned that the public will pay just as much for a poor quality of food as a good — and like it! " He thrust a biscuit under his shaggy moustache and washed it down with a large mouthful of chocolate. For a moment he could not speak, then he continued — " We used to make biscuits almost as good as English biscuits. Now, look what we have, and the makers have the cheek to advertise them as ' English Style Biscuits ' — whatever that may mean."

" It 's just too bad," said Miss Trent, critically biting into another biscuit.

" And bread," went on Nicholas. " The baker's bread is uneatable, yet the advertisements are full of drivel about its excellence. Thank God, Mrs. Wragge can make good bread."

" It 's delicious," agreed Miss Trent. She loved to hear Nicholas go on like this.

" Baker's bread," he continued, working himself up, " has no crust. The bread is made to suit the people of to-day. They're too lazy to chew. When they are as old as I am they won't have any teeth. I have twelve. Seven upper — five lower." He dipped a biscuit in his chocolate.

"When we were children," put in Ernest, "and were hungry between meals, we were given hard crusts of delicious fresh homemade bread, with butter and brown sugar on them."

"And the sugar was *brown*," added his brother. "Dark brown, with what a flavor! Not the tasteless yellowish stuff that is called brown to-day."

"Then there is the fruit," said Ernest. "What a difference in the fruit!"

Nicholas blew out his breath in contempt. He said — "The new generation have never tasted a good banana and never will. Fifty years ago we ate only the large red banana, rich, mellow, really good. Then came the yellow banana, not so good but still eatable. Now we have the green banana that rots before it ripens."

"And the peaches," almost chanted Ernest, "with their crimson cheeks, their golden flesh! Now the wretched underripe fruit is covered by red netting to make it appear ripe."

"The variety is no good to begin with," growled Nicholas. "The growers discovered coarse-grained varieties that ship well, and the good old kinds are pushed off the market."

Ernest chimed in — "Piers tells me he can't sell our little snow apples. I don't suppose you ever tasted a snow apple till you came to Jalna, Miss Trent."

"No — and I adore them."

Nicholas fixed accusing eyes on her. "You *adore* them! Yet it is you Americans who have taught us all these tricks."

Ernest gave him a warning look.

Nicholas chuckled and added — "I confess there never were apter pupils."

"I'm afraid we started it," agreed Miss Trent, smiling.

"Of course you did," said Nicholas. "You can't deny that." He heaved himself about in his chair and glared at her. "You have taught us to call our soldiers *boys*. We used to call 'em *men*. You've taught our *boys* to call their sweethearts *babies,* to call their pals *buddies,* to call their full-grown dogs *pups!* Younger and younger! More and more inane."

"I agree with all you say." She patted his arm comfortingly.

"That's handsome of you. Still, I'm ninety-two and have a right to say what I think."

"At this minute," she said, "you don't appear a day past seventy."

"Ha, and what of that old fellow?" He pointed with the stem of his pipe at his brother.

"Sixty-five!" she declared.

Ernest was pleased. In truth, with his pink complexion and blue eyes, he looked many years younger than his age.

"Boys — buddies — babies — pups," growled Nicholas. "Bah, it's sickening." Still with his pipe he pointed at the radio. "Take that thing," he said, "can one get any pleasure out of it nowadays? No. Two thirds of it is advertising, the other third flaccid sentimentality. And the songs!" He could not continue for the disgust that made his utterance unintelligible.

Ernest continued for him. "They have revived the word *ballad,*" he said, "which once conjured up the thought of a charming old song. But I always say that the ballads sung over the radio are composed by the illiterate, sung by the illiterate, for the pleasure of the illiterate."

Nicholas had got control of his voice. "*Crooners,*" he growled. "Just enough vitality to crawl to the microphone and be sick into it."

"Nick!" reproved Ernest. "Remember that Miss Trent is here."

"I don't mind," she laughed gayly. "I feel just the same."

"But you Americans invented it."

"We invented a good many things that have got out of control."

"Then you ought to be ashamed," Nicholas returned brusquely.

"Let us talk of the opera," said Ernest, soothingly. "I think the Metropolitan opera is splendid."

"I like light opera." Nicholas lighted his pipe and drew on it with some placidity. "I like Gilbert and Sullivan. Do you have Gilbert and Sullivan down there?"

"Do we! I guess there is n't a country in the world where their operas are presented so often. I just wish you could have seen the jazzed-up version of the *Mikado* at the World's Fair. It was the funniest show you can imagine. Now we have two versions of *Pinafore* running on Broadway. One is a Negro version. The other is called *Hollywood Pinafore*. It 's terribly clever."

As these words fell from Miss Trent's lips, Nicholas's pipe fell from his, into his shaking hand. His jaw dropped.

"Is there no law against it?" he demanded.

She stared. "Against what?"

"Such — sacrilege? The *Mikado jazzed up! Pinafore* done by *Negroes! A Hollywood Pinafore!*"

"Oh, no, I don't think so. Don't you like the idea? That 's too bad. I 'm sorry I told you."

He returned sonorously — "*Like* it? *Like* it? There ought to be a law against it. There ought to be a law prohibiting any but the English from doing Gilbert and Sullivan. They are the only people with the voices, the personalities, to present them properly."

Nicholas took a large silk handkerchief from his pocket and, spreading it over his face, laid his leonine head against the back of his chair.

"I'm sorry to appear unsociable," he said, "but I'm an old man and I need a little nap. Please excuse me." A moment later a bubbling snore fluttered the handkerchief against his moustache.

"I must apologize for him," said Ernest, coloring, "but I'm afraid I agree with him."

Outside, in the hall, Finch said to Rosamund Trent: —

"You must n't mind what my uncles say. They find some of these changes hard to bear. They think they 're changes for the worse."

Her handsome face lighted with a good-natured smile. "One thing is certain," she said. "I would n't have those old dears changed. They 're perfect as they are."

"As for that loan," he continued, "you should not have paid all that interest on it. In fact, I 'd forgotten all about it."

She threw both arms about him and gave him a hearty hug. "My only fear is," she said, "that I have not given you enough."

When they separated a few minutes later, Finch went straight outdoors. He felt extraordinarily young and carefree. There was a high, pale blue sky, a piercingly fresh wind with the dampness of melting snow in it. The thin layer of snow that accented the irregularities of the ground soon would disappear. The red berries on the barberry bushes shone out. The sound of horses' hoofs came sharply from the road. Finch swung his arm like a flail and ran down the drive, the wind blowing through his hair. His eldest brother, on horseback, was trotting in at the gate.

"Hullo," he exclaimed, as he saw Finch. "You look nice and sportive."

"You 'd feel sportive too," laughed Finch, "if you 'd just had happen to you what I have."

Renny drew rein. "Tell me," he said. "What was it?"

Finch caressed the smooth shining leather of Renny's leggings. "Rosamund Trent has just paid me the ten thousand dollars she borrowed from me — with five thousand dollars' interest."

"The hell she has!" Renny's hard features broke into an expression of complete astonishment. "How splendid! You *are* in luck."

"I never was so surprised. I'd long ago given up any hope of the debt's being paid. But just now she took a check for fifteen thousand dollars out of her handbag and simply forced it on me."

"*Forced* it on you! You aren't telling me that you had to be *forced* to accept it, are you?"

"Well, not exactly forced, still — it was embarrassing."

"I should think the embarrassment would have been on her side. What are you going to do with it?" He looked down into Finch's face with a genial smile.

Finch gave a little laugh. "Oh, I shall find lots to do with it."

"You'll not need to save it for your boy. He will have as much as is good for him."

Now Finch was stroking the mare's muscular chestnut neck. He said, hesitatingly — "You know, Renny, I'm not altogether happy in the life of a pianist."

Renny's smile took on a sardonic gleam. "I don't know what you could do," he said, "that would make you happy. You're just not the happy sort."

"I suppose I'm not. But — I want to see — to experience a different sort of life. I'm not ambitious."

"You don't need to tell me that."

"I think I've worked damned hard," exclaimed Finch hotly.

"Of course you have. What you mean is, you're not particularly ambitious to be rich or famous."

"Yes."

" I think you 're right," said Renny. " You want to enjoy life. Not be a slave to your profession."

" Yes. I 'll just invest this money till I need it."

" Good. What shall you invest it in? "

" I have n't thought about that. I have n't had time."

His elder brother looked down at him speculatively. " You must be cautious."

" Oh, I will."

" No lending it to an irresponsible person."

" No, no. I 'll put it into some sound stocks."

" It 's hard to tell," said Renny, combing the mare's mane with his fingers, " just what stocks are sound."

" I suppose so — in times like these."

Renny regarded him almost tenderly, then he said : —

" If I were you, I 'd invest it in Jalna."

" In Jalna? "

" Why not? You could n't make a better investment."

" But Renny — just what do you mean? "

" I mean that the stables have got run-down during the war. They need building up. I mean that there is going to be a lot of money in horses when the war is over — as it will be in a few months. If I had fifteen thousand dollars now, I could double it — there is no knowing what I could do with it."

" Well — but what," stammered Finch — " just what do you want me to do? "

" I want you to invest this little windfall to the best advantage, to yourself and to Jalna. Come along to my office and I 'll tell you exactly what I have in mind. You 'll catch a cold standing here."

The mare had grown impatient. The gravel showed a groove where her hoof had pawed it. Now Renny let her go at a gallop toward the stables. Finch stood looking after them. He remembered all that Renny had been through. And now he was apparently as well as ever, able to gallop off on a new quest, as though he never had had a care in the world. Well, there was no reason, thought Finch, why he too could n't be carefree. He had nothing to worry about. Absolutely nothing in the world to worry him, except that his feet were cold as ice. Again swinging his arm like a flail, he set off after horse and rider, at a jog trot.

XXXIII

INTO THE YEAR 1945

ALAYNE should have felt happy, with Renny restored to her, not only in the flesh, but in soundness of spirit. What had happened to her that she was not happy, she asked herself. Was the power of happiness atrophied in her by long disuse during five years of war, to say nothing of the harassment of the theft? Was her spirit no longer flexible enough to resume the shape of happiness? She could feel sudden joy — experience an hour's content. But happiness was a different thing. It came as easily as breathing to the children, when all went well with them, but was hurled aside on the slightest provocation of anger or discipline — to be as easily resumed. The two old men were better at it than she, Alayne thought. Morning after morning they came downstairs cheerful, after a night's sleep. The dark days of early winter did not depress them. They listened with rapt interest to every detail of Renny's plans for improving the stables in the following spring. They accepted the loan to Renny of ten of the fifteen thousand dollars as an excellent thing. It filled Alayne with a kind of shamed anger, for even though Finch were paid a high interest on the money, she did not believe the principal would ever be repaid. She was ashamed for Renny, who, with this money in his pocket, showed a hardy forgetfulness of everything but the pleasure of spending it. It was hard for Alayne to forgive him for not telling her of the presence of Finch's child in the house, before the child was put in her arms to embrace. There had been something callous in that, she felt, and she realized afresh how impossible it was for them to look at any event from the same point of view. She could not even guess what his point of view would be, except to be certain it would be different from hers.

Alayne was willing to accept Dennis as a member of the family. The friendship between her and Finch was of such long standing, and so dear to her, that she was willing to make this sacrifice in its support. Sacrifice it was, for Dennis was a spoilt child, excitable and highly strung. But she admired the self-assurance with which he encountered life at Jalna, though it must have been strange to him. He came into a room as though certain of his welcome, his green eyes alert below his fringe of fair hair. He took possession of what he saw that pleased him, and only a will stronger than his could force him to let go. There were few wills stronger than his. Archer's was one of these and soon there were screams and stampings, as Archer proved the fact. Once Renny put him across his knee and smacked his seat with a hard hand. Set once more on his feet, Dennis looked at Renny in astonishment and said — " That hurt."

" See to it," said his uncle, " that you behave yourself or you 'll get hurt again."

" I don't like you."

" Yes you do. You like me very much."

" You don't like me."

" I like you when you 're good."

" I 'm good now."

Renny picked him up and kissed him.

" Dennis is a fine little fellow," Renny said to Alayne. " You must try to be a mother to him."

She looked doubtful. She found it trying enough to be a mother to her own two. Soon the holidays would be upon her, an exuberant young girl in the house, and she so tired! It would take her a year to rest, she thought. She would like to go away, with Renny, to some balmy, relaxing climate for a year. Then the thought of Renny in a balmy, relaxing climate made her smile. Surely he would take the balm out of a South Sea island and turn it into something northern.

She yearned over Archer, with inexpressible longing for him to develop into a man worthy to be the only grandson of her father. Archer had inherited the high, noble brow, the penetrating blue gaze, of Professor Archer. Sometimes he made remarks so profound for his years, it seemed to her, that she was filled with elation. At other times, in truth at most times, she could have wept at Archer's insane egotism, his senseless chatter, his preoccupation with things that were worse than useless. Renny was more tolerant of Archer's peculiarities than she. " He 'll come through it all," Renny would comfort her. " I 've seen boys act like imbeciles before this."

Archer's fancy would be captivated by some word or phrase that he could not get out of his head. He would go about as though in a daze, muttering or chanting the charmed words. If they had been beautiful words or phrases, Alayne would have been happy. She would have thought her boy was going to be a writer of distinction. But no, the words that fascinated Archer were not distinguished or beautiful. Sometimes they were embarrassing, and his craze for them lasted so long. For a month, for perhaps two months, they were his constant companions. Alayne was thankful that Rosamund Trent was not there to hear his latest spellbinder. It was the one word *saliva*.

Up and down, in and out, Archer would go declaiming the horrid syllables, his head up, his back so straight that he seemed almost to lean backward. Alayne reasoned with him, she ignored him, she used every device she had read of in her books on child training. Nothing impressed Archer but the one word, *saliva*.

" Oh, saliva — saliva — saliva," he would chant, while his hallucinated gaze saw what she dared not guess.

Finch was not helpful. He just went into shouts of laughter. Renny was not helpful, for he joked about Archer's obsession. " Saliva, is it? " he would say to Archer. " Well, spit it out. Get rid of it."

But Archer did not smile. There was nothing funny in it

to him. He continued in his singlehearted impervious way. After standing by the piano singing Christmas carols, with a look so pure it went straight to Alayne's heart, he would stalk away chanting " Saliva — oh, saliva."

The singing of carols each afternoon before the childrens' tea was begun by Finch's playing the piano for the uncles at that hour. Someone had started a carol, all had drifted in from other rooms and joined in the singing. An artist, with a taste for large colorful canvases, might well have enjoyed painting the scene. There stood the old piano reflecting the firelight, the mirror with its tarnished frame reflecting the family group; Finch at the piano, singing as he played, Alayne standing with one elbow on the instrument, one arm about her son's shoulders. At Finch's other side Adeline, now home from school, looking, as it seemed to Alayne, fairly ready to push her elders off the face of the earth by her exuberance. How was it, Alayne wondered, that boys never looked like that? Boys might look strong and healthy but they did not look like that.

The mirror also reflected Nicholas and Ernest, at ease in their padded chairs, little Dennis perched on the arm of Nicholas's chair, his little pipe joining with the not unmusical rumblings that came from his great-uncle's chest. The mirror did not reflect Renny who always sat somewhat apart on the window seat, the cairn terrier and the bulldog on his either side, the sheep dog at his feet. The dogs thoroughly disliked the singing but so enjoyed the warmth of fire and of human companionship that they endured it with tolerance.

Almost every evening Piers and his sons joined the group. No one of the family enjoyed singing more than Piers. His fine baritone was a great addition to the volume of song, and both Nooky and Philip had charming trebles. Finch arranged " Good King Wenceslaus " as a part song, and it was in the treble part that the two had their chance to shine. They stood up straight, singing with all their might. It was hard to believe they were ever anything but sweet and good. In truth Nooky seldom was but Philip's days were spent in getting into scrapes and getting out, with considerable disturbance to schoolmasters and family. Pheasant usually did what she could to conceal his misdeeds from Piers, but now and again she stepped aside and let him get what he well deserved.

Meg and Patience, with Roma, often joined the carol singers. The term at school had done wonders for Roma, who now also was in glowing health. Mr. and Mrs. Fennel too, and Miss Pink, but the best addition, in the way of music, was the coming of the Griffiths. Their voices had a spirituality, a strange wildness, as of the hills where they had been bred. It was Finch who had urged them to come to Jalna for the singing. It was some time before they could make up their minds to cross the ravine, enter the house, and sit down among the family whose doings were at once so familiar to them and so remote. It was Althea's doing that her sisters were shy and distrustful of themselves in the company of outsiders. Garda was naturally sociable. Gemmel was naturally bold. Both were under an influence they scarcely were aware of, in Althea's ethereal presence.

Eugene Clapperton was no singer but he liked music and he bitterly resented not being invited to join the party. Instead of being thankful that Gemmel was able to go to Jalna with her sisters, he reiterated to himself that she was ill, that no one had a right to ask her to go where he was not invited, that she should not want to go where he was ignored.

One day Renny Whiteoak met him face to face on the road. It was a day of slushy snow and dim sunshine. Squirrels sped from tree to tree on last-minute urgency of business. It was a colorless day, of wan foreboding of winter. It was one to make the average human being look his worst. The squirrels had looks to stand it. Black or red, occasionally gray, they were pretty as ever. But Eugene Clapperton was not pretty, as he doggedly plodded along the road. He was out for exercise. He was not going to allow himself to get soft, not with a young bride awaiting him in the spring. Next winter he would take her south. They would leave slush and snow behind them, stroll in warm sunshine in Florida, if he could find a place that was not horribly overcrowded. His face was sallow, his lips were blue, his eyes the color of oyster shell. He was a contrast to the figure he now saw approaching. It was the master of Jalna, riding his handsome old mare Cora. Horse and rider were warmly colored, yet in their warmth they harmonized with the scene in its bleakness. They had had their troubles. Pain might be ahead of them, but as Cora planted her hoofs nonchalantly in the slush, as he drooped in the saddle, they shared an enviable serenity of spirit. Eugene Clapperton wished he had gone in the other direction. He gave a quick glance up into Renny's face, his lips scarcely moving as he said : —

" Good day."

Renny drew rein. " Not very Christmaslike weather, is it? " he remarked, genially.

" It 's abominable."

" Walking pretty bad, I guess."

" Bad! It 's vile. But I must have exercise." He straightened himself. " I never let weather stop me."

The geniality in Renny's voice took on an almost tender note. " I admire you for that," he said, " but walking on a road like this is hard work. Better let me sell you a horse."

Eugene was suddenly afraid. He had never mounted a horse. He distrusted them, and yet —

" Riding is the best exercise there is," said Renny. " All your insides get exercise without any effort on your part. Now tramping through this slush is quite a strain on the heart. But perhaps you have a particularly strong heart."

"Well — at my last physical check-up — I have one every year — X-rayed from head to toe — the doctor told me to take things a little easier. Nothing organic wrong. I was just to slow down a little. I've lived a very strenuous life. Mentally, I mean, Mr. Whiteoak."

"I'll bet you have. Men don't arrive where you are without an effort."

"True. Very true."

"Now what you ought to do is to conserve your strength for the enjoyment of a long life."

"Yes. I guess that 's so."

"It 's not going to help you to enjoy life or conserve your strength, to plod along a bleak country road in December."

"I 'm certainly not enjoying it."

"And it is the same all through the year. You 'd always be better on horseback than on foot. With your figure you 'd look mighty well on a horse."

He had struck the right note. A smile trembled on Eugene Clapperton's pale lips. But he said doubtfully: "I 'd probably break my neck."

Renny laughed in scorn at such an idea.

"You? With your physique? You 'd have a good seat and good hands. I thought that the first time I met you. Now I have a little horse — quite a small little horse — but strong and reliable and gentle as a lamb. To tell you the solemn truth, she has one knee a little stiff from a fall, so she is no good for jumping. But she 's the perfect horse for you. Mind you she 's not cheap. You 'd not want to be seen on a cheap horse — a man about to be married to a pretty young girl."

"Can't ride," said Eugene Clapperton sulkily.

"I 'll teach you. And I may remark that I am a good riding master. As for the mare, you could n't fall off her if you tried."

As he talked, Renny's enthusiasm heightened, in the sheer

pleasure of an expected sale.   He would have taken pleasure
in selling a horse to the devil himself.   " I have the very
mount for you," he would have said.   " A horse accustomed
to a rider with hoofs and tail.   As for temperature — this
horse just revels in the heat."

Eugene Clapperton was won over.   He was grateful.
After a pause he said — " I 'll come and look at the mare,
Colonel Whiteoak.   And right here I want to say I appreciate your friendly attitude.   I appreciate your taking that
incinerator away — also the piggeries."

Renny Whiteoak showed his fine teeth in a cheerful grin.
" If we are to be neighbors for life — if you are to marry
into a family I 'm attached to — we should be on friendly
terms."

" I did wrong, I freely admit it, in suspecting you in that
miserable affair.   I should have known better.   I 'm very
sorry, Colonel Whiteoak."

The smile faded from Renny's face, but he still spoke
cheerfully.   " I have put all that behind me," he said.   " On
my part I appreciate your giving up the plan of building a
lot of small houses."   He could not bring himself to speak
of these as constituting a village.   The idea was grotesque.

Eugene Clapperton's face broke into little wrinkles of
weakness and shamefaced pride in that weakness.

" I gave it up," he said, " to please my fiancée.   She
could n't bear the thought of outsiders infringing on our
privacy."

Renny toyed with Cora's luxuriant mane.   " I like her
for that," he said.   " I 've always liked her but now I shall
like her even more.   You 've made a good choice in her."

" I know I have."

" And she in you."

" Thank you, Colonel."

" Now about the mare.   What about coming to see her
now?   We are near my gate.   Then, after you have looked

her over, I hope you will come to the house for a drink.
We 've been singing Christmas carols every evening lately.
Perhaps you would like to join us."

Eugene Clapperton agreed. He could not help himself.
He felt hypnotized. Also to go indoors out of that hateful
slush and sing carols had a kind of celestial lure in it. He
turned in his tracks, entered the gate he never had thought
to enter again, and plodded to the stables.

Renny was there considerably before him.

"Wright!" he called. "Put Belinda in the big loose
box and groom her a bit. She 's sold!"

Wright was a happy man in these days. He had been
downcast in the months when Renny's self-suspicion had
darkened the lives of all at Jalna. But now he had thrown
care aside and was straining toward the spring when he and
Renny would set about the pleasant task of rebuilding the
prestige of the stables. The colt jointly owned by himself
and Adeline was developing magnificently. The two had
great hopes of him. Renny had offered to buy Wright's
share in him at treble the cost but Wright firmly held on to
his prize.

Now he leapt to obey orders. By the time Eugene Clapperton reached the stable the mare, standing in deep clean
straw, showed a glistening hide and freshly combed mane
and tail.

"You look cold," said Renny. "Better come into my
office and have a drink. I keep a bottle of Scotch here."
He led the way into the little room that somehow looked inviting to Mr. Clapperton.

"Sit down," said the master of Jalna, "and make yourself at home."

It was a strange new world to Eugene Clapperton, whose
days had been passed in city offices, hedged in by clicking
typewriters and glossy-curled stenographers. Here there
was the smell of clean straw, of harness oil, the sound of

powerful bodies quietly moving in the straw. Wright was an honest, jolly-faced fellow, Eugene Clapperton thought. He felt strangely exhilarated, muscular and a little tough, as, with the drink inside him, he strode with Renny to inspect the mare.

Shortly she was his and, again at Renny's side, he walked toward the house to join in the carol singing. Its windows glittered red in the light of the setting sun. Eugene Clapperton felt exhilarated and a little shy as he pulled off his galoshes in the porch and then entered the house. The bulldog and bobtailed sheep dog greeted him with a terrific barking, but it was the little cairn that raged about his legs and had to be picked up by Renny and carried. Instantly its expression became one of angelic sweetness. More than twenty people were in the room. Some of the young ones were sitting on the floor. Every mouth was open and from every one issued lusty singing. Mr. Fennel's mouth in the midst of his beard, Nicholas's beneath his shaggy moustache, the children's like newly opened flowers. The carol came to an end just as Mooey sprang from his seat and offered it to Eugene Clapperton.

" Thank you, thank you," he murmured, dropping into it.

Renny bent over Nicholas and whispered: —

" I 've got a visitor here somewhat resembling old Scrooge, but be nice to him. He 's just bought Belinda at a mighty good price."

" What! " growled Nicholas. " That horrid old fellow! Must I be nice to him? "

" Just to please me, Uncle Nick."

Nicholas turned his massive head and grinned at the newcomer. A crumb of cake fell off his moustache on to his waistcoat.

Eugene Clapperton hurried over to shake hands with him. " I do hope you are well, sir," he said.

" Very well. Very well. Enjoying the singing. Let 's

go ahead with it.   Kind of you to join us.   Glad to see you."

" Good King Wenceslaus," announced Finch.

Eugene Clapperton decorously resumed his seat.   But he had seen Gemmel and his heart was pleasantly quickening its beat.   He opened and shut his mouth, pretending to sing. He was very pleased by the turn events had taken.   He regarded the fair-haired small boys with an almost affectionate interest.   He strained his ears to hear Gem's voice but it was hushed, now that he had come into the room.

Several carols more had been sung when a loud knock on the front door sent the three little boys scurrying to answer it.   If they had waited for Rags to answer the knock, he would have had more sense than to usher in Renny's two horse-dealing friends, Messrs. Crowdy and Chase.   The boys escorted them into the midst of the room with ceremony, though they hung back and would have preferred waiting in the hall.

At first glance Renny was delighted to see them but almost instantly he remembered how ill they would mix with many of the party.   He always took care not to inflict their presence on Alayne.   Already he could see the surprise on her face, that look about the nostril as though she smelled horse. In truth the pair always brought the smell of stables with them.   Meg disapproved of them; Mrs. Fennel openly stared at them in curiosity and wonder; Miss Pink threw them a look of alarm.   The small boys brought chairs from the dining room for them.   But before seating themselves they bowed from side to side, with the air of star performers at a concert.

Finch played the opening bars of " Silent Night " and Crowdy and Chase were forgotten, but not for long.   They knew the carol by heart.   Crowdy, in a rather hoarse but powerful bass, Chase in a high penetrating tenor, now took the lead, overcoming all opposition.   They sang slowly and with great solemnity.   If they had spent their lives in carol singing, instead of horse trading, they could not have done it with greater proficiency. The singing lasted longer than usual. The room grew very warm. Before leaving, Chase bowed low over Alayne's hand and said, " Thank you, Mrs. Whiteoak. I have not spent such an evening since I was a choirboy. You 'd never believe I was one, would you? "

Crowdy, extending his left hand, palm up, drew on it a design with the forefinger of his right — a habit he had when moved — then exclaimed : —

" This evening will never be forgotten by yours truly, ma'am. It 's been very dee-lightful."

When all were gone, Alayne threw open the windows. She stretched her arms wide and took a deep breath. " What air," she exclaimed. " I could scarcely breathe."

She and Finch were alone, except for Archer and Dennis. The little boys were tired. Archer wound his wiry arms around her waist.

" Only three more days till Christmas," he sighed. " How can I wait? I wonder what Santa Claus will bring me! " He looked pale and tense.

" He will bring me the best," said Dennis, from where he lay against Finch's shoulder.

" He won't. He always brings me the best."

" I shall lie awake all the night listening for him."

" I heard the little reindeers' hoofs on the roof last Christmas."

Dennis's eyes were like stars. He bobbed up and down in his joy.

Alayne said — " Now children, it 's very late. You must go to bed. Help Dennis to undress, Archer. If you are good, I 'll come up and tell you a story."

When they had gone she said — " I do wonder if we are right in encouraging their belief in a myth. There are psychologists to-day who say it 's very bad for them."

Finch gave a hoot of derision.

" Bad for them! They get a greater thrill out of it than out of anything that comes later in their lives."

" Many experts believe they get too much of a thrill. They say there always is fear mixed with it and that their nerves may suffer afterwards. It may give them some form of neurosis later." She looked anxiously into Finch's eyes.

" Alayne," he said, " I hope you are not going to be taken in by this sort of twaddle. If the psychologists want to start a campaign to protect children from fear, let them begin on the crime plays that come over the radio — the hideous pictures in the comics — but no, they 'll never do it! They 're afraid to. There 's too much money at stake. There 's no one to protect poor old Santa Claus. Even the department stores do their best to spoil him. But I want Dennis to believe in him. I want him to have the feeling I used to have when I woke on a Christmas morning and smelled the greenery and thought of the Tree and thought of Santa Claus — no fairy but jolly flesh and blood who had come down the chimney the night before with presents for me. Gosh, the man who would take Santa Claus from the children and leave a kind of Mother Goose in his place is about the meanest and stupidest man on earth."

Alayne laughed and shut the windows.

" I do like you, Finch," she said.

In the hall she found Archer not yet halfway up the stairs. She looked up at him and asked: —

" Archer, do you believe in Santa Claus? "

" Do you want me to? " he countered.

" That has nothing to do with it. Just answer Mother quite simply. Do you or don't you? "

" I 'm not sure. But I won't tell Dennis. He believes, all the time."

" You have no feeling of fear about him? " she asked anxiously.

Archer gave one of his rare smiles.   " All I 'm afraid of," he said, " is that he won't bring me what I want."

He continued on his way up the stairs.   From the twilight of the upper passages she heard his chant.   " Saliva! Oh, saliva! "   And far above in his room he still lingered on the fascinating word.

There was snow and to spare for Christmas.   Never since the house was built had it been so buried in snow.   It had begun to fall quietly one afternoon in mid-December, just like an ordinary snowfall.   In the night it had become a blizzard.   The house had groaned and its shutters had rattled in the storm.   When calm clear morning came it could be seen that more than two feet had been added to the depth of whiteness on the level ground.   But the drifts were as high as a man's shoulder between house and stable.   It was necessary for everyone who was able to wield a snow shovel to put his strength into the clearing of paths.   Even Dennis, in a scarlet snow suit, set to work.   Nicholas and Ernest never had seen any snowfall to compare with it.   A hundred generations of birds had had no such struggle to find a morsel of food.   Pheasants, blue jays, juncos, and even a pair of cardinals, came to the very door for the great bowls of cut-up bread and basins of wheat, scattered for them by Mrs. Wragge.   For five days no grocer, baker, butcher, or postman could reach the house.   But it did not much matter. Mrs. Wragge baked delicious bread, a pig and a number of chickens were killed.   Who wanted newspapers or letters? An enjoyable isolation cut off the family from the rest of the world.   Piers's boys and Patience came every day on skis.

At last the roads were cleared by snowploughs.   The dogs ran between walls of dazzling marble whiteness.   Christmas came and went.   It had seemed a long year but like the snow it came to an end and the New Year dawned.

XXXIV
SETTLING DOWN

WITH domestic help so difficult to secure in these last months of the war, it was impossible to guard Pheasant from overwork. As her bulk became noticeable her strength grew less. Two men and two racketing small boys required more effort in housework than she was capable of. Piers helped her all he could but his leg was a handicap to him. Maurice hated work. The very thought of physical work depressed him. He liked his books and was getting on well at the crammer's in town. It was arranged for him to board near by during the early months of the year, not returning home until after the baby's birth. This disposed of him but left Nooky and Philip to be coped with. They could not be taken to Jalna because of the old uncles. Meg was willing to have them for a fortnight at the time of the birth but she could not house them for the winter. It would be impossible for her to control Philip. She knew it and he knew it. He was an obstreperous small boy and it did not shame him to be known as such. He was a bad influence on Nooky, who was by nature obedient. The two combined were never at a loss to think of things to do which they should not do. Piers delighted in their high spirits but at times he came down hard on them, always the hardest on Philip. When he considered his years in the prison camp and what his life now was, he could not be really angry with them.

What the boys needed, said Nicholas and Ernest, was the discipline of boarding school. They themselves had gone to boarding school and Renny also. The old men were very fond of Pheasant. It troubled them to see her with dark circles beneath her eyes and that tired look about the mouth.

They put their heads together, and considered how they had not much longer to live and how they might as well spend their money to the advantage of the family. So they proposed to Piers that they should pay half the school fees of the boys, if he would pay the other half. Piers with gratitude accepted their offer. This left Archer in prospect of being without companions of his own age. He was now beyond Miss Pink's little school. Because of the immense snowfall he could not be taken to a school in the town. There was little gasoline for the car. Alayne was forced to agree to let him go to boarding school with the others.

Therefore, in mid-January, Renny set off on a bitterly cold morning, with his two nephews and his son in tow. The passengers in the train were mostly boys of seven to eighteen. None was more composed than Archer. He had said goodbye to Alayne with no sign of emotion. The last words she had heard him say, as he shouldered his boy-scout kit in the hall, were — " Saliva — oh, saliva — " in a shrill chant.

Now there followed at Jalna a period of such quiet, such tranquillity of spirit, as had not been known there in years. The health of the old uncles was remarkably good, considering their years. They had nothing to worry about. The war was drawing to an end. Occasionally they had spirited words over what should be done about Germany and her leaders. Their ideas clashed. Those of the gentle Ernest were drastic, but Nicholas was weary of violence. Let there be an end to violence on both sides, he said. What he wanted was assurance and peace.

Finch was off on another tour. Wakefield had gone to New York to see what chances there were for him in the theatre there. In New York, he again met Molly Griffith, as he had feared he would, but the meeting was not so full of pain as he had expected. He talked to her with less constriction of the heart than he would have thought possible. She was so calm, it helped him to control himself.

Wakefield urged her to visit her stepsisters, who could not understand her reluctance to do so. She must be with them for Gem's marriage if it were possible, he said, and she promised she would, as though she longed to do what he wanted her to. A dangerous, half-melancholy friendship now sprang up from the ruins of their blighted love. Now they sought each other's company. They were always in each other's thoughts. He never sent her flowers, he never gave her presents, but he would take her to as quiet a restaurant as they could find and there they would sit, after their meal, smoking, talking of the days before the war and the vicissitudes of their experiences in the theatre in London. Sometimes they would laugh over these but it was seldom that their eyes met for more than a moment. His eyes would rest on her hands or on the rising and falling of her breast. She would look straight before her but above the heads of the others in the restaurant, as though she actually were seeing pictures of their loved past. They would talk of Wales and his visit to her family.

At Jalna, Renny and Alayne had time for a happier companionship than they had known for many a year. They went about more often together. They sought out old friends, and made a few new ones. They gave a few dinner parties, though it was difficult for guests to come from more than a short distance. Alayne looked and felt well but the harassment of the months after the discovery of the theft had taken something from her that would not return.

On the anniversary of Eden's death Pheasant gave birth to a daughter. It was a normal birth but Piers worried over her more than ever he had before. He was delighted to be the father of a little girl, though disappointed that she did not look like Pheasant. She was to be like him, he thought, though Ernest said she would be like Piers's mother. Ernest was strong on resemblances and knew where every feature of each member of the family had come from, though he had been put to it to account for Finch when he had arrived.

The child was christened Mary Pheasant, which meant, young Philip said, Happy Bird. And she indeed started off happily for, instead of crying when Mr. Fennel sprinkled water on her face, she smiled. It was a festive occasion in the Easter holidays when all the children were home. Meg and Alayne were the godmothers, Renny the godfather. Nicholas and Ernest were there — Ernest the first to have been christened in the church, of which he reminded everyone present. The winter safely battled with and now behind them, the two old men spread their spiritual plumage in the approaching sun of summer. They got out their best clothes and donned them with zest.

Maurice had looked on the approaching birth with aversion. In hours of depression he had been convinced that his mother would die. But, when he held the tiny sister in his arms, his heart went out to her and he knew he was going to love her.

" Ha-ha," teased Adeline, " you 're old enough to be her father. I 've never heard of such a thing ! "

" Count up the years between Wakefield and your father then," retorted Maurice.

" There were two marriages."

" Never mind. This infant is my sister and I 'm dotty about her."

" So am I. She 'll be like my own child, as I 'm never going to marry and have any. Let 's make an agreement, Mooey, never to marry but always to be friends — sort of partners in living, proud and single — and have little Mary for our child."

Maurice caught her almost roughly by the wrists. " Adeline," he said, " you are the last person on earth I 'd make such an agreement with."

Something in his eyes deepened the color in her cheeks.

" Oh, Mooey, you are a silly! " she exclaimed and began to wrestle with him.

What with skiing, skating, and hockey she was no mean opponent. All that winter Maurice had lived a soft life of study and more study. He was humiliated by the onslaught she made.

" Gosh," he panted, " what do they teach you at that school? "

" To be ladies. Lily-handed ladies."

Maurice suddenly quelled her and gripped her against his chest. He looked unsmilingly into her eyes.

" I wish you were eighteen," he said.

" I wish I were! I 'd show you! When I am eighteen I 'll be as strong as you."

" Oh, I did n't mean that! " He released her, almost pushing her from him.

They stood regarding each other with challenge in their eyes, then turned away, he half-angrily, she puzzled by his look but still teasing.

Patience, Adeline, and Roma all were excited by the approaching marriage of Eugene Clapperton and Gemmel Griffith. He would have liked to have a large wedding but she refused this. In the first place, she said, she did not feel able to bear the strain of walking down the aisle under the gaze of a lot of people. The use of her legs was still too new to her, she might become nervous, be forced to sit down and propel herself to the altar in the old way. How would Eugene like that she asked, with a smile that, to him, was too droll to be seemly.

So they were married by Mr. Fennel, who gathered them in as stray lambs, with no others present in the church but Gemmel's three sisters — Molly had come from New York for the occasion — and Sidney Swift. The groom was very nervous but the bride bore herself with statuesque dignity.

Garda mourned to think that there was no admiring throng
to gaze at Gemmel as she moved slowly down the aisle, her
hand barely touching Eugene Clapperton's arm.

Afterward they held a reception at Vaughanlands to
which not only most of the Whiteoak family came but a
large number of Eugene Clapperton's friends from the city.
It was from these that the wedding presents which loaded
several large tables came. No Whiteoak had bought a
present but, from the corners and cupboards of the old house,
they had unearthed articles presentable enough to keep them
in countenance. Alayne had thought that Piers and Meg
had small right to do this but Renny seemed not to mind.
She herself had never felt that Jalna or its contents belonged
in any way to her, so made no objection. But quite un-
witting of its value, Meg had given a little china figure that
had been in her room when she was a girl, and to which she
felt she still had a right. It was not till one of Eugene Clapperton's friends, who was a connoisseur in china, picked it
up, examined it, and exclaimed in delight, that Meg realized
what a mistake she had made. It was the most valuable
present of all, declared the connoisseur, and asked Meg, who
happened to be standing beside him, if she knew who had
given it. In a faint voice Meg had answered that it was she.
Fortunately none of the family was close enough to overhear
but the day was spoilt for Meg. That night she lay awake
for a long while considering how it might be possible to get
the china figure back.

After three weeks in Quebec, the Clappertons returned to
Vaughanlands to find Gem's sisters already established there.
Indeed they were so thoroughly established that Eugene
Clapperton experienced almost a feeling of shock when he
entered his home with his bride. The two girls had left
their mark everywhere. In the living room Garda had taken
down several prized pictures, one of them a painting of Ni-

agara Falls, and hung in their stead strange drawings done by Althea. They had brought gaudy cushions and strewn them, it seemed to him, all over the house.

Garda's goloshes were lying in the middle of the hall and a pair of pink bedroom slippers halfway up the stairs. She had a passion for small creatures. The verandah was strewn with bread crumbs for the birds. On every sunny window-sill were boxes containing unpleasant-looking cocoons from which, as the days went on, there emerged various large moths that laid their eggs, in great numbers, on rugs and furniture. Eugene Clapperton traced a really nasty smell to a cage of white mice in a corner of his own private room — the very room from which the money had been stolen. Garda also collected shells and odd stones which decorated every avail-able shelf and tabletop. Sidney Swift had been careful of his bicycle but Garda threw hers down wherever she alighted from it. There was no order in her habits but she was al-ways happy and smiling. She was almost too happy and smiling to please Eugene Clapperton. She took all the bene-fits he showered upon her as though they came as easily and naturally as sunshine. She never seemed to consider how hard he had worked to make so much money.

Althea now possessed a great Dane given her by Finch, who, for some obscure reason, felt it was just what she needed. It was an enormous creature, with a profound and melancholy bark and a blood-chilling growl. When Althea was not taking him for long walks she was spending most of her time with him in her attic studio. He was young and his romping sounded on the ceiling of the rooms below like the prancings of a cart horse. Whenever he saw Eugene Clapperton, he growled at him.

In truth the benevolent man found his three girlies, at times, overpowering. He could not have believed how com-pletely they would take possession of his home. In Quebec it seemed that he had made Gem implacably his, with no desire to have a will of her own. But now she drifted back into the atmosphere of her sisters just as though she had had no new and epoch-making experience. The three had private jokes to laugh at. In a room they grouped themselves close together, making him an outsider. He never regretted what he had done. His marriage to Gem had given his life a new meaning but he could not restrain certain moments of pensive dwelling on his ordered days with Sidney Swift.

The fox farm was let to new tenants. Renny was having the house redecorated, painted without and within. It was impossible to engage men to do the work, so Finch and Wakefield had undertaken it and were making it look like new. They joked and sang at their work in the variable spring weather. Now, on a Sunday afternoon, Alayne and Renny had come to inspect.

"It looks fine, does n't it?" he said.

"Very nice. Thank goodness, you have let it to people who will pay a good rent."

"Yes, yes," he agreed, and visions of the past tenants flashed through his mind.

"I hope they will be more congenial to me than the sisters were."

"Oh, I think they will. I 'm sure you 'll like them."

They walked through the rooms.

"It 's a sweet little house," she said. "I wonder what it would be like if you and I lived in a house like this. Just the two of us."

He turned to her surprised. "Would you like it?"

"In some ways I think I should."

"Leave Jalna! Desert your children! And the old uncles — and all the others!"

"I 'd have you."

"That 's the way to talk," he exclaimed, with a gratified grin. "After all you 've been through with me — after all the worry I 've caused you!" He put his arm about her and laid his cheek against her hair.

In the grass outside she found a fragile pink flower.

"What a backward spring," she said. "This is the first wild flower I 've found. It has seemed as though the flowers never would find courage to come up."

"They always do," he said. "They 're like you. They 've lots of courage — when necessary."

Adeline was home for the mid-term week end. She now came running across the grass to join them. She pushed her body between theirs and, turning her head, smiled first into Alayne's face, then into Renny's.

"It 's glorious to be home!" she exclaimed. "I wish I might never have to leave it again."

Renny smiled down at her.

"What about that visit to Ireland with Mooey?"

"Oh, bother Mooey!" she exclaimed.

"Bother Mooey," repeated Alayne. "I thought you and he were great friends."

"We are," laughed Adeline; "but still I say — bother him — bother him — bother him!"

Maurice appeared as from nowhere.

"What 's that?" he demanded. "What 's that about me?"

"I say, bother you and Ireland, too."

"Just for that," said Maurice gravely, "I will take you there and keep you forever."